M000003997

CHARLES M. BOYER

HISTORY'S CHILD

A NOVEL

New Issues Poetry & Prose

Western Michigan University
Kalamazoo, Michigan 49008

First American Edition, 2016.

ISBN-13: 978-1-936970-39-1

Library of Congress Cataloging-in-Publication Data:
Boyer, Charles M.
History's Child/Charles M. Boyer
Library of Congress Control Number: 2015948021

Editor: William Olsen
Managing Editor: Kimberly Kolbe
Layout Editor: McKenzie Lynn Tozan
Copy Editor: Sarah Kidd
Art Direction: Nick Kuder
Cover Design: Jacquie Timm
Production Manager: Paul Sizer
The Design Center, Gwen Frostic School of Art
College of Fine Arts
Western Michigan University

This book is the winner of the Association of Writers & Writing
Programs (AWP) Award for the Novel. AWP is a national, nonprofit
organization dedicated to serving American letters, writers, and
programs of writing.

Go to www.awpwriter.org for more information.

CHARLES M. BOYER

HISTORY'S CHILD

A NOVEL

NEW ISSUES

 WESTERN MICHIGAN UNIVERSITY

Acknowledgments

First of all I would like to express my gratitude to the novelist Mary Gaitskill, who, as the judge of the AWP Novel Award contest, chose my manuscript out of what undoubtedly was a number of other deserving novels.

I'd like to thank the Association of Writers and Writing Programs more generally for holding such contests, and for all it does to encourage writers and to further literature.

I'd also like to express my appreciation of the talented team at New Issues Press, who helped my book through the publication process with skill and insight, especially to Sarah Kidd, McKenzie Lynn Tozan, and Kim Kolbe.

Finally, I am grateful to my longtime academic home, Montserrat College of Art, for its support in the writing of this book with a sabbatical leave.

This book is dedicated to my parents, Merle and Eunice Boyer, whose everyday deeds and ideals inspire me still; to my wife, Anna Lebed-Boyer, whose support and love make each day possible; and to Anna's father, Edmund Lebed, who lived the epic life of which this book is the fictional shadow.

Foreword

History's Child is a work of natural beauty—or rather the beauty of its artifice is so intelligently and lovingly constructed on such fine-grained level that it *appears* natural; it mimics the natural world with seeming artlessness. I mean, by that last part, that this book masterfully renders the subtle electricity of life as it flows and flashes through the eyes of people and animals, animating the wings of insects and the strange hearts of human beings; it renders the beauty and mercilessness of the world.

Specifically, *History's Child* is about life in Poland and Belarus during World War Two and the years of Soviet occupation, particularly the brutality of life in the Gulags. It is especially about Tadek, an intrepid young Polish boy riding his bike through that clumsy chaos in which normal village life is slowly transformed to accomodate guerrilla warfare, genocide and familial betrayal. It is a story of anonymous people caught up in the mechanical gears of political power and war, how they strenuously resist it, and how, win or lose, they become crushed or changed. It is also about how, in some private and untouchable place, they may abide.

While reading the book, I was tangentially reminded of a line from Michael Ondaatje's novel *The Cat's Table:* "What is interesting and important happens mostly in secret, in places where there is no power." *Power* can be a slippery world, but I believe Ondaatje (or Ondaatje's character) refers to worldly power, and indeed the worldly power so well portrayed in *History's Child* is not only cruel but oafish, petty, profoundly uninteresting and finally unimportant. The resistance to such power matters a great deal to real people and to historical outcomes; it was and still is a matter of life and death. But nonetheless the most interesting and important moments in the book are those in which that power is barely present even when it is all around: the gifts of honey and jam at the birthday party of a beautiful young girl (which one boy gives her "as if it were an admission ticket," the other "as if she were a servant taking [his] coat"); an ice-skating boy calmly eluding wolves; an old machinist in the Gulag composing a mediocre poem in his head and trying to make Tadek commit it to memory before he is worked to death; an uneducated peasant with a shrewd, wrinkled badger face who cures prisoners of typhus with "bark and herbs...scents and intuitions;" a hive of bees in an apple orchard, Tadek's grandfather "sweeping them with smoke and removing the dripping slats full of honeycombs."

History's Child is not about a place and time that we, as Americans, pay much (or any) attention to at the moment; World War Two and its Cold War aftermath are now the stuff of old movies and airport novels, and, in our perhaps fatally distracted, internet-addled imaginations, Poland is neither a pivotal nor powerful country while Belarus is practically non-existent. I imagine that this lack of real-world presence in the American imagination is why this beautifully written and quietly passionate book did not attract the attention of mainstream publishers: To say that a book describes the "way that we live now" is a form of high praise that seems to have an extremely narrow idea of who "we" might be. *History's Child* is very much about Poland and Belarus and the spirit of those that live there. However, it is also very much about people anywhere and everywhere trying to maintain humanity however they can in a world of gross power and abuse. As such it is something that "we," as citizens of what is still the most powerful country in the world, would do well to pay attention to.

—Mary Gaitskill

"Without a global revolution in the sphere of consciousness, nothing can change for the better in the sphere of our being as humans, and the catastrophe toward which we are headed—be it ecological, social, or demographic, or a general breakdown of civilization—will be unavoidable....

We are still incapable of understanding that the only genuine backbone of all our actions, if they are to be moral, is responsibility.... Responsibility to something higher than my family, my country, my company, my success—responsibility to the order of being where all our actions are indelibly recorded and where and only where they will be properly judged."

—Václav Havel, Address to U.S. Congress,
February 21, 1990

Map Drawing: Elliott Grinnell

PART I:
THE
VILLAGE

Chapter One: The Patriarch

August 1939, Eastern Poland

As soon as Zygmunt Belyawski heard of the Molotov-Ribbentrop Pact, pledging peace between Stalin and Hitler, he went to his barn to fetch six canning jars full of his homemade apple vodka, and drank all of two and most of a third before he passed out beneath the ancient oak tree across the street from his house. His daughter and her husband had to come and haul him to bed, shaking their heads at his absurd reaction to a piece of paper concerning two distant scoundrels. But he was right and they were wrong.

Zygmunt was a lean, hulking man, with a heavy limp, and high, knobby shoulders. He had high cheekbones and an aquiline nose and his eyes stared out unsettlingly from beneath gloomy brows. He gave the impression of being dark even though he was only slightly less fair than the rest of the village. He'd been the local blacksmith when he was younger and his forearms and hands seemed preternaturally hard and sinewy even when he was into old age. But he'd determined early on that no one ever got rich sweating over a forge. For a decade with every hammer blow on the anvil, he'd thought of the land he would buy, a plan he gradually set into motion as he began to purchase, lot by lot, the marshy strip along a stream north of town that ran into the Niemen River. By the time he was sixty his plan consumed his every waking moment. At formidable expense he drained a bit of the marsh into the creek and built two houses to rent out. But those were short-term investments. The long-term plan, which Zygmunt kept deliciously secret, was to set up a private ferry where once years before there had been a bridge, burnt in retribution after some futile uprising against the Czar. The land, now useful only to beavers and storks, would surely become valuable once the ferry turned the road away from Grodno, siphoning off traffic on a more direct Baltic route than the Niemen River, which wound its way beneath a bluff at the edge of the village.

Suspicious of Jews, he nevertheless admired what he considered their acumen in affairs of the world. He frequently trekked the ten kilometers into Grodno to argue and do business, consulting so often with Levy Reznikoff, the owner of a textile shop and an occasional investor, that it was difficult to tell animus from friendship. When Zygmunt had been a teenager, he had rampaged with his classmates in one of the pogroms inspired by the distant governmental powers, for reasons as obscure as the causes of the weather. They chased the Jews out of a nearby shtetl, flinging dirt-clods and epithets after their fleeing carts, while Cossacks in their high fur hats stood by astride their horses, hands on the pommels, watching with approval. But the mature Zygmunt and Levy made mutual investments, in the crop of a wheat field near Bialystok, or in a forestry enterprise near Wilno. They were small investments, it's true, but the length of the two men's deliberations increased in indirect proportion to the project's size, as if what they could not take out in zlotys they were determined to extract in conversation. Together, bit by bit, Zygmunt and Levy had profited during the years of Polish independence. Even after First Marshal Piłsudski's death, when the sentiment against Jews was growing, laws were passed restricting their admission to universities, and their harassment in the streets became common, Zygmunt continued to visit Levy, inspired less by idealism or altruism than ruled by his own mulish, contrarian instincts. Besides, he respected Levy's opinion and his devotion to his family, and often forgot to hold against him his peculiar liability of being born a Jew. As Zygmunt drank shot after shot of vodka slumped beneath the oak tree, he had brooded over the wisdom of the Jews. Levy had always told him: keep your assets liquid. And he'd been right. They knew. Zygmunt had always said, "Land, land, you must have land!" and Levy just sat back and sipped his tea and shook his head. They knew better than to trust in land. Especially they knew better than to trust the governments of the world.

Zygmunt woke up from his first wave of drunkenness only to resume his assault on the remaining jars of vodka, finishing the last just as, on September 1st, a week after he'd started his drunk, Hitler invaded western Poland. A wave of nauseating sobriety and clarity swept over him: he'd been right, and he was ruined. He staggered to the barn only to discover that his daughter had removed the rest of his vodka cache, which he'd thought had been well hidden. First he cursed his daughter. But knowing his pleas would not move her, he began searching for a few more hidden jars, for there were levels beyond levels to his secrets, and he'd hidden more vodka for just such an emergency. Unfortunately the inspiration to hide liquor commonly visited him just as he achieved the apogee of his drunken state. Often he could not remember the hiding place afterwards, and so he cursed himself in turn.

Two weeks later, after Zygmunt had returned to excruciating full sobriety, Stalin invaded eastern Poland. With new determination Zygmunt now tore through the house and the barn and the back buildings, finally finding a few jars of alcohol—on a shadowy ledge an arm's length down the well, perched on a rafter in the barn loft, up with the pigeons. Sipping gratefully, he collected apples and fired up his still to make certain he couldn't be caught short again. He was determined to follow his drunk through to its natural ending, since he could control nothing else in the world. Seated on a stool beside his homemade distillery in Liaski, he could hear the bombardment of Grodno ten kilometers away.

The bombardment continued the next day while Zygmunt drank hard, as if to somehow counter the artillery. But even muffled in his alcohol haze he couldn't avoid the stories his friends came to tell him: of much of Grodno flattened, of a fourteen-year-old boy, captured after throwing a Molotov cocktail, dragged behind a tank until dead as a message to the rest of the populace, of leading citizens or just people in the wrong place at the wrong time, lined up against convenient walls and shot outright.

The Red Army had triumphed. The jails were stuffed with the luckier Poles who escaped execution, and the remnants of the Polish Army scattered into the forests, some making their way to free Europe to fight, others reforming themselves into bands of partisans. Zygmunt drank on.

Liaski, and the land that Zygmunt's ancestors had farmed when the Swedes invaded in the 1600s, was declared to be Poland no more. Henceforth, it was part of the Byelorussian Soviet Socialist Republic. Polish landowners, kulaks such as himself, would no more be tolerated—that was made clear.

The repeated drinking bouts to escape the calamities of politics ended for Zygmunt with a stroke. From his bed where he lay, the right side of his body paralyzed, he could hear the pounding of Red Army reinforcements marching through the streets of Liaski on their way to Grodno.

Chapter 2: The Grandson

Through all of 1940 Zygmunt refused to die. He would talk politics ceaselessly to his bedside visitors, through his drooping, half-paralyzed mouth. In February of '41 his visitors told him that the Russians were arresting anyone of import in the cities—intellectuals, industrialists, politicians—and putting them on trains that headed east. In Grodno several thousand citizens were rounded up and sent away toward the frigid, lethal, nether reaches of the Soviet Union. Only a few in the small village of Liaski were considered important enough to be arrested: their mayor was taken away, and a man who owned a small tile factory in Grodno. The worse the news, the more satisfaction Zygmunt seemed to experience, as his low estimation of the world was confirmed.

One day an old friend visiting from Lwow said, "Our entire army officer corps has disappeared."

"What do you mean, disappeared?" he asked, the clearest sentence he'd spoken in months.

"Vanished. Gone."

Zygmunt recoiled, then gave a cynical, slitted look with his eyes, making for an unpleasant combination with the sour smile he wore: "The Kremlin magician has worked one of his tricks."

His reinvigorated hatred of Stalin gave him new life, and the next week, he got out of bed for the first time in months. A few days later he began to walk again. Even his mouth looked better and he was soon spouting his predictions and anathemas with a slightly lower volume but as much vehemence as ever.

Living in the house his father had built was Zygmunt's favorite child, his daughter, Krystyna, and her husband and son. The house was of dark, unpainted beams, with an orchard, garden, small barn, and sheds out back, all surrounded by a wire fence, which set it off from the neighboring houses, all likewise sunk in trees and vegetation and bordered by fences. The first massive waves of Soviet collectivization had subsumed the surrounding countryside, while these small village plots had been ignored.

Krystyna's son and Zygmunt's favorite grandchild was Tadeusz Gradinski. As Zygmunt's health improved, Tadek went on short walks with his grandfather through the garden and orchard, back to the beehives. Tadek had been almost eight when the Russians moved in, and he still thought of his grandfather's stroke as the primary damage done by their invasion. He was now grateful to have Zygmunt standing on his own again after almost two years. Zygmunt could just shuffle along with a cane in one hand and the other resting heavily on Tadek's shoulder.

Tadek's earliest childhood memories were of tagging along beside Zygmunt as he would stride through the backyard to take care of the fifteen beehives that ran in three rows at the end of their plot of village land. Zygmunt would slap a beekeeping hat on himself and another one on Tadek, a giant one, with the veil coming down to the boy's shoulders. As Tadek watched through the twilight of the mesh, Zygmunt would wave a few puffs of smoke over a hive with a significant, practiced motion like a conjuror's, and then remove the slats of honey one by one, while bees staggered drunkenly up and down his arms, their wings humming, covering him like a shirt of moss.

Tadek would help him remove the honey and carry it to a shed where Zygmunt, up until the day of his stroke, would take off his shirt and vigorously spin a hand centrifuge to separate the honey from the wax. The grandfather and grandson would sit on wooden benches across from each other on either side of an unpainted table and jar the honey and paste labels on each jar. Tadek and his mother would sell them at the market on Mondays. He would make Tadek swallow dripping spoonfuls of honey, claiming that it was a cure and a preventative for any malady, be it asthma, grippe, impotence, shyness, stuttering, or cancer. His first comprehensible word after his stroke had been the word "honey," whispered as a desperate plea, and he credited the elixir with bringing him back his health.

Though Zygmunt was too ill to care for the hives any longer, this Sunday he had asked for Tadek to walk with him as they'd used to do. He seemed to have a lot to say. It was a mild summer day in June, with widely spaced cumulus clouds drifting overhead. Tadek's barefoot steps kept up with Zygmunt's heavy limp and stabbing cane as they made their way to the barn. Here he lifted a lid on a feed bin to survey his concealed still, a whirligig of copper tubing and jugs, now gathering a depressing layer of dust. He shrugged and let the lid fall, and they continued on through the garden and to the orchard and hives on a dusty path worn through the knee-high grass. They had a white cat named Bandito that had been caught in a trap in the woods and had lost a leg. He followed behind the two as they walked, hopping gamely along on his remaining legs like a peg-legged sailor.

"This hive is over a hundred years old," Zygmunt said. His voice was gravelly and intense, as if he had to reach deep inside to pull out the words.

"I know, Grandfather."

This was the sixteenth hive, a hollow tree. "My grandfather found it in the woods when he was a boy and brought the hive here."

"I know."

To hear Zygmunt tell it, the Belyawskis and the bees had a special kinship that carried on through generations and transcended the life of any one person.

"His wife didn't want him to bring it in the yard. She was afraid of bees. Don't listen to what women tell you!" Zygmunt kept a taloned hand on Tadek's shoulder, and every once in a while he'd grip it hard for emphasis. He limped to the next hive and laid a hand on it as if saying hello, ignoring the intense, humming orbit of the bees.

"All right, Grandfather."

"Except your mother. She's a smart woman."

Tadek wished Zygmunt hadn't made that exception: he'd glimpsed a tantalizing doorway to liberty and now saw it close.

"And don't die for any fucking governments!"

Tadek laughed. But the talons dug into his shoulders.

"I won't." The talons retracted and Zygmunt resumed his halting progress forward.

"But don't let these assholes rule over us Poles as if we were nobodies! The Russians are dolts and clowns and the Germans are barbarians who think they shit flowers!"

Tadek laughed. He didn't know anyone else who talked like his grandfather.

"If Piłsudski were still alive, we wouldn't be in the shape we're in now. He crushed the Russians outside Warsaw and he'd do it again." He paused his limping steps to laugh out loud. "Boy, he really kicked their asses!" He sobered as he turned to his grandson. "Remember this: Hitler is not your papa and Stalin is not your mama!"

"I know."

"Say it!"

"Hitler is not my papa and Stalin is not my mama."

"That's right. They divided us up like a plate of *alatki*! Remember that. And remember always that the Polish poets are the best! Especially Mickiewicz!

'My country! You are as good health:
How much one should prize you, he only can tell
Who has lost you.'

"That was when Poland and Lithuania were one! We were a Commonwealth! All sorts of people lived together and got along then. But of course Mickiewicz was Polish, a master of our mother tongue. And you, you're a Belyawski in your soul, even if your name is Gradinski."

"Okay."

"Okay? Okay? Good and goddamn right okay!" Zygmunt stopped and eyed the gnarled tree at the end of the orchard. "This apple tree was planted by my father. Remember the white apples this one gives?"

"Yes."

"We'll get many baskets of apples off this tree, and they look as white as a virgin's thigh and taste like honey. We need the bees to pollinate them to get fruit. You know that?" He bent to scoop up the cat and gave it punishing head strokes with his bent hand, making it squint in bliss.

"Yes."

Though Tadek had been eating the apples for years, his grandfather's words made them significant. At summer's end the tree would bear off-white apples that were a precise blend of sweet and sour.

"My father was good with trees. He planted those cherry trees too. He had more patience than I ever had. To plant a seedling and wait for it to grow and to bear fruit. That's patience! Do you have patience, Tadek?"

"I don't know." He thought of how his restlessness always got him into trouble. "I don't think so."

"That's okay. You're like me. Use the strengths you have. But don't forget to eat honey, Tadek," he said with sudden intensity, as if these were his most important words. "Honey will keep you healthy!"

"Okay, Grandfather."

"I'm tired now. Take me back." He dropped the cat onto the ground. With shuffling steps he turned around in the path and headed back to the house. That was the last time he walked in his orchard.

Tadek's mother was waiting in the doorway. After she helped her father inside, she gave Tadek a few of the despised rubles that had been forced on Poland by the Soviets, to buy some salt from the little shop on the square. For months salt had been a rarity, but recently some mysterious powers had loosened their grip on the commodity and let it trickle down to the small village. "Don't get sidetracked," she said. "Come right home." She wore a white blouse and blue skirt with matching blue scarf. In looks she took after her delicate mother, who had died young, rather than her strapping father. Those close to her, though, said she had a will that could challenge even Zygmunt's. She was Zygmunt's youngest child and, Tadek believed, the most beautiful woman in the village. She had an angular face, clear, almond-shaped blue eyes, and cool, long fingers that remained elegant despite her work in the kitchen and garden.

"All right."

"Are you sure you know the way?"

He nodded. "Yes," he added, to her scrutinizing gaze. Tadek readily ran all over town on his own and had done so as far back as he could remember. He had been to the store with his mother numerous times.

"I can rely on you?"

He nodded again, a touch insulted by her doubts.

"All right."

With the coins clicking in the pockets of his shorts, feeling the weight of new responsibility, he opened the gate and stepped into the street. The late afternoon sun still sailed over the rooftops of Liaski as he walked toward the center of town. Most of the streets consisted of packed dirt and gravel but this didn't bother Tadek's feet, toughened from a summer without shoes. The houses on each side of the street sunk into the surrounding vegetation, fruit trees and lilacs and sunflowers. Each had its garden and its well-kept fence hedging it from the next. A teenage boy with a cocky grin trundled a wheelbarrow full of horse dung in the opposite direction from Tadek. He kept grinning without the slightest change of expression as he looked at Tadek, as if a kid of Tadek's age might as well be a rooster or a squirrel, meriting no acknowledgement. An old woman hobbled toward him with a side-to-side rocking walk reminiscent of the wheelbarrow. She held a dark wicker basket full of eggs in the crook of her arm and smiled at him with a few amiably crooked teeth. "*Dzień dobry*, Tadek." He knew her by sight, but didn't remember who she was.

"*Dzień dobry*," he responded.

A few dogs of different breeds and sizes trotted past him, all staring intensely forward as if on some mission. Tadek felt immensely happy, full of his own mission, delighted by the sights of the village, which always seemed fresher and more full of possibilities when he was on his own.

A young woman holding an empty canvas bag cut diagonally across the lane, and Tadek swerved aside and hurried his step so that she didn't cross in front of him. He knew very well that an empty bag carried across his path could condemn his errand to failure.

Relieved at this near mishap, he reached the town square. Brick pavement edged the square and a half-dozen ancient sycamores, with large patches of peeling bark, framed an open space with benches and rails where farmers tied their horses on market day. On one side of the square was the police station and on the other was a low wooden building that served as town hall, both buildings with large red stars painted on their walls, echoing the red stars on the flags overhead, and on the vehicles parked out front, and on the caps of the soldiers standing about, smoking. Tadek made a circuit around the group, ignoring them. That was how everyone treated them, like unwelcome houseguests who needed to leave soon. The queasy peace of defeat had settled on the village in the past two years.

An assortment of shops filled out the rest of the square, except for a gap like a carious tooth filled only by a heap of charred beams and a blackened smokestack. The Russians had burnt a store in their first day of occupation after shooting its owner, for reasons that had never come clear. Tadek had heard the story, but had missed the events, hiding in the rootcellar with his family, and felt that there was something unreal about the heap of charred beams because he hadn't witnessed the flames himself.

A few old men sat on one bench and a babushka with a baby carriage rested on another. As Tadek passed her, she lifted a foot to rock the carriage, making clucking and cooing sounds into it.

Right after the square was the Friedlanders' shop, a

storefront of dark blue paint that seemed to be perpetually chipping and perpetually repainted. Tadek opened the door to the ringing of the bell above him and stepped into the shadowy, shallow front room filled with shelves high as the ceiling. The shelves were about half-full with tins and sacks lined in ordered rows. Behind the worn wooden counter that stretched wide as the room stood Benjamin Friedlander, a tall Jew dressed in black, with the long sidelocks Tadek thought so odd, and yet appropriate on Friedlander somehow. Friedlander looked up from a pile of buttons he appeared to be sorting, studying Tadek not unkindly through wire glasses that had slipped halfway down his nose. He said tersely, "Ruth," to his daughter, a slender teenager sitting on a stool at the other end of the counter, her chin cupped in her palm, propped by the elbow, looking down at a book. Expressionless, the daughter stood up and looked down at Tadek. "Yes?" she said, with the impatience befitting a teenager forced to speak to a nine-year-old.

"A hectogram of salt," he said. "*Proszę,*" he remembered to add.

She weighed out the salt and Tadek slid his coins across the counter and received smaller coins in return plus a small, solid, paper packet. He stood for a second looking up at the girl before turning to go.

"Ruth," her father said again, casting a glance, and the daughter reached behind her to bring out a plateful of day-old fig biscuits, offering them to Tadek. He took one and looked up at the girl who nodded encouragement. He took a second one.

"*Dziękuję.*"

Instead of returning home as he knew his mother expected, he continued onward, turning down a side street to walk past his friend Pawel's house. Closer to the center of the village than his house, it had a smaller yard and garden, but was similarly made

15

of dark, creosote-soaked timbers. The trim was painted a bright blue. Tadek went to knock on the door. He wanted to see what Pawel was doing. But there was no answer. No one was ever very far away in Liaski and Tadek anticipated running into Pawel as he continued on.

He walked on out of town to the bluff overlooking the curve of the Niemen River that held the village in its crook. From Liaski, the vast forest stretched to the north, the west, and the south. To the east there were patches of forests, but then the vast grassy steppes stretching forever. Now Tadek could look down over the unbroken tops of the trees and down to the riverbank where men fished with long poles. He sat down on the thick grass and took the cookies out of his pocket. They were plump squares with pieces of figs in the center. He ate both of them, the first one quickly and the second as slowly as possible. Dusting off his fingers, he looked out across the river and over the treetops that stretched into the distance. Cloud shadows moved over the surface of the forest like the shadows of boats on the bottom of a lake. Closer, he watched one leaf on a linden by the river whirling madly about, though the leaves next to it scarcely stirred.

He lay back on the long grass and locked his hands behind his head. The lowering sun still beat full on his face. He closed his eyes, feeling the sun on his eyelids. When he opened them, he saw two storks floating overhead, coasting to the other side of the river, their legs hanging down. He closed his eyes again, listening to the flat, matter-of-fact voices of the fishermen down below. It seemed as if beneath his back he could feel the earth turning around, as if he were lying on some invisible axis. He could almost feel the leaves and grass growing around and under him. When he turned his head to look over the treetops he watched them stir in the wind and he sensed them bristling and changing. Everything was growing older and newer at once. He squinted at a cloud crossing between him and the sun, and after a while he dozed.

Excited shouts from the fishermen below woke him. He stood up to see better. Four or five men clustered along the bank, shouting, moving crabwise along the bank. Tadek scrambled down the bluff to the river's edge. One of the men was wading cautiously into the water up to his thighs, then, as if making an abrupt decision, suddenly splashing in up to his chest. The river was high and moving fast. Another man stepped in and grabbed the first man's hand and another stepped in and they made a chain now stretching out into the river, and the first man was pulling on something, something red, bobbing in the river, something about to escape into the current, but the man held on and Tadek saw that it was a red shirt caught in the current that the man was pulling into shore. The man slipped and went under, losing his grip on the chain, but then emerged and paddled with one arm and dragged the shirt with the other. He regained his footing at last and all the men circled the red shirt. They turned it over with a splash, revealing a bloated purple face, bobbing in the water, staring with astonished white eyes up at the sun. The dead man's hands looked like horrible sausages about to explode. Tadek watched in stomach-turning fascination as they pulled the dead man into shore. Their effort seemed excruciating, as if death had made the man as heavy as a stone sculpture. They flopped him onto a sandy ledge and covered their mouths and noses with their arms and stumbled back at the odor. Still more people were crowding forward to see, streaming down the bluff. Tadek was thrust out of the crowd and darted here and there through the thicket of legs, not wanting to miss anything. There were shouts to go get the Soviets, and mutterings also, "They probably did this, their friends in Grodno."

But someone else said, "Maybe he was a collaborator."

"No, it's a warning to us from the NKVD. See, shot in the

back of the head. Their trademark."

"That doesn't prove anything!"

Two local Polish police officers, instead of the Soviets, came to the top of the bluff and began making their way down the slope. They were not young men, one fat and one thin. They were the butt of frequent jokes in the town, but now they both wore faces expressing the strenuous gravity of their role, and the other townsmen silently parted for them to pass. The tall one Tadek had always thought was strange looking, with slumped shoulders and a caved-in chest, a prominent Adam's apple, and a blade-like nose. But his looks didn't make him reticent and he now began to shout in a surprisingly high, cutting voice. As the crowd shifted Tadek tried to follow the policemen into the thick of things, but felt an arm on his shoulder holding him back. He tried to tug his shoulder away, but it held him. He tried to tug away again and felt himself jerked out of the crowd.

"Tadek, what are you doing?"

It was his mother.

"There's a body…"

"Yes, I know. But you're coming home. You don't need to see this. It's not a gypsy-show. It's serious."

"But…"

"Come on!" That was her voice that permitted no argument. He fell to and trudged behind her up a sandy path back toward the village. Craning over his shoulder from the top of the bank to see what he was missing, he could see that someone was leading a donkey-cart diagonally down the bluff toward the river.

They walked on in silence. The sun was getting lower and a cool breeze came off the river. When they approached their house, his mother asked, "Did you buy the salt?"

A panic shot through him. "Yes."

"Well, where is it?"

He looked at his empty hands as if he expected the package to appear. "I don't know."

"Where were you? What did you do with it?"

"I'll get it!"

"Tadek, wait!"

But he was gone, running back through an alleyway he knew as a short cut. In a minute he came to the grassy river bluff where he'd rested. Two men were standing near where he'd lain, watching below as the donkey and cart, with the blanket-covered corpse in back, crested the bluff fifty meters away and headed into town. Tadek kicked about the men's feet as they watched him with amusement. He was astonished at the perversity of a world that could make things vanish like this, and felt tears start to scald his eyes. The dead man or the salt, the dead man or the salt. The words made a ridiculous jingle in his mind. Dead man or salt, dead man or salt. It hadn't been that he'd actually chosen the dead man, but that air of excitement around the crowd had pulled him like an irresistible current and he'd forgotten all about the salt.

Just then his foot touched something and he parted the grass. The mischievous tan paper package reappeared, intact, feigning innocence. He snatched it up and ran back to meet his mother, who was walking to meet him.

That night after he said his prayers, his mother came to tuck him in, sitting along the side of his bed and combing his hair off his forehead with her cool fingers. Though Tadek often slept in the haymow in summer, tonight he automatically curled up on his cot behind a curtain in a corner of the kitchen. The yellow kerosene light came through a split in the curtain and fell over his mother's shoulder and down the length of her arm.

"Mother?" he said.

"What?"

"I'm sorry I almost lost the salt. I had to see what was happening."

"I understand. But sometimes its best to run away from what's happening instead of straight toward it."

"I guess so." He was unconvinced. "What's a collaborator?"

"That's someone who likes the Russians."

"Who likes the Russians?"

"No one."

"Then why would someone…?"

"No one we know."

"Is that dead man a collaborator?"

"No one knows."

"Who killed that man?"

"It's idle to speculate."

"What do you mean?"

"We just don't know." She was growing impatient as his questions strained her powers of reassurance. "Now try to sleep."

"Was it the Russians?"

"Nobody knows."

"But somebody killed him?"

"Yes, that's what everyone's saying. But it's all a dirty business and you should stay out of it." She ejected a sudden stream of breath upward from her underlip, blowing her hair away from her face, shook her head, then smiled. "You do have a nose for trouble! Remember, it's okay to stay away! Now sleep! Don't dream about dead men. I'm glad you found that salt."

But Tadek did dream about the dead man. He was swimming in the river which was still his cot when the dead man put his arms around him and began with slow strength to pull him down through the cot, through the floor, down into the ground that was like water. He awoke with a shock, immediately forgetting the dream, just sensing the residue of its emotion like a thick smoke that swirled within him, but exciting and frightening. Crickets rasped outside his open window. He felt his heart thumping. He'd soaked his bedclothes in sweat. He wanted to run to his mother but restrained himself because he didn't want to again raise the issue of his wandering down by the river and losing the salt. He stared at the ceiling and forced himself to bring his emotions under control. After a long time, he was pulled back under by sleep.

The day after Tadek saw the men hauling the corpse from the water, Hitler invaded Soviet-occupied Poland.

Chapter 3: The Funeral

Operation Barbarossa, June 22, 1941

Destined to lead a life synchronized with history, Zygmunt suffered another stroke the day of Hitler's invasion, and was laid back in the bed which he'd escaped for two years. Everyone assumed that it was the shocks of history that had caused this stroke, yet when his eldest son Kazimierz whispered the news of the fleeing Soviets to him, Zygmunt managed a rancorous smile. He was thinking what a rarified irony it would be if he could manage to pry his land free from the grip of one tyrant, because of a second tyrant's perfidy.

Tadek stood beside his grandfather's bed and heard Kazimierz whispering the news, and Zygmunt's whisper back, "I knew the two vipers would strike each other." He attempted to turn his head to take in the roomful of his family, but failed, falling back in his pillow to say one more time, barely audible, garbled, understood only because everyone in the room knew the phrase like their name, "Hitler...not Papa...Stalin...not...Mama." He closed his eyes and slept. Everyone was shooed out of the room.

The family and neighbors crowded the house, pushing through

doorways two at a time, their shoulders bumping against walls and each other, creating a forest of legs and belt buckles Tadek roamed about. No one seemed to know what to do with themselves or with the leaden time of waiting, until Tadek's Aunt Jadwiga, Uncle Janusz's wife, chased all the men out of the kitchen, and then, for good measure, out of the house, dismissing them as if they were children. Outside they gathered beneath the ancient oak, the men arranging themselves, sprawling on a log bench or leaning against the tree. This was Zygmunt's favorite drinking spot, and as if in necessary homage to Zygmunt, a bottle of vodka appeared, and the men began applying themselves to it with sustained concentration.

They talked of Zygmunt, and then their talk gravitated to the Germans. The front was approaching Grodno and now artillery fire could be heard in the distance like a low, indecipherable mutter.

"It's still a long way away."

"They'll be to Grodno soon. The Soviets are already cracking."

"We're leaving for Minsk tomorrow," a neighbor said.

"They'll be in Minsk in a week."

"Maybe they'll stop."

"Why would they stop?"

"Well, what do they want?"

"They want everything."

Tadek sat on a fence rail and listened to the men, trying not to be noticed so that he wouldn't be chased away. After the first bottle was vanquished, a few of the neighbors drifted away, and there remained Uncle Janusz, Uncle Kazimierz, a few older men, friends of Zygmunt, and Tadek's father, Roman, who lingered indecisively halfway between Tadek's place on the fence and the group of men, who lounged on the log bench or stood in a semicircle fronting the bench, passing a new bottle. Roman waved off the bottle, enduring some teasing, and came to lean against the fence by Tadek. He was a tall man with narrow shoulders and a narrow, heron-like face and glasses. He had been a young accountant brought along to visit a factory in Grodno by his bosses from Warsaw, aware that his father knew of a man named Zygmunt Belyawski near Grodno, who had arranged for him to meet his daughter. He fell in love with Krystyna at once, and deserted the city he had been born in to marry into a family that would always see him as the outsider.

He looked over and smiled at Tadek who smiled back. Tadek loved his father, but he worshipped his Uncle Kazimierz, and he followed his every word.

Kazimierz was the center of the group, and though he didn't talk as loudly as his brother, Janusz, when he spoke, everyone listened. Kazimierz was Tadek's mother's younger brother, and like Tadek, he tended to be in motion, and he knew everyone in the town. He was a handsome man with very blue eyes, a long mustache, and an assured smile. Though shorter than Zygmunt, he had his father's strong arms and shoulders. He always shook Tadek's hand in greeting, as if Tadek were an adult, and the casual strength of his hand would leave Tadek laughing in amazement. He was just a construction worker now, and did specialty carpentry work when there was a chance, and a little farming like everyone else, but he gave the impression to Tadek, when he saw him walking the streets with his energetic, bouncing gait, waving to friends and laughing, that he was the unofficial mayor of his hometown, even though Kazimierz now lived in Shabany, the next village downstream from Liaski, with his wife and two small children.

Tadek watched him take a sip of the jar of vodka and pass it to his brother. Tadek's father seemed to have a change of heart and he left Tadek alone on the fence and went to join the circle of men. Janusz took a pull on the apple vodka and then pretended to pass the jar to Roman, then pulled it away, then motioned to give it to him, then pulled it away, laughing. "Do you want some too, Roman? Perhaps you should ask permission from our sister?"

Tadek watched his father pretend to laugh, finally take the jar from his brother-in-law, take a cautious sip and pass it on. Everyone knew Tadek's Uncle Janusz had some rough edges, and he liked to tease Roman in a way that made Tadek uncomfortable, even though Janusz was Tadek's godfather and had always treated him well.

Tadek had a memory of a younger, thinner, happier Janusz wrestling with Kazimierz at a family gathering: it was just a few years earlier, at Kazimierz's marriage, when, drunk, laughing with flushed faces, the two brothers had placed their hands on each other's shoulders and circled and grunted, and tried to trip each other and finally tumbled into the grass, rolling over each other, still laughing, getting up, hugging and kissing each other frankly on the cheeks. "Big brother," Janusz had said, "you have married a true beauty, and she has married the love of my life! I toast to you!" and everyone had raised sloshing glasses of beer.

That was before Janusz took his fall from the top of the barn where he'd been replacing shingles, and shattered his ankle, giving him a permanent heavy limp. With the limp came a large weight gain and a souring of his temperament.

"I heard from someone who had been to Moscow," said Jan, turning serious. "The man told me that some people, some intellectuals and officers from Lwow and Wilno, who had been arrested and sent to Siberia, are now going to be released to fight for the Communists."

"Those the Russians haven't killed already!" scoffed Kazimierz.

"I heard they're shooting all the Polish political prisoners in the Grodno jails before they retreat," an old man said. Everyone looked at the ground and let this news settle in. No one could respond. Even Tadek could taste the bitter helplessness in the silence.

A barrage of artillery sounded in the distance, just a shade closer and louder than before. It seemed to come falling out of the sky itself. It was a cloudy day and the sound might well have been thunder if everyone didn't know better. The men listened to it as if they were reading omens in its gravelly voice.

Jadwiga stepped out of the house. She was a large-breasted woman with a round, flushed, mocking face. Long-legged, she seemed to have almost no waist. She usually seemed angry about something too vague or deep to be fixed.

"Come on," she said brusquely. "Come on and eat. People are dying, here and elsewhere, but you still have to eat. Nobody likes me to tell the truth, but it's still the truth!"

The men all quieted down again as they re-entered the house where their sick progenitor or friend lay. They passed plates filled with herring and potatoes and beets, silently at first, but Jadwiga's matter-of-fact attitude seemed to dismiss their piety. She began slinging the dishes onto the table only to remove one or two of them a moment later and replace them with different plates, as if after being generous enough to make the meal, she now regretted it and resented the men for eating it. The men winked behind her back as they began to eat, gripping their plates to protect them from her. The conversation regained traction, circling the same questions. People were fleeing the Germans already, but no one knew where to flee.

"We'll just wait for them to pass by us the way the Soviets did before," Jan said. "Nobody cares about the little people. It was the rich people Stalin took."

"Don't be too sure. It was the rich and then plenty more."

"Yes. But there's little to do."

"There are people fighting still."

"A few partisans in the woods? What good are they? It took the Germans all of, what? Three weeks to destroy our army in the west."

"And now the Germans and the Russians will destroy each other for us," Kazimierz said, tearing off a chunk of bread. "And I know these partisans. They won't give up!"

"Well, it's all bad news for the Jews, that's for sure," Jadwiga said.

"How do you know that?" her husband argued.

"You never listened to Hitler's speeches?"

Krystyna stepped into the doorway. Her presence made everyone realize how loud their voices had become, and they immediately silenced. She looked stricken, a blanch spreading up her throat and then her face as she looked at them, as if only the sight of them made her father's situation real.

"Kazimierz." She motioned him into the other room. "Now."

A minute later Kazimierz came out and said in a flat voice, "He's gone."

No one said anything for a few minutes, just sat around the table full of half-eaten plates of food. Tadek didn't know precisely what he felt. He knew his grandfather was dead but didn't believe it. He couldn't imagine Zygmunt looking like the purple sopping corpse they'd pulled from the river. He looked around at the adults all turned to statues, staring at the potatoes and turnips.

Eventually Jadwiga began to circle the table, removing all the plates this time, whether the men were finished eating or not. "Well," she said, "don't look so morose. It was time. And we all know Zygmunt would've wanted to go out in the middle of a political argument rather than any other way. He's probably just angry he couldn't get his own last word in."

* * *

The funeral was held the next day because of the advancing Germans, who had reached the outskirts of Grodno, and were bombing areas still in ruins from the Soviet's attack two years before. In the morning the family could hear the antiaircraft guns from the city and see the black smoke rising from the bombs. When Uncle Janusz dispatched the frightened gravediggers to do their work, the German bombardment had spread to the east of Grodno. A few shells had begun to land on the main road from Grodno and in the fields surrounding Liaski. The Germans' destruction was spreading methodically across the entire countryside.

Uncle Kazimierz shrugged: "Where can one hide, anyway?"

Fatalism was widespread, since everyone knew that this part of Poland had always been the first stop on the highway for invaders, the first step over the Niemen. There still lingered tribal memories of the Norse sweeping down the rivers on slave-raids, and the Mongols coming out of the east and crossing here into Europe to clash against the Teutonic Knights. The Cossacks and Tartars, too, came out of the east. More recent armies had made this the pathway from the west toward Russia. The Swedes had crossed here in the 1600s, and later Napoleon, greeted as a liberator. Occasionally still a stray saber from his army was unearthed in the fields around Liaski. After Napoleon, the heavy weight of the Russian bear pressed down again from the east. Now it was Hitler's turn to try his luck, the west pushing against the east again as if the two directions were primal antagonists rather than abstractions sketched on a map.

A small group of relatives and acquaintances followed the coffin on a crude cart headed to the ancient church, which lay across a field and a kilometer out of town on the site of the old town, burnt by the Swedes, who had spared only the church. One look at the road told them progress there would be impossible. It was jammed with throngs of people on foot and with horsecarts and handcarts fleeing eastward out of Grodno and the surrounding villages. The carts edged along, jostling and obstructing each other. They were all loaded with trunks and chairs and glazed-eyed children, some with cows or goats tethered behind them. Soviet soldiers too were fleeing. A troop carrier came by, driving the carts off the road, followed by soldiers on horseback, on bicycles, on foot, casting looks over their shoulders toward the west, their clay-brown uniforms making a muddy stream through the crowd. Tadek was amazed to see the road crammed as far as he could see where it disappeared into the distant woods, and wondered where so many people could've come from.

A younger child Tadek knew was sitting on the back of a wagon, and they looked at each other awhile, but both were too awed by events to even wave or acknowledge each other.

A man stood beside a fallen horse whipping it with all his might as if this would right it, but it kicked and squirmed in the mud, unable to find its footing in the ditch. Kazimierz dashed at the man and pulled him away from the horse. Janusz, with his lumbering gait, backed up his brother and the irate man turned away. Left alone, the horse righted itself with a violent heave, and Kazimierz grasped its bridle, stroked its neck, then turned it loose in the direction of its scowling owner. Kazimierz and Janusz caught up with the knot of mourners on the side of the road, surrounding their father's coffin.

After a moment's indecision, the funeral procession angled away from the crowded road and took a parallel cowpath and forest path, struggling over ruts and, on precarious stepping-stones, over muddy streams. Still they seemed to progress faster than those jammed on the main road, whom they could see through a curtain of trees.

The church had been closed off and on by the Soviets during the past two years, but no one was left to chase away the priest now. He was a tall man with wire glasses and unruly tufts of gray hair. He stood in the doorway hurrying everyone inside with a circular motion of his hand. His eyes swam, magnified, behind his glasses as he stared at Tadek entering with his mother. Fewer than twenty people were scattered through the church: the nearest family and only a dozen old friends of Zygmunt, though he'd lived in the village his entire life.

The men carried in the coffin and placed it on two sawhorses in the front of the church, and then, to Tadek's horror, removed its lid and leaned it against the coffin's foot. From the back of the church Tadek stared with dread and pain at his grandfather's rigid profile. A lady came up to Tadek's mother, her steps down the aisle mincing but determined. Lowering her voice she said confidentially, "You know that devil's mark on Tadeusz's neck?" There was a red mark the size of a *zloty* on his neck. This woman was known in the village as a *znacharka*, a woman who knows. "If you touch it with a dead man's hand, it will disappear."

"I know," his mother said. This was common knowledge. "But now's not the time."

"All right. If you don't want it cured. It'll bring ill luck, but it's your decision." She moved away, pressing her hands together and shaking her head.

"You won't touch Grandfather's hand to my neck, will you?" Tadek asked.

"No, Tadek. But you must say good-bye."

They approached the coffin, his mother's hand holding his, dragging him after her steady, unrelenting steps. As they walked, Tadek's eyes kept darting to the grim, white profile of his grandfather, and then away as if scalded by the sight. The bloated corpse from the river had held no emotion for Tadek compared to this: he kept expecting his grandfather to rise up on an elbow and issue one of his edicts or curses. At the front of the church Tadek and his mother knelt in front of the coffin for a moment of prayer. Tadek's prayer was little more than a few moments of squinty-eyed concentration on his own misery and confusion as his mind chased in vain for something to think or say. In relief he followed his mother's lead and crossed himself, signifying the end of the prayer. She stood and leaned over him and kissed her father good-bye. She asked Tadek if he could pat his grandfather's hand to say good-bye and he reached up to touch the frigid fingers. His grandfather's mouth was set in a stern frown, as if being dead was serious work.

Tadek and his mother went to sit down in the front pew. Everyone knelt together at some hidden signal. Silence. A gap in time, into which everything could fall. In a few moments of fidgeting, awkward waiting, a thought occurred to Tadek, a sharp suspicion that it was his grandfather's death that had precipitated the Germans' invasion, creating a vacuum into which the bombers and the troops were now rushing.

The priest stepped hurriedly to the front of the church and cleared his throat. The shockwave from a bomb on the Grodno road rattled the windowpanes, causing the priest to gulp and clear his throat again and then begin a rapid, mechanical run-through of the mass, during which Tadek could feel through the soles of his feet when the bombs struck in the distance as the vibrations came through the earth and the floorboards.

Afterwards, outside the church, the small group dispersed. "I must go now," one old man said to Tadek's mother. "Forgive me for not accompanying my old friend to the graveside, but," he gave a weak smile, "the Germans, you see."

"Of course. Thank you for coming."

So only family and the priest remained to follow the cart the two hundred meters to the cemetery, hidden in a pine grove. They walked fast, hurried by the explosions in the distance. Glancing back to the road, they could see that the Germans were through with Grodno and were moving on. The bombardment had now begun in earnest around Liaski. Leading the attack were crooked-winged dive-bombers that screamed overhead in their dives, dropped their one bomb, and then strafed the ground below them before pulling upward and after a minute's respite circling back, looking for more prey. Their crooked wings seemed to mimic the swastikas twisted on their tails, creating the impression of something full of perversity and malice.

Higher up, emitting a grinding muffled roar, were other bombers, which though distant were no less dangerous, dropping their regular rows of bombs which crossed the fields and into the forest in a deliberate, crushing rhythm.

Tadek held his mother's hand as they stumbled along the path back into the woods. He felt numbed and looked to her for assurance. He thought she looked blurred and withdrawn in the black veil she wore. Her blue eyes today were deepened and gleaming with tears. She seemed lost in emotions of her own too deep to permit fear of the Germans to penetrate.

His other hand held that of his father, who was now even quieter than usual, surrounded by the widening chaos and by his wife's family.

The small black-clad cluster hurried through the pinewoods to the cemetery. There, each family plot lay separate, engulfed in vegetation, sequestered by a small fence just as the houses in the village were. Why should a decent respect for privacy be of less importance in death than life? The sounds of the bombs came closer. The family watched helpless as a bomber roared overhead and released a bomb, which was left silhouetted black against the sky as the bomber swept away. At first the bomb seemed to float weightlessly above them, and then it became apparent it was traveling quickly past them, turning its nose earthward, gathering momentum, then plowing heavily downward, striking across the cemetery, exploding with a sharp yellow flash, shattering monuments, as if intent on killing the dead a second time.

The gravediggers turned and fled, dodging among the tombstones and disappearing among the pines.

The priest blurred his rushed words into a stream, his voice now quavering. He shook his aspergillum over the coffin, muttering Latin, then, sketching a cross in the air as he turned with a gesture that was more a goodbye than a blessing, hurried away toward the church. The only men left were Jan, Kazimierz, and Roman, so Tadek took the other end of one of the ropes, with Jadwiga stepping up behind him to help, as they lowered the raw pine coffin without ceremony. When it snagged on the edge of the grave, Jan nudged it with his toe. It disappeared beyond the rim of earth. The ropes burned Tadek's hands. With a thud the coffin hit the bottom of the grave. That was that. That was how a life was finished. Jan and Kazimierz took up the abandoned shovels to quickly fill the hole. For a time there was only the sound of their rhythmic shoveling and the more distant ambient sounds of occasional explosions and the monotonous droning of airplanes.

With the blade of a shovel Kazimierz chopped a rough cross into the pine tree near the head of Zygmunt's grave. "We'll give him a real marker," he said, "when the war is over."

When the war is over! The fantastical sense of the phrase didn't have time to settle before the buzz of an approaching bomber grew to a roar. The bomber swung wide of them, but they had already turned away from the fresh grave and were walking quickly back through the high trees.

The family stopped at the edge of the woods across a field from the road, along the length of which now were strewn abandoned carts. The civilians had all scattered into the forests once the German strafers had begun to work their way up and down the road.

Tadek saw that a cow had been struck with a bomb and lay nearby in pieces in the field, its organs indiscriminately mixed with mud and sod. As Tadek looked more carefully, he saw in the distance half a dozen bodies stretched here and there on the road and partially hidden in the tall grass of the field. A few days ago the corpse in the river had been the first body Tadek had ever seen, and this morning his grandfather had been the second, and now he'd suddenly lost count of how many he had seen. The more he looked, the more he saw.

A wind was blowing the ferns that grew there in the woods' edge in a gentle whisking motion against Tadek's thighs. For a moment the war seemed to have gone somewhere else, seemed to momentarily be in a tense pause.

The family mumbled their goodbyes, exchanging brief hugs, already moving quickly their separate ways. Kazimierz and Jan and their families headed through the woods northward to the next village over, while Tadek and his parents took the quickest way home, down the cowpaths. They would try to avoid the road, cross several fields, and duck into the woods when they could. They made their way across one field and discovered at its edge two ragged Russian soldiers crouched, hesitating in the undergrowth. The soldiers—haggard, slack-jawed, red-eyed—looked vacantly at the young family as if nothing was quite in focus. One soldier stood up and began gesturing and explaining himself to Tadek's parents in earnest Russian, incomprehensible to Tadek except for a few words. He seemed to feel it was very important that they understand his situation. He seemed to be apologizing for something. The other soldier said nothing but took off running east, across the field the family had just crossed. After a moment's hesitation, the first soldier abruptly gave up talking and started after him.

A moment later a monotonous overhead drone swelled into a roar and a dive-bomber flew overhead so close that Tadek, looking up between the trees, could count the rivets on its wings. The plane started strafing the empty road and then with a sudden cat-like pounce swerved back over the field after the two soldiers.

Tadek wanted to see whether the soldier who had talked to them would make it across the field and into the woods, but his parents grabbed his hands, and they ran together away from the field and deeper into the woods.

Finally they were in the village and at their gate. Tadek's father fumbled at the gate latch and they rushed into their yard.

They filled a box with food and blankets and hurried into the packed-dirt potato cellar, a place of dampness and spiders, where there was just room for the three of them, and the grownups could not stand upright. They sat down on an old rug and wrapped themselves in blankets to wait for the Germans to pass through. Tadek could hear the bombs falling and with each bomb some dust would shake down from the floorboards.

Just as he started to relax there came the thumps of a volley of rifle bullets hitting the side of their house, then smashing a window, then quickly moving on. They all squirmed together in hunched silence, their arms around each other.

After that the only shots heard were more distant.

Tadek had a blanket that was of rough wool but smelled clean, and he nestled his head into his mother's lap. They turned off the kerosene lantern. In the darkness the odor of the earth floor crept through the smell of the blanket; it was a dense, homey odor that comforted him. "Try to sleep now," his mother said, stroking the side of his head with her slender fingers.

"Will I have school tomorrow?" he asked his mother, and

was surprised to hear her laugh. Though it was summer now, underground Polish-language classes continued as best they could year-round to make up for weeks missed throughout the year.

"No, Tadek." She stroked his hair in the dark. "No. The Germans have given you a holiday. But try to sleep. There are worse things than school and we must be ready for them."

He could hear the sadness in his mother's voice and remembered that she had just buried her father. He pressed the side of his head against her thigh, wondering what the Germans would bring, confused as to what he should be feeling. He remembered the profile of his grandfather's rigid white face in the coffin and his heart constricted but he didn't cry.

He lay listening to the bombs walking away from the house across the fields and into the forests like the steps of a lumbering giant. He concentrated on his parents' conversation. What would the Germans do? Rumors from western Poland had been dire, though no one under the Soviets had sympathy to spare. Would the Belyawskis get their land back now? This house and the plot of land around it were all that the Russians had left them.

The bombing gradually moved away into the night. Tadek felt himself sliding down the gaps between the bombs and into sleep. Thinking that he was still awake, he dreamt of running across a field with his mother. They were running for the woods in front of them, the sounds of airplanes above them. A shadow swept over them, following them. Tadek realized that a huge bird was clawing at his back from the sky. He tried to turn and strike away its huge talons. A hand pulled him and he continued to run. Now it was his grandfather holding his hand. He was surprised, because his grandfather was dead, and he was about to say, You're dead, grandfather, when Zygmunt picked him up and ran with him, not at all the limping old man he'd known in the final days, but a sprinting demon. In the woods suddenly, they were safe. But now his grandfather was his uncle Kazimierz, and he was carrying him deeper and deeper into the woods where the sound of the airplanes faded away. Tadek, who had been certain he was awake throughout his dream, realized that now he was truly awake.

The bombs outside had stopped, leaving a huge, heavy silence that seemed to press against Tadek's skin.

"Do you need to go to the outhouse?" his father whispered. He must've heard Tadek stir.

"Yes." Tadek whispered too.

"Come with me."

His father pushed open the trapdoor, took Tadek by his hand, and led him up the small ladder. "You must be quiet," he told him. Upstairs, his father inspected the house in the dark. There was one broken window where the house had been hit by the rifle-volley, but beside that, everything looked intact. Tadek's father grunted, acknowledging that things could've been worse.

Outside, there was a reddish three-quarters moon low in the sky, eclipsed and then revealed by low, fast clouds. Tadek and his father made their way down the garden path. A bomb had splashed into the end of the orchard, destroying an apple tree, and Tadek's thoughts flashed to the bees. Were the bees all right? He knew that's what his grandfather would care about. But there were the three rows of hives, phosphorescent white in the moonlight, unharmed.

When he and his father passed the bomb crater, Tadek could smell the burnt earth and metal and powder and imagined that he could still feel the heat from the explosion on his cheek. It all seemed very foreign, as if a meteorite had struck, and it seemed to knock loose all the strangeness of the day within him. He felt the pressure of a bubble growing within his chest, and in an instant the dream came back to him in one complete image, and for the first time he realized that he would truly never see his grandfather again—knowledge more a sensation than a thought—and the bubble rose through his throat and burst through his eyes into tears.

He hugged his father's belly, crying as silently as possible, finally succeeding in stifling his tears and stepping away.

"Are you all right now?" his father asked.

"Yes."

"Good. You first," his father said, gesturing toward the outhouse, and he went into the closet so familiar he needed no light and when he emerged his father entered. "Stay here," he said.

He felt just empty now as he waited for his father. He began hearing rustling and crackling noises, faint at first. Then voices. He saw them then, streaming through the colorless night, soldiers stalking down the streets on either side of their house, silent except for the shuffling of boots and an occasional barked order. The German language sounded queer and rough to his ears. There were a few shots in the distance, ahead of the troops, eastward where they headed. After the first vague line of shadows, there were more and more of them, line after line of them. Under the moonlight, Tadek could see them in the field beyond the houses, stretched out in wavering but relentless lines. On the road a cluster of soldiers passed by in a half-run, half-walk, their gear shuffling and jangling. They were gray as ghost soldiers in the moonlight.

Watching these invaders, the pain and emptiness he felt at the death of his grandfather melded into quite a different emotion, a shame and anger at the violation of everything he knew.

He watched the shadowy soldiers trooping through the town, stretched out into the open fields, as at the same time he sensed the contours of the dream within him as one multi-sided shape that he could examine facet by facet. He knew he could not explain the dream to his father or to anyone, but he felt exactly what it had meant; not only the dream, but the corpse floating down the river, the rows of beehives white in the moonlight, the death of his grandfather, the infinite lines of gray soldiers he saw walking through the streets and fields of his country. All of these things were part of the core of the dream that was almost tactile within him, telling him that he would never be whole until all the invaders were gone from his land.

The moon slipped behind a cloud again. The troops had passed. Tadek's father grabbed his hand again. "Come." Tadek's footsteps knew the path through the darkness back to the house.

Chapter 4: Pigs

Black and red swastikas rippled from the antennae of staff cars, snapped in front of town hall, and emblazoned every troop carrier and wall, replacing instantaneously the red star that had seemed so triumphant only a few weeks before. The taut rhythm of marching boots filled the streets. The Russians had been shambling and disorganized and rough, and would crush you with their unbearable weight. The Germans were hard-edged and precise and would rip you apart.

Much had to be done quickly to adjust to the new order. Tadek's Uncle Janusz had called upon him and his father for help in butchering his pigs. With a few discreet bribes, Jan had been able to keep the pigs out of the hands of the Bolsheviks, who gave useless receipts instead of cash for any food appropriated. But now he'd decided to salt the meat and hide it away rather than count on the Germans being as conveniently corruptible.

Jan lived past the village of Shabany, five kilometers downstream from Liaski, in an isolated farmhouse up on a bluff near the river. It was there that Tadek and his father were bicycling this late September day. Sometimes after fishing his father would take him to his uncle's for lunch, so Tadek knew the way well.

Halfway there, by a bridge over a little creek, a convoy of German troop carriers, led by a staff car, a *kubblewagen*, with an officer, rumbled at them around a corner, driving in the middle of the road. The beds of the trucks were full of German troops in their gray-green uniforms.

Tadek and his father had to jump off of their bikes and leap with them into the dusty bushes along the road to avoid the convoy. They watched them pass, three, five, seven trucks, the men with their helmets pulled low, impassively inspecting Tadek and his father as they passed. One German held up his gun and took careful aim at Tadek. He took a pretend shot and his friends laughed. Dust hung in the air after the vehicles were gone, settling on the clothes of Tadek and his father, coating their mouths and hair. Tadek looked at his father. His face was stony. He turned to his son and squeezed his shoulder. Tadek understood. There was nothing they could do. But Tadek also felt again the very personal shame and anger he'd felt the night of his grandfather's funeral. He stared at the receding convoy, wanting to somehow rid himself of those emotions. As the dust from the convoy settled, his father clambered back on his bike, gave Tadek a thin smile, and they continued toward Jan's as if nothing had happened.

There was a small pen and barn behind Jan's cottage, where they found both Jan and Kazimierz. They were both dressed in long leather aprons. Kazimierz was honing a knife on a whetstone wheel. Jan was outside in the pen trying to chase a large sow through a chute into the barn where the slaughtering would take place, on ground hard as concrete with a trough dug in it for the blood. "Are you here to help, Tadek?" Kazimierz called.

"Yes!"

"Well, these pigs are in trouble then!"

Kazimierz gave Tadek his fine, confident smile that seemed

to deny any doubts, quite different from his father's always anxious face. Kazimierz continued to whet the knife with quick touches to the stone, shooting out sparks and shrieks.

Uncle Jan had given up on the pig for the moment and, leaning over the rail of the pen, turned to Tadek's father. "How about you, Roman, are you ready for this?" he asked. Tadek felt his father grow tense for the second time that day.

"Of course. I've slaughtered pigs before," Tadek's father said. He took off his black jacket and vest, folding them carefully over the back of a wooden bench. He took down an apron hanging from a peg on the wall.

Tadek's father Roman was from Warsaw and was an only child. After he'd moved from the city to Liaski to marry Krystyna, he hadn't found a job quite up to his abilities—or hadn't had the humility to work at anything requiring sweat, rather than a pencil, depending on who told the story. He'd been an accountant at a small firm in Grodno when the Soviets invaded, but they'd closed it down as inessential, so he'd become a supervisor in a granary outside Grodno. In some towns the Soviets had lined up the men and had them stick out their hands, palms up, and gone down the row, shooting anyone with soft, uncallused hands, so Roman, counting himself lucky to have escaped thus far, began working the machinery with the men just to keep his calluses in shape. In the granary he had to deal with the Soviets on a regular basis, as they demanded a steady supply of wheat and barley. This caused some resentment to come his way within the village, but the job had kept them from conscripting him into the army. Some nights now, out of nostalgia for his old status, he would read calculus books for amusement, sitting at the kitchen table and saying little, smoking his pipe.

"You had pigs in Warsaw?" Jan scoffed, seeming to want some sort of proof. That Roman was from Warsaw always seemed to be a source of personal offense to Jan. Tadek was never certain how seriously to take his godfather.

"Of course they had pigs in Warsaw!" Kazimierz set aside the knives and clapped Roman on the back. "They even had kielbasa! Here, Tadek, put these on." He found a pair of rubber boots lying under a bench and handed them to Tadek. "We aren't going to church! You too, Roman."

Tadek sat on the bench and pulled on the knee-high boots, his toes groping for their ends. Kazimierz gave him an apron, too, which he had to fold almost in half because of its length. He picked up a long, rusty knife lying on a worktable. When he appeared at the barn door in his floppy regalia, everyone turned to laugh.

"Ready for business!" Kazimierz cried.

Jan grabbed a thick plank of wood and re-entered the pen, where three sows clustered together against the opposite railings. Tadek looked them over with a sort of horror. They were massive, easily as heavy as Jan was, and covered with sheets and clots of gray mud along their flanks. From their lowered heads, they eyed the humans with slitted, suspicious, intelligent eyes.

Jan took the plank and jabbed and pried at one of the pigs, which grunted and reluctantly gave in to his pressure, edged toward the gate, then panicked and bolted away, circling back with the other two. Kazimierz went into the pen to give his brother help. The two men approached the three pigs warily. Kazimierz clouted one pig in the snout with a metal fence stake, separating her from the group. The sow stood facing the two men, now between her and the safety of the group, and she glared at them, her eyes gone venomous, the four pegs of her hooves stubbornly dug into the earth. The two men approached side by side, stake and plank in hand, prodding, and with a sudden snort the sow wheeled and trotted, now its head held proudly, through the gate into its killing pen. Jan swung the gate shut.

Kazimierz and Roman grasped the pig by its front and back legs as it struggled and set forth shrill squeals. They motioned to Tadek and he grabbed hold of one of the rear legs, which pumped in his hands with amazing strength. The pig kicked and pumped his legs, squealing insanely, almost throwing Tadek to the ground. The two men and Tadek managed to hike the pig's rear legs into the air and, after a couple of failed efforts, that seemed unending and futile to Tadek, as the pig's legs pumped and pumped and he held on with both hands, dodging the sharp hoof, Jan finally fastened a chain around the pig's rear legs and, tightening the chain with a winch, started hiking the pig's rear legs into the air on a block-and-tackle fastened to a beam. Finally the entire pig swung from the chain.

Everyone stepped away and took a breath. Jan, in a leather apron mapped with old bloodstains, unsheathed a long knife and walked toward the pig, his legs spread wide for balance as if he was on a boat battling high seas. The knife's handle had been broken and mended with tape. Tadek was astounded at the length and narrowness of the blade, worn down by years of sharpening. The broken handle, the long blade, the continuous squeals, all seemed to make the death more squalid. Without a pause Jan plunged the knife into the pig's neck behind the ear and cut downward through the stream of blood. After one shrill shriek, the pig was silent. Tadek saw a shudder ripple down its flank, and it went slack.

"Let it bleed out."

Kazimierz slid a battered tin basin under the pig to catch the thick blood draining over its face.

Tadek watched as the men relaxed, wiped their hands, lit up cigarettes. The late afternoon seemed to take a pause to settle around the pig's death, as if more than blood was draining away, and the men talked about the Germans, how they were setting up their organization in the town hall, how the Polish schools would continue underground just as they had with the Russians.

The men finished their cigarettes and laid the pig on the dirt floor and stepped back. Jan gutted the pig with a quick slice from groin to chest, spilling the steaming intestines onto the floor.

"Are you all right?" his father asked Tadek. Whenever pigs had been slaughtered before, Tadek had always walked away as soon as he heard their squeals.

"I'm all right."

"You look a little white!" Kazimierz said, gripping Tadek's shoulder and laughing.

"I'm all right," he repeated. But now, as though the questions had stirred up a reaction, he felt his knees wobble and took a couple of steps backwards to quickly sit down on a stool. The men turned back to their business.

They slaughtered two more pigs that day. The other two pigs, which had listened to the terrifying fate of the first, had to be forced into the barn by all three men, armed again with boards and the stake. Tadek sat out the second slaughter, but by the third slaughter he got his legs back again and tried to help once more, mostly working the chain and tackle at the men's directions and cleaning up afterwards, sloshing buckets of water over the floor to clear away as much blood as he could. The blood smelled like brass or how he imagined brass might smell if you could somehow crack it open, and it created a peculiar ache in the roots of his teeth. The flies already coated the floor like a rippling carpet and they would rise with each bucket of water and then settle again. There was blood all over Tadek's shirtsleeves that he knew would leave permanent stains. The truth was that he'd been more of a mascot than a helper, but still he was determined to take the bloodstains on his shirtsleeves as a mark of pride.

They gutted and quartered the hogs. Jan had a large table

next to the slaughtering floor. Though he was a large man with a heavy belly and an awkward limp, he still managed to move about that table with a rough grace, especially in his shoulders and arms as he switched from cleaver to large knife to thin blade like a surgeon, dismantling the meaty apparatus of the pig's life with sure, gentle cuts. He would properly butcher them later and salt the meat in a huge salting chest they'd hidden in their fruit cellar. Then he'd send everyone his share. For now, with the quartering done, they washed off at the well. They filled a basin with water and each took turns before a mirror nailed to the side of the house. Tadek was surprised to see his own face freckled with blood. He knew his father would take him to the public baths tomorrow to clean him up, a fate he reluctantly accepted, hating the baths full of naked men standing and talking.

They sat down outside at benches around a stump, next to a lean-to under which Jadwiga was cooking on an outside stove. Seeing Jadwiga again at a stove gave Tadek a pang of grief, reminding him of the day his grandfather died. As usual she was in a hostile but sociable mood, as if her obscure grievances with life needed to be doled out to others to maintain equilibrium.

"Sit down and eat! What are you waiting for? Would you stand there and starve without me here to tell you when to open your mouths and when to chew?"

As they ate the men talked. They talked of the ham, the thick bacon, the ribs, but also the snout, the pigs' feet. Don't forget the lungs! Yes, they too could be good. And intestines make perfect sausage casings, and stomachs too can be used for blood sausage. Fried ears, those would be good in winter! Yes, they were all right, but ears and tails in a pot of beans add savor. Save the hooves for gelatin. Don't forget the headcheese!

Jadwiga began to fry a liver steak from the first slaughtered pig. Folk wisdom had it that if the liver steak was good, the pig was good. The sizzle and savor of frying meat filled the air. The bounty of a slaughtered pig seemed inexhaustible. Usually a pig was slaughtered at Christmas, so a celebratory mood had infiltrated the day, but gradually the reality of why they had killed the pigs prematurely settled upon the men, and they grew silent.

"An angel passed over," said Jadwiga after a while. "Or the devil!"

"You know of the partisans in the forests near here," Kazimierz said, shifting his elbows onto his knees and leaning forward, as if he had a secret to reveal. Usually amiable and smiling, now his brows thickened, showing a vertical mark between them like the nick from a hatchet. "These partisans are now part of the Home Army. They work with London." He let this sink in.

He selected an onion from a bowlful on the stump after turning over several in his hand. "I have young children. I didn't want to leave them without a father." He pulled a knife out of his belt and, guiding the end of the blade with his thumb, slit, then removed the brown skin in one motion. "But I will go with those who are in the woods," he announced. His dark look vanished now that he'd gotten the news out. He bit into the onion as you would an apple as if now he could enjoy himself. "I've been spending more and more time there anyway, to stay out of the Russians' grasp, and doing some jobs for the *lesni ludzie* already. My children, they seemed too young to leave for long."

"They're still too young to leave!" Jadwiga said emphatically, as if she was settling the matter.

"Don't you want the Germans to defeat the Russians?" Janusz asked.

"I want a free Poland and that is all that I want!"

"And you will provide this for us?" Jadwiga scoffed, standing behind the men with her arms crossed over her apron.

"Me and the rest of Poland fighting together."

Jan and his wife scoffed together.

"And you will abandon your wife and your children?" Jadwiga challenged again.

"I told you I'd thought of them. I'm abandoning no one. I will be nearby. But I don't want them to be slaves!"

"They will suffer without you."

"They will have to be strong."

"Your wife's a pretty slender reed to hold so much!" Jadwiga wouldn't relent just because others' feelings were being bruised.

"She's stronger than you think! And she'll have to be stronger yet! And you will all have to help her, too!"

"We all want a free Poland. We would also like to be alive to enjoy it," Jadwiga said shortly, shrugging and turning her back on the men as if they weren't worth talking to anymore. She'd let the liver steak cool in the frying pan. Now she stabbed it with a fork and dealt out a small plate of meat and onions before each man as if dismissing them one by one. The men smiled and made faces behind Jadwiga's back, cutting the liver and delving it into a jar of mustard. For a while they ate in silence.

"They would take me away anyway, sooner or later," Kazimierz said, picking up the thread of the conversation. "I might as well fight."

"I'm no good to them." Jan tapped his bad leg. "With this leg like a rock."

"No, brother, but I expect you to help me when I need it."

"Whatever you need and I can do, I'll do it," Jan swore.

They tapped their glasses of kvass together.

"I'm just an accountant," Roman said. "The Germans have their own accountants. I'm no good to them for that. And they'll need the granary to keep running, so maybe nothing will change there."

"Don't be too sure," Kazimierz said. "They'll find their own uses for all of us if we sit and wait."

Later they moved inside to avoid the mosquitoes and, as the adult conversation continued, Tadek grew bored and strolled about the room before stopping by a chess game set out on a corner table. Jan's eyes had followed him. "Do you play, Tadek?" Jan asked, dropping his gruff manner for a moment.

"No."

"Do you want to learn how?"

"All right."

While Roman and Kazimierz continued their talk, Jan brought a kerosene lamp and set it beside the board and went through the pieces one by one for Tadek. He picked each up and explained its magical properties, contained in its shape and switched on by the position on the board, creating a conflicting ground of shafts and interlocking angles of force fields—powers, complex alliances, magnetic attractions and repulsions. Tadek's eyes grew large. It was like the world of politics and armies compressed into a miniature square.

Jan talked him through a few simple openings.

Tadek had never liked the way his Uncle Janusz taunted his father, though Roman seemed to shrug it off. Still, with Jan teaching him chess, he remembered how he could be, like when he'd scuffled and laughed with his brother on Kazimierz's wedding day. He had the Belyawski toothy white smile and deep blue eyes that could charm when he let himself relax.

"Look at him," Kazimierz exclaimed. "The young grandmaster!"

"I never see him sit still like that!" Roman commented, standing and putting a hand on Tadek's shoulder. "I can't get him to concentrate for two minutes! But come, Tadek. It's time to leave. I will give you a set for your birthday."

Tadek looked up, alarmed: "But I want a football!"

The men laughed, and then laughed again louder at his surprised expression, and finally reassured him that such dreams came true, even in wartime.

It was evening as he and his father headed home. As they approached Liaski, Tadek suggested shortcuts that he and his friends used, through fields and backyards, in order to avoid the Germans.

"You know your way around here better than I do," his father said. He accepted the compliment in silence, knowing it was true. He'd been running these fields since his legs could support him.

"Will you go into the forests too, Papa?" he asked. They were walking their bikes over a rough field.

"No, I need to stay with you and your mother as long as I can." They walked in silence. "Do you want me to go?"

"No. I want you to stay."

"Good. I am not like your uncle."

"No." Tadek loved his father and was glad he was not going, but he was in awe of his uncle.

"Let's stop for a minute, Tadek. Look!" They'd reached a lane that ran between the field they'd crossed and the woods, and when they turned back toward the field, the stars shone above them in rare numbers. "See that broad belt of stars? That's the Milky Way. And straight above us, that's the Northern Cross. These three bright stars that form a triangle, there, there, and there, are Deneb, Altair, and Vega, in three different constellations: the Northern Cross, Aquila, and Lyra, a musical instrument. Over here . . . . " He bent down and put a hand on Tadek's shoulder, turning him slightly to the east. "That's the Great Square of Pegasus."

"It's big."

"Yes. Pegasus was a winged horse."

"A winged horse?"

His father laughed. "In mythology, anyway. And those stars over there are Andromeda, a maiden who was chained to be eaten by a monster. And down by the horizon is Perseus, who rode the horse Pegasus to save Andromeda. But here's some more practical knowledge. There's the North Star. Count over three lengths from the end stars of Ursa Major. It's always due north. Square yourself off toward it and your left hand is west and your right hand is east."

"I see."

A gunshot came from across the field, in the woods behind them, toward Gombachy, the next village over. Then came faint shouts and a peppering of shots, as of a hunting party. But what would anyone hunt at night? Tadek's father's hands had stiffened into a tight grip on his shoulders. He let go and began to walk his bike quickly down the lane. "Come."

"What was that?" Tadek asked.

"Nothing. Nothing good. Come on! We must hurry!"

Chapter 5: The New Order

It turned out the Germans didn't forage through the town for food, the way the Russians had done more than once. Instead, junior officers came to knock on the front door and ask for eggs and milk. Sometimes they asked politely, sometimes with a sneer, but all the villagers knew that they could not be refused without consequences. Nevertheless, they paid cash for the food.

The Germans swept through Liaski, leaving it seemingly unscathed, hurrying after the collapsing Russians. To Tadek, compared to the drab and ragged Russians, the Germans had a fine, honed style, especially the SS in their dramatic black uniforms. Though when they went marching through the streets in tight, stomping formations, singing in full-throated arrogance their song, *Heili, Heilo*, Tadek understood that this style was nothing he could share in, but was a weapon against him somehow, and it served to stoke his resentment.

It wasn't only their marching that was tightly organized. They had an ordinance prescribing all imaginable behavior. The joke made the rounds, "Whatever is not verboten is required." The commandant in charge of Liaski made the residents whitewash the town hall. His soldiers shot wandering dogs. He made the Gradinskis' neighbor clean up his yard and made sure that the ruins of the first few days' of fighting, and even the ruins still lingering from the Soviet invasion, were cleared from the street. No garbage was allowed to accumulate. He had the fence running along the railroad station whitewashed, and in general the whole town looked trimmer than it had under the Russians.

It wasn't long before the Germans began to reveal themselves more fully to the eastern Poles, mostly in the reprisals for the partisans' activities. Tadek listened to anything to do with the partisans with keen attention, since Kazimierz had done as he'd promised and taken his hunting rifle and disappeared into the forest the first week of German occupation. Stories sifted into Liaski about forty, fifty, one hundred Poles killed for every German killed by the partisans. So the partisans were always gathering, always preparing, usually abstaining from direct action against the German personnel in order to protect the civilians. There were lists in every town of the citizens who would be punished if local cooperation wasn't satisfactory.

But the partisans acted anyway, calculating to a fine degree what might not elicit reprisals from the Germans. Mostly they struck at the railroads. One day the line heading out of Grodno was sabotaged, derailing a trainload of German troops, and everyone had looked at Tadek differently that day, assuming as he did that his uncle Kazimierz was involved. The leader of the local partisans was called Kowal, the blacksmith, and those who knew Kazimierz, who had taken over his father's forge for a time, had suspicions who this Kowal might be.

There was no genuine news in Liaski, just the posters and loudspeakers in the town square proclaiming the Germans' triumphs, past, present, and future, replacing the posters and loudspeakers that had proclaimed the marvels of the Soviets. It was illegal to listen to the British radio, and difficult to tune in anyway, if someone had a radio that had not been confiscated. But as the German occupation settled in, the stories of their treatments of Jews began to be whispered everywhere. In November the order went out from the German command that all Jews in the area were to move to Grodno into one of two ghettoes that had been established by closing off the sprawling, informal Jewish Quarter with gates. The Jews, it was said, would be given work assignments. They had three days. All contact between Jews and gentiles was banned.

Tadek heard later how the Jewish storekeeper Friedlander and his family were among those who left town in their own cart, headed toward Grodno, under the disdainful eye of the Gestapo. First over the loudspeaker had come the order for the Poles to go inside and to close their shutters. Still, some people stood silently and peered through half-open doors on the side streets and watched the Friedlanders and the few other Jewish families in Liaski pack and go. Some looked the other way or walked away and went back to their business. What were they to do? Fight the Germans? They'd already tried that. That, at least the open resistance, was done. The Germans were going to do whatever they wished to do with anyone they wished. Most in Liaski were too in shock by the recent events and fearful of what was yet to come to voice an opinion. Some shrugged and were indifferent and others were pleased, saying, "Good, the Jews deserve it. They were never like us." Others felt a growing nausea, sensing the beginning of a great wrong.

Tadek didn't know what to think. If he'd been asked he couldn't have precisely said what a Jew was, beyond describing their dress, nor could he have said why they were so different and controversial. He knew that they'd demanded that Barabbas be freed, instead of Jesus, though he'd always been mutely baffled as to why they would want to do such a thing, since it seemed such a peculiarly bad choice. Thinking about all of that just confused him further. Liaski itself was mostly Catholic. There were the Friedlanders, who had been kind to him, and the other Jewish families whom he'd see pass through town in their odd black garb headed toward the Temple in Grodno on Fridays, speaking their strange language. There was also Levy Reznikoff whom his grandfather had visited in Grodno, taking Tadek along sometimes when he was a young boy. Tadek would sit or wander through the dim, silent shelves of the fabric shop while his grandfather sat over tea with Levy. Their voices would rise and rise as they argued, and the more they argued, the more pleased they both seemed. But that had been years ago and the memories were already fading. Once Bolek Kosokovski had called him a Jew and he'd come at Bolek swinging, even though Bolek was much bigger than Tadek, because he knew it was meant to be an insult. Bolek had laughed and fended him off with one hand.

Everyone knew that the Catholic Poles were considered *untermenschen* as well. At first, when the Germans had entered western Poland, there had been little news. But by now stories had filtered across the country about the Germans' slaughter of Poles, in the tens of thousands, especially army officers, journalists, teachers, doctors, and lawyers. Now the vicious reprisals meted out by the Germans taught everyone that, hard as it was to imagine, they could be as bad as the Russians. New rumors were coming now that the Germans had begun to clear all the Poles out of large swaths of western Poland for resettlement, putting Poles into railroad cars and shipping them east with no provisions or housing at their destination, or shipping some directly to camps.

Still, it had been good to see Stalin's soldiers running away like frightened children.

PART II:
THE SCHOOL
OF WAR

Chapter 6: The Basement School

Under the Soviets school had been sporadic, and when it was in session, Tadek and the other children of Liaski attended only now and again. The study of Russian was required, though some lessons were in Polish. Yet the imported teachers were so deficient in Polish that the lessons became a theatre of miming and misunderstanding. He remembered one teacher, an obese Byelorussian woman, who told them, resorting to mangled Polish for this important lesson, to pray to God for candy. She walked around the room, looking up at the ceiling, wondering out loud, "Where's the candy? Where's the candy? Where can it be?" Then she told them to ask Comrade Stalin for candy. She slipped on a painted paper maché mask, tying it in the back of her head with a ribbon. It was obvious whom it represented, with the heavy black mustache and thick head of black hair. Humming to herself as she walked down the aisle, continually readjusting the loose mask, she doled out one piece of caramel candy to each student. The students gawked, dumfounded by this performance. Did she on some level truly believe that her metamorphosis into the Supreme

Leader himself was convincing to their docile minds? But then they shrugged and bit into their candy. Only Tadek sent his piece flying by the teacher's head when she turned away.

The German educational plan for the Poles was no better. Schools were closed for all Poles beyond the sixth grade, since they were just *sklavenvol*, the slave people, who needed no refinements. They were to be taught simple addition and subtraction for numbers only up to five hundred, and enough basic German to take orders. They needn't learn to read. This indifference rankled Tadek's parents so much that either Roman or Krystyna read with him every night.

Elena Swyokla, an aging, alcoholic poetess with an unfortunate weakness for Goethe and Heine, staffed the official German school. She was helped in these duties by her niece, Danuta. As with the Russian school, attendance by the children of Liaski was spotty, with mostly those children attending whose parents were the most fearful of the German authorities. Others such as Tadek went only when the Germans began to take too close an interest in their comings and goings.

Under the Russians, underground Polish-language classes had moved about the village, first at the church and then from house to house, finally settling with some stability at the home of a pair of retired teachers from Wilno, the Krzaczeks, who had at first been wary of setting up classes in their own home, but had grown bolder over the years. Now classes continued unchanged under the German regime. Often Tadek stayed home to help his mother in the garden or orchard, but when he did attend, he was surrounded by the same children he'd grown up with, Pawel Karposovich, his best friend; Halinka Nowak, the beauty of the town; and Sabina Jablonski, Halinka's only rival in looks and her best friend. Also included were the musical Borovski twins, Yanek and Franek; and Bolek Kosokovski, who was already almost as big as an adult, and carried the other children on his back as a lark.

The Krzaczeks owned one of the larger houses in town, a two-story brick house a street from the main square, surrounded by cypresses and shrubbery, through which the children could slip one by one before darting between the acacias and into a side door and down into their basement, making the Krzaczek's an underground school in all senses. The basement smelled of mushrooms and mildew. In two large rooms, the students sat on crates and make-shift benches and listened to Mrs. Krzaczek in one room, with the younger children, and Mr. Krzaczek in the other, hold forth in disorganized lectures in their native tongue. Then the two would switch rooms, though their methods were identical.

Mrs. Krzaczek's specialty was the glories of the Polish-Lithuanian Commonwealth, especially the poetry of the era, and it was amazing how such seemingly tranquil language could result in such an apocalypse of chalk as she slashed line after line onto a piece of slate nailed to the wall. Her husband, also a vigorous chalk-smasher, gloried in the movements of regiments and battalions under the great Piłsudski as he defeated the Russians, again and again, on the battlefield of the chalkboard. The children sat with crumpled and stained lesson-sheets in their hands, full of dates that seemed doomed to fade in their minds—yet the heroic martyrdom of generation after generation came through clearly enough.

Mrs. Krzaczek would recite huge swaths of Mickiewicz out loud, looking up from the book at the low, cobwebbed ceiling, peering into her dusty but defiant memory.

> I knew he'd tell his story in the end.
> (Ex-convicts like to speak to an old friend
> About their prison days.) I'd learn the truth,
> The truth that tyrants hide, the Polish truth.
> It flourishes in shadows. Its history

Lives in Siberia, where its heroes die.

While her quavery voice unspooled line after line, Tadek squirmed in his seat and tried to catch the eye of his best friend Pawel, to make him grin. Pawel, who had astonished everyone by declaring when he was seven that he wanted to be a priest, had given up that goal, but was still considered a model student compared to Tadek, who would only sit still for the stories that his parents read to him. Mrs. Krzaczek began to go around the room in an attempt to force the students to memorize the poem a stanza at a time. "This is our heritage! Our life! You need it inside you!" Tadek stared down at the lesson sheets in his hands, now trying to keep himself from laughing—he didn't know why.

Both Krzaczeks agreed that Tadek had been born restless, and he seldom made it through a day without a reprimand for speaking out of turn or bouncing up and out of his seat. Still, he felt that both teachers secretly liked him, despite his missteps. He felt that they liked him personally, but also because his grandfather had been an important person in the town, and maybe because of his Uncle Kazimierz's whispered fame for his work in the resistance, taking place somewhere in the mysterious depths of the surrounding woods.

At night, after feeding the chickens and the two goats that the Gradinskis kept, Tadek would cross the village to Pawel's side of town, nearer the river. He would weave through the back streets to avoid the Nazis in the town square. His memories of Pawel went as far back as his memories of himself. When they were both younger, Pawel had lived two houses down from him, and as soon as they had been able to walk they were together, and as soon as they were allowed out on their own, they were running all over the village as if it were their private playground. Whether Russians or

Germans claimed their land, the boys felt instinctively that nature owed them a childhood.

Even at ten Pawel seemed tall and slender and walked with a grace as if his joints had been well oiled. He never did anything wrong, which maddened Tadek, but still he was Tadek's loyal follower as long as no trouble with adults was involved. It was Tadek who made the decisions for them, where they would go that day or with whom they would play. The only oddity of Pawel was that his grandfather, as everyone quite well knew, hadn't been Polish, but a Byelorussian, creating one of the few wrinkles, beside the few Jews, in the solid Polish town. Pawel, however, followed the religion of his mother and went to the Catholic Church in Liaski along with everyone else.

Before the Germans' bugle-call to mark the curfew, the children had a few hours of twilight and evening to play. Tadek and Pawel and as many as twenty village boys and girls would gather, ignoring the Germans, whose only presence away from the square was two soldiers who would circle the village every half hour, smoking and chatting, far from the front. The children quieted a little and let them pass, then continued with their games, playing tag, crowded into the intersection of two streets, or scattering for Go Hide, through the streets and alleys, taking in the smell of the ash-heaps and the chicken coops as they ran.

Almost every house had its garden out back and fruit trees and outhouse. Although these gardens were fenced, Tadek knew every low, jumpable hedge, every missing fence board, every ill-tempered dog. He knew the overgrown shrubbery where you could crouch unseen until the seeker would be brushing the leaves inches from your leg, and then you could burst running out of your lair and easily beat him to the base.

For those moments Tadek could be fully alive within these

gaps in the adult world, running bare-footed down the streets and then hiding in the mothy shadows. In his heart of hearts, he craved perpetual motion more than anything, and the moments of quiet hiding only made the wild release of the run that much sweeter.

The two child beauties, Halinka and Sabina, were among those who would play. Pawel and Tadek, Halinka and Sabina had all known each other since their mothers used to stop and chat while they would stare wide-eyed at each other from their baby carriages. Halinka had blonde hair pulled into a long braid and a narrow, delicate face. Already now at the age of eleven, she was taller than the other girls and many of the boys. She was slender, regal, and shyly aloof, looking down upon the world with a kind and enigmatic superiority. Her father had been conscripted by the Soviets, and this added the sense of a deeper sadness and impressive strength to her silent beauty. Though she was still too young to exercise her power over the boys, and they were too young to be captured by its spell, they could sense it already, growing in its potential everyday, like a fairytale potion that first needed aging in the dragon's lair.

Sabina was shorter than her best friend, with darker hair and a heart-shaped, impudent face and plump mouth always ready with a joke, poised exactly halfway between affection and hostility. Tadek fought constantly with her as if she was his sister. She could run faster than most of the boys, and when they tugged at her dress, she would give them a serious punch in the arm with her small clenched fist, hurting them enough to make them think next time before they teased her.

The last game of the night, he wanted to say to Halinka, come hide with me, but he couldn't make himself say the words. Instead he found that he and Sabina were running toward the same thick cluster of lilacs, flush against a fence. He ducked into them right after her.

"Hey!" she protested.

"Shh," he said. Together they watched the seeker prowl the other side of the street in the moonlight. He listened to her breath in the dark. They were both panting from running. As his eyes adjusted to the shadows, he could see her open lips, her flushed cheek, her wide eyes peering through the leaves. It was Halinka he wished he was with, Halinka and her clear, pure beauty. But Sabina had a remarkable plump lower lip that gave her a pout when she wasn't laughing, and on an impulse, compelled by that lower lip, he leaned over and kissed her, managing to land the ill-aimed kiss half on her mouth, half on her cheek. She turned and looked at him as if he'd just dropped from the moon, begun to dance some lunar dance, and warble some lunar song.

The steps of the seeker were coming toward them. He leaned and kissed her again, aiming more surely for that lower lip. Inches from his face, she laughed her surprise and scorn. Then she turned and shot running out from under the branches, leaving him to be caught by the seeker.

"Did you kiss Sabina?" one of the Borovski twins asked as the kids regathered. The word was out. The girls clustered together, looking over their shoulders, giggling.

"Sure. Why not!"

"Do you like her?"

"No, I like Halinka."

"Then why did you kiss Sabina?"

"I'll kiss who I want to. I don't care."

The fact was that he felt more at ease with Sabina, as if he could show himself, while Halinka made his mind go numb and his hands turn to wood.

The next time he saw Sabina was after mass where most of the village gathered on the lawn in groups of three and four to talk. While their parents chatted, he found himself next to her. She just made a face at him and dismissed him: "You're so strange. I know you like Halinka, not me. Just tell her." Of course he wasn't about to tell Halinka anything. He looked over his shoulder at Halinka, who was walking away with her mother.

"I don't like anybody," he said. "Certainly not you."

"I don't care. I think you're stupid."

"Good!"

He tried to step on her foot but she skipped away. "Ha-ha!"

Near the end of summer, Tadek and Pawel spent three days building a tree house in an apple tree behind a house that had been bombed and abandoned. It was just a small platform, no more than three meters off the ground, but it was on a small rise, and from there they could survey the town and look across the road down the bluff to the river. At the back of Tadek's mind was the thought that the Germans wouldn't like their tree house, but the tree could not be resisted once the idea for the treehouse formed in his mind. The boys stopped work each time they saw Germans circling on the road and froze, hidden amid the leaves. When it was done, they snapped thin, flexible branches off the tree and took out their pocket knives and sharpened them. They picked a burlap sack full of green apples and sat with their legs dangling over the side of their platform. Each boy pierced an apple with a branch and used the branch to fling the apple far into the air, slicing across the road. They couldn't believe their fortune when Halinka and Sabina came walking down the road which ran above the river, arm in arm. With a quick whip of the branch with his wrist, Tadek sent an apple bouncing in front of them. The girls stopped, puzzled. Conferred. Sabina saw the tree house and pointed and they walked over to it. Tadek stood and sent an apple arcing as high as he could toward the river. The girls looked up at them.

"What are you doing?" Sabina asked.

"We built this," Tadek answered.

"No, you didn't."

"Yes, we did."

"Just you two?"

"Yes."

"Pretty nice," Sabina admitted grudgingly.

"I can almost hit the river from here."

"Pawel, this isn't like you," Halinka said, fretting.

"You're going to get in trouble," Sabina said confidently.

"No one lives here anymore."

"Well, you'll still get in trouble."

"I don't care, anyway." Tadek jammed another apple onto the pointed stick and turned to send it flying toward the abandoned house. It smashed through a window fragment with a satisfying crash.

"Look at you. That was ridiculous," Sabina mocked. "Show off!"

"I just wanted to."

They stood arguing for a while, mostly Sabina and Tadek, with Pawel and Halinka as their audience.

"I could hit you easy from here," Tadek threatened to toss one of the green apples down on the girls.

"Don't!" They backed away from the tree, laughing, while Tadek tossed an apple up and down.

The laughter stilled when the kids saw two German soldiers appear around the corner of a house. The soldiers saw the kids and veered off the road toward them.

"We'd better go! Watch out!" The girls hurried away.

One of the soldiers began shouting at Pawel and Tadek in German. Tadek shook his head. When they drew close, the soldier barked again in German, but Tadek didn't understand and just shook his head again. He was surprised to see their individual faces—one narrow and pockmarked and tense, the other round and ruddy. He was used to just seeing their gray-green uniforms from a distance. It was odd to be so close to them, to see them as separate people.

The round-faced man ran forward, took a step up the ladder the boys had hammered into the tree, and reached up to grab Tadek by the ankle. "Hey!" Tadek clung for a second to a branch, then to the platform, before plummeting down to smack on the ground.

For a moment he couldn't get his breath. He lay there breathing hard, but seemed to get no air. Tears came to his eyes. He could smell the distinctive odor of German boot polish as the men stood over him in their shiny boots. They moved away. When he sat up, still gasping, he saw that Pawel had climbed down and was walking away, turning and watching from the road. The soldiers took their rifle butts and were smashing the boards upwards. One of them climbed up the ladder, and began to rip the boards away from the tree one by one. It took just minutes to dismantle it.

"*Verboten!*"

"Okay, okay." Tadek joined Pawel and they walked away, not wanting to fall into the Germans' clutches. They knew if they were hauled into the police station, there would be no end of trouble. Still, they couldn't help but linger and watch as the two soldiers hauled the boards down to the river and threw them in. They floated away, turning on the current.

A few nights later Halinka and Sabina walked by the boys who were gathering in the dusk. "Are you two okay?" Halinka asked.

"Sure," Tadek shrugged.

"We were scared," Halinka said.

"I wasn't," Sabina protested.

"All right," Halinka ceded, smiling her shy smile, so cryptic to Tadek. "You're brave! But I was."

"They didn't have to tear up our tree house," Tadek said. "It's not going to kill any of them."

"That's the way they are," Sabina said.

"Obviously!" Tadek was sick of talking about it. He remembered that helpless feeling as he'd been ripped out of the tree house and into the air. He remembered gasping for breath and he wanted to forget the event. "Are you going to play?" he asked impatiently. "It's almost dark."

"No," Sabina informed the boys. "We're getting too old for this."

"That's right," Halinka said, as if they'd rehearsed it.

"And besides," Sabina continued, "summer's over." Halinka gave Tadek a pitying smile. The girls walked away hand in hand.

"I don't get them," Tadek said. "They aren't so grown up."

"They think they are," Pawel said.

Instead of playing, the boys stood around arguing.

"Why don't you go to the Krzaczek's school?" Tadek asked the Borovski twins, on hearing they were going to the official school the next day.

"We will, but our mother wants us to go to the above-ground school sometimes, so we don't get in trouble."

"Well, I'm not going," Tadek said.

"You're in seventh form. You don't have to go."

This was true. The twins were a year younger.

"I wouldn't go anyway."

Something was coming to an end. The boys walked up and down the alleyways off the square, disgusted as one of the last nights of August went to waste.

They walked by a half-painted fence, and as they turned the corner, Tadek noted a can of paint with a brush atop it tucked behind the fence. In the next alley they came upon an escaped piglet, its back to them, trotting in an exploratory, zigzagging fashion down the alleyway. Tadek put two ideas together. "Shh." He put an arm out to stop his friends. "I have an idea," he whispered. "Let's catch the pig."

"What for? What's your idea?" Pawel was wary.

"I'll tell you. Just get in front of the pig. Cut him off."

The four boys slowly crept around the pig. He noticed them and stopped to look up at them with mistrustful eyes. But it was too late. One of the twins dove upon it, pinning it against the cindery alleyway, and all the boys grabbed hold of the squealing beast.

"Wait here!" Tadek ran back to the half-painted fence and found the brush and paint. "Hold him down!"

"What are you doing to do?"

"Watch and see!"

As the other boys held down the piglet, Tadek pried open the can of paint and dipped in a corner of the brush. The squirming piglet made a difficult canvas, but the dark paint showed up well. Tadek wrote with a corner of the paintbrush, dipping and dabbing, dipping and dabbing. "Hold him still!" After the third letter, rough and smeared but legible, the boys knew what he was writing.

"Oh my God."

"We're going to get in trouble."

"They'll kill us."

"I'm leaving," Pawel said. He seemed suddenly angry. "It's almost curfew anyway." He walked away.

The twins and Bolek didn't seem to know how to react. They seemed in awe of what Tadek was doing. "They'll arrest us."

"They tore down our tree house!" Tadek said. The other boys hesitated. They all understood the justice of the claim. Everyone hated the Germans anyway, but the boys could sense how seeing the tree house float down the river had stung Tadek in a personal way.

"Just let me finish," Tadek said, working on the final syllable of the Führer's name.

Tadek wondered, too, if he'd gone too far this time, but he felt a compulsion to finish what he'd started.

"There. Okay. I'm going home too. I'll give you a head start. But give me the pig. I'm dropping him off by the square."

They carefully handed Tadek the pig, backing away, before they took off running. He held it tightly against his chest, a leg in each hand, the painted side away from him. In seconds, the alleyway was empty. The pig squirmed, but Tadek held it tighter and it quieted. He trotted down the alleyway, thick with inky shadows, till he turned the corner from where he could see the square, with its German guards standing in front of the townhall in a harsh light. He set the pig free in the alley, blocking its escape. "Shoo! Shoo!" he waved his arms. The pig turned away from him and bolted towards the square. Tadek waited until he saw that it was trotting into the light before he turned to run himself, laughing at the sound of a few shouts in German before he disappeared down a shortcut between two houses and finally into the fields on the edge of town. From there he knew he could work his way back to his own house unseen.

He tried to make his way past his mother in the kitchen.

"Why is there red paint all over your hands? And what's this?" His mother grabbed him by the shirt. "You've ruined your clothes! What have you been doing?"

As he explained she grew more and more astonished. She grabbed a brush and soap and pulled Tadek by the arm out to the pump, where she scrubbed his hands till they were raw in an attempt to remove the paint.

"Don't provoke them," Tadek's mother warned, finally relinquishing her grip on him and giving him a steady look from inches away until he returned that look and held her gaze in acknowledgement. "Don't provoke them," she said slowly, intensely. "Do you understand me?"

"Yes." But Tadek thought that he knew how much he could get away with better than she did. He'd known his escape path before he'd ever written the first letter on the pig.

She made him stay home from school for two days, giving his hands vicious scrubbings until she was satisfied that they were free of paint. She had him burn his shirt in the ash pit at the back of the garden.

Yet nothing could ruin the success of the prank. It turned out that there had been an audience of both Germans and Poles in the square when the pig came trotting happily by. A sergeant had deciphered the red letters along the pig's flank and had ordered two guards to capture it, but the pig took them for three circuits of the square before disappearing up another alleyway and into the night. The German commandant assigned a few soldiers to spend much of the next few days trying to get to the bottom of the crime. In other villages, there had been reprisals for offenses only slightly worse than a pig with the Führer's name written on his side, but the Germans were finding that blanket reprisals just increased the perverse will of the stiff-necked Poles.

Then there was an attempted sabotage of a railroad bridge on the line to Wilno to remind the Germans of more serious things, and the incident was forgotten. The assumption in Liaski was that it was the work of the partisans led by Kowal. Often these partisans seemed rumored into existence, flimsy and evasive as ghosts, but it was upon these spirits that the Poles hung their attenuated hopes.

In the meantime the Nazis rolled ahead, their formations of Junkers and Heinkels overhead, their troop carriers and trains full of fresh troops headed east. They weren't interested in Liaski.

It was just a pebble over which their river of troops poured, chasing the Russians, who were collapsing, falling back hundreds of kilometers as the flood of Germans closed in on Leningrad, Stalingrad, and Moscow.

Chapter 7:
A Knock on the Window

November 2, 1942

Tadek slept on a cot in an alcove of the kitchen behind a curtain. His father pulled back the curtain and folded the cot for him every day, leaning it against the wall. He considered the setup perfect, since one side of the alcove was formed by a Dutch oven built into the wall that vented directly into the chimney, heating the whole house in winter, and making his alcove toasty on the coldest nights.

One night that fall he lay on the cot not yet quite sleeping, half-dreaming about a football game they'd played that day. He played over in his mind a steal he'd made, the rush down the sidelines, the ball skimming in front of him as he raced toward the makeshift goal of two rocks. With a start he woke up. He realized that he'd been hearing for some time, without being fully conscious of it, a rustling outside in the shrubbery. He stiffened and listened. Voices. Someone bumped against the wall.

A timid rapping came at the windowpane directly above his head. He propped himself up on his elbow and pushed himself up till he was staring at a man's pale face right next to the pane not two feet away. They both started and fell back.

When Tadek looked again the man's face had disappeared, but as he waited, it returned, a lean, young, clean-shaven face, a finger to its lips.

"Go get your parents," the man whispered in lightly accented Polish that Tadek recognized but couldn't place. "Tell them it's Ephraim Reznikoff and his family."

"Who's there?" he heard his mother calling from the next room. "Tadek? Tadek? Who's there?"

"It's Ephraim Reznikoff." Now the accent made sense.

His mother, grasping a thin nightgown at her throat, rushed from the bedroom to the window. Outside the young man stood behind some bushes, underneath Tadek's window, spotted by moonlight. Craning at the window, Tadek could just make out other forms behind him: a woman and two children crouched in the shadows.

"Of course. I didn't recognize you at first. Come around to the door, Ephraim." His mother gestured to them to go around the house. Tadek went to light the kerosene lantern.

"What are you doing?" Tadek's father whispered angrily to his wife.

"Shh!" she turned and hissed over her shoulder.

His father went to the lamp and turned it down until the yellow flame just fluttered weakly.

Krystyna went to the door and leant out into the night. One by one the family came in and everyone stood in the small kitchen, clustered together, as though embarrassed and not wishing to take up much space. The woman and her two children, one on each side of her, each under one of her hands, stood by the door, prepared to be driven away. There was a boy of about seven dressed all in black, and a younger girl. Tadek stared at the children and they stared back. They had round, dark, sad eyes.

"Thank you," Ephraim said. "We've had to flee the ghetto."

"Of course," Krystyna said, taking the lead when her husband was silent. "Tell us what happened."

Ephraim stood wiping a hand down across his brow and eyes very rapidly. His wife began to cry. Ephraim hugged her. They seemed unwilling to fully trust the relief that they had begun to feel, smiling doubtfully and looking around the room as if some treacherous beast might make a run at them any moment.

"They took my father away first thing." Ephraim turned to Tadek's parents. "Relocated, so they said. And my mother died soon after...heart attack. I don't know if you knew that."

"No. I'm sorry."

"She'd seen too much already and would not have wanted to see the rest of this."

"No."

"You know, we've all been in the ghetto for the past year?"

"Yes, I knew." There was another embarrassed silence that Tadek struggled to understand. Bandito, their three-legged cat, limped into the room and, ignoring the visitors, made his way over to his food bowl in a corner. Everyone stopped and watched him for a while, as if expecting something more from him.

"Friends of your brother Kazimierz, from the woods, brought us some food," Ephraim continued. "Not much, but something."

"Did they?"

Tadek remembered seeing the man in his father's shop in Grodno when Tadek had gone there with his grandfather: a young man with flushed cheeks behind the cash register calling out questions to his father, orders to the help in the store. He had looked different then, dressed all in black, with sidelocks, beard, and skullcap. Now he had shaved off his sidelocks and beard, and his bare face looked younger—surprised and naïve. He was very frightened and his complexion, which had been flushed, was now an alarming white. As if divining Tadek's thoughts, his hand went to his cheek, and he began to stroke it tentatively as he spoke.

"Well, they've begun what some of us have been expecting," Ephraim started to explain. "An *Aktion* in the ghetto. And my family and I, we have nowhere to go. They rounded up some community leaders last week. I was warned just minutes before they entered the ghetto this morning. It has taken us all day to walk this far. We hid in the fields during the day.

"Your brother is with the partisans...at least I have heard... and I remembered your grandfather's visits . . . . That was why I came here. There was nowhere else."

"We'll think of something," Krystyna said. Roman, standing behind her, said nothing.

"Thank you."

"But you must hide. Tadek, put your shoes on and take Mr. Reznikoff and his family around back. There's that lean-to behind the hen house. Clear the way to it. It's small, but that's good. It won't be noticed. We will bring you food."

"Thank you."

"Leave the light, Tadek," his father said, in a voice that was too loud for the room. Everyone turned to look at him, as if they'd forgotten he was there. "No light," he said more quietly.

"Okay."

The path to the henhouse through the yard was mostly in shadows, but it was so familiar to him that Tadek could've walked it with his eyes closed. Bandito limped ahead of him on the path, a dim white beacon assuring him of his steps. But he heard the family stumbling behind him. He paused midway and let them catch up. "Give me your hand." He took Ephraim's hand and they all formed a linked line. "Watch out for the stump." He led them around the chopping block where chickens were slaughtered. "The outhouse is down this path, if you need…"

"Yes, I think we do," Ephraim said. "Please, show us the way. The dark . . . . "

He led them further into the yard. Here the path was straighter and, embarrassed, he let drop Ephraim's hand. They went through the garden and orchard to the very end. There Tadek and Ephraim sat on a stack of lumber while the mother helped the two children into the outhouse one by one. The yard ended with a tall wooden fence covered in vines, but on the other side of it one could occasionally hear someone passing on the street, so he and Ephraim were silent, until Ephraim said cryptically, "I shouldn't, but I have to," and withdrew a paper and tobacco from a pocket and skillfully rolled a cigarette. After glancing around at the borders of the fence, he backed into a dark pocket of shrubbery and lit the cigarette, cupping the match carefully in his hands.

"Can I have one?" Tadek asked on impulse. Tadek was eleven, and had never smoked, but the strangeness of the moment seemed to call for a memorable action. He felt the man looking at him in the dark.

"No, you are too young."

"I smoke all the time," he lied.

"No," the man said firmly. "You don't."

Tadek shrugged, oddly pleased that the man's refusal confirmed something he'd expected but wanted to test.

The rusty hinges of the chicken coop's door made a screech that made them all cringe and stop and wait in silence for a moment. "Step over the board here," Tadek directed. The ammoniacal odor of the chickens enveloped them. An unsettled rustling of the hens and a few squawks accompanied them on their way down the narrow aisle between shelves of sleeping fowl. At the back there was a panel that served as a door to a lean-to. With Ephraim's help Tadek moved a couple of bales of hay and then removed the door.

Inside were stacks of rusty hoes and broken rakes that he passed out to Ephraim, who laid them in a corner of the coop. They tried to work quietly. No one spoke. They then broke up the bales of hay and spread them on the dirt floor. The roof was so low that Ephraim couldn't stand upright, so the family sat down together on the hay. There would be just enough room for them to stretch out to sleep. Tadek started to apologize but found he didn't know what to say. "I'll get some food," he finally got out and they thanked him.

Back at the house his mother handed him a basket of food and a folded blanket. As he walked down the narrow chicken-coop aisle for the second time, he listened for the family, but they were frozen still, holding their breath. He placed the basket on the ground, lit a candle, overturned a wooden crate, and placed the basket and candle on it. The family was sitting on the ground in a semi-circle, hunched as if to make themselves small, their dark eyes following his every motion as he unpacked the basket: a bowl of beans, a loaf of black bread, a small pitcher of milk. They thanked him again. The girl took two bites and then turned aside, lay down on the ground, and vomited. The mother smoothed her hair back, apologizing again. Tadek scooped up the straw on which she'd vomited and threw it into the chicken coop.

He retraced his steps to the house, where his mother waited in the kitchen.

"They need more blankets."

"I'll take them. You go to bed, Tadek."

Later from his cot in the kitchen he could hear his mother and father arguing. He tried to get his mind back to where it had been, the ball skimming smoothly off his foot ahead of him, the gang of kids rushing after, the goalie with spread legs and arms, but try as he might he couldn't maintain that vision through to the goal.

"I knew him," his mother was saying. "My father knew his father. Others are hiding Jews!"

"Others are turning them in too!"

"Don't talk like some *szmalcownik*—or worse."

"I didn't mean that."

"What did you mean?"

"It's a dangerous business, that's all. Half of them are Bolsheviks anyway!"

"You don't know that!"

"They put on red arm bands and welcomed the Soviets into Grodno!"

"They! How many? Five? Eight?"

"The Bohatkiewiczes were shot for hiding Jews in Shabany." Tadek could gauge his father's frustration by the way his voice was becoming ever more intense as it went lower, like a thin stream of water spraying under incredible pressure.

"They were stupid. In an apartment above the tailor's in the center of town!"

"It's dangerous, this is. Maybe they can stay one night. Only out in the fields. Or down by the river. We can give them some food."

"They can hide in the chicken coop until they're ready to go!"

"Shh! Keep it down!" Roman's voice said that he was relenting, accepting. "It's just, this is a dangerous business."

Tadek understood. It wasn't just the Jews who were in trouble.

Finally he fell asleep, dreaming of the dogs the Nazis had, and the sound that their tanks made as they plowed through the fields like metallic dragons, and of their boots stomping in unison down the dusty main streets.

Chapter 8: Disappearing

Tadek worked about the yard the next day. He fed the goats, chopped wood, pumped water, and gathered eggs. All the while he felt the alert, tense, silent presence of the lean-to at the back of the chicken coop. It was little more than a cluster of slanted, unpainted boards, surrounded by thick weeds and shrubs. Its original purpose was now forgotten and it was used to store items on the brink of disposal. He'd half-forgotten about the shed himself.

Once a patrol of German soldiers passed on the street at the end of the yard. Tadek heard their confident German voices and knew that the Reznikoffs must hear them too. That night at dinner he could feel the tension between his parents. At first they tried to argue in hushed voices and only when he left the room, but the argument soon grew beyond these boundaries. His father said the Reznikoffs had to leave, but his mother refused to evict them until they knew where they were going. He'd never seen his parents both refuse to give in like this.

When it was fully dark, Tadek led the Reznikoffs again to the outhouse. They paced to stretch their legs in the small, packed-earth clearing between the small barn, the house, and the henhouse. Krystyna brought a basket of food and they all moved into the tool room of the barn. Krystyna passed out plates and boiled potatoes, chicken, onions, and black bread.

"I'm sorry...the plates...I don't really know about...." Krystyna said.

"It's all right," Ephraim said dryly. "We're hungry and we have to eat. We thank you."

The family ate in the dark while standing up to stretch their legs, since they'd been cramped all day. They stood close to each other and whispered in Yiddish as they ate.

Ephraim told Krystyna and Tadek about what had happened in Grodno. Tadek remembered the year before, '41, when the Friedlanders had left town with all of their possessions in the back of a cart as the Germans rounded Jews up from the countryside and sent them to the two ghettos of Grodno. Ephraim said that those who made it to the ghetto were the lucky ones: the Germans had just shot many Jews in isolated spots in the woods as they came upon them in shtetls, which they left in flames. The conditions in the ghettos had been terribly crowded as they swelled from 20,000 to over 30,000. For the past year, no one knew what their fate would be. But now the Aktion had begun.

The Germans had come in trucks and emptied the buildings, beating old ladies and children, driving them into the marketplace square. Ephraim had been out early and rushed home when an acquaintance told him he'd seen Germans in troop carriers heading for the ghetto. He found his wife and children and grabbed a few bags of valuables. He shaved off his sidelocks and beard and they changed their traditional clothing to don clothes he'd bought earlier that would let them pass for gentiles. The Germans had built a two-meter-high wall around the ghetto, but the Reznikoff's house was on the border, and a window that looked over an alleyway had only been boarded up. Through the alleyway they made their way onto a larger street. After just a few paces they saw a patrol of Germans turn the corner a block away and come trotting toward them. They ducked into the first doorway, a butcher shop. Ephraim had never done business with this butcher, but they'd seen each other in the streets. Now the man stared steadily at Ephraim and his family, with wide, blue, blood-shot, protuberant eyes, as they stood there catching their breath. Ephraim said he'd never forget that look as the butcher stood there: a big man with a shock of white hair, wearing a bloodied apron and holding a cleaver. Ephraim knew from that look that the man recognized him—despite his metamorphosis—but he had no way of knowing what the man would do. He didn't think the man had decided. The Germans rushed by on the street, and the five of them stood in the butcher shop, watching each other. Ephraim said that he could almost see the man's mind spinning through its options as their gazes locked.

Ephraim leaned out the door to see that the Germans had turned the corner and, muttering an apology, hurried his family out into the street and away. They ran down the street to the next alleyway. In this manner they found their way zigzagging through the side streets toward the edge of the city. The sound of distant shouting and shooting chased after them through the streets.

As soon as they were beyond the city gates, they wended their way into ever-smaller lanes until they were on a path that ran along a little wooded creek. On this path they continued as far from the road as they could, finally just curling up in the thick grasses and waiting out the day.

When it grew dark they made their way the ten kilometers to Liaski through the fields and along the edge of the woods, circling around the village until they saw the Gradinski's house on the eastern edge.

"Tell us," Ephraim said. "What are they saying?"

"Just as you say. They are emptying the ghetto. The Jews . . . your people . . . are being moved to Kielbasin to the west. It's a transit point. Some are still saying the plan is to use them as laborers."

Ephraim scoffed and looked at Krystyna with bitter eyes. "Surely you know that they have been shooting Jews in the woods since they arrived?"

"Yes." Krystyna barely whispered.

"Do you think they have suddenly developed a soft spot for us now? That they will keep us alive through the war, when everyone else is dying?"

She didn't answer.

"I talked to a man who escaped from Kielbasin," Ephraim continued. "They put those they transport on the trains. They are sent to Oświęcim or Treblinka. No one ever comes back."

"But they need workers!"

"They will kill us all!"

His voice barely raised but its intensity was chilling. Tadek felt he was getting a glimpse of the way things really were, as if someone had peeled back the skin of the world to reveal the white tendons, the blue veins, stripes of red muscles, and the dark, pulsing organs.

Krystyna didn't say anything for a long time.

"What are you going to do?" she asked at last.

"I know . . . I know we can't stay here."

"It's . . . it's dangerous . . . " Krystyna said. "For everybody. Roman...he isn't comfortable with you here."

Again there was that air of embarrassment.

"*I understand*," Ephraim said, a bit stiffly. "I don't want to endanger your family."

There was a long silence.

"I was thinking perhaps we could make it to Riga. We have

friends who may still be there. From there, maybe across the Baltic to Sweden."

"Listen, Ephraim, that may not be such a good idea. A while ago, Jews were going through Wilno, especially from Germany. It was neutral. But that was a long time ago, and now it's quite dangerous there. You've heard about what happened at Ponary?"

"Yes, I've heard."

The name seemed to weigh upon them and for a long time no one spoke. Tadek had heard that many Jews were killed there.

"What else can we do? We will go around Wilno to Riga. The Baltic and then to Sweden is our only hope."

"That's possible, but it's a long way. I can help you get started. If you travel through the woods, it might work. You need to find a way to the river unnoticed, and then across it. The Germans have a floating bridge, but it's guarded day and night of course. My brother has a boat and he can help get you across. Tadek, are there back ways to Jan's?"

"I know ways out of town so we won't be seen. Going by the reeds along the river and then if, if we circle inland along the woods around Shabany . . . ."

"Not 'we,' Tadek. I'll take them. I can't risk you in this. But I know the way that you mean."

"But I know the way better . . . ."

"I said I know the woods you mean, Tadek," she said impatiently. "The half-moon of woods that goes around the north side of the village. Don't argue." Krystyna turned to the Reznikoffs. "Then I can take you to Shabany." They all had stopped eating and were just holding the bread in their hands, imagining this mysterious, wonderful route to safety. "My brother lives outside Shabany."

"Is it Kazimierz?" Ephraim asked.

"No, Janusz, my other brother. He has a boat there."

"All right."

"I'll talk to him tomorrow. He's not like Kazimierz, but he'll do this. He's got to. And there are people in the resistance who have been helping Jews. He can talk to them and see if they can provide you with a guide on the other side."

There was nothing more to say. Just then there were loud, light-hearted German voices at the end of the garden, on the other side of the fence, as a patrol passed.

They were all still until the voices faded away. It was a mild night for early November, but even so they were all chilled. In the west the moon broke through the clouds behind the apple trees. Tadek led the Reznikoffs back to their hiding place where they curled up in the hay. He replaced the panel that served as a door, leaning a rusty shovel and stacking a pile of hay against it to disguise it.

In the house, Tadek's father was standing in the kitchen in a swirl of cigarette smoke. "I don't want to hear anything more about them," he said.

Two days passed. Krystyna went to see Jan and told him to arrange for a guide on the other side of the river. They awaited a response for another day. Just after dusk Tadek had returned from playing in the streets to find his house dark and empty when he let himself in the garden gate.

He lit the kerosene lantern on the center of the table and cut himself a slice of black bread. He put a couple of pieces of wood in the stove. There were still warm coals and he blew on them to get the wood going.

His mother's steps came running down the path from the street. She dashed into the house. Her face was pale and stricken, the way it had looked the day her father had died.

"They are searching the village for Jews," she whispered.

She began to throw some potatoes and onions and apples into a canvas sack.

She led him quickly back through the yard to the hen house. The chickens rustled in the dark as they brushed past their shelves of nests. "Ephraim. It's me," she whispered hoarsely, warning them before she began to remove the door. Inside, Tadek could barely make out the frightened pale faces. His mother explained the situation. "You must leave at once."

Without a word the family picked up their few belongings and followed them out into the night.

"Tadek will show us out of town," Krystyna said. Ephraim nodded. "From there, we'll follow the path he talked about, skirting the woods around Shabany to my brother's. He'll take you across the river and set you on your way there. There's supposed to be a logging road that will take you to a house where people live who will help you, but my brother should know about that by now. That's the best we can do."

"All right."

"Are you ready? Hurry."

Tadek led the way through the orchard. They all gathered at the bottom of the garden by the back gate, a little-used entrance surrounded by leafless rhododendron bushes. They all crouched in the shadows.

"Go ahead and see if anyone is in the street," his mother said.

"There's a cut-through down a house."

"Okay. You'll show us."

Tadek went through the gate, where there lay a back street, empty except for a cat slithering around a cottage corner. Tadek ducked back into the shadows.

"It's okay."

Five shadows followed him as he quickly darted across the

street, into a gap between gardens that ran through to the next street. They followed him down this narrow path, usually only used by dogs and kids. It wended right and then left. A dog barked two houses over. There was a wire fence that kids had bent down until one could step over it. They emerged on the edge of the village beside a flat, empty field. Alongside it grew a row of small trees as a windbreak and a low scrabble of bushes. "Thanks," Ephraim said. He put a hand momentarily on Tadek's shoulder.

"You go home now and clean up everything in the chicken coop," Krystyna said, and started toward the fields, followed by the Reznikoffs. "Make sure you get everything. It's important."

"All right. I will."

Tadek watched his mother's dark form merge into the hedgerow. The family, one by one, disappeared behind her as thoroughly as if they were vanishing under the ocean's waves, and standing there for a moment alone, he felt his own smallness surrounded by the vast, forbidden circles of the world he yearned to explore.

When Tadek had let himself in through the back gate to the garden, he could hear Germans moving through the town two streets over, pounding on doors, their electric torches slashing through the darkness. He went to the back of the coop and lit a lantern. The small room looked like a nest for deer, the scattered straw pressured into a circle. He kicked the straw around in a random fashion and brought back the broken hoes and rakes from the henhouse and leaned them and tossed them in chaotic fashion about the lean-to. There were four plates in a corner he picked up and put outside in the henhouse. Just as he was leaving he saw a small, wooden, top-like toy one of the children had left, with Jewish lettering on it. He'd seen children playing with toys like these in Grodno on the warped wooden floor of Levy Reznikoff's textile shop. He picked it up and put it in his pocket.

On the way out, he picked up dust from the floor and scattered it over everything. He lifted his lantern and looked over the hut. Satisfied, he closed the door and found more tools and a few sacks of grain to pile against the door, sprinkling more straw over everything. He picked up the four plates and stepped outside into the night, where he could see that the Nazis were already at his neighbors. He hurried into the house and scraped and washed the plates, drying them and putting them away before stepping back outside again. The Germans had already broken the gate latch before he could get there to let them in and their dark forms rushed toward him under the grape arbor. Three soldiers in black uniforms came sweeping into the house with their electric torches, shoving him out of the way, crashing through the rooms in their heavy boots, seeming too big for the rooms. "Juden?" was all that they said. "Juden?" They immediately glimpsed the fruit-cellar trapdoor, half-hidden under a worn rug, and kicked aside the rug and pried up the door, turning away disappointed. "Juden?" Tadek followed them as they moved outside, prodding in weedy corners and kicking over bins, out to the barn, where one lifted the feed bin to find Zygmunt's still. He waved another over to look at the still and they laughed, then let fall the lid and climbed up to the barn loft where they poked through the piles of hay.

Tadek stood by the well and watched the third soldier, a tall officer who moved, unlike the other two, without hurry. He strode past Tadek, looking down at him without acknowledgment, and headed directly to the chicken coop, sending the chickens squawking down from their roosts. Tadek wanted to follow him into the coop, to see what he saw and how he reacted, but he made himself stand still. Tadek could follow the path of the German's light through the cracks in the coop's flimsy walls, and he could hear as the German progressed to the back, kicking, thumping, scattering the irate chickens. Finally he could hear the German at the end of the coop tossing aside the tools and swinging open the lean-to door. He could hear the two Germans shuffling through the barn and some distant shouts. But now the German at the back of the henhouse was silent.

There were two figures standing at the entrance gate. Instinctively Tadek walked toward them a few steps under the shadows of the grape arbor. He was surprised to hear that they were speaking Polish. One of them held an electric torch in his hand and was waving it nervously up and down the road. The two men shared a match, trying to light a cigarette. He could see them clearly through the skein of the grape vines. The match misfired and one man took out a cigarette lighter and lit both cigarettes. They were laughing and talking about the lighter. The man with the torch wore a long leather jacket of the type that Tadek already knew collaborators favored, in imitation of the Germans. He turned to speak in fluent German to some soldiers passing by. The other man was in a farmer's jacket that seemed too small for his long arms and body, giving him, despite the situation, a comic and incompetent air. He was a very tall, slouching man, not young, with a blade-like nose, narrow face, and dark, pouchy eyes. He looked familiar to Tadek. Maybe he'd seen him on market days. He heard the man speak again in his high-pitched, nasal voice, and then Tadek remembered him. It was the man who had served as a policeman under the Soviets, who had helped haul in the drowned body from the Niemen.

Tadek slipped back down the shadowy lane.

Finally the officer emerged at the chicken coop door, flashing his torchlight onto Tadek's face. The light crawled down his body. Tadek's hands were in his pockets, his fingers touching the Jewish toy he'd found. The man stepped closer to scrutinize Tadek. He was so close that Tadek could, once again, smell the distinctive odor of black polish on a German's high boots. On the man's collar was pinned a metal skull insignia, which also seemed to be studying Tadek.

"Where are your parents?" Tadek got or guessed at the gist of the German.

"*Arbeit.*" One of the words he'd picked up.

"Hm." The man growled something Tadek couldn't understand and fixed him with a hard look.

In the distance, shots rang out. The German, lowering his light from Tadek and seeming to forget about him, lifted his head and sniffed the air. He strode over and called to the soldiers in the barn, '*Schnell! Schnell!*' Together they made a quick march through the orchard and then circled back past Tadek, without even glancing at him now, and out into the street.

When he went over to look at the broken gate-latch, his father approached out of the darkness, a bit breathless. He'd been trying to avoid the Germans as he made his way late from work, taking a roundabout route through the woods and fields. Tadek told him of the events and they waited up late together for Krystyna. Finally they heard her at the door. Relief washed through Tadek when he saw his mother, wearing the belted wool jacket she always wore, enter the kitchen. She reported that she'd delivered the Reznikoffs safely to Janusz, and seen them rowing away across the Niemen, headed toward Janusz's connections and, eventually, the Baltic Sea and Sweden.

Tadek told her about the two men speaking Polish. Of the one in the leather jacket, his parents nodded and said, *volksdeutche*, but of the other one both his parents grimaced and shook their heads and his mother wanted to hear every detail of description, twice. His father nodded in recognition. "He's found another master to serve," he said, looking at his wife. She nodded.

"I'll pass on what you've told us," Krystyna said to Tadek.

"It's very important to notice everything. You did a good job. Someone will take care of it."

"Take care of it?"

"Yes." She exchanged another, complex look with her husband, and the table fell quiet. Something was beyond Tadek and he struggled to understand.

It was very late, but everyone was too stirred up to sleep. Tadek pulled the small top out of his pocket and spun it on the table, wanting to show it off for his parents to see their reaction. Everyone watched the top spin about the table, skirting the edge and then, as if aware of its danger, veering back toward the center and almost off the edge on the other side. Gradually, it started to wobble. "What in the world...?" His parents' eyes grew wide. "What are you doing with that?" His mother lowered her voice for some reason, but her whisper was vehement. Tadek snapped up the top before they could take it from him.

"They left it behind. I didn't steal it."

"That's not what I mean. Go get rid of it. Smash it with an axe into small pieces, and then bury them. Or better, burn them in the ash pit. That toy could get you killed. Now!"

His curiosity more than satisfied, he picked up the top and went out into the night. The Germans had finished their searches and the night was quiet, at least on their side of the town. There was a swollen moon setting in the west, which meant it must be well after midnight. A breeze stirred the leaves of the trees in the orchard and in the grape arbor. All was peaceful. A night bird called, and Tadek crossed himself. He went to the barn and found a hatchet, weighing it in his hand, but then set it back down. For some reason he couldn't make himself destroy the toy and, disobeying his mother, walked to the corner of the barn where he took a trowel and shifted the rain barrel, digging a hole and burying the top before replacing the barrel, thinking that someday the toy might somehow be found again and somehow redeemed.

Chapter 9: The Frozen River

December 1942

For a week after the Reznikoffs left, every time Tadek walked past the shed behind the chicken coop, he felt their absence. His mother had warned him he must never speak to anyone about what had happened, and they had all disappeared so quickly, quietly, and thoroughly behind that hedgerow, that this warning hardly seemed necessary. It seemed as if the family had just been phantoms of some feverish dream he'd had, stirred up by the war, vanishing when daylight came.

A few weeks later Tadek and Pawel, with Bolek Koskovski, were headed back to the village from the river bluff along which they'd been playing. It was dusk and time to go home for dinner. At the edge of the village they met the Borovski twins, who told them excitedly that a man who had formerly been a policeman in Liaski had been found hanged from a tree outside his house near Gombachy, a scrap of paper on his chest saying that this was the fate of all collaborators. All the boys started talking at once. A few more children trotted up to add and hear more excited tidbits of information.

Tadek walked away from the boys, steering his steps into the shadows of buildings. The other boys called after him, but he waved them off, calling simply, "No," and kept walking, turning his steps toward home. He needed to hide in these shadows. Images were flashing through him: the man in police uniform, dragging the corpse out of the river, the man lighting a cigarette at the end of the lane, the man swinging from a tree. He didn't know what he felt or was supposed to feel, but was grateful for the growing dark that hid the confused tears that burst out of his eyes, breaking a tension he hadn't realized he'd been feeling. He ended by kneeling alongside the road and vomiting into some weeds.

Before he went into the house, he tried to thoroughly wipe his eyes and make certain that he had stopped crying. He went to the water pump and tried to wash the taste of vomit out of his mouth. He was glad his parents weren't there when he let himself into the house, but his mother said to him as soon as she came through the door, "You've been crying."

"No."

"It's all right. You've heard what happened?"

"Yes."

"There was a trial," his father said. They both leaned close to him, anxiety in their looming faces. "You were right about him. It wasn't just you."

"Don't take it on yourself," his mother took her turn. "You hear me? Others knew him too. Kazimierz handled it. It's over now. It was what had to be done. Don't ever mention him again. Do you understand? And never mention the Reznikoffs again. Nothing that happened that night. Nothing. Never. To anyone. No matter how much you think you trust them. Do you understand?"

He was more than a little frightened by her intensity, but he nodded his head.

"You already said that," he said. He didn't want to know any more about anything that had happened. "I want to go to bed now."

"So early?"

"Yes."

He was angry and ashamed that he'd cried. Why had he cried? And even vomited. It was like a betrayal, to have shed tears over a traitor's death, even to have vomited, because of a traitor.

He didn't hear himself scream that night, but suddenly found himself sitting up in bed with his mother sitting next to him.

"Are you all right?" she asked. "You were shouting 'No, No,' like someone was attacking you." He didn't even recall what he'd been dreaming. He half couldn't believe he'd been yelling at all, but knew that she wouldn't make up something like that.

For the next week he woke up every night shouting at some invisible assailants. He began to dread bedtime itself, when he would have to face these opponents. During the daytime, he tried to steel himself against the memory of that tall Polish man with the blade-like face, blade-like nose, and prominent Adam's apple (but how that noose must have pressed against it!).

Over the next month or so, Tadek's day-to-day life reasserted itself as these memories, never fading, were pushed down beneath other events. His childhood continued to unfold in the spaces between the convoys of troops and under the rain of loudspeaker pronouncements in a foreign tongue.

There was a gully cut by a stream north of town. The stream twisted its way through fields (once owned by Zygmunt) before feeding into the Niemen, and it froze weeks before the river did, attracting both adults and children to sit on the logs lain alongside the creek, strap on blades, and then hobble the few feet to the ice where the skaters turned weightless and agile and free. The children played hockey and tag until dark, and there'd always be a fire going on the bank to warm their hands and feet. On Sunday afternoons the most sober adult villager would skate meditatively up and down the stream with his hands behind his back. In the heart of the winter, eventually the river itself froze over, and there were times when the entire village seemed to move down to the edge to cluster along fires or skate across and back, the eternal barrier of the river having transformed into the medium of the villagers' access to the other side.

Pawel and Tadek and most of the children from their school spent all afternoon skating up and down the early-frozen creek one December Sunday. The Borovski twins were there. They were slender blond boys, uncompetitive and playful. And Bolek Kosokovski was there, lumbering along the sidelines, having never learned to skate. Sabina and Halinka were there, Halinka, with a red scarf and a matching red cap on her blonde head. She skated with thoughtful, elegant strides up and down the patch of ice where the boys of the village clashed and dashed in hockey. They used crooked sticks broken off a fallen tree to guide a crumpled tin can as a puck. Tadek scored a goal and noted Sabina and Halinka were skating arm-in-arm far down the stream. Eventually the boys gave up on hockey and began jumping over four barrels laid out on the ice, something Tadek took to naturally, flying over them all, farther than anyone else dared attempt.

Tadek sat on a log on the edge of the ice to relace his skates. They were hand-me-downs from his mother, bought by Zygmunt for his favorite child when he had felt momentarily flush with cash. They were still too large for Tadek and had paper wadded into the toes. But he considered himself lucky to have them: many people just lashed blades to their heavy leather boots.

Sabina skated up to him and sat down beside him. He gave her an irritated look. "What do you want?"

"To talk to you."

"Okay, so talk."

"You're rude."

"I don't care." But even as he was rough with her, he had to admit that he liked the attention of her little pink face turned towards him. She pursed her lips together when she was thinking and squinched her level eyebrows that seemed to testify to a forthright nature.

"Do you like Halinka?"

"Why?"

"Do you think she's pretty?"

"Yes, I do."

"Do you think she's beautiful?"

"Why do you want to know this?"

"I just do."

Tadek could see that Halinka and Pawel were standing down at the bend of the streambed, talking. He got up and skated madly in the other direction, then came back, swerving through a cluster of boys, and with a shout leapt over the row of barrels. The boys cheered. He kept skating as fast as he could, swerving behind Halinka and Pawel, and with a quick motion, he pulled off Halinka's long cap and skated away, ignoring her protests.

She skated after him. "Tadek, give it back!'

"No. Come and get it," he taunted.

"No. Give it back."

"No."

He slowed and let her approach him. She wore a threadbare brown coat but was taller than he was and as she neared he felt the power of her beauty, her tolerant smile, her kind eyes and long, modeled face of perfect facets and curves. "Come on, Tadek. My ears are cold."

"Ha!" He skated away. Unable to restrain himself, knowing

it was a terrible idea, but needing to do something dramatic, he turned and flung the cap up into the branches of the tree above him, where it snagged on a branch and swung above them.

"Oh," Halinka gasped in frustration. "I can't believe it."

"Serves you right," Tadek cried, and skated away across the stream.

After a consultation with Halinka, Sabina skated after him. "Are you going to get Halinka's hat down?"

"No."

"Why not?"

They skated side by side for a moment.

"I don't know."

The cold air made the edges of her nostrils pinkish. "You don't have to act that way, brat," she said.

"You can't tell me what to do."

"You have a turnip where you should have a head."

She skated away from him, swiveling neatly to skate backwards, her tongue sticking out at Tadek. He laughed.

Pawel got a long branch and retrieved Halinka's cap for her. It grew late as the kids skated in circles or played tag till they were tired. They had all been skating for hours by the time the day wound down, the sun lowering over the forest across the river in the distance, the air growing bluer and colder. Tadek and the rest of the kids sat down on the stumps and logs surrounding the ashes of the fire and pulled off their skates. The kids started walking in a shambling group down a lane along the river toward the village. The fields were frosted with a slight cover of snow.

They all made their way along the edge of the frozen river. They rounded a bend before the village and were wending their way through a stand of leafless poplars when they heard shouts. A group of kids was standing on the edge of the river, shouting at a small black dog that was ten meters out on the ice, his legs sprawled out, unable to stand up straight or move. Some kids were throwing rocks and others were shouting. Tadek didn't recognize them and thought they might be from a nearby village, Gombachy or Shabany.

"Cut it out!" Tadek grabbed the arm of a boy who was about to throw a rock. The boy was a string bean, taller than Tadek but about his age, with gangly arms and legs. He and Tadek stood staring at each other, squaring off their shoulders, circling. A fight would feel good now, Tadek felt. The boy had a lazy eye that was looking at Tadek's ear, but even so he managed to give Tadek a poisonous look. Insults floated through Tadek's mind—freak, fisheye, boiled-egg eye—but they seem to surface to his lips and die there, and after a moment, both boys turned away from each other.

"What happened?" A few younger girls, in tears, came up to Tadek.

"Somebody threw him out there, and now he's too confused to move. He's not much more than a puppy."

"I'll get him," Tadek said, sensing that, according to an ill-defined law, if he saved the dog now, it would redeem him for earlier stealing Halinka's cap.

"Don't, Tadek," Pawel said. "No one's tested the ice yet." After a hard freeze the police would go out into the river, pulling a rowboat behind them, and take ice samples to see the depth, but with the Germans in charge, no one had bothered. To skate on the protected creek was one thing, but the fast current and the broad expanse of the river sometimes kept it from safely freezing all winter long.

"It looks safe." Tadek let his skates slide off his shoulders onto the shore and took a few sliding steps onto the river. In the back of his mind was a doubt, but he felt Halinka's eyes on him, the eyes of the crowd of kids, and knew he couldn't back out now.

"You can't tell by looking," Pawel warned.

"It's fine."

"Don't go, Tadek." Halinka called. "You're making me worried. I can't look." She turned away, covering her eyes.

"Fool!" called Sabina. "It'll break. You're going to get soaked and probably die."

"Ha!"

He took a few steps further. Here the ice was black with silver bubbles trapped like large pearls. He could almost feel the black water rushing beneath. Where there had been a crack, he could see that the ice was about two inches thick. "Come on, Pawel," he taunted.

"No. It's too risky."

Tadek walked out on sliding steps another few meters. The dog was standing splay-legged, looking at Tadek with abject eyes, barking and whining miserably.

He took a few more sliding steps before he heard a sharp crack shooting out from his feet, leaving its trace in a long jagged line toward the shore. He turned back to say something to Pawel when the ice buckled in two sheets beneath him and plunged him under. The cold water took his breath away. He felt waterweeds wrapping around him. Something black brushed beside him and rushed away in the current. His toes touched a sandy bottom and he pushed off of it, but at the surface the ice sheets had risen back overhead and his hands slid helplessly along them as he felt the current pulling him along.

When his toes touched bottom again, he pushed up and shoved against the ice, and the whole sheet heaved up and then came down again.

The tinny, underwater sound of the bubbles breaking around him, the sensation of his fingers slipping against the pane of ice, the beautiful bubbles in the ice against which he pressed— all these things slowed and revealed themselves with the vividness of a hallucination. He noted them all and was calm. He too slowed down. He too was a sort of hallucination. He was bobbing off the bottom and pushing against the ice sheet over his head, moving along it, pushing against the current so he wasn't carried further away. He was just bobbing along. The bubbles were luminous and fascinating. Even their sound was intriguing in its brightness.

But despite his calm he knew that he had to act, and when his toes touched bottom again, he shoved up and the sheet heaved up again, and this time he managed to lunge forward to the edge of the main sheet of ice and hang on as the sheet he'd shoved up crashed down on his arms and head and shoulders. The water was pulling him under, but his fingers had some slight grip on the ice surface, and he pulled himself up to his elbows. Something nudged his arm and he grabbed a hold of it: the metal runner of a child's sled. He grabbed hold of it and felt it pulling him. He kicked and lunged, his elbows sliding on the ice, and found himself sliding on his belly across the ice, still holding the sled, face to face with Pawel, also belly-down on the ice, hanging on to the other side of the sled.

Other children had run out and held onto Pawel's feet, and as they pulled, Tadek scrambled away from the hole, hanging onto the sled and sliding after Pawel. Near shore he sprung to his feet, hugging his arms, laughing through his rattling teeth, knowing he was free from the river. Pawel was angry. "You're crazy," Pawel said. "That was stupid."

"Where's the dog?" Tadek didn't want to face Pawel's criticisms. He turned away and his eyes searched the river, a featureless gray plain except for the black jagged star where he'd fallen in. The dog was gone.

"Where is he?"

"He fell in with you. He went under."

"No!" But Tadek remembered now a brief flurry of motion

from a black mass as it was swept away under the ice.

"He would've been okay if you hadn't tried to get him." This was from the edge of the crowd, from the kid Tadek had stopped throwing rocks.

"Shut up!"

"Well, it's true," he laughed.

"Shut up, you!" Tadek pushed through the ring of kids around him to stand in front of the tall boy with the lazy eye. "You were throwing rocks at him!" Tadek's eyes went out over the bleak stretch of ice again, searching across the river to the edge of the woods, down to where the river bent out of sight. He tried to will the dog into sight.

"Look at you! You're shaking!" the kid laughed.

"Shut up!" Tadek yelled again, taking a step forward to shove the kid, but it was true: his arms and legs were shaking so hard he felt he could scarcely stand.

"Come here, you," a man said, throwing a blanket around Tadek. "Haven't you had enough for the day?" He picked Tadek up and carried him up the hill to a cabin where a woman waited at the open door. They settled him down in front of a fire and Tadek gave in to crying and shivering so hard his teeth clattered like castanets.

"Get out of your clothes," the woman said matter of factly. She was a plump woman in what seemed to be several layers of sweaters, green on top of brown on top of red. She was neither old nor young. A look of amusement lit her eyes. Her house smelled of earth and spices and the wood fire.

"What?"

"Get out of your clothes. Here." She handed him a towel and a blanket. "I won't look, sonny. Not that I haven't seen it all before."

By the time Tadek's mother came through the door, he had stopped shivering and was sitting in front of the fire, wrapped in a blanket, wearing pants much too large for him, and drinking tea with honey. "Tadek? What's all this? What's happened?"

"I tried to save a dog but he fell in the river with me," Tadek admitted. "He...he . . . . " He couldn't bring himself to say, "he drowned."

A man gave Tadek and Krystyna a ride across the village in the back of a wagon. Snow was spitting out of a dark sky. His mother put her arm around him and he watched the broken icy puddles pass beneath his swaying feet. He felt glassy and dazed. At home she gave him soup and put him to bed. He fell asleep immediately. He woke to the sound of voices and rose to wander into the kitchen. His uncle Kazimierz, now bearded and bundled in a heavy coat, smiled broadly to see him.

"The winter swimmer!" In a step he was across the room, hugging Tadek hard and lifting him off the ground.

"What? What are you . . . .Why are you here?" Tadek felt he was still dreaming. He hadn't seen his uncle in over a year. To Tadek, Kazimierz seemed to fill the room with an air of anticipation, as if he were about to pass out gifts.

Yet in the midst of his happiness, he thought of the dead dog and choked back tears.

Brother and sister smiled and shook their heads at Tadek's confusion.

"Here, calm down, dear," his mother said. "Let me feel!" She put a hand to his brow. "You're very lucky, you know. You shouldn't be so reckless. I've told you before."

"I know."

"Do you feel all right?"

"Just tired. I would've been all right. I'd touched bottom.

I wasn't drowning," he protested, and was a bit confused again by their renewed laughter. It seemed as if no one had laughed in a long time.

"But the dog drowned," he said.

"Tell me all about it," his uncle said.

Their three-legged cat limped out of his bed of rags beneath the stove and rubbed the top of his head against Kazimierz's calf. He picked him up and plunked him on his lap and looked to Tadek, who told his story while his uncle tamped his unlit pipe and gazed at him with his round, dark blue eyes, nodding as if, of course, of course, it was all natural. After Tadek was done, Kazimierz nodded and lit his pipe, making tiny puckery sounds with the side of his mouth. The cat leaped away from the smoke.

"Well, Tadek, you tried to do what was right. Maybe tried a little too hard."

"Too hard," his mother agreed.

"I got into trouble a few times myself."

"You almost drowned saving Janusz once."

"Yes, that was before he was fat! Now he'd just bob to the surface. But I was thinking of when I got hungry out in the fields and ate old man Bohatkiewicz's lunch when he wasn't looking."

"Or when you drank papa's apple vodka."

"I had some help with that from Janusz."

Soothed by his uncle's words, pleased that he could be in any way like Kazimierz, Tadek sat at the table, wrapped still in a blanket, and listened to his mother and her brother talk, gradually growing sleepy. Kazimierz talked about his wife and two daughters in Shabany, and how he tried to sneak into the village now and again to see them. "But it's dangerous, coming out of the forest like that. If you could get them something now and . . . . Who's that?" With one quiet movement Kazimierz set down his pipe and reached into his jacket. He didn't stir from his chair, but a revolver had suddenly appeared in front of him on the table, next to his pipe as if it were a cup of tea. Tadek hadn't heard a sound.

"It's Roman. I'm sure," Krystyna said. Roman more and more just did the menial work at the granary during the day and so often had to stay late to finish his managerial duties. The factory where he'd once worked in Grodno was still closed, and to go into the city to look for work brought one into constant contact with the Germans and was too dangerous.

"Go see," Kazimierz said.

Krystyna hurried to the front door and out onto the porch, then out into the night. She'd left the door ajar and frigid air rushed in.

Kazimierz took another pull on his pipe and turned to Tadek and winked. But he kept his hand near the pistol.

Krystyna came back making palms-down, calming motions with her hands, smiling slightly at Kazimierz's vigilance. Roman followed in a black raincoat, his shoulders and hat covered with snow. He took off his coat and hat and brushed off the snow. He smiled—a bit tightly—and shook Kazimierz's hand, glancing at the pistol on the table.

"Are you going to shoot me before I get supper?" he asked. Tadek knew that his father liked Kazimierz, but could see his discomfort at having any partisan, even a brother-in-law, in his kitchen. It was as if he wanted to stay outside the currents of the times, as if by ignoring them they would sweep by and ignore him.

"Relax, Roman! We didn't invite our German friends to visit tonight! Don't worry!"

"You needn't invite them. They aren't shy. They'll invite themselves whenever they feel like it."

Kazimierz told them about life in the woods. They had gathered together a group of almost a hundred men and were in contact with similar groups of partisans scattered throughout

Poland. Food was always a problem, but they had received some aid from London, money and guns, and the peasants would always support them, with what little to spare they had.

"We have word from England that the Russians are holding at Stalingrad. That will stop the Fritz. They're freezing in this winter cold. What it all comes down to is, the Germans are going to lose."

This news seemed to drop into the room from another world. No one had ever said these words before, few had dared to think them, and yet he said it with casual authority: the Germans were going to lose!

"Now we all say," Kazimierz continued, "'God send us the Red Plague to rid us of the Black Death.' First the Germans. Then we will deal with the Russians."

"You've got your work cut out for you, then," Roman said, stirring a spoonful of sour cream into his steaming bowl of borscht. Tadek watched as his father's thin, pensive face and his uncle's candid, smiling one exchanged a long look.

"You too, Roman," his uncle finally said. "This concerns us all."

"Sadly, I think you're right."

"I'm glad to hear it. We need help. I was talking about food! Not only for my wife and children, but my fighters can't spend all their time foraging. I can give you money if you can get bread made for us."

"I can do that," Krystyna said. "I can get others to help."

"My wife or Jan will be in town on market day and you can give it to them."

Roman nodded. "We'll do what we can."

When Kazimierz was ready to leave, Krystyna said, "Come, let's all sit."

"Oh, sister, so formal!" Kazimierz protested, but Krystyna made the four of them all sit around the kitchen table together in silence for a moment. Tadek could hear the flakes of snow hitting the window above the sink like gentle paws that wanted in. The wind whistled under an ill-fitting window frame.

"Fine!" Kazimierz broke the mood and stood up, hugging his sister, shaking hands with Roman, and clutching Tadek briefly to his chest and kissing him on the cheek with his rough, tobacco-smelling mouth.

When he was gone, and Tadek lay in his cot with the curtains open as his mother tidied the kitchen, Krystyna said, "You know you can't tell anyone that you saw your uncle, you know that?"

"Yes."

"Not even your best friend. No one. Just like with the Reznikoffs. Never. Not a word."

"I understand."

"Or anything about the food we're giving to him."

"No. I understand."

Tadek lay in his familiar cot with his mother alongside him stroking his forehead. "No fever," she said. "You'll be all right."

"Yes. I'm all right. Mother, I want to be like Uncle!"

"You'll do best to not be like him," she said. "He leads a dangerous life."

"But he's doing the right thing?"

"For him, yes. For us, yes. For you," she paused, and gave him a long look. "I hope not."

"Mother? I just wanted to save the dog, but because of me he drowned."

"You don't know that."

"Not for sure."

"Be more careful next time. It's okay to be bold. But not reckless. I think what you did today was very reckless. Foolish."

"Okay."

"You understand me?"

"Yes."

"Good night then."

No one knew that he'd just tried to save the dog to impress Halinka. Still, that didn't stop him from feeling miserable about the dog—the way it was whining and sliding on the ice, staring at him with those abject eyes.

Tadek dreamt that he was swimming in the river. It was summer and he was on the open river, but it was cold. He swam underwater with the black dog beside him. It grew so dark underwater that he could see nothing. Somehow the dark water became the dark forest beyond and there were vast hidden movements in the forest that Tadek could not stop, that not even his uncle could stop. They were obscure and powerful, but if he stayed very still, maybe they would not sense him, and maybe they would sweep away the dog into the darkness instead of him.

At the Krzaczek's basement school on Monday, he ran down the stairs and entered the low room and felt the eyes of the other children turn to him. "We heard you fell in the Niemen, Tadek!"

"I like to go for a dip in the afternoon," he said, "to freshen up!" There was something about the formal way that he said "freshen up" that made the whole class laugh.

Mrs. Krzaczek stood in front of the room frowning. "Take your seat, Tadek."

"Are you all right, Tadek?" Halinka turned around to ask when he slid into his seat behind her. Her long honey-blonde hair was in a thick braid that lay between her shoulder blades, where Tadek could study it during the day. The escaped strands of hair at her temples were so light and fine that they stirred at the slightest breeze.

"Yes, I'm fine."

"What did your parents say?" Pawel asked later.

"If I'd've drowned, they would've been sad, but since I didn't, they could just be mad."

They both laughed. Tadek wanted to share with Pawel some of the excitement of the visit from his uncle, but caught himself in time.

"I knew I could get out on my own," he told Pawel. "I'd hit bottom and could just bounce till I broke through the ice. But thanks anyway."

"You would've just bounced out!" Pawel mocked. "You didn't look like you were bouncing!"

"Now I have to save your life so we'll be even," Tadek said.

"It's a deal."

Sabina passed him and poked him in the side with the stub-end of a pencil. "You're a simple fool, aren't you?" she said with a mocking smile. "Trying to swim in December. Who ever heard of such a thing? I told you you'd fall in."

"You did, didn't you?" Tadek admitted.

"Of course. I could see it all happening just like I'd read it in a book. You should pay more attention to me. I'm usually right."

She walked away smiling as if she'd just won a point in a long-running contest, the rules of which Tadek could not quite understand.

Chapter 10: Taken

February 1943

After a few hours of school in the Krzaczek's basement, Tadek walked Pawel home. They often did this for each other, to spend a little more time talking together before returning to their families. They talked about the Krzaczeks, about the other children, Halinka and Sabina, the Borovski twins. Nothing was quite firm in either's mind until it had been discussed and argued over with the other. A snow had been falling all afternoon, and they said goodbye with lobbed snowballs they easily dodged.

Tadek continued on by himself toward the town square, his head lowered, keeping his eyes on the ground where a few inches of snow mixed with mud and gravel, covering patches of ice he tried to avoid. The snow was turning to sleet, whipping sideways in the wind between the houses. Approaching the square, he heard shouts and motors roaring, snapping him out of his reverie. He turned the corner to see a German staff car and two trucks with open beds, lined up on one side of the square. About twenty German troops were surrounding a dozen men in mufti. A crowd of Poles had gathered a little distance away and were shouting at the Germans as they herded the small group of men, heads lowered against the wind and snow, into the back of one of the trucks. The other vehicle, with an open bed and high rails, already had eight or so civilians looked over by German guards. Tadek's steps hastened. He pushed his way through the crowd. He recognized a black jacket, a light blue scarf his mother had knit, a familiar navy-blue cap.

"Papa!"

Roman, prodded by a soldier at his back, was just climbing into the back of the truck. His head whipped around.

"Tadek!"

Tadek ran closer but a German stepped in his way and pushed him away with his rifle across his chest. Tadek slid further down the line of Germans closer to the bed of the truck. "Papa! What are they doing?"

Roman was being shoved further back into the truck bed, shouting over his shoulder, "Someone said we'll be laborers. No one knows."

"Shut up!" said a guard, stepping between Tadek and the truck, shoving Tadek away. The guard spoke in German but Tadek understood and slid further down the line.

"When will you be back?" The back of the truck slammed shut. The engine roared and lurched into gear.

"No one knows. Tell your mother that I . . . ." Tadek couldn't hear what he was saying over the engine and the wind in his ears and the sporadic shouts of the crowd behind him.

"What? What did you say?"

"Tell your mother I . . . ." He half-rose to make himself heard. A German guard shoved him back down with a rifle butt. The truck pulled away. The convoy was pulling in a circle about the square and Tadek cut across to run along side. Roman watched helplessly as Tadek ran. He made a slight waving gesture to Tadek with his hand. It seemed placating and resigned. The German guard stood directly over him, watching as Tadek ran after. Tadek was shouting, he hardly knew what. He watched as his father ducked his wind-pinched face down and away from the sleet. The trucks pulled away toward the Grodno road and Tadek ran after them till he slipped on an icy patch and fell. Picking himself up, he saw the convoy accelerating in the distance, and he turned back.

An old woman stood in a doorway cursing after the Germans. She spat on the ground before her and then closed the door without looking at Tadek. He walked through the square. A crowd of people gathered around him. Someone placed a hand on his shoulder and said something in a kind voice, but Tadek shook it off and ran from the square.

As he slowed to a walk near home, he met his mother running toward the square. The neighbors had already told her what had happened, but as he repeated the story to her, bending down there in the street beside him, he watched as her face changed, as if something not hard but durable that had been hidden inside her rose to the surface and took over. They each put an arm around the other's waist as they turned toward home. She did not cry in front of him, but that night he would hear her crying in her bed alone, just that one time, and then never again.

For a long time it seemed achingly peculiar without his father's presence around the house. Tadek realized now something that he had never thought of before—how little his father talked. His mother had always told her husband everything about the day, while he would nod and tamp his pipe, and Tadek would tell him too, as if nothing was real until they'd told this silent man about it, though Roman seldom told them anything about his day. Now without him there—at the dinner table, or strolling home from work in the dark, or sitting at the card table he used as a desk, reading his calculus books—Tadek felt the sharp stab of his absence in his throat and had to fight the choking and the tears.

* * *

At the end of winter, Kazimierz stopped by briefly. He came through the back garden and tapped on the kitchen window, then circled around to the doorway. He was wearing a long olive green coat and a black leather cap. He brushed snow off his shoulders and shook off his cap and stamped his feet. Krystyna hugged him.

"Thank God, Kazimierz! I heard you were dead!"

"I heard that too!" he laughed.

His mother had not mentioned this rumor to Tadek. He looked at her and she looked back. "No, I didn't tell you because I didn't want to worry you," she said to Tadek.

"Anyway, that's what we want people to think," Kazimierz said. "But I'm still here." He picked up Tadek and hugged him to his cold chest, grunting with the effort. "You're huge! Next time we meet, you pick me up, all right?"

"Okay."

Kazimierz gave his confident smile. "It's good to see you two! My favorite people!" But his smile evaporated as he came into the kitchen and serious talk began. Tadek saw that his drooping mustache had some gray strands in it and his eyes were nested in new wrinkles.

"I haven't heard anything about Roman," he said. "No one has. We're guessing everyone was taken to work in Germany."

"To work? Are you sure?"

"No, I'm not, but that's what people are saying has happened to many of the non-Jews they've taken. And you've heard about the Grodno ghettoes?"

"I've heard terrible things. Fighting everyday."

The first Aktion that had spurred the Reznikoffs' flight had been only the beginning. They came in unpredictable waves, each one carrying away more Jews and increasing the suffering of those who remained in the ghetto.

"Not fighting. No, not fighting. We got a little food into them, but that was weeks ago." He looked around the table, an appeal in his eyes. "There wasn't much we could do. The Aktions, they are all over now."

"How many are left?" Krystyna ask.

There had been over twenty thousand Jews in Grodno. Almost twenty thousand more had been crowded into the two ghettos from the countryside. Their grandfathers and great grandfathers had grown up there, people like Friedlander, whose daughter gave Tadek cookies, or like the Reznikoffs. For five hundred years there had been Jews in Grodno.

"No," Kazimierz said. "No. The Germans have finished their work. There are none left. None."

Chapter 11:
Football and Trains

That summer Tadek and Pawel and their friends spent every free moment playing football in the open field across the tracks and behind a thin wall of birches from the train station. The Germans had banned all of the organized clubs, but the soldiers ignored the kids in the field. So after their chores, before or after their intermittent schooling, between long hours sometimes spent in the field, they would chase the ball up and down the hard-packed ground till sweat flushed in sheets down their sides and dripped into their eyes. At breaks they would wander over to a water pump closer to the station. Usually the guards would ignore the boys when they slipped through the birches to get a drink of the perfect crystal liquid, which they sipped from a dented tin cup hung on a hook by the pump. Other times the guards would become possessive and chase away the boys, especially if a train was in the station.

The boys were used to troop trains headed east going by while they were playing football. The Germans could be put in the background of life, when you were rushing down the field with the football rolling before you, jittering over pebbles, with a defender shadowing alongside you. But one day a different type of car stopped at the station. This train was headed west, and the engine pulled six stockcars, one troop car full of soldiers, and then the caboose. Guards were posted atop each car. The boys stopped playing to watch as the guards went to the first car and threw the door open on a jumbled tangle of humans. From the darkened doorway of the stockcar, the boys could feel dozens of gazes upon them where they stood silently watching. The guards gave orders and two ragged men got down from the car and took a metal bucket toilet around to the side of the train where they dumped it. The same chore was repeated at the next car. To the third car, the guards had the prisoners bring a wheelbarrow, into which they shoved a man's body from out of the car. Then another body, a woman's, made to balance precariously on top of the first one. The boys stood watching in silence. The prisoners wheeled the corpses around the train and, as the boys stepped around to watch, loaded them in the back of a truck, which promptly drove away.

"What's that?"

"I don't know."

"It's Jews. They're Jews."

The next day, there was another such train. The day after that, another one.

Tadek and his mother were gathering eggs one morning, the three-legged white cat hopping along beside them. He remembered what he had been wanting to ask her: "Where are the trains of Jews going?"

"What do you know about them?"

"We play football next to the train station."

"Of course."

Krystyna looked at her basket of eggs. "Do you think the

chickens are giving fewer eggs now?"

"Yes. But where are the trains going?"

"That's the last one. Let's head in. Leave the cat outside."

"She'll get in anyway, sooner or later. Where?"

Krystyna brushed the hair away from her brow and finally said, "People say probably to Bialystok. Then Treblinka."

"Then what?" They walked back toward the house. The summer dusk was coming early. Clouds were thickening and seemed to be heavy with impending rain.

"Then what? It's a camp. Nothing good. They work. Or they get killed." She stopped before the house door and gave him a pensive look. "There's nothing that can be done."

"I know. Is there any word on Papa?"

"No. Just the same old rumors."

Some said that he had been conscripted into the German Army and had been sent to the eastern front, others that he was in a labor camp in western Poland. In truth no one knew. Pawel's father and Sabina's father were taken in the same sweep. Halinka's father had been taken earlier by the Russians, so she had the most practice at being a half-orphan, but most of the rest of the children of the village were catching up. Tadek felt now as if he had a greater sense of Halinka's quiet, constant sadness. There were no letters, no messages in any form from any of the fathers. It seemed to Tadek that it could be now as if his father had never been born, except for the figure of absence that was pressed into Tadek's life and that he felt everywhere around the house and yard like a ghost.

"We just have to wait," Krystyna added.

"I miss him."

"Me too. I'm sorry you have to grow up this way."

"I miss him. Besides that, it's not so bad."

"No?" She gave a little laugh. "Well, you only have one

childhood. What would you compare it with? How was football?"

"I scored three goals."

"You're very good, aren't you?"

"Yes, I'm fast."

"It's good to be good at something."

"Yes," he said. "It is." Yet as he thought of playing—the wonderful rushing over the turf, the clashing of feet—he felt his chest squeezed hard by a regret he didn't understand.

"Enjoy it then." She turned into the house and he followed her.

One day the train stopped while the boys were drinking water from the pump near the tracks. Most of the other boys finished drinking and kicked the ball down the tracks, moving away from the train. Most of the guards, too, had moved away, to the other side of the train, supervising the emptying of the latrine and the removal of corpses if need be. Tadek and Pawel stood alone at the pump, where maybe twenty meters away the last train car sat, with a tangle of hands and arms waving out of a high, small opening, crisscrossed with barbed wire. Tadek finished drinking from the tin cup and passed it to Pawel, who pumped the handle and let the water gush out, overfilling the cup. From the dimness of the car, the haggard faces of men stared at them, the sunken eyes of women. "Water," someone called. The call was echoed by another. A dozen arms waved through the small opening like some sort of many-armed god or monster. Faces pushed at the openings, mere slits between boards.

One woman's eyes caught Tadek's, and he could tell her look also caught Pawel's eyes. Pawel was standing with the tin cup in his hand, staring across at the train full of prisoners. He filled the cup again and stood for a while, staring, forcing a confused laugh out of Tadek. As if overcome by some force, Pawel started to move toward that woman's eyes, the cup still in his hand. He stepped over the first set of tracks in a slow, somnambulatory walk. The cry of water, water, had become general. Pawel kept plodding, oblivious to everything but the cries from the cars. Tadek saw that two guards had noticed Pawel's approach to the car. "Pawel!" Tadek called, but Pawel ignored him. "Pawel!" Pawel stumbled on over the tracks.

Tadek ran up behind Pawel. The two guards were running toward them down the tracks. Tadek grabbed him by the arm, jerking at the cup and spilling the water. A tortured cry of disappointment came from the car. Tadek pulled Pawel by the arm, turning him around, trying to hurry him away from the railroad car. The soldiers were upon them. One smashed the butt of his rifle into the cup, knocking it out of Pawel's hand. "*Streng verboten!*" Tadek kept pulling on Pawel's arm, leading him away from the soldiers, who now stood, a bit indecisively, watching the boys retreat. On the other side of the trees, the rest of the boys swarmed around Pawel and Tadek.

"What were you doing?"

"I don't know. I wanted to give them water I guess."

"You know you can't do that!"

"It was just one cup of water."

Tadek was astounded by his friend. Didn't he know what the situation was here? What sort of strange, idealistic world had infested his friend's mind? Tadek looked at the side of Pawel's unhappy face as if he might read answers to these questions there. Signs were posted in the town's square and the loudspeakers told them every day: to help a Jew was punishable by death. It was against the law for a Pole to talk to a Jew. Tears were welling in Pawel's eyes.

One guard, having made up his mind that more action was needed, pursued the kids down the rail line, up the slight rise and through the trees, waving his arms at them, shouting at them in angry German, the words incomprehensible, the meaning unavoidable. As a group the boys sullenly retreated, step by step, as he pursued them until it was clear that he wanted them gone from their football field. The group broke up and the boys returned to the village streets.

"Thanks, Karposovich!" said one of the older boys, one of the better players, respected by all. "They probably won't let us play here anymore. All that for the Jews."

Pawel hung his head. Tadek could tell it hurt, to lose face before the older boys. Tadek felt himself turned around by swirling currents that he felt sometimes in adult conversations between his parents and his uncles. The suffering of the Jews, the contempt of the older boy, Pawel's instinct to help, the brutality of the Nazis— all pulled and twisted on him like the currents of the Niemen during spring rains.

A clattering sound came from behind them. The train was starting to pull away from the station. All the boys were glad to see it go.

Tadek walked Pawel home, feeling bad for him. He shook his head at Pawel's naïveté: how could he think of doing such a thing? Everyone had known where Pawel was headed with the tin cup of water, but Tadek had pulled him back before he had actually offered it to the Jews, and this permitted the Germans to overlook the seriousness of what he had done.

Pawel walked slowly, his eyes at his feet, evidently ashamed of his behavior. Tadek wanted to tell him about the Reznikoffs, so he wouldn't feel so bad, but he knew he couldn't. To help Jews could be not only dangerous for one's family, but for neighbors and entire villages under the Nazi policy of collective punishment.

It took a few days for the boys to regather at the football field, tentatively, further away from the tracks where the turf was inferior. They were all relieved that the guards ignored them. But when they tried to drink at the water pump, they were chased away, and Pawel was blamed for everyone's thirst, increasing his misery and guilt. After two weeks without water, when Tadek saw by the pump one guard whom he judged less hostile—just on a hunch, because of a slight wistfulness to his gaze—he walked over and grabbed the metal handle and pumped up and down till the water gushed out. The guard jerked his head around at the sound, walked a few paces toward Tadek, then waved his hand as if to say—who cares, you're just a kid—and turned and paced away again, saying something dismissive in German to the other guard.

Tadek stuck his head under the stream of water and let it wash away his sweat and dirt. The other boys crossed the tracks, casting glances at the guards, who had turned their backs. The other boys could finally forget Pawel's reckless actions.

After that all the boys kept their distance from the stock cars as they came through. Sometimes they would stop playing football and from a distance make throat-cutting motions with their hands at the train. Sometimes they would just stop and watch the cars in silence, feeling the silent gazes out of the darkness settling upon them like a weight. Sometimes, more and more as they got used to the sight, they just played on.

Before the trains stopped in the late summer, even at night Tadek could hear them passing. They would pull into Liaski out of the vast eastern plains and would stop at the station a hundred meters from where he lay and the Germans would load the trains with water and coal. He could hear the coal's coarse rush down the metal shoot and its clattering into the bin, its sounds changing as the bin filled. Once he was jolted awake by a few abrupt gunshots. Those brief shots seemed to kill every other sound in the night.

Slowly after the shots the night sounds began again—a barking dog, a hooting owl—and among these sounds he thought he discerned or maybe just imagined the moaning of the people in the boxcars, a misery that distilled out into the night air, insinuating itself everywhere like the slowly accumulating sound of the crickets, seeping into the porous earth like a stain.

Chapter 12: Hunger

By the fall of 1943 and through the winter of 1944, the lack of food had become a serious problem for all of Liaski. Even the Germans, who had been precise about protocol when they first occupied this area, paying the villagers for any food that they required, now abandoned such niceties. One day a group of soldiers came, led by an officer with a sheet of paper that he brandished in front of Krystyna. Despite her protests, which ended with the officer pulling out his Luger and waving it at her while shouting in German, they took away the last remaining chickens. At any time of the day or night Tadek might see several gray-clad soldiers roaming through the garden, kicking at weeds, digging in the dirt.

Some beets and potatoes escaped the Germans. Krystyna and Tadek harvested these at night and buried them in a tin at the back of the garden and covered the fresh ground with a moldering pile of weeds. They picked the white apples at night too, harvesting those from the top of the tree that the Germans hadn't reached. Luckily, the Germans hadn't the time to do anything with the bees. Their honey was liquid gold, as good as currency with the other villagers. In the autumn Tadek had processed it at night and hid it in the rafters of the barn, underneath the chicken coop, and in a bucket hanging on a line far down in the well. For a while these resources kept them from hunger. They passed on some food to Jan, who promised to pass it on to Kazimierz and the other partisans in the forest, but the time was done when they and other families had the spare flour to bake bread for the partisans.

In general the fields surrounding Liaski were ill-tended, with many of the men of the village gone for the war, forcibly conscripted or taken as laborers into Germany. Who was working what fields and what would be done with the food were decisions made in an erratic fashion. Most of the food raised in the fields was confiscated for the German troops. The Poles hid away as much as they could. Later that winter as the Gradinski's resources depleted, Krystyna sent Tadek out foraging in the nearby onion, beet, and turnip fields at night. The Germans patrolled the fields and had picked them clean during the day, but still it was worth a try. He would find himself in the frosted fields surrounded by the shadows of elderly ladies, also digging for turnips, all of them hunkering down behind a fencerow as a two-man patrol of Germans passed by on the bordering lane. Occasionally the beam of an electric torchlight would stab out over the fields. To be caught stealing food was a serious crime. It was safer for Tadek to do the foraging than his mother, since his age might bring some mercy. Sometimes he would kick and paw through the snow-frosted fields by moonlight to find a few frozen turnips, beets, or onions no bigger than marbles. He'd bring a pocketful of them home to his mother, who would look at them with an expression that managed to be rueful but not ungrateful, because that was all they'd eat that day.

Fishing, one of Tadek's pastimes when he was younger, now was a necessity. He and Pawel drilled holes in the ice of the Niemen and sat for hours a few yards apart, tending their lines. Nobody went to school anymore. Nobody played any of the games of their childhood. One day Tadek noticed that he hadn't seen their three-legged cat Bandito for several days. Usually he was seen bobbing around the corners of the barn, adroitly catching mice with one paw and his mouth. But he didn't show up day after day. He had vanished. The unspoken fear was that someone had killed the cat for food.

Tadek knew what it was like now to wait for a tug on the end of his line that would make the difference between going to bed with a cramping, vacant belly or with the taste of fried fish in his mouth. He knew what it was like to feel that tug and, over-eager, attempt to set the hook with a tug too quick and hard, jerking the hook out of the fish's mouth, and come home empty-handed, and go to bed empty-bellied, not because of bad luck, but because of his own mistake.

If Tadek came home empty-handed after a day of fishing, his mother would purse her lips and another new line would appear on her forehead. She would just say, "Oh," or, "They weren't biting, then?" She would have to improvise a dinner out of stale bread and a few dried-up beets.

One day she said, "There's nothing to eat. I'm sorry. There just isn't anything.

"I'm sorry I didn't catch anything."

"It's okay, Tadek." But he knew it wasn't. "Maybe we should just go to bed now."

"It's so early."

"I know. But to stay up and not eat will be torment. Tomorrow we'll come up with something."

He hadn't realized how hungry he was until he'd realized that there was no food. He lay in bed and, for some sick reason he could not fathom, imagined that he was lying in the grave next to his grandfather, beneath the pines, with the bombs dropping overhead to no effect. Some dark part of himself extracted a disturbing solace from the fantasy. Finally he slept.

In the early spring the ice became rotten and the river swelled and it was difficult to fish, but in the late spring and then into the summer Pawel and Tadek fished as often as they could. The fish to go for was the speckled pike, which had weapon-like jaws and fought to the death. Some days they had to compete with women and old men for spots along the river's edge, but if they were lucky they found their favorite spot unoccupied, a grassy ledge that hung over the river just where the ice-skating stream entered the river, creating a back-eddy by a fallen tree where the large fish lurked in shadows.

One day the Borovski twins came by on their bicycles, poles clutched in their hands, projecting forward like lances. They pulled next to Pawel and Tadek and discussed whether the football teams of Warsaw, Lublin, Bialystok, and Grodno would ever play again.

Pawel and Tadek set their hooks with bait of worms, crickets, berries, almost anything, following the rumors of the day, but once the poles were set, there was nothing to do but to lie back in the grass and watch the clouds overhead, just keeping one eye on the tip of the poles. They lay down in the shade of a birch tree where they could watch their lines and also gaze at the storks floating overhead, as if the birds were swimming in another river far above the boys, their legs drooping down like a wasp's. It was the duty of the storks to leave every autumn on September 10 and return every spring on March 25, a duty they fulfilled with eerie accuracy. When they were a day or two late or early, talk of imminent apocalypse filled the conversation of the villagers.

By late afternoon the sun was lowering over the forest across the river, and the Borovskis gathered their things and set off for home. Pawel and Tadek had recovered their stringer of fish from the shallows of the river. Tadek thought of the potential meals hanging on the line. There were three perch, always tasty, and two *lecsh*, a large, flat, sweet fish, that Tadek's mother could simply fry on the stovetop and they could eat with a slice of good black bread, if there was any. Also, Tadek had caught one pike, primordial, as long as his arm, with its sinister, narrow, machine-like jaws, now gaping and clamping in agony in the air. Krystyna could make a soup call *uha* with the pike, cooking it with, if they could find any, some barley, carrots, and potatoes, adding the rest of the fish in large chunks at the end. If they had any sour cream—which they did not, but Tadek couldn't stop his dreaming—then they could add that to the soup at the table.

Tadek and Pawel walked up the ridge from the river, cresting it onto the road where two German soldiers were walking.

One of the soldiers said something in German, sounding indignant, and strode up to the boys. Usually Tadek and Pawel took the long way around town to avoid just such confrontations, but caught right at the riverside, they'd had no chance to avoid the soldiers.

"*Documenti*," he said in Polish. "*Documenti.*"

"We don't have any papers!" Tadek said, though it was obvious the German didn't understand him. The soldier gave Tadek a clammy smile and held out his hand to take the stringer of fish.

"No!"

The soldier kept his arm stretched out. The other soldier loosened his holster flap and rested his hand on his pistol.

"Give it to him," Pawel said, disgusted. Tadek handed over the fish.

"We have to eat too!" he said, but the two soldiers had

already turned and were walking away, the stringer of fish swaying along beside them.

Furious and disgusted, Pawel and Tadek walked aimlessly around the town. They'd wasted the entire day. They would have no food for their families.

They walked by the football field next to the train station. Two younger boys were kicking around a ball in the growing shadows. The games had gotten smaller and smaller and less and less animated as the war wore on and the boys had less and less food to eat.

Tadek and Pawel stood talking with the other boys, kicking the ball back and forth listlessly, telling them about what had just happened with the Germans. The familiar sound of an approaching train didn't cause them to even look up, but when this train came by, its sound was different. The boys stopped kicking the ball to watch the train. The German guards, too, stood watching. The train moved very slowly, dragging behind it a heavy metal claw that tore up the ties as it passed, leaving a devastation of shattered ties and twisted tracks in its wake.

Slowly everyone realized what this apparatus meant. There would be no more arrogant strains of *Heili, Heilo* echoing through Poland, accompanied by the sound of pounding boots. There would be no vast eastern *lebensraum* for the Reich. There would be no more troop or supply trains, headed east. The Germans were retreating.

Within a few days the gray-green-clad troops, now as haggard and haunted-eyed as the Russians who had fled before them, were shuffling west, back towards Germany. The guards disappeared from the railroad station, from Liaski, from Grodno, leaving no one in charge.

Chapter 13:
Operation Bagration

Summer 1944

Tadek heard voices at the gate to the street before it crashed open: they'd smashed through the latch. From the window he saw three Russian soldiers, in their khaki green tunics and cloth caps, with high black boots, striding boldly into their yard. Up the path under the shadowy grape arbor they came, two of them, rifles swinging from their shoulders, continuing into the sun past the house to the barn and the henhouse. The third came to kick against the door. Tadek stood behind his mother as she went to meet him. "Do you have anything to eat?" he asked in Russian, a language Tadek had heard when he was younger, but now not for years.

"We have to feed ourselves," she replied, also in Russian. The language sounded extraordinary coming from his mother's mouth, though he'd known she could speak it a little.

"We have liberated you. Now we have to be fed." The soldier's eyes ran up and down Krystyna. A loud squawking came from around the corner of the house and Krystyna ran out to see the other two soldiers coming back from the henhouse, each holding a wing-batting hen upside down in one hand. They had just recently managed to trade honey for two new chickens with the hope that these chickens would put an end to their hunger.

"What are you doing? Put those back! You want us to starve?"

The men stopped and grinned stupidly at her, both giving her the same slow, raunchy look, up and down. Krystyna hit one in the chest and tried to grab back a chicken. He laughed and hid it behind himself and together they turned in a circle, with him laughing and her swearing and reaching for the chicken. She stopped when the first soldier stepped in and she bumped up against his chest, his unshaven face close to hers, his ravenous eyes suddenly quite serious. She stepped back as he edged closer.

"Hey, Anisim. The kid." The other gestured with his head.

Tadek stood in the doorway with a hatchet in his hand. He couldn't even recall turning into the mudroom and grabbing the hatchet out of a corner.

The man just gave Tadek an empty glance. He might have been looking at a boot alongside the road.

Another soldier, an officer by the red star on his cap, stepped through the gate and stood in the shadows of the grape arbor.

"Come on!" he called. "You! No more of your nasty tricks! Save it for the fräuleins in Berlin. Bring the chickens!"

Grinning, the three men began backing away down the lane, their eyes still on Krystyna. But as soon as one turned his back, she lunged forward and, grabbing a chicken's scaly legs, jerked it out of the surprised man's grip, turning and running away several feet, scowling. "This is ours!" she snarled.

"Come on!" the officer called again. The soldier who'd lost the chicken cursed and took a step toward her, then laughed abruptly. He retreated with the other two down the pathway, tilting his head back and laughing at the sky, a bit hysterical.

"We'll be back, little rabbit!" he tossed over his shoulder.

"We'll be back."

"Lock the gate behind them, Tadek. Wire it shut. And what's this?"

She gestured to the hatchet in Tadek's hand. He thought she might scold him, but she just nodded: "All right then. You're ready. We'll slaughter this chicken now so no one else has a chance to take it."

Her tone was light but when she tried to steady the chicken's head with calming strokes, her hands were shaking so badly that she finally thrust the bird and hatchet into Tadek's hands. "You do it."

First with a knife he just nicked a blood vessel in the neck of the chicken and let it quietly bleed out, the way his grandfather had taught him. Only then did he chop off the head with one quick blow. Together they plucked and gutted the chicken. Krystyna rolled it in salt and hid it above the cupboards. All the time they kept the hatchet nearby as troops kept passing on the road, raising a fog of dust. Only late that night when most of the troops had passed through town did she quickly boil the chicken whole and fry its innards. She cooked in the dark, with the windows closed, so that the smell wouldn't give them away.

"Eat as much as you can," she urged. Together they devoured the bird, the most they'd eaten in months, the most they would eat in coming months. "Those were our chickens," she muttered. "They had no right." Tadek saw that her hands were still trembling; from rage or from fear, he didn't know. They locked the doors and windows and then let themselves down into the root cellar crawl-space just as they had when the Germans had been bombing. With the trapdoor half-down, she pulled a rug to fall over it when closed. They huddled together under a few blankets. She kept the hatchet by her side that night. Tadek couldn't help but remember how the last time they had slept there his father had been with them.

PART III:
THE
RESISTANCE

Chapter 14: A New Recruit

When the end of the war came in May of 1945, it seemed to change little in Liaski, so there was no celebration. The *lesni ludzie*, or forest fighters, continued their war. As soon as the Russian soldiers came in, they treated those who had been fighting the Germans for years as their new enemies, especially the Home Army, the AK. Sometimes they attacked them directly, and sometimes they promised amnesty and then arrested them as soon as they lay down their arms and packed them on trains for Siberia. So battles continued in the Polish countryside, now looking more like a civil war between the Russians and their allies and those who wanted independence from Moscow.

One late August evening in 1945, Tadek had been sent for water from the pump in back of the house. He hooked the bucket over the spout and with both hands jerked up the creaking metal handle and gave it a hard thrust down. Nothing. Another, and the water began to sputter out. On the third thrust a torrent of water gushed out and he grabbed the bucket with one hand to steady it, keeping the handle going with the other. He looked up and stopped pumping.

Three shadowy silhouettes had let themselves in at the hidden back gate and were making their way down the long path through the orchard between the rows of trees. Tadek thought of running for the hatchet, but he knew that would do little good, and something about the silent certainty with which these men moved made him wait for their arrival. They came through the garden and into the clearing made by the barn, toolshed, and henhouse. Only when they were within a few feet of him did he make out the smiling face of Kazimierz and relax. With him was Jan—Tadek had unconsciously recognized him by his limp—as well as another man whom he didn't know.

Kazimierz hugged Tadek and he felt the scrape of a pistol stuck into his uncle's belt against his chest. "You're getting big, Tadek." Tadek smiled to himself. Kazimierz always said this, but Tadek didn't mind. Tadek knew it wasn't really true, anyway. He was still short for his age. He consoled himself that indeed he must've grown since Kazimierz had seen him. "How old are you?" Kazimierz asked.

"Almost fourteen." Kazimierz released him and Tadek nodded at Jan and the other man, a small, bowlegged man. The man wore an open-mouthed grin on his face that made him look as if he'd just finished a raucous laugh and had some secret joke that was about to cause him to burst out laughing again.

"Time's a thief, Tadek!" Kazimierz said. "Enjoy yourself now. How's the football?"

"Good. We've started to play again."

"What position do you play?"

"Center. Sometimes goalie."

"You like it?"

"Yes! There's always something happening. I like that."

"I bet you do. Here. I'll take the bucket!" With a one-armed thrust he worked the handle and water gushed to fill the bucket the rest of the way. "Go run and tell your mother she has guests. And they have news! Kozel." This was the smirking stranger. "Get the packs." Kozel turned and disappeared again into the orchard's shadows to return in a moment carrying two bags on his shoulders.

Inside Kazimierz said, "Krystyna, sit down over here. No, please. First, I've talked to someone who claims to have seen Roman—alive!"

She stared at her brother's face for a moment as if she didn't understand him. Her face went through a terrible constriction. "Tell me everything," she finally said, slumping down in her chair.

"There's a man named Olenski from Grodno who'd been with the Boesky partisans, in the forest south of here, and then joined with the Russians when they came through, and fought with them into Germany. Anyway, he knew Roman. He'd worked with him in the Grodno shop before the war. He said he saw Roman among a group of forced laborers who had been building roads outside Ravensbruck. The Russians had arrested them all for fraternizing with the enemy."

"Fraternizing!"

"They'd want him anyway because he's an educated Pole. They hate that we are more cultured than they are!"

"But how did he look? How was he?"

"Olenski said he was all right. Skinny, but intact. Alive, anyway!"

Tadek rushed to get a seat at Kazimierz's elbow.

"What's that?" Tadek pointed at a badge on Kazimierz's chest.

"That's the Black Madonna of Częstochowa. She watches over me and Poland. So she's very busy!" he laughed.

Kazimierz smelled of the woods, of rain and wood smoke. He had grown a full beard that was shot with gray, and it made him look wild. Yet he seemed revitalized since the last time he'd stopped by, and his blue eyes and white teeth gleamed in the chaos of the beard. He winked at Tadek and gave him his carefree smile, erasing years. "Let's eat something, sister, all right?"

"We don't have much food right now. I'm sorry."

"Today, we have food for you! Kozel! Show us what you brought!" He pursed his mouth and lifted his brows with a judicious self-appreciation, nodding. "You'll be surprised what your brother's brought you, Krystyna." She was smiling, so happy to see her brother that it immediately cheered Tadek.

Kozel pulled off the floor a burlap bag and shook out of it some packages onto the table. From another bag he shook a bottle of vodka, which Kazimierz grasped and opened with a grin. "Do you have glasses? And can you boil us some of those potatoes?"

"Yes, and yes! Tadek, help me."

First Tadek poured vodka for the adults. They toasted to the fall of Hitler, which had finally come. They toasted to the fall of Stalin, which was unfinished business. They toasted to Poland. Together they heroically downed the shots in a toss of the arm and slammed their glasses down on the table as if to signal they'd each won a race. Krystyna coughed and her eyes glistened with sudden tears. Kazimierz made a puffing sound with his lips, hitting the bottom of his glass to the table in applause and request for more.

Despite Kazimierz's energy, Tadek could see that he had lost weight, and in lulls a shadow crossed his eyes. Kazimierz noticed Tadek looking at him and said for the second time, "Time's a thief, Tadek."

The men pounded another shot before Kazimierz sent Kozel to keep watch outside. Krystyna talked to her brother while she cooked. "How long are you in town for? Did you see Helena?"

Kazimierz's wife, Helena, was a thin, fretful blond who had lost even more weight during the years her husband had been a fighter. She seldom left her house in Shabany where she stayed with

144

their two children. Neighbors took care of the family, bringing them what food they needed. Sometimes when her anxiety would be too much for her, she would walk the five kilometers to Liaski to sit with Krystyna till late at night. She didn't get along with Jan's wife, Jadwiga, whom she considered ill-tempered and rude.

"Yes, I'll be there tonight, and then back to the woods."

"Oh, Kazimierz." Krystyna leaned across the table to hold and rub her brother's arm with both hands. "Why don't you come home to stay?"

He smiled and patted her hands, then stroked her cheek affectionately with a knuckle. But he shook his head as his smile waned. "No, when we come in from the woods, they just shoot us or arrest us. We're better off in the woods. The AK has been formally disbanded. We have been told to implement Polish independence as best we can, and that from now on, 'you are your own commanders.' So, I will command if I must. I will implement. We will continue."

"And what about Helena and the children?"

"And what about Poland?"

Krystyna didn't say anything. She turned away and pulled a pot down from the walls and busied herself at the stove for a moment, her back to the room.

"Did you hear what they did to the pitiful Swyokla women?" Kazimierz asked.

"Yes, of course."

"Well," Janusz said, "they collaborated. What should they expect?"

It was true that the new Soviet regime was uncompromising. One day when the old poetess, Elena Swyokla, and her niece showed up at the schoolhouse, an NKVD officer told them that they were both under arrest for collaborating with the fascists. Elena fainted in a puddle of old gray wool at his feet. Her niece stood with tears streaming behind her glasses, down her face, tears she didn't bother to wipe away, as if she could disavow their presence. Both of the ladies had to be picked up bodily by the secret policemen, and placed in the back of a Black Raven. They were driven away toward Grodno, and never seen again in Liaski.

Everyone's thoughts dwelled on the two women. There were many other stories such as theirs, and the adults discussed a few of them and the uncertain future faced by both Poland and Liaski, now that it was part of Byelorussia.

"Tadek, get a jar of honey from the barn."

"And tell Kozel he can come in and eat!" Kazimierz laughed and said, "Kozel always gets stuck standing guard."

Tadek stepped out into the night and walked down the familiar path to the barn. In the moonless night his feet had to remember the steps one by one. He smelled smoke before he looked up to see the tip of a cigarette hovering in the dark: Kozel, leaning with one boot propped backwards flat against the wall of the barn. Kozel made a sort of grunt to greet him.

"Kazimierz says you should come in and eat."

"Kowal?" Though Kozel was a scrawny, hungry-looking man, his voice was deep and hoarse, as if coming from another creature within him.

"Yes, Kowal."

"Good. When I finish this cigarette. Want one?"

Tadek didn't like Kozel's snaggle-tooth smile and unshaven face, but he shrugged and said, "Sure." Kozel pulled out a bag of tobacco while Tadek went to find the honey still hidden on a beam from foragers. When he returned, Kozel handed him the cigarette. He put it in his mouth and Kozel lit it for him.

He choked on the first inhale and Kozel laughed, but the second time he was more careful, and felt the nicotine rush to his head. Kozel was staring at him with an unchanging smile that seemed unrelated to any specific event.

"Tadek! What's keeping you?" His mother was at the porch, light spilling over her silhouetted form. "Are you smoking?"

"No."

But when he entered the kitchen, his mother turned and, before he could dodge, smacked him twice smartly on the back of his head. "The first is for the cigarette and the second is for lying," she said, turning away as if he wasn't worthy of further attention.

"Here's the honey," Tadek said, putting the jar on the kitchen counter and slinking away against the wall, hoping the incident would soon be forgotten. Both of his uncles tossed back their heads and laughed at the ceiling, then looked around the room and at each other, tremendously amused. Kazimierz's white teeth against his black beard brought back Tadek's memories of the younger Kazimierz, and Tadek grinned with him. Janusz spun an empty glass on the table, still laughing.

"Listen to your mother, Tadek," Kazimierz advised.

For a time everyone ate in silence, spearing the steaming potatoes out of a large bowl and slicing them with their forks.

"That land to the west of Poland, that used to be Germany, where they want us to settle now, that's not really Poland. It's Germany!" Janusz declaimed. "And this is not Byelorussia, it's Poland! It's going to be no good for Poles here. I'm too old to leave. And too crippled." He lifted his bad leg and clumped it back on the floor. "But I'm sick of the fighting."

"You? Fight?" Kozel said, the leering grin still on his face.

"I didn't say I fought!"

"You just run errands."

Jan gave Kozel a long, bitter look.

"Shut up, Kozel!" Kazimierz said. Jan kept staring at Kozel while Kazimierz talked. Kozel's grin stayed oddly fixed on his face. "Jan does his job, you do yours. But I'll tell you this. I'm not about to start standing up and saluting whenever a new government tells me a new lie!" He slapped the table with his hand and the dishes jumped. More calmly he turned to his brother. "We have to take what is ours and leave the rest for others to take. That land is Germany. Leave it to the Fritz! This is our land! This is Poland! Just because a group of criminals who call themselves a government says it is now Byelorussia means nothing! A country is more than lines on a map. Where are our ancestors buried? You know our ancestors fought the Swedes here!"

After Kazimierz's outburst, no one said anything. Things were settled in the Belyawski family, in the Gradinski offshoot, and with the local partisans. They would fight on. All the governments in the world might sign all the peace treaties they wished, but the war was not over in Liaski.

While Kazimierz and Jan ate the potatoes and soup, Kozel took a raw egg from his bag and placed it on the table, took a knife from his belt, and nipped a hole in one end of the egg. Into this hole he then sprinkled a pinch of salt, then of pepper, making subtle brushing motions with his none-too-clean thumb and forefinger. He next upended the egg into his mouth and in one giant suck cleaned it out. He crushed the empty shell in his hand, let it fall on the table, and breathed a contented sigh. "That's how you eat an egg, kid." He looked at Tadek with his red eyes. "Raw! It goes right into your blood and makes it red." Again Tadek was struck by the dark gravelly sound of the man's voice, an octave too low.

Everyone laughed. "You're scaring the boy, Kozel!" Kazimierz said. "We won't tell him you eat chickens about the same way!"

"Can I try it?" Tadek asked.

"Tadek, no," his mother said.

"Okay."

After the men ate they fell into a detailed adult conversation, and Tadek paid less and less attention. He sat on the kitchen counter and leaned against the cabinet as he tried to stay inconspicuous, so that his mother would not send him to bed. He heard Kazimierz saying, "We need someone we can rely on to take messages from Liaski down river to Jan. Someone who can go back and forth without suspicion. Not someone from Grodno. The traitors around us would know they don't have any business there, and would pass word on to the NKVD. That's what it's come to!"

"What about Jan?" Krystyna asked.

"He's slow," Kozel growled.

"Yes, he is," Kazimierz agreed.

"You don't think I know it?" Jan said. "I can't help it!"

"And he thinks the NKVD is watching him," Kozel gibed.

"Yes. They are!"

"Do they know you're the leader, Kazimierz?" Krystyna asked, alarmed. "And they know you're Kazimierz's brother, Jan?"

Both men shrugged. "They may suspect both," Kazimierz said, trying to restart his pipe again, covering the top with a chip of wood and puffing out the side of his mouth. "It may take some time for the Soviets to catch on to how things run around here. Kowal is still supposed to be dead, remember?"

"Oh, that's a bad thing to even say! Don't taunt fate!" Krystyna said.

"Anyway, we need someone else."

There was a silence around the table, and then Tadek felt Kozel looking at him. His vodka-fueled gaze was gleaming and hot. It made Tadek squirm.

"Send the kid," Kozel said.

"No!" Krystyna said. "He's just a child!"

"Well, someone's got to do it," Jan said harshly. "He's not that young."

"Just fourteen next month," Krystyna protested.

"Anyway, he's certainly not a child," Jan insisted.

Kazimierz nodded to himself. "Young is good. Jerzy Tomasz, he was only sixteen when he started with us during the war, right?" He looked at his brother and Kozel, who both nodded.

"Sixteen!" Krystyna cried. "That's two years older! No comparison!"

"Taking a message to the AK," Kozel said, "when he's just a kid with some rutabagas for his aunt? It's perfect."

"Sure. If the Russians stop him, he can say he was just visiting us," Jan continued. "He heads our way all the time. He helped you lead those Jews out of the village, didn't he?"

"He was just a lookout." Krystyna said.

"Still, if he'd been caught..." Kazimierz reminded her.

"It was an emergency."

"This is too," Jan answered.

"For him to go all the way to the camp would be too far," Kazimierz thought out loud. "But still...he can drop any messages off with you." He indicated Jan with a nod. "Then you can cross the river to us."

"Think of what you're getting him involved in," Krystyna said.

"Something everyone should be involved in now," Kazimierz said. "We need messages sent from Grodno. We need a regular link. Also information from Liaski about the NKVD staffing and movements. We can't have Jan hanging out here. It's suspicious, and we can trust fewer and fewer people every day."

A silence expanded in the room, and after a few moments, Tadek realized that everyone was looking at him.

"Tadek, will you do it?" his mother asked.

"Yes!" He would've done anything for his uncle.

So it was decided.

"It's going to take a month at least to set things up," Kazimierz said. "Just be prepared."

"All right."

"Be out on the streets. Let the Russians see you and get used to you. Don't avoid them."

"All right."

Krystyna, seeming to look at Tadek in a fresh way, put a hand on his shoulder as if she could protect him.

The men slipped away into the night.

Chapter 15: Friends

Sabina ran a few steps with a bright blue kite in her hand. When the wind gusted, she tossed the kite into the air where it rose before veering sharply to the ground. "Oh!" she gave a knock-kneed, fingers-spread pantomime of disappointment.

"Get it higher," Pawel, who manned the reel of string, advised.

"Let me try it," Tadek said.

Sabina picked up the kite and handed it to Tadek. "I guess you have to run faster than I did. The wind should be good!"

"You can do it, Tadek!" called Halinka.

Tadek and Pawel repositioned themselves at the start of the river bluff. The wind swept over the bluff from the west while Tadek started to run. "To your left, your left!" Pawel shouted.

"Toss it! Toss it!" Sabina shouted.

Tadek lifted up the kite and could feel the wind rippling it. He felt he was running off the side of the bluff, but he didn't want to take his eyes off the kite.

"Toss it!" Sabina shouted, but he ran on, lifting the kite higher till he felt the wind take it full on, billowing it out, and he tossed it, and instead of careening to the ground, this time the wind snapped it taut and it lifted up and up and up, over their heads and, as Pawel fed it string, over the village itself.

Even before the war had ended, a sense of the possibility of normal life had seeped into Liaski from the outside world, despite the continuing struggles of the partisans and the new regime of the communists. Half a dozen of the youths of Liaski had become inseparable. They had chores and schoolwork, but Sunday afternoons were theirs, and usually Halinka and Sabina organized picnics on the river bluffs.

Today Halinka, Sabina, and the Borovski twins met with Pawel and Tadek. The girls had somehow taken charge of the group. They seemed to know something now that the boys didn't, and, their attention elsewhere, smiled askance at the boys' roughhousing and pranks. Sometimes their group would walk the streets of Liaski at night, a group of girls five meters ahead of a group of boys, casting glances, whispering, creating shifting allegiances and fine nuances of intimacy and alienation which the boys could not quite comprehend.

Tadek watched the kite go higher and higher into the air, rippling and swooshing. When he turned back, Sabina had knelt down on the picnic blanket and was talking there with the Borovski twins, one of whom cradled a guitar in his arms. Halinka, willowy and smooth, stood next to Pawel, who was playing out the string as the kite rose higher. As Tadek walked back, Halinka slipped her hand into Pawel's. They stood framed together by the sky and the view of the woods to the west.

Imaginary romances often bloomed and faded among the kids. The more a boy was attracted to a girl, the less he would speak to her, until finally the awkwardness became unbearable, and they would hold hands for several nights, kiss once, and then break up. But the casual warmth with which Halinka leant against Pawel told Tadek that his friends had grown out of that stage and left him behind. He stood there for a time while the kite rippled in the wind over his head and the sun beat on his face. He felt Sabina and the Borovskis looking at him and knew that something was expected of him, but he had no idea what it was.

Halinka oohed as the kite veered toward the ground and Pawel righted it, letting it soar higher. Tadek, squelching his uncertainty, walked toward them, but their eyes were fixed on the kite, and they didn't look at him until he was just a few feet away. Halinka dropped Pawel's hand. They both gave Tadek a puzzled look as without a word he took out his pocket knife, pried open its blade, and cut the string to let the kite escape over the village and the fields, disappearing eastward toward Russia, as so many people had done over the years. He watched it for a moment, then turned and walked away, feeling their eyes on his back, disciplining all his will to continue walking slowly and not run away through the village like a child.

The next day he heard Pawel, as usual, calling from the gate in the evening. He stood there bouncing a football on his knee and, as usual, Tadek took a few quick bites of the food left on his plate and hurried down under the grape arbor to join him. "Let's go! Hurry up!"

"I'm here."

Pawel kicked the ball down the road and hurried after it. Tadek caught up, nudged the ball away from Pawel with his toe, and dribbled ahead. "Hey!"

They trotted in this way, dribbling and passing ahead to the other, until they neared the field by the railroad station and slowed to a walk.

"So," Tadek said. "You are Halinka's boyfriend now?"

"Yes. Why not?"

"When did this start?"

"I don't know. It just happened. Besides, it's none of your business."

Tadek kicked the ball away from Pawel, sending it bouncing across the field to where a few other footballers had already gathered. He stood in front of Pawel, blocking his path.

"You've got to stay away from Halinka."

"Stay away from her! What are you talking about? Is she yours?"

"You're my best friend. You knew I liked her."

"Sure. The same way we all do."

Tadek shoved Pawel in the chest and Pawel took a step back. "Hey!" He stepped forward and shoved Tadek in turn. They stood facing each other. Pawel was at least four inches taller than Tadek, but Tadek was tight-knit and hard and Pawel, though the strength in his long arms and legs could be surprising, was slender, even graceful.

The other football players had noticed and they ran into the street. "Hey, what's wrong, you guys?" Big Bolek Kosokovski stepped between them. When Tadek kept trying to dodge around him, Bolek just put his arms around Tadek and lifted him out of the way. "You guys, cut it out," Koskovski said. "Let's play."

"You better stay away from her."

"I'm not going to."

"Ah, it's a girl!" someone called from the soccer field.

"Not just a girl! It's Halinka."

"Ooohhh," the kids echoed knowingly.

Tadek turned away, but he recalled the sight of Halinka and Pawel holding hands, his mind filled with a red mist, and he turned back, dodging around Bolek and shoving Pawel in the chest. "Stay away from her!" He knew this was futile, even as he did it, but it was the only thing he could do to rid himself of that image.

"Leave me alone." Pawel attempted to walk around him. "I'm not going to fight you."

"Then I'll have to do all the fighting myself!"

Tadek took a swing at Pawel, who was so surprised he only tried belatedly to block the blow, throwing up his left arm. The blow caught him on the side of his head and he took a step back, shaking his head as if to clear it.

Pawel's long arms gave him a reach advantage, but he was reluctant and Tadek was the one fueled by jealousy. Pawel kept pushing Tadek away and Tadek kept coming at him. Bolek kept trying to step between them, holding first one, then the other, but Tadek fought around him. Finally they both shook free of Bolek and Pawel stood his ground and they slugged away. With each blow Tadek gave, even with each blow he received, he felt some of the pain flow out from him and transform into a lovely flower of external pain that blossomed and faded. It was the pain of seeing Halinka holding Pawel's hand but also the pain of his father's absence and the pain of standing by helpless as Russian soldiers eyed his mother hungrily, as a German passed by on a troop carrier sighting him with his gun and laughing, and the pain of picking through frosted turf for a few frozen turnips the size of acorns to take home for his mother to thaw out and try to turn into soup.

Tadek felt arms on his shoulders. Bolek finally succeeded in pulling the two boys apart, almost throwing Tadek to the ground, holding him. When Bolek let go of Tadek, he turned and swung at one of the twins, who laughed and danced out of reach. Tadek scowled and turned and walked away.

After church on Sunday, the families of Liaski gathered in small groups to chat, joined by the body and blood of Christ, most of them momentarily lighter, better, relieved of their pettiness and sins. Not so Tadek, as he watched Pawel leave with his family. He stood scowling at the pebbles on the ground, which he tormented with his toe, while his mother finished talking with a friend. Out of the corner of his eye, he saw Halinka walking over to him. Reluctantly, his eyes surrendered the pebbles for Halinka's long, lovely face.

"Why do you fight with Pawel?" she asked.

She wore a dark blue dress with white flowers and she gazed at him with serious eyes that he felt on his face like the brush of a hand. He was glad even for this attention, but looked away, embarrassed. "I don't know," he said. "I don't like you two together."

"Well, I don't like it when you two fight. You've been friends so long." Her voice softened with sadness.

"That's none of your business, is it?" he responded, surprising himself with his rebellion, not wanting her sadness for his friendship with Pawel. He walked away, head up, but having to restrain the urge to hit his head with his knuckles.

Tadek avoided his friends for a week, skipping school and working in the orchard, but finally could no longer restrain the urge to play football. When he went up to the boys at the football field beside the train station, he again took his ground in front of Pawel, feeling a duty to a cause that he must throw himself behind, consequences be damned.

Pawel pushed him away but wouldn't swing. Again the other kids pulled them apart, some of them laughing at Tadek. After he felt he'd demonstrated something obscure that he couldn't name, he turned away.

"Okay, just remember . . . . " Tadek said.

"Yes?"

"All right then . . . . Let's play football."

"Okay."

"Just remember . . . . "

A few days later Pawel came knocking at the door for Tadek as if nothing had happened between them. Usually people called from the gate, which had a trick latch and wasn't easy to open, but Pawel knew the trick, a hidden latch that you could feel but not see, and which had to be twisted before pulled.

"Come on out, Tadek."

"What do you want?"

"Football, of course."

"Okay."

When Tadek came out Pawel had returned to the street and was hitting the ball with opposite knees, juggling it. He kneed it high then let it come down to his foot, catching it with his insole and tossing a soft pass to Tadek. They passed the ball back and forth trotting down the street to the field without a word passing between them.

"If you're still mad about Halinka, we're not together anymore."

"Oh, yeah?" Tadek feigned indifference to the news.

"Yeah."

"Well, I don't care."

"Okay."

"Well then . . . . "

"All right then."

* * *

One night they were all sitting on the stoop of a closed shop on a side street, listening to one of the twins play the guitar, accompanied by his brother on the accordion. They'd had musical instruments in their hands since they were young enough to lift them, and both seemed to walk and move with their own inner music, no matter what armies were marching through the streets.

A large man turned the corner and stopped—just a shadow in the dim street. "Halinka!" He took a few halting steps forward. "Halinka, is that you?" the coarse voice asked. Sitting on the steps, she shrunk behind her friends briefly, as if she could deny her identity, and his.

"Yes, Papa!"

The shadow wobbled. He stepped forward a few steps. He was a tall, formidable-looking man, with a laborer's plank shoulders, stiff with muscle.

"Get home now!"

"Yes, Papa." With bowed head, muttering, "Sorry," to her friends, she leapt from the steps and dashed away, around the drunken man and around the corner.

"Huh!" her father grunted, surveyed the kids slowly, and then walked on past them without another word. He wore a long dark mustache that drooped around his mouth, accenting an unconscious sneer, and he could not have been less like his elegant daughter. The quiet, energetic, hard-working man who had left had been replaced by an empty-eyed drunk, who woke in the night screaming, still fighting the Germans across the Ukrainian steppes. Tadek watched him walk by and sized him up as an adversary, an instinctual skill he'd begun to apply even to adults.

On the next Sunday afternoon, Halinka and Sabina were sitting on the blanket by the river with their legs tucked under their skirts, leaning together, talking seriously to themselves. "What's the matter?" Tadek asked. Halinka looked away. Her eyes were glistening. She had a mole in the hollow below a high, proud cheekbone.

Sabina asked her, "Can I tell him?" Halinka nodded, still looking away.

"Her father's drinking again. He beat up her mom."

Halinka's tears disturbed Tadek. The thought that he could do nothing about it disturbed him more.

"Well, I'll beat him up!" he said.

"Oh, Tadek." Sabina turned away from him in disappointment, and Halinka just shook her head, still staring away across the river. Tadek knew he'd failed. He'd wanted to help. He'd do something. Something amazing.

"Watch this!" He ran down the hill where Pawel and Bolek Kosokovski sat on a ledge, kicking their legs in the air above the water. When he reached them he didn't slow but jumped over them, his legs still running as he plunged into the river. When he surfaced, he saw that Pawel and Kosokovski had leaped up in surprise at his feat. They yelled to Tadek as he swam to the shore, wrestling with him when he strode sloshing onto land and clambered up the bank. Pawel and he tried to throw each other into the water. Bolek came at them sideways and tried to push them both in, but they grabbed him at the last moment, and they all tumbled in the water in a laughing, splashing chaos.

As Tadek swam to shore again, he looked up the hillside to where Halinka and Sabina had been talking. They had stood up and were walking away, oblivious. Tadek remembered when he and his mother had gone to early mass once at the beginning of that summer. It had been a rainy day, and fewer people than usual were there. Sometimes before the start of mass, old men and old women would prostrate themselves before the altar, lying face down for half an hour on end. In abasement? In hope? In prayer? Tadek wasn't sure. But as he and his mother were moving along the side aisle to find a place, he'd recognized a dark blue dress with white flowers, and saw that Halinka was lying prostrate before the altar, before God and Liaski. Thinking of that moment now and watching her walk away, he realized how little he understood her.

Chapter 16: Chopin

October 1945

It was late afternoon when Tadek was on his way home from one of his few days in school. The Polish school lessons in the Krzaczek's basement became more infrequent than ever under the weight of another Russian invasion and with the increasing fragility and fallibility of the aging teachers. There were other scattered efforts at lessons in Polish, and the official Byelorussiaian school, but Tadek had decided, though he had not told anyone yet, that he would soon quit school and just work. He already had a handful of part-time jobs around the village and much preferred the activity of the work world to sitting in a room listening to words, words, words, spewed at him like a stream of endless pebbles.

Rounding a corner, he glimpsed his mother up the street, walking home from the bus into Grodno, where she'd gotten a job in the office of a fertilizer factory. He waited and their steps fell in together. It was early autumn, and Tadek noted that they both wore light jackets covered with patches. Tadek's jacket had once been his father's and was too large for him. Reading his mind,

Krystyna put her hand on Tadek's shoulder as they walked. "Your father would be proud of you if he could see you."

Tadek stopped walking. He wondered, why would he be proud? But a second thought occurred to him, and what he asked was, "He's not dead, is he?"

"No," she seemed as alarmed as he was at the thought. "Don't even say that. When you talk about bad things, you can make them happen."

Tadek already knew this and was angry with himself for what he'd said. "I was just afraid . . . . "

"Yes, I know. Don't worry about it. No, we haven't heard anything new."

"Okay. I'm going to go kick the football around over by the tracks."

"That's okay. But is your bike in good shape?"

"One of the tires is flat." It was still difficult to find rubber for patches, though some of the wartime shortages were starting to ease up.

"Well, fix it, whatever it takes. I'll pay. You're going to need your bike."

"Why?"

"To run a message to Jan, for Kazimierz, the way we were talking about."

"When?"

"In two nights."

More than a month had passed with no word from his uncles, and Tadek had worried that they'd forgotten about him, that it had all been one of those inexplicable adult actions that he couldn't comprehend. Caught up in the fights with Pawel over Halinka, for a time he'd almost forgotten the plans himself, but it was still something that he felt eager to do, drawn compulsively to the unknown, to the next thing.

When the night came Krystyna passed on to him instructions that she had received from someone in Grodno—who this was she wouldn't say. They wanted to accustom him to being on the road, so this would just be a trial run. He would carry nothing, just a bike-basket full of vegetables for his aunt. He was to bike along the road to Grodno for a kilometer and then take a gravel road down to the riverside where there was a bombed-out mill. At the mill he would meet someone who would say—and here Tadek sensed the ghost of his grandfather Zygmunt speaking through Kazimierz—"Henryk is not my father." He was to reply, "Svetlana is not my mother," and the man would tell him what to do.

He biked past the Russian troops hanging out in front of the police station in the town square, a few coming in and out of the town's inn. There were maybe half a dozen of them, and they ignored him as he pedaled through the square and out of the village. The sun was setting and it was a beautiful autumn evening. Tadek felt both cool and warm at once—cool with the wind rippling around his arms and legs, but warm in his papa's canvas jacket and with his cap pulled down to his brows.

He pumped the pedals, weaving between the puddles from an earlier rain. The setting sun caught some of the puddles and lit them red. He turned onto the paved Grodno road and picked up speed, and then he saw the turn his mother had described and coasted off the road and down the gullied gravel lane. In minutes he saw the ruins of the mill before him down the hill, with the dull glimmer of the river behind it. He started pedaling faster, causing the bike's chain to come off with a clatter, and he came to an abrupt halt. He had forgotten how this happened now and again. Cursing to himself, saying words that would get an ear-slap from his mother at home, he hopped off and, grabbing the greasy chain, pulled it away from the larger wheel, guiding it carefully back onto the sprockets while turning the pedal. He hopped on again and continued, careful not to pedal too vigorously.

He leaned his bike against a tree and stepped over the collapsed rails of a fence. A gray cat slinked away at his approach. The mill had had a stone foundation on which its wooden frame had been set. Much of the wood had been hauled away for firewood, but the stones and a partial wall still stood, screening Tadek from the road and yet giving him a view down the bank to the river. He walked into the empty clearing of the ruins and waited. It was growing dark. Tadek wished he smoked, so he'd have a way to pass the time. He imagined himself lighting a cigarette, put two fingers to his lips in a sophisticated manner and inhaled imaginary smoke. A peasant on a wagon pulled by a gray horse clopped by with a lazy cadence, the horse and driver nodding together in rhythm as if both were lost in the same dream. A crow flew overhead, following the path of the river. Tadek was wondering if there had been some confusion in his mission when from behind him, from the riverside of the mill, someone said, not asking but stating a fact, "Tadek."

"Yes?" He'd been startled.

A man detached himself from the shadows and walked quickly forward to within a step of Tadek.

Where had he come from? Had he been there all along?

He was a narrow-shouldered man, not young, dressed in a severe black suit and wrinkled white shirt, with rimless glasses on his nose. He had a pinched, censorious face and a small blond goatee.

"Come down the other side of the lane next time," the man said. "It loops around. You'll see anyone following you that way. Understand?"

"Yes. Where the cart came from."

"Yes."

"Where did you come from?"

"Don't worry about that."

The man withdrew a thick envelope from within his jacket and began patting it with his hand in a nervous motion. He stood so close that Tadek could smell the acrid scent of smoke and the vinegary odor of dried perspiration. The black suit was comforting to Tadek. It said to him—city, experience, knowledge—and instilled confidence, though the odor undermined the effect and left a lingering doubt.

"Here. Take this," he said, handing Tadek the envelope. "Put it under your shirt. No one will stop you."

"They said that this was really just practice. Until the Russians were used to me."

"Who said that? You obey orders now. That's all there is to it. This is not practice. Do you understand?"

Tadek nodded. He didn't want to fail in his first mission. "All right." He unbuttoned his shirt, put the envelope flat against his chest, and rebuttoned it. The man patted him on the chest and looked him up and down. "Good. How old are you?"

"Fourteen."

"You're short for your age. That's good. They won't search you, anyway. Now your jacket." Tadek buttoned his jacket.

"You look fine. Now go!" the man said.

"Wait! Who are you? What's your name?"

"You mean my real name? Don't be stupid. You think I want you to know my name? Why would you even want to know my name? That's even stupider. Then they could beat it out of you. Remember, you don't want to do know anything more than you have to." The man lit a cigarette and inhaled till his cheeks sucked in, and Tadek could imagine the skull beneath the man's flesh. "I'm Chopin. They didn't tell you that? For that's what I'm called."

"Sure. Okay. You're Chopin." Tadek wasn't sure if the man

was joking or not, but he didn't want to show his uncertainty.

"Good. Be back here the first Tuesday of every month at the same time. Do exactly what we say and nothing else. No word to anyone. You hear me?"

"Yes."

"If we need to see you besides that, we'll get word to you."

"I was supposed to say, 'Svetlana is not my mother.'"

"Shut up with that nonsense. Do you think I would be giving you messages if I didn't know who you were? You are Kowal's nephew, son of Krystyna Belyawski."

"Gradinski."

"All right! You live on the east side of Liaski in the house with the grape arbor and the large orchard. I know all about you. You don't need to know anything! You just need to do what you're told."

Tadek didn't respond. The man evidently thought better of his outburst. "You're fighting for Poland," he said in a different voice. "That's all you need to know. Now leave. And use your head." He sneezed. Both of them looked at each other significantly and nodded together. People said that if someone sneezed, it confirmed the truth of what had just been said.

Tadek headed out on his bicycle, shrugging off the man's contempt for the passwords. He liked that the man wanted to get things done.

He pumped the pedals hard, while still keeping an eye on the chain. He'd planned his route. Not back into the village, where the Russian soldiers patrolled, but around it, away from the river, on little-used roads, through fields where there were paths along the fencerows. He knew these ways better than anyone. He wended his way around the edge of the village with no problem. The moon rose and began dodging over his shoulder through the branches of trees. He left the back way and circled back toward the river, eventually crossing the hump-backed stone bridge that told him he was nearing his uncle's village.

Shabany's central square was just a few buildings huddling together as if for reassurance along the river on one side and along a widening of the gravel road that served as the town's center on the other. A few more houses were scattered up a slight rise into the encroaching forest. The sight of Shabany usually gave Tadek a sense of disappointment, as if the village had always aspired to be different from how it ended up, but had now thoroughly resigned itself to its fate. But today when he turned into the square, his heart thumped in his chest and tried to escape up his dry throat, and his hands clenched the bike handles.

A few soldiers stood before a makeshift shed they'd built to break the wind, one with his foot up on the bumper of a staff car. Tadek made himself slow down and look at the soldiers as he passed. One glanced at him. Tadek felt his heart quiet and a calm seeped down his limbs as his gaze held the soldier's. He looked casually away before his look became challenging. The soldiers were all listening to someone tell a story. The man finished the story and they all laughed as Tadek passed down the road.

The chain came off again with a clatter. He ground to a halt. He'd unconsciously been speeding up. He hopped off and once more pulled loose the chain from where it had jammed around the axle and guided it back onto the gear teeth. Without looking at the soldiers, who were listening to a follow-up story, he hopped back on the bike and continued on his way.

As he turned the corner off the square out of sight, his nerves sang. He'd done it! He tried to control his impulse to pedal faster out of sheer elation. The moon had risen higher in the sky and helped to light Tadek's way. In ten more minutes he was at his uncle's, an isolated wood house and a few outbuildings that sat, beyond a row of trees, on a small rise one hundred meters from the river.

Tadek slung his bike against the fence and knocked on the door. He no sooner finished knocking than the door opened. Jan's massive frame filled the doorway. He wore a leather vest over his ample belly, and stood looking over Tadek's shoulder into the night. "Were you followed?"

"No."

Jan seemed skeptical and peered again over Tadek's shoulder. Finally: "Put your bicycle all the way behind the shed. People pass by down the hill and they can look up and notice a strange bicycle. Yes, yes, they notice everything. Someone notices everything in this world, especially when you have something to hide. Remember that! Now hurry."

Inside the house smelled of Jan's cigars and frying bacon. Jadwiga stood by the stove and turned to watch Tadek enter. There was just one kerosene lantern in the room, giving off a faded, yellow light that seemed secretive.

"It was behind the shed, uncle."

"No, it was not. I could see it. It's all the way behind now, right?"

"Yes."

"From now on, you must listen to everything I say. I am no longer your uncle. You are no longer a child. These are orders and they might save your life and the lives of others."

"I understand."

"Just do what I say. Listen to me! Did you see that couple walking toward you on the road the other way?"

"No."

"No, you didn't! They passed five minutes ago and probably stopped along the river. Keep your eyes opened, and when you see anyone else on the road—I don't care how innocent they look— just keep on going!"

"I understand."

"Understand...understand . . . . You understand nothing."

What Tadek understood quite clearly was that his uncle was afraid, and the knowledge of his fear planted a seed of doubt in Tadek more serious than the moment of tension on the square.

"You are stupider than I thought. Come here! How do you like this?" He cuffed him on the ear.

"Ow!"

"And another for the sake of your brains that refuse to function!" Tadek ducked away from his raised hand, eluding the second blow.

"Cut it out, you!" Jadwiga said to her husband. She rapped his knuckles with a wooden spoon. "Come, Tadek; sit down." She motioned to a place at the table, a glass of kvass and a slice of buttered bread already set for him. "What's the matter with you?" she said to her husband.

Jan shrugged his heavy shoulders and went again to the window. When he turned back, he seemed truly remorseful. "I'm sorry, Tadek." He kept pacing though, going to open the door to peer out again into the dark. "You might have been followed," he said. "You need to be careful. This is very important."

Tadek sat down and began to unbutton his jacket and shirt but stopped, glancing at the strip of night-black window visible between the curtains. Jadwiga followed his eyes and went to pull the curtains completely shut. Jan nodded. "Good boy. Now you're thinking."

Tadek removed the envelope and handed it to Jan, who took it and without looking inside put it in a canvas bag hanging besides the door.

In a low voice, as if someone was listening at the window, Tadek told them what had happened: where the soldiers had been, how they had reacted. His aunt and uncle listened carefully. Jan asked him twice about where the soldiers had been and how many of them there were. Tadek told him about his chain falling off.

"Well fix it! You can't be so sloppy about things."

"Yes, uncle." When he saw his uncle had run out of questions, he couldn't resist asking, "It's still early. Do we have time for a game of chess?"

This was his uncle's weak spot. He hesitated. "Oh, okay. We can start one, and finish it up next time. Just the opening, all right?"

"All right."

Away from the chessboard, Uncle Jan was overweight, clumsy, slow, angry, profane, and lame. But over the chessboard, Tadek saw another Janusz, one who was complex, precise, and ruthless. They had developed the habit of playing over the years whenever family gatherings brought them together, and even if they only had time to make a move or two on the continuing game set up at each of their houses, they would carve out that time. In game after game Jan conquered Tadek, but he would always take time afterwards to demonstrate a few of the crucial errors that had led to his downfall. The game could hinge on the slightest pawn move, he emphasized over and over again. His Uncle Kazimierz was his favorite, but Tadek respected this surprising side of Jan. Though Jan had tough hands that seemed strong and insensate as wrenches and that struggled to pick up a piece, though his body was lumbering and awkward, Janusz had a mind that was always racing ahead and probing behind appearances.

Tonight they only sat over the board for a few minutes and made a few moves before Tadek became aware that Jadwiga was clearing her throat every few seconds, wiping and re-wiping the tabletop, dimming the lantern, peering out the window.

"You'd better go, Tadek," Jadwiga said. "They will think it strange for a boy to be out so late."

"Yes."

At the door she warned him. "Keep your head down." She briefly hugged his head to her ample chest. "Don't pull any more stunts like your Hitler-pig." While his aunt and uncle chuckled at him, Tadek gave an embarrassed grin. His uncle sobered. "I was too harsh on you! But you must take this seriously, more seriously than you've ever taken anything!" He gave Tadek an assessing look. "Do you understand?"

"Yes, Uncle."

"Do you now?"

"Yes."

"Don't talk to anyone about what you're doing," his uncle reiterated. "I mean it."

"I know."

"Good job," his uncle said gruffly. "So far."

His aunt gave him a burlap sack of turnips, beets, and onions to place in his bike basket, and he was off again into the night, following the hard dirt road on the shoulder above the river. Bats fluttered and jerked overhead in the light spaces between the trees and out over the surface of the river. Once another biker passed him going the other way, and twice he whizzed by the dark form of a stroller along the side of the road. When he approached Shabany, he saw that the staff car was gone now, and only three Russian soldiers stood before the shack. This time he did not slow, but to his surprise a soldier stepped forward and cried, "Halt!" He slid to a stop.

"It's just a kid," one of the soldiers said.

Tadek could understand this much Russian—learning it had become a necessity and he'd discovered that he had a knack for languages and mimicry. He had picked up phrases of German quickly during their occupation and now was doing the same for Russian, though he'd found the Germans' barking accents more fun to imitate.

He was surprised, though, when another soldier stepped forward and said in accented Polish, evidently for Tadek's benefit, "Little worms grow up to be snakes." This last speaker came up to Tadek, shadowed at his back by the other two, who craned curiously over his shoulder as he poked and prodded at Tadek's basket. He snapped on a torch and peered into the basket, where he found the burlap sack. He roughly shook out the sack, spilling some vegetables in the road.

"Beets," he said indignantly. He picked one up by its rat-tail, made a distasteful face, and dropped it down again. "Turnips. Onions." He prodded them with his boot toe.

"I told you," another soldier said.

The more curious soldier turned to Tadek. He was a large man with a coarse, squarish face and bloodshot eyes. "Who are you?" he asked again in Polish. "Where are you going?"

Instinctively, he half-lied. "Tadek Dobrinewicz, from Liaski. I was just getting some food from my uncle. Their garden did better than ours. I'm just going home."

"Let me see those onions," one of the soldiers said, prodding at Tadek's bike basket with his barrel. He selected a couple and put them in his jacket pocket.

"That's the penalty for interrupting our conversation! Get going!"

Slowly, gritting his teeth, understanding that he had to restrain himself, Tadek picked up the onions and beets that had fallen into the dust, replaced them in the basket, and pedaled off into the night.

Chapter 17:
In the Marketplace

Through the fall of that year, the first months of so-called peace, Tadek and the other boys of Liaski still played football near the railroad station, after work or after school, more so than ever, now that they were better fed and had more energy. Though the nationalities of the guards had changed, little else had. Two sentries would sit on the benches and smoke while the other two would walk up and down for half an hour, and then they would switch. One day Pawel gave a mighty cross-field pass to Tadek, but had too much on it. The ball bounced awry out of bounds, through the scrim of trees, down the bank and over the tracks, twisting across the gravelly ground to hit, as the appalled boys watched, the back of the calf of one of the Russians walking back to the platform.

This was the sergeant in charge of the group, regular army, not NKVD. He turned and swept an assessing gaze over the boys, who had gathered trackside in a mute row. The sergeant was a tall man with heavy shoulders.

To Tadek's relief and amazement, the sergeant laughed, the

laughter transforming his face, making him for the moment kid-like, almost innocent himself.

He said something to the other soldiers, one of whom ran to take his rifle from him.

Another guard stepped forward to take a pass from the sergeant. A third formed another corner of a triangle and for a moment their military roles dropped away as they kicked the ball back and forth in their heavy boots. Tadek had just started to worry that their ball had been stolen when the sergeant said something to the others with a laugh. One passed the ball back to the sergeant. He juggled it with his knees a half a dozen times, then began dribbling the ball toward the boys on the gravel beside the tracks, surprisingly agile in his booted feet, playing it back and forth fluidly from boot to boot, till he paused and gave the ball a precise kick that lifted it neatly over the railroad tracks to land at Tadek's feet. Tadek stilled it with a toe. It had been a perfect pass. The boys and soldiers all applauded and laughed.

"*Spasiba*," Tadek called to the sergeant.

"*Nezashto*. What's your name, kid?" the sergeant called.

Tadek sensed instinctively what the soldier had asked him. "Tadek."

The man said something more in Russian, followed by "Tadek," but since he didn't fully comprehend, Tadek didn't reply. There followed a silence. The sergeant smiled and shrugged, and then, as if embarrassed, each turned back to his group, and each group folded into itself.

He met this same sergeant a week later, on a market day when he and his mother went to the town's square to meet Kazimierz's wife, Helena, and her two children.

Helena preferred to remain inconspicuous, both by temperament, because she was a shy person, and because her husband was rumored to be Kowal—the head of the Liaski partisans. She lived like a recluse in her house in Shabany, a small place on the way into town which Tadek would bicycle past on his missions. He never stopped there, though sometimes she came into Liaski and stopped to see them, Krystyna being one of the few people she trusted.

Many people said that Kowal was dead, a status which lent a supernatural aura to his partisan forces, which still struck out at the Soviets now and again and then dissolved into the forests. Helena dressed in black like a widow, and let people assume what they wished. She was a slight, pretty woman with a narrow nose, almost translucent skin, and huge eyes. Today she wore a black scarf over her thinnish blond hair like an old babushka and had on a tatty black cardigan that was missing buttons over a black dress. One hand rigidly clutched it shut at her chest in a gesture much older than her years.

Krystyna and Helena, after walking through the stalls of vegetables, sat away from the crowd on a bench against a wall.

"Why don't you walk with your cousins, Tadek, so I can talk with your aunt?" Krystyna said. Basia, the younger girl, looked up at Tadek with solemn eyes and took his hand. She was fragile like her mother, seemingly made of a fine porcelain. Genia, the elder girl, now seven, was more full-faced and solid like her father. Before reluctantly taking his hand, she made an odd expression, popping her eyes and lifting her brows. Inside Genia, Tadek sensed a mulish resistance. Tadek wondered how often they saw Kazimierz, whether their house was watched by the NKVD. Their whole lives their father must have been a mysterious, hushed, but elating presence who came and went at night like the wisp of a dream that they'd doubt in the morning.

"Do you want a cookie?" he asked the girls. Basia nodded, shy.

Genia made that odd popping expression with her eyes and asked, "What type of cookie?"

"I don't know," Tadek replied. "Whatever you want." She made the odd expression again as she thought, and Tadek wondered what adult pressures had seeped into her life and been transformed into this peculiar mannerism.

An enthusiastic puppy, making the rounds in the marketplace, ran squirmingly up to the two girls, who cowered shrieking behind Tadek. Tadek smiled and shooed the puppy away, stooping to reassure the girls before moving on.

They went to the store that had been owned by the Friedlanders years ago. Now it was a bakery run by a cheerful man with a full mane of silver, wavy hair. "Hi, Tadek," the man greeted him, and Tadek smiled and waved, though he was unsure of the man's name. He bought his two cousins each a large cookie sprinkled with squarish granules of sugar and they walked back toward the marketplace, each child holding the cookie in one hand and Tadek's hand in the other.

As they crossed the marketplace, a Soviet soldier called to him from a bench near the town hall entrance. "Kid! Kid!" Curious and suspicious, Tadek edged closer. It was the same tall sergeant from the railroad station. Up close Tadek could see he had a lantern jaw and sunken cheeks that gave him a ravenous look, complicated now by his open smile.

Tadek nodded to the children gripping his hands, but the sergeant called anyway, "Come back. I want to talk to you!"

Tadek walked across the square to his mother and aunt. Helena withdrew her daughters' hands from his, giving Tadek an unfriendly look. But his mother said, "You'd better go talk to him, Tadek." Tadek looked over his shoulder and the sergeant was still looking at him. He gestured "come here" with his hand.

"Yes, all right."

The sergeant was standing amid a group of soldiers round an officer who sat on a chair. The sergeant said something to the officer in Russian and they both looked at Tadek.

Tadek had never seen the officer in Liaski before. He was a thick-chested man wearing rimless glasses on a pockmarked face with slightly Asiatic features. He was unimpressive to look at but had a confident air, and the other soldiers circled him in a deferential way, listening to his every word. He wore the blue tabs of the NKVD on his shoulders. The sergeant called him Captain Orbatov as Tadek approached.

He said to Tadek, "You speak Russian?"

"Just a little."

"What are you? Byelorussian?"

"I am Polish."

"Ah, I see. What does it feel like, to lose a war?"

Tadek surprised himself by understanding what the Captain said, but replied heatedly in Polish: "We beat the Germans!"

The man understood, at least, Tadek's emotions.

"Yes, that's right." The man said, still in Russian, laughing. "I forgot." The soldiers around him laughed as well. Tadek could smell onions and vodka on their breath, and he thought—and we will win again against the likes of you!

The man stopped laughing and gave Tadek a long look. The sun glinted on the disks of his glasses. Tadek put a simpleton's grin on his face as he sensed the pressure of the man's scrutiny.

To Tadek's surprise, the man switched to rough but passable Polish: "Well, not your fault, I suppose, to be born a Pole." He leaned back with an easy grin which he shared with his companions. "Though it wouldn't've been my choice. Here, take this across the way to the tavern and give it to the Russian with the officer's cap. See?"

"Okay." Tadek took the envelope and crossed the square to

hand the envelope to another blue-tabbed NKVD officer sitting at a table. This one fished into his pocket and brought out a couple of small coins to give to him.

Tadek joined his mother, aunt, and cousins, and they began walking back home in silence. A little way away from the square, Krystyna asked what had transpired. "How can you talk to those people, Tadek?" Helena gasped. "Despicable!" He saw tears were in her eyes.

But Krystyna said, "No, he did the right thing. It's good to get them used to seeing his face, to lure them into trust." Helena thought about this and nodded. She bent over and kissed Tadek on the cheek.

"I'm sorry, Tadek! I know what you're doing is for us!"

"It's all right. Is Kazimierz coming to Liaski soon?"

"Don't ask your aunt about Kazimierz, Tadek. Sorry, Helena."

"That's all right, Krystyna. I never know when he'll arrive, Tadek."

Tadek put his hand in his pocket and felt the coins that the officer in the tavern had given him. Without saying anything about it, as they walked along he took the coins out and tossed them unseen into some weeds alongside the street.

* * *

Tadek shared the incident with Chopin. They were both standing in the shadows of the mill. Chopin's ascetic, humorless face kept nodding, nodding as Tadek talked. Chopin was tall and narrow-shouldered, and there was something vulture-like about him, with his hunched shoulders beneath his top-buttoned black coat. He was of Krystyna's mind, and encouraged Tadek to befriend the Russians. Chopin thought that Tadek might pick up interesting information. He made Tadek tell him about the envelope again, but Tadek was convinced there was nothing important in it.

To further aggravate Tadek, Chopin also told him that in any spare time Tadek had, he should bicycle by the Russian troops in the square, carrying nothing. If he could take a pointless trip to Shabany, that would be good. If the occasion arose, he should strike up a conversation with the Soviets, even hope to be searched. The goal was to accustom them to the sight of him on his bicycle, coasting through the towns and fields.

He'd been told this before, and thought it was easy for others to assign him pointless tasks to waste his time. When he was riding his bike through the square, sometimes he would nod to the lanky, lantern-jawed sergeant, or the round-faced, Polish-speaking officer. But even these interchanges made him feel queasy. He remembered Helena's tears and her gasp of "despicable," and even though she had said that she was wrong, her reaction seemed just and correct to him, and though he didn't argue with Chopin, he would only go so far in his obedience to his order and would never befriend the Russians.

Chapter 18:
The Boy from Gombachy

In the spring Chopin sent him with a package for a small group of partisans who were in the forest near Gombachy, the little village east of Liaski.

After riding down a back road, bordered with looming sycamores just starting to leaf, he arrived at Gombachy, which sat on the border between a flat expanse of potato fields and the beginning of the vast forest. Just like Shabany, Gombachy seemed to Tadek inferior to Liaski. There was just a muddy street that stretched between a cluster of a few houses, a store, and a smithy. Tadek was supposed to go through the town and then look for an even smaller side street, take that until he hit the woods, walk his bike through a field, and wait until a partisan came to get his package. But as soon as he was biking through the town, he noticed another boy following him on a bike. He tried to ignore the boy and took the almost unnoticeable turn onto the side street, little more than a path. To his annoyance, the boy turned onto the path and kept following him at a steady distance.

Tadek stopped. The boy stopped. Tadek turned and bicycled

toward the boy, who was a lanky youth about Tadek's age. The boy hopped onto his bicycle and biked away, laughing. Tadek let him go and turned around, continuing on toward the fields beyond. But again the boy was behind him. Tadek kept pedaling, but as he approached the meeting point, the boy was still there. He couldn't let a partisan come out of the forest to be seen. Furious, Tadek turned and biked after the boy, this time continuing, gaining on him. Almost back to the village, the boy stopped and let Tadek catch up to him. He turned to face Tadek, laughing again. Tadek stopped his bike and they faced each other five meters apart.

It was the same gangling boy who had been throwing rocks at the dog stuck on the ice years before. Tadek studied him hatefully. He had a flat face and flattened eyes, one of which was lazy and roamed around disconcertingly, staring behind Tadek as they faced each other.

"What are you doing?" Tadek asked.

"What are you doing?" the boy mimicked, laughing. When he laughed, his teeth disappeared, so his mouth seemed all gums.

"Don't follow me."

"I live here," the boy said. "This is my town. You get out."

"No." Tadek threw aside his bike and ran toward the boy, who hopped on his bike and with a few quick pedals coasted out of distance.

"If you follow me again, I'll beat the crap out of you."

"No, you won't."

"What's your name?"

"What are you, a policeman? You don't look much like one," the boy sneered.

"Who are you?"

"That doesn't matter."

"Shit."

The boy laughed some more. "Stay away," Tadek said.

He didn't think he'd ever hated anyone as much as he hated the mocking, skinny, fish-eyed boy. He remounted his bike and pedaled once more toward the meeting point, but his shadow followed. When Tadek stopped abruptly and the boy coasted too near, Tadek jumped off of his bike and ran after him, running alongside him while the boy tried to speed up and fend Tadek off with one arm, but Tadek grabbed ahold and pulled the boy to a stop. The boy leapt off his bike, and he and Tadek tumbled together into the weeds alongside the road. First Tadek was on top, trying to get a good hit at the boy, whose long arms and legs made him difficult to restrain, and then the boy flipped Tadek, trying to keep him down and repay the favor with his fists. Tadek too squirmed away and both boys leapt up, faced off, and stood swinging wildly at each other, aiming for the face but hitting each other's arms more often than not. They both got some good blows in. They separated, panting, flushed, hating each other and calling each other names they'd scarcely been aware they had known.

"Get out of here!" the boy shouted. A vein throbbed in his forehead. His face was flushed and sweaty.

"I'll go wherever I want to!"

"If you ever come back here, I'll beat you up again," the boy warned.

"If I ever come back here," Tadek answered, "I'll kill you."

They both paused to think about this. Tadek glanced at his bike and saw that his package had rolled out of the basket amid a pile of beets. Tadek went to replace the package and cover it with beets, noticing the boy's eyes growing large as he followed Tadek's every move. The boy had seen the package and grown thoughtful. Tadek righted his bike, stepped on a pedal, slung his leg over the seat, and pedaled back down the lane, taking his time.

He gave up. This was no way for a quiet handoff with the partisans. He retraced his path through Gombachy and back toward home, with, infuriatingly, his shadow following behind him on his bike until Tadek was well away from the village. Tadek felt his cheek and ear stinging where the boy had caught him with a couple of his long-armed punches. The knuckles of his hand remembered stingingly how hard the boy's skull had felt as he'd hit him on the back of the head, and he hoped the boy's head remembered the blows too.

Chopin sent word to meet him the next week, and his handler had some unpleasant news for him. When Tadek began telling him of the boy from Gombachy, Chopin nodded impatiently. "Yes, yes. I've found out all about him. It was just a mix-up. He's a bike messenger too."

"He's on our side?"

"Yes. That's why he was tailing you. He didn't know who you were."

"Shit!"

"Don't swear! You're too young for that. Anyway, you have to meet him on the first Thursday of each month. If I haven't given you anything for him, then he may have a message to bring back to me. This way we'll have better communication with them."

"I'm not going to meet him!"

Chopin seemed genuinely shocked. He moved as if to slap Tadek, who skipped out of his reach. "You'll take orders like everyone else!" Chopin said. "Meet him exactly where you were last time, where you fought. Give him this." Chopin handed Tadek one of his thick envelopes.

Tadek didn't mind flouting the NKVD or the Soviet army for the good of Poland, but that he had to put up with the insolence of the kid from Gombachy seemed to be asking more than could be stomached. He knew he had no choice though, and so he directed his bicycle toward Gombachy the next Thursday. As he wheeled down the path between the field and the forest, he saw no one. Then a shrill whistle called him back and the lanky kid stepped out of the forest and gestured to him with a curt motion. Tadek turned his bike down a little gulley, through some weeds, and into the forest, where the boy stood next to a tall, dead tree.

"No one will see us here," the kid said.

"Okay."

They stood looking at each other a few feet apart, as if their bodies were remembering their fight, measuring each other again. In the forest shadows Tadek observed the boy's lazy eye, his flat face, his long, gangling arms that, he knew, could pack a punch, and he didn't like him any better than he had before. He didn't care whose side the kid was on: Tadek's body still wanted to fight him. The boy seemed to feel the same way. Reluctantly, he turned away from the brief face-off with Tadek. "Follow me," he said, and biked into the forest a hundred meters to a clearing with a large, uprooted tree at its center. He overturned a flat stone in the pit left by the uprooted tree to reveal a hollowed out space.

"You can hide messages for me here, if we don't meet up."

"Okay."

"What do you have?"

Tadek reached into his shirt and pulled out the envelope. The kid took it and, without a word more, Tadek stepped onto a bike-peddle and spun away.

Retracing his path back to Liaski between the rows of sycamores, he saw almost no one. When he went to Shabany, he had to wend his way past groups of Soviets, but the back way to Gombachy seemed abandoned by armies, governments, and fate. Tadek had to admit the wisdom of the plan as a way of keeping in touch with the Gombachy partisans, though he hated to give up his personal spite, and thought scornfully that not even the Soviets cared enough about the miserable little village to patrol it.

Chapter 19: Circling

Over the summer Chopin sent him more and more frequently to Gombachy, to meet with the disagreeable native whose name, Tadek learned, was Lech Sosna. Tadek hadn't exactly gotten to like Lech, but he realized that there was a bond between them that was more important than affection, more important now than his bonds with his friends from Liaski: they held each others' lives in their hands. They both always showed up, exactly when and where they were supposed to. Tadek appreciated this in Lech as much as he prided it in himself. Lech insisted that Tadek call him Diabeł.

"That's my *nom de guerre*," he said.

"What's that?"

"That's what people call you so that they don't use your real name."

"Oh." They were meeting again in the forest clearing with the fallen tree. Tadek handed Lech, or Diabeł, a heavy, tightly wrapped package of a type he sometimes carried—the size of a loaf of bread, but much heavier, dense with mystery and dark potency.

"You need a nom de guerre, too," he advised.

"I don't think I need one."

"You need one," Lech insisted, unnerving Tadek a bit with his lazy eye, which seemed to see all around them but never focused on Tadek himself. "Everyone should have one."

"See you, Lech," he teased. Tadek was damned if he was going to call him Diabeł, and he leveraged himself onto the bike and slowly pedaled away. Lech made an obscene gesture with one hand, but put his other hand on Tadek's handlebars to stop him.

"Let me go."

"No. Do you want to see something?"

"What?"

"Something."

"What?"

"Follow me."

Lech swung onto his bicycle. Despite his reservations, Tadek followed. They rode straight into the forest. Lech knew paths that wove between the trees and around the underbrush. The going was surprisingly easy over the spongy pine needles, and for a few moments Tadek forgot about everything except the joy of being young and alive, jouncing around trees, racing with Lech. After ten minutes, Lech pulled up at the edge of a ravine, a look of success on his face. "Look!"

Tadek pulled up next to him. He didn't see anything. Just a ravine filled with fallen pine needles and branches. "What?"

"Look again." Lech was looking at Tadek with what wasn't quite a smile.

Tadek did look again, studying the shadows. Shapes formed themselves underneath the litter of leaves and rusty pine needles. Maybe six or seven shapes half-buried in the ravine. The complex bone-architecture of a hand, the unmistakable shape of a jawbone, the cavities and convexities of a skull. They were just skeletons, a few tattered rags. They must have been in a shallow grave and the erosion of several springs had washed away the covering earth.

Tadek turned away, choking down a gagging sensation that brought vomit to the back of his throat.

Lech looked at Tadek, waiting for a reaction. Tadek's shocked silence prompted a nervous giggle from Lech.

"Who is it?"

"Jews."

"How can you tell?"

"Their clothes. What's left of them. That hat."

"Well, you need to tell someone."

"I will."

"Somebody should bury them. Or do something."

"There's no reason to be angry." There was something that disappointed Lech about Tadek's reaction. "I didn't do it."

"Well, go tell somebody." Tadek turned his wheel away and rode off, hoping he could find his way back to a road. He pedaled hard, away from the discovery. He was angry that he'd been fool enough to follow Lech. The truth was, Tadek believed in ghosts, and sometimes woke up at night in a sweat when a branch scratched at his window. While he'd been making treehouses, human beings were being murdered in the woods and left to rot there, forgotten and unmourned. Though he'd told Lech to tell someone about the bodies, for some reason, Tadek could not bring himself to say anything to anyone about what Lech had shown him. He tried to forget, but now he had the secret, too.

* * *

Chopin told Tadek that he would be taking no messages or packages for a while. He was to continue to keep a presence on the streets of Liaski, but would be carrying nothing incriminating for a time. "Lie low," he said.

"What's happened?" Tadek asked.

"You don't need to know anything more."

"Is something going to happen?"

"Don't ask."

Later that week, a small group of Soviet soldiers, who were pushing on foot deep into the forest near Gombachy, were ambushed by about twenty partisans armed only with small handguns. Three of the Soviet soldiers were wounded and one of them died a week later.

When Tadek next saw the lantern-jawed, football-playing sergeant, he took in Tadek with a vacant, preoccupied gaze and turned to call an order to a pair of soldiers who were with him. Tadek was satisfied that the sergeant was still alive—he had nothing against him personally—but also glad that a clearer demarcation had been established.

Later that day, bicycling homewards from fishing with Pawel, as he approached the town square, he saw that a crowd had gathered. He saw the familiar khaki-green uniforms of the army, plus a few NKVD officers. The bespectacled, round-faced Captain Orbatov stood up in a staff car, surrounded by a platoon of his troops. When he stood up, even in the car, Tadek could see how short Orbatov was.

He was haranguing the Poles, who were closing up their market stalls, or lingering at the corners of the square out of curiosity. He spoke through a bullhorn in high-pitched, comical Polish, informing the Poles that they were foolish to support the resistors, like those who had dared to attack the Soviet army in the woods near Gombachy. These banditos would all perish into the dust of history. The shutters of the buildings closed around the square. The few Poles shuffled their feet and looked up at the sky and drifted away. Tadek circled around the square on his bicycle.

Orbatov reminded the Poles that the Red Army had driven out the Germans and liberated them, that Marxist-Leninism was the future and that all things would be equal and all people would prosper. Tadek kept circling. The closed shutters seemed to listen and to watch. A dog urinated in a corner of the square. Orbatov turned to his troops and told them that they were the pioneers of history, settling the future for the generations to come. Around went Tadek. Around the knot of men under the seven sycamore trees. Each time he circled behind Orbatov, he could feel Orbatov's urge to turn to follow him. He sensed the vulnerability of the back of Orbatov's head. When his circle brought him within the Captain's sight, Tadek could see the flashing discs of his spectacles turning to watch Tadek even as the Captain continued to speak into the bullhorn. Tadek knew that Orbatov could not see everywhere. Tadek knew that the Poles would win sooner, or later. Tadek also knew that Chopin wouldn't approve of his being here, but he couldn't stop himself. He had to watch the NKVD captain as he shouted and gestured. The flash of Orbatov's glasses caught him as soon as he circled to the front and the glinting glasses turned as Tadek turned over the hard-pounded ground, between the trees, to finally escape the captain's eyes as he circled behind him and around the gathering of soldiers to recapture the captain's gaze on the other side. Orbatov's voice finally trailed off into a disgusted dismissal. He sat down in his staff car. "Get that kid!" was his final order, before driving off toward Grodno.

Tadek veered off, down the same alley where he'd once let loose a pig, and peddled helter-skelter down a narrow path between houses. When he shot out the other side, it was an easy ride of a minute across the village, cutting through more alleys, to his back garden gate and safety.

PART IV:
LOVE AND
VIOLENCE

Chapter 20: Working

January 1949

After Tadek had given up on school for good, it had taken him a while to find a decent job, but now he was an apprentice machine repairman in a shoe and textile factory in Grodno. The job appealed to him in several ways, much more so than school ever had. He liked getting up in the blue-black dawn and making his way to the stop for the Grodno bus with the handful of other villagers who worked in the city. He liked making his way against the flow to the fields of the *kolkhoz* workers in the morning. He liked the noise and crowds of the city and enjoyed finding his way around it. Sometimes he thought that despite the overshadowing presence of the Soviets, there might be a future for him somehow.

The factory was really two factories, with the shoe building and the textile building separated just by a narrow cinder alley. Tadek's boss's name was Stronski, and Tadek liked him too. Stronski was in charge of maintaining all the machines in both factories. He was a wiry and sly septuagenarian with darting blue eyes behind wire-rim glasses and long white hair he combed back in a mane that looked grandiose on such a short man.

Tadek spent the morning in the shoe building, carrying a bulky box of repair tools, hung by a leather strap over his shoulder, trailing the old man from sewing machine to sewing machine, oiling and repairing. Next came the stamping machines, a row of dwarfish, thumping machines into which hunched women fed sheets of thick leather from morning till night. One particular arm that gave the downward force its leverage tended to get misaligned and needed to be oiled and coaxed and observed like a fussy dowager.

Tadek and Stronski ate their lunches wordlessly in a closet filled with metal racks of spare parts. Sometimes Stronski would pick up a machine part and look it over while he ate, the lump of steel in one hand, a sandwich in the other.

"What's that?" Tadek asked once.

"It's a magneto."

"What's a magneto?"

"So you want to know what a magneto is?" Stronski asked, mocking.

"Yes."

Stronski lifted his eyebrows and shrugged: "All right, kid. Pay attention."

In the afternoon they made their way across the alleyway to the textile building. Having one technician in charge of maintenance for all the machines in both plants was efficient and redounded to the greater good of the Soviet Union.

Here Tadek observed how Stronski took apart the complex, spider-like looms, and how he put them back together with an exact sequence of exact tools from his repair box. He then replaced the exact tools in an exact reverse-sequence that seemed, after Tadek had seen it enough to appreciate its discipline, like a miniature dance.

Stronski projected an air of skepticism, as if, Tadek felt, he was secretly afraid of being made fun of or fooled somehow. But Tadek was an optimist, and rather enjoyed Stronski's company as he danced a bit from side to side behind the man in impatience at their slow progress down the long rows of whirring machines. He smiled and nodded as the old man demonstrated what had gone wrong with a machine and how it needed to be corrected, unconsciously emulating the man's meticulous manner and gradually winning over his guarded nature.

As Stronski lifted each tool he would make a verbal introduction, and as he pointed out each vulnerable point in each machine, he would similarly take the opportunity for a little oratory, but these weren't wasted words. Tadek respected him and listened to him. Indeed, except for the complex workings of an ingenious chess opening showed to him by his godfather, he'd never known anything quite as intricate, logical, and beautiful as the rapidly clicking innards of these machines, or the carefully arrayed tools, minute screwdrivers and tiny hooks, graduated in size, that fit into the smallest velvet slots in Stronski's toolbox. The order and precision awakened within him a longing for something in his life that he hadn't known existed.

For the past three years, his missions to Shabany and Gombachy had continued, usually about once a month. In Liaski the Soviet troops circulated through, and he forgot their faces. There would always be new ones, who would pass through themselves in six months or so. As the occupation, as everyone in Liaski called it, entered its fourth year, the regular army troops were thinning, but there were still NKVD stationed in Liaski, considered a center of stiff-necked resistance. (The NKVD had been split into the MGB and the MVD—"so much prettier," everyone had agreed—but everyone in Liaski would never call them anything but the NKVD, refusing to let anything they'd ever done be forgotten through a shuffling of initials.)

Now at seventeen, Tadek realized that he was viewed with less casualness than before by the Soviets. He was outgrowing the disguise of boyhood. Glances that used to sweep over him with supercilious negligence now paused for an extra half-second of scrutiny. Still, after a month or so, the new troops too would get used to him bicycling around the square and start to ignore him as just a part of the village scenery, like an old crone or the village drunk.

The activities of the Liaski partisans were low-key and infrequent. Mostly the partisans were just trying to stay alive and avoid the fate of their colleagues who had made the mistake of trusting Soviet offers of amnesty. But sometimes still there were partisan raids. A shipment of ammunition disappeared in Grodno, or a drunken soldier ended up at the bottom of a cliff. Once the railroad bridge over the Niemen was damaged, and though the official story was that it was closed for routine repairs, everyone nearby had heard the explosion in the night and had seen the twisted rails and the shattered remnants of timbers the next day. Sometimes Tadek had difficulty putting together his bicycle rides around the area with the events in the broader world, though he assumed that the packages he carried were weapons, the smaller ones handguns, the larger ones dismantled submachine guns.

Uncle Kazimierz in the guise of the near mythic Kowal had been rumored wounded in a raid near Bialystok, and again everyone said that he was dead, but in two days Krystyna heard from Helena that he had snuck into Shabany to visit her, the wound was superficial, and he was delighted by the rumor. His buoyant spirits never deserted him, and Helena was the one to feel the weight of his years in the forests. Though she was a young woman, still delicate and beautiful in an anxious, poignant way, the years drew their lines on her face, two streaks down either side of her mouth as dark and distinct as if drawn with crayons.

A few weeks after these rumors, Tadek bicycled to meet Chopin at the abandoned mill. At first it seemed no one was there, but when Tadek wheeled his bike further into the ruins, he saw Chopin sitting on an old millstone, looking down at the half-frozen river, where very black water rushed beyond a border of delicate ice. "Chopin!" he made a stifled call, and the man whirled his head around in alarm. He gave Tadek a rare smile. They made their exchange: a package for the Liaski partisans, and an envelope from the partisans for someone in Grodno, Tadek guessed. Chopin's smile seemed genuine, but came out of raw edginess that was unsettling to Tadek. Chopin paced, his jawbone pulsing in his cheek, wiping a hand along his goateed chin as Tadek told him about added patrols through the main street of Shabany and how he'd had to evade them.

"The Soviets are tightening down," Chopin said, "That's certain. They have controlled things in the west and now can concentrate on us." Sometimes he made an odd, involuntary shrug of his shoulders, as if to rid himself of something. He wore the same severe black jacket that he always wore, under an equally severe black winter coat. He and Tadek stood together in the center of the ruins, their breath turning into plumes of steam. "You did well," Chopin said, "You're getting good at your job." Again a glint of smile, this time almost a grimace. He wore no gloves and his hands were chapped from the cold and he kept clearing his throat, as if he was about to make a speech that never came. Tadek saw that this man, who had always been so determined, stoical, and focused, giving Tadek the confidence and guidelines he'd needed, was now uncertain and doubtful.

"We can't meet here anymore," Chopin said. "Not for a while, anyway. They're searching places like this now. There is a new strategy from Moscow, or from the traitors around us. They're not content to let things simmer forever. Orbatov is a butcher, but he's sloppy and lazy. Someone is behind him, making him do things differently." Rarely had Chopin opened up this much to Tadek about any thinking beyond the strict focus on Tadek's mission. "I can't take unnecessary risks," he said, and Tadek felt a constriction in his stomach as he saw the depth of Chopin's anguish. "I'm married now," he said candidly, turning a direct gaze on Tadek. "Things are different."

"Yes."

"I really do like Chopin, the composer, you know," he said from nowhere, following up a train of thought that seemed to have been running in his mind for a while. "The Preludes especially." He hummed a few sorrowful notes to himself. "Number two, A minor. That's why I picked that name. That's also why I fell in love with my wife." He shrugged his shoulders and lifted his eyebrows, as if such things were beyond comprehension. "That was the start, at least." He stared off down to the black rushing river and seemed to forget Tadek.

"Anyway . . . " Chopin reassembled his wits and pushed himself off from the stonewall he'd been leaning against. He patted Tadek on his upper arm, a bit diffident. "We'll meet somewhere else. I'll contact you soon."

Chapter 21:
Friends and Lovers

Tadek stopped outside the gate to Pawel's house by the leafless shrubbery, and stuck his two little fingers in his mouth, and gave a shrieking whistle. He was picking Pawel up on the way to Halinka's Saturday afternoon birthday party at Sabina's house. In a moment Pawel stepped down the path, wrapping a blue knitted scarf around his neck. "Nice scarf," Tadek said, and grabbed the ends of it, miming as if he were choking Pawel. Pawel slid out of his grasp laughing.

"Thanks. My mother knit it."

It was good to see Pawel. He'd seen his friends less since he was working in Grodno. His secret life as a bike messenger distracted him and sheathed him in hidden obsessions. So the thought of seeing them all today set him in a playful mood. At the same time, the truth was that Tadek really was envious of the scarf, though he knew the smallness of this thought was something he should hide from Pawel.

Tadek's mother didn't have time to knit since she worked full time. Pawel's father was back from the war, working, and making money, and though no one had much, some people now had a little, and Tadek was conscious of the patches all over his too-tight, brown corduroy coat, especially a faded pink patch on one elbow. He had slid cardboard into his boot to cover up a hole in the sole and could feel the cold of the road creeping up through that foot.

They both carried presents for Halinka, both, wrapped in their brown paper and string, obviously jars.

"What did you get her?" Pawel asked.

"Honey."

Pawel nodded somber approval.

"You?" Tadek asked.

"Blackberry jam."

The similarity of their gifts reassured them. They walked along the frozen road, Pawel's lanky stride contrasting with Tadek's springy one. Occasionally Tadek would run a few steps to slide on a larger ice patch. Their breathing made puffs of steam in the cold air.

Pawel had grown so serious! It was as if he was reverting to his childhood self, who had been teased by the other kids because he'd wanted to be a priest. He studied constantly, especially science and math, at the official school. Even under this cloud of Soviet domination, Pawel had ambitions. He wanted to find a way either to immigrate to Poland (but how could he leave his parents?) or to find his way into a profession, engineering or medicine, despite the Soviets and their attitudes toward Poles in Byelorussia.

Today Pawel was serious about other things as well.

"I'm going to ask Sabina if she wants to go to the St. Tomas dance with me in Grodno," Pawel said. He looked pale and stricken as he said this, and Tadek laughed. Seeing his friend's shyness, which always surprised him, made his envy less severe.

"Exactly when is it?"

"Three Saturdays from now."

"So do it."

Pawel laughed nervously, his eyes darting about. "It's not so easy. You know what she's like. So mocking and confident. What about you and Halinka?" His eyes worried the road ahead of him.

"I'll ask her too." Tadek was glad at this prompting. He wasn't shy like Pawel but never knew what he wanted from Halinka. As he grew older, rather than gaining on the girls, he felt as if he was falling further behind: they still had older minds and were privy to secrets he only dimly guessed at. He had lately felt a tension whenever Halinka was around, that made him start studying her with wary, sidelong glances as if there was something treacherous about her now. This date would be an intensification of their relationship that he felt was due.

"Okay, it's a bargain." They stopped and shook hands in the street. "Now I'll have to do it," Pawel said, more stricken than ever.

Tadek laughed. "Go ahead. She likes you."

"Oh, as a friend, sure. That's how I used to feel too, but I don't feel like that anymore. Now it's different."

It was different for everyone. Tadek was reminded how different when Sabina answered the door wearing a pale blue dress with a tight waist that showed her figure. She turned her heart-shaped face, with its mocking, rosebud mouth, to the boys, then laughed over her shoulder at something someone had said behind her, waving Pawel and Tadek in. Definitely some magic potion had been administered to the girls of the village, granting them new powers.

Tadek looked over Sabina's shoulder to see Halinka. It was her face that was burned into the insides of his eyelids. She looked at him and smiled and then turned away, flushing, reaching down to a punchbowl. He studied the clear line of her face in profile:

from brow to curving cheekbone to delicate, definite chin, an artist of skill and sensitivity had etched it.

"Don't stare! It's not polite!" Sabina poked him in the stomach. His gaze hadn't been as subtle as he'd thought.

"What do you mean?" he laughed.

She winked and made a dismissive face, pretend-frown, but more of a smile. "You know what I mean!"

Sabina was attractive to Tadek too, but he was glad Pawel and she were getting together. He felt he knew her too well. She was too much like him, sharing a defiant, independent streak. But Halinka was tall, cool, elegant, with long fingers like a queen in a fairy tale, and with that mysterious reserve that set all his senses on alert and made him feel as if he'd been drawn willy-nilly into an intricate game, even trickier and with higher stakes than the chess games with Jan.

Sabina took Tadek's and Pawel's coats and flung them recklessly over a chair. Abruptly she took Tadek by the elbow and pulled him aside. "Did you hear?" A look of concern came to her face as she leaned toward Tadek. She whispered with amazement: "A miller from Gombachy, Henryk Bohatkiewicz, asked Halinka to marry him!"

"Is she going to?" Tadek asked, not trying to hide his shock.

"Who knows? Maybe." She seemed to rebel against her own concern and said, "You should see your face!" in a mocking tone, moving away.

Pawel and Tadek followed Sabina into her sparsely furnished front room that served as living room and dining room. A warped picture of Pope Pius XII on the wall, next to one of the Sacred Heart of Jesus, together presided over the proceedings. A square, tiled stove stood at one end, overheating the crowded room. Some modest snacks had been set out on a few small tables that had been put together, covered with tablecloths that didn't hide their uneven sizes. The arrival of Pawel and Tadek made about a dozen guests. Franek and Yanek, the Borovski twins, on the accordion and clarinet, sounded the first notes of a polka.

"Make room for dancing! Give us space!" Sabina moved around the room pretending to shove people out of the way. She and Halinka began dancing together, creating their own space where Sabina's pantomime had failed. Two other couples joined them. When the music stopped, all three couples slowly twirled to a halt, laughing at themselves and clapping for the twins, who put down their instruments and, reaching their hands in front of them demonstratively, clapped for the dancers in turn. Franek was ten minutes older, and if one looked very carefully, one might discern a slightly more relaxed expression on his face than his younger brother's, which tended to look a bit stressed. Each had the same constellation of three moles on his right cheekbone. Franek was the more talkative of the two, while Yanek sat back and observed.

The moment the applause quieted, both Tadek and Pawel stepped forward and thrust out their presents for Halinka.

"Here."

"Here, Halinka."

"You handed your present to Halinka as if it were an admission ticket!" Sabina teased Pawel.

At first Pawel just looked at her with baffled eyes, slowly smiling at the others' laughter. "And you," she turned to Tadek, "handed it to her as if she were the servant who was taking your coat!" Everyone laughed. She'd captured their abrupt, mechanical gestures exactly.

"Halinka, are you going to marry that Gombachy man?" Tadek couldn't keep himself from asking, partly to change the subject, and the entire room laughed at the awkward lurching of his question.

"What's so funny?" he asked, offended.

Halinka smiled slowly and half-turned away from the group toward a window. She was scarcely the skinny girl with whom he'd played Go Hide, but a willowy blonde with a narrow, sensitive face and tender voice. He could imagine half of Poland, or Byelorussia, wanting to marry her and felt a panic.

"Yes, Halinka, are you?" others chimed in teasingly.

Halinka, acknowledging that the question wasn't going away, turned back and groaned and said, "Not that again."

Then, seeing Tadek's confused expression, she moved to him and put a hand on his arm and said, "No! Of course not! He's older than Noah, I don't even know him, and he asked my father without even telling me!"

"You're kidding! You're just eighteen!"

"I'm older than you!"

"I know. But you don't have to always act like you know more, too." Tadek wouldn't be eighteen until the next September.

"Some people say eighteen isn't so young! Bolek's sister got married at fifteen. But I agree with you. Isn't he disgusting, too? He slicks his hair back and smells like rotten turnips."

"Everyone from Gombachy smells like turnips."

Though the three neighboring villages were indistinguishable to an outsider, each possessed a fixed character in the minds of the others' inhabitants. It was certain knowledge in Liaski that Gombachy, the smaller town, was full of unambitious, out-of-date hicks, lost as it was away from the riches of the Niemen and kilometers off the main road from Grodno. At the same time, people from Gombachy thought those from Liaski were corrupted by their proximity to Grodno, which made them snobby, greedy, and dilettantish. Both villages took as an eternal verity that Shabany people had a reckless, atavistic toughness that made them treacherous—no matter how shy or intelligent they might be individually—while the people from Shabany considered themselves shrewd and realistic compared to the residents of the other two villages, who everyone knew were given to wool-gathering and easily duped.

"Her father wants her to marry him!" one of the twins said.

"I've got to get out of that house."

The other twin played the opening chords to a wedding march on his accordion.

Everyone laughed at Halinka's suitor. But her home life wasn't a matter for humor. Her friends knew that it was scarcely tolerable for her, with her stormy, vodka-loving father. Halinka's party was at Sabina's house because Halinka's father made her own house off limits.

After some fussy tuning of instruments, the twins began the Rosamunda polka. Tadek danced with Halinka, his hand riding precisely on her narrow waist. Then he danced with Sabina, whose electric breast brushed against his chest twice, and then with a small, inconspicuous girl transformed by the music and the dance into a twirling nymph. The dancing partners switched indiscriminately. Tadek could feel the warmth of the girls' bodies pressing against his. They flushed and laughed, their teeth flashing, their lips red. They smelled of bath salts and something else. The poorly made floor sagged beneath everyone's weight, the nails straining to pop loose. Franek and Yanek kept switching from mandolin to violin to clarinet to accordion, displaying their virtuosity. They played a sprightly *krakowiak* folk tune, and the reckless, spinning *oberek*, with each dancer taking a turn while the others clapped, finally all collapsing, laughing as they tried to catch their breath.

Sabina's mother brought platters of cakes and biscuits for the teens. Tadek's eyes went from Sabina's round laughing face to Halinka's slender face with its mysterious half-smile. He'd known them since he was five, but how they had changed. A miller from

Gombachy had asked Halinka to marry her. He pondered this fact, still dumbfounded.

"Come on, let's open presents. Halinka! The place of honor!" Sabina drew out the chair for her friend at the head of the table. The presents were modest. "Look," Sabina noted. "Pawel brought a jar of preserves and Tadek a jar of honey. They're both showing their sweetness."

"Oooh! How sweet!" one of the twins mocked. One brother trilled on the clarinet while the other gave a sonorous chord from the accordion with a pump of his elbows. Often they were more apt to sing like birds than speak like people.

"How analytical," Pawel observed dryly, irritated. Tadek too felt a bit wounded by Sabina's constant gibes. He was a little ashamed of his gift.

"But berries have thorns and bees have stingers!" Halinka remarked. "That must mean something, if we're to analyze in depth."

"Yes," Sabina agreed.

"It's a symbol of their dual natures. Their dangerous sides! Do you have a hidden side, Tadek?" Halinka turned to ask him directly.

"Doesn't everyone?"

"But I don't think you do, Tadek. You always say exactly what's on your mind," Halinka said.

"That's why we all love you," Sabina said.

"Don't get fresh!" he kidded back. He knew his personality appeared a good cover for his partisan activities, but felt a pang at the distance that had grown between himself and his childhood friends.

"And you, Pawel, you have hidden depths, don't you?"

"Certainly. I'm very profound and deep."

So they'd noted Pawel's deepening seriousness too. But he'd

always been serious, and was now just becoming more thoroughly who he was, less susceptible to outside influences. He sometimes irked Tadek by reading when Tadek wanted to go fishing or kick the football around, and Tadek teased him for being a bookworm.

"We all see that. And that's what we love about you," Sabina continued her discourse.

"I'm glad I'm included in the lovefest too."

"What about us," one of the twins said. "You can't leave us out."

"You can never complain. Look at the girls surrounding you two musicians," Sabina said. Five or six circled them like petals on a flower. "Musicians are always popular."

"You're the one with secrets," Tadek teased Halinka as they stood apart from the others.

"I am?"

"Yes. You're the dangerous one." He didn't really think she was dangerous, except in the power that her beauty held. But he knew that he didn't understand her. She seemed to have an invisible force field around her, spun out by her poise and intelligence, and he wanted to crash through that field and know who she was behind it. "Most particularly that mysterious smile of yours."

"I have to smile. It's my philosophy." Sometimes her smile did have a pained fixedness to it. As he stood next to her, she tapped with one hand on the back of the other in an odd nervous gesture he'd noticed she'd developed. He grabbed her hand to cease the tapping and led her to dance.

When the guests started leaving, Tadek, Pawel, and Halinka lingered and helped to clean up. There seemed to be an unspoken conspiracy shared by the four of them.

"Did you ask her yet?" Tadek whispered aside to Pawel.

"No, not yet. You?"

"No."

At the door, Tadek asked Halinka, "Can I see you home?"

"You can't see me to my door. You know...my father . . . . "

"Yes, I know."

"Everyone knows! But, yes...we can walk a ways."

"Oh, it's sleeting again." Sabina stood at the open door. She had gathered Halinka's presents into a wicker basket, which she handed to her. "I hope you don't get soaked."

They stood at the open door, hesitant to step out into the winter afternoon. The day was prematurely dark under charcoal clouds. Sleet slanted at an oblique angle across the doorway.

"Is it awful?" Halinka asked.

"It's just bitter, not that wet," Pawel said. Pawel wrapped his neck in the blue scarf, and Tadek eyed it seriously again but said nothing. He noted that Halinka was wearing the same black, knee-length coat she'd worn last year. This made him feel a bit less self-conscious about his corduroy coat, worn shiny at the elbows, with its pink patch.

Halinka gave Sabina a kiss on each cheek and slipped a hand through Tadek's arm. Pawel lingered behind with Sabina, so Tadek and Halinka walked ahead, stepping nimbly around the puddles to the corner of the next house. They turned to look behind them: Sabina's door had closed. Halinka smiled. "I guess Pawel is staying."

"I guess so." They both wavered, smiling at each other for no apparent reason, before starting to walk together, their heads bowing against the spitting sleet. "He wants to ask Sabina to the St. Tomas dance in Grodno."

"Oh, yes?"

"Yes. Would you like to go with me?"

"That would be nice."

"All right then . . . . " He caught her smiling to herself as if she'd received an unexpected birthday present. That was easy, Tadek thought. He knew Pawel would be going through torments to ask Sabina, and he was glad he wasn't like that.

The couple walked on a while in silence, steps crunching, carefully navigating the ice.

As they rounded the corner of a house, he gently touched Halinka's sleeve and pulled her into the lee of the wind. He held her elbow, steering her back against the bare wooden boards of the house, half-hidden by leafless shrubbery. She widened her eyes in bemusement, still smiling. He leaned forward into her warmth and kissed her.

"What are you doing?"

"You see."

He kissed her again, lingering wonderingly. Her lips softened as they kissed. He could taste the cake they'd all just eaten on her mouth, a hint of the cider she'd drunk. And just the taste of her, which was what he craved. She didn't argue anymore and kissed him back for a while before breaking away. "Tadek! I must go. Anyone could see us!"

"I don't care. I love you!"

"Oh, you don't love me!"

"Yes, I do."

"Well, I can't stand around kissing on street corners, anyway," she said, as she grabbed his arm and pulled him back down the street. Out of the corner of his eye he saw her slight, introspective smile as they picked their steps between the hard ruts and frozen puddles of the street.

Tadek's cardboard patch in his boot had slipped out of place with all the dancing and he could feel the cold ground pressing against the ball of his foot with each step. They both tilted their heads again in the same direction away from the sleet.

"Horrible weather for a birthday," Tadek said.

"I had a great day anyway. I hate to go home now."

"Your papa?" Tadek asked.

"And Mama too. She's so sad all the time now. Ever since her brother died, really." Tadek knew that Halinka's uncle had died at a work camp in Germany. "That caused it even more than Papa."

"That's difficult."

"Yes. His death, and Papa," she repeated. "She sits in the kitchen all day doing nothing."

He squeezed her hand and they looked at each other, probing the depths of this new relationship.

A noise down the street broke into their moment.

"What's that at the square?" Tadek asked. A crowd had gathered beneath the leafless sycamores. As they neared the square, they could see three groups of people. A group of Russian soldiers, identical in their long brown coats, were leading three prisoners around the square. The prisoners' hands were bound and they stumbled as they walked.

A sullen group of Poles—mostly old men in dark jackets and caps and women with their heads wrapped in babushkas—followed the spectacle. They kept a distance, but moved about in one mass behind the prisoners and soldiers. "Oh my God," Halinka breathed. Tadek hurried to the square and she followed him. They found a place at the back of the crowd of Poles. From here Tadek could recognize the short, stocky NKVD captain, Orbatov, directing his soldiers. He shouted an order and his men brought the prisoners to a halt.

Tadek ignored Halinka and pushed to the front of the crowd. Now he could see the prisoners: two rugged men in rough, patched jackets, dressed like peasants or partisans, and a third prisoner, a narrow man all in black. The crowd moved, forcing Tadek back, and he lost sight of the men. He pushed forward again. The two peasants were ill-shaven and looked more angry than frightened. The man in black looked at the crowd and then right at Tadek, whose heart leapt—it was Chopin. Tadek let the crowd push forward around him so he sank into the back ranks. Someone hit Chopin in the back of his head. He stumbled and his glasses flew off his face to the ground. It pained Tadek to see the normally confident Chopin momentarily bewildered.

"Comrades!" Orbatov shouted into the sleety wind. "These are traitors who are fighting against the Soviet Union!" His face was very red and he took out his handgun and gestured, pointing to the men and then to the crowd to make his point. "These are betrayers of their fellow workers. We caught them with these weapons. Comrades!" He pointed with his gun and two soldiers followed his direction, piling two rusty rifles and three or four pistols onto the frozen ground between the crowd of Poles and the soldiers. "They are spies for France, England, and the United States. These sorts of people will do anything for money. They have no loyalties to Byelorussia. We are building a future together as equals in the Soviet Union, but these are only vipers and vermin and parasites!

"Soldiers! Shoot them all!"

Anguished, angry shouts arose from the crowd. The soldiers hesitated, not knowing exactly what the order meant.

"Against the wall!" Orbatov shouted impatiently. "Put them against the wall! Now!" The soldiers prodded the group with their rifles and herded the men across the square against the stone-wall of the police station. More curses and cries from the crowd. Orbatov glared about as if to find and punish the shouters. The two peasant-partisans looked angry and defiant. Tadek had slid back into the crowd next to Halinka and watched Chopin: his face was white, but he seemed to find something he'd been grasping for inside himself and lifted his head and started to shout something, perhaps "long live Poland," but all he said was "long" before a messy volley of shots ripped into him and the other two partisans. Tadek saw the jolts of the bullets jerking Chopin's chest and destroying his face in a red mist. The three men fell into a muddled heap on the earth. Smoke drifted over the square as the echoes of the shots faded and startled pigeons circled through the trees and away. The crowd was silent. For a moment there was dead stillness and no one seemed to know what to do.

No more than a minute later a flatbed truck drove into the square and swung around to back up to the wall. Orbatov shouted orders into the cold air, and other soldiers rushed to grab the bodies and tossed them without tenderness onto the truck, which pulled away with what had been the three men flopping and rolling around in its bed.

Several old women rushed to the ground where the bodies had bled, dabbing at it with kerchiefs. This was holy martyrs' blood, which they would have blessed by the priests and press close to their chests from then on.

Orbatov saw what they were doing and barked angrily at his men to chase them away, but the women moved out of range of the soldiers' swatting rifles and soon crept warily back. Orbatov marched away with his men to where two more trucks waited and drove away, leaving behind two sentries at the townhall. The sentries chased away the old ladies a time or two, but finally gave up in the face of their determination and looked away as they swooped down upon the ground to soak up the precious blood.

"I can't walk," Halinka said, and Tadek helped her to a bench. He also felt his knees about to give way, and sat beside her. They slumped together on the bench, just around the corner from the square. They said nothing. A surly crowd of Poles stood across the square from the police station, talking amongst themselves and casting glances across the square at the two sentries.

"They're no different from the Nazis," Tadek finally said.

"You're right. They're frustrated with the Resistance. The Russians won't go away, and neither will the Resistance. Everyone says that the partisans are doomed," Halinka said.

"Don't say that," Tadek said. "I know they'll never give in."

She didn't reply. Almost everyone in the area was for the partisans, but no one could figure out how they might win. The war had been over for almost four years now.

Tadek didn't know what he felt. The image of Chopin's face dissolving in a red mist did not fade. He felt the seriousness of what he'd been doing in a way he never had before.

Kazimierz. Kazimierz would have to know what had happened.

"I must go!"

He stood up and Halinka looked up at him, surprised.

"Where? Is everything all right?"

"What could be all right?"

"I mean, with you."

"Yes. But you'll have to see your own way home. Oh, come on. Let's hurry."

He grabbed her elbow and lifted her up and started walking briskly down the street. Halinka lived in a little cottage sunk in mulberry trees along a row of similar houses on the north side of town. When they glimpsed this gray tangle of bare trees, he just squeezed her hands, all romance now gone.

"I still love you!" he said.

"All right," she said, questions filling her eyes.

He took off briskly walking through the sleety twilit streets. When he was out of Halinka's sight, he broke into a run.

His mother was not home. She was probably in Grodno, where she worked overtime whenever possible. He decided he would ice skate directly to the partisan camp himself.

Chapter 22: Wolves

By the time Tadek had packed a bag and written a note for his mother—vague enough, he hoped, that only she could understand—it was fully dark. She surely would hear about the executions in the square. He wished she had come home so that he could consult with her, but he thought he was making the right decision. To stop to wait for Janusz would create an unnecessary delay. Chopin had given him directions to the camp. "In case of an extreme event," he'd said, doubtless not foreseeing his own death.

When he stepped outside, the sleet had stopped, and a pale patch of sky showed the moon fighting through the clouds. He made his way down the orchard path, a dark line through the low covering of snow on either side. Each bump in the path was familiar beneath his feet. He slipped out the back gate and across the back lane into a narrow path between the neighbors' gardens, then through another row of houses, and then out across the fields along a path that hugged the hedgerow. At the end of the field, he cut over to where the land sloped down to the river through a poplar grove. Next lay an almost impenetrable thicket of reeds. Tadek trotted alongside the thicket looking for a path he knew, the clouds now crumbling in front of the moon, allowing him to see his way. From a specific angle only, the path opened as if magically before him, and he slid into the opening and trotted down the path to the frozen riverside. There he sat on a log, removed his skates from his backpack, and put them on. Once he'd had to pad the toes with paper wadding, but now they pinched his toes. When he stood up on the ice and took his first stride he felt liberated.

He headed downstream, keeping in his mind the directions: he needed to skate to Shabany and then another seven kilometers, then look for an outcropping of rocks on his left in a wide curve of the river. There he could wait for a lookout to make his rounds, and Tadek could tell the lookout who he was and what his mission was and hope that he was believed.

He skated in almost complete silence except for the long slicing sounds of his skate blades and his rhythmic breathing. The moon slipped between the clouds and followed him over his shoulder. The ice was beautiful—a hard black marble with bubbles encased in its depth like gigantic pearls.

Thoughts and images surfaced like murky bubbles rising within him—kissing Halinka, Chopin's body tossed onto a truck-bed, Orbatov waving his gun and shouting—and he tried to push his thoughts away and just focus on the skating, the movement. He skated on and on, driven by the memory of the executed partisans, watching the landscape gradually shifting on either side of him.

His legs were tiring and he slowed down to a pace he thought he could maintain.

Eventually he was making his way through the village of Shabany, a few disheartened buildings strewn along the riverside for two hundred meters, with a thickening of the buildings at the town center, a few of them rising to two stories. The woods pushed on all sides of Shabany, shoving at the buildings and roads and the meager fields, like a herd of beasts relentlessly, silently pushing toward the water, threatening to crowd out the signs of man.

Outside Shabany he passed where he knew his uncle's house would lie up the bank, a hundred meters inland behind the thicket of trees, but he could see nothing but thick shadows there. Later he passed a mill along the right bank, a tall wooden building with a paddle wheel that had been lifted out of the frozen river for the season.

On the left side of him now was the impenetrable black wall of the forest, and on his right lay a river bluff, beyond which stretched farm fields. The bluff went up and down, sliding sometimes down to the river's level, and then rising, punctuated by an occasional small grove of trees. During one empty stretch, when there were no farm buildings or trees at all, Tadek glimpsed a dark form moving along the riverbank through the low weeds. He skated away into the center of the river and thought he might have imagined the movement. He made his way around a slow bend. There it was again, definitely following him. More than one. Low and fast, much too fast for men, more like shadowy demons, keeping pace with his hurtling speed.

He heard them barking to each other: wolves. The barks sounded like encouragement: keep after him. We can catch him.

The bluff lowered down to the river's level, giving access to a beach, and a wolf was suddenly running at Tadek's level. The river narrowed here and Tadek and the wolf went side by side. He could hear its panting and he was sure it could hear his breathing. He kept up the smooth pace. The wolf turned toward him, venturing out onto the ice. As soon as it found itself past an edge of hard snow onto the pure ice, it lost its footing and started to slide, yelping its surprise. Tadek heard its claws scratching for traction, but they didn't gain enough control for it to keep up with Tadek and he left it whimpering in frustration behind.

The rest of the pack continued dodging after him along the bluff. He stayed in the middle and stuck to his pace, and after a few kilometers more they gave up, leaving him to the rhythmic exchange of sounds between his breathing and the slicing of his blades over the ice.

His legs were growing heavier and he was struggling to maintain even a slackening speed when he saw the outcropping of rocks at the elbow of the river's bend. He skated up to the shore. "Hello," he called, in a voice meant to be firm but not quite a shout. No answer. The wind was picking up, shaking the tree branches. "Hello?" Again, nothing.

He slumped against a boulder and let his breath try to catch up with his heart. Gradually they both slowed. He hadn't realized he'd been working that hard. He sat down on a rock and began to remove his skates. He was having a difficult time seeing exactly how the laces were knotted, let alone getting his numb fingertips to grip them, when he heard a step on the snow behind him and turned to see the silhouettes of two men a few meters away, stepping out of the woods with their rifles trained on him. One stepped onto the ice and immediately slipped and fell heavily. "Shit!" But the other ignored his partner and stepped forward steadily right up to Tadek where he prodded him in the armpit with the gun barrel, the way you might prod something you found lying in your path on the ground. In the blue moonlight, Tadek could see that the man had a lean face with a dark, scraggly beard. There were rags wrapped around his head that gave him a piratical look.

"Who are you then?" he said. "Before we shoot you." His voice was idly curious.

"Tadek Gradinski. Kazimierz's...Kowal's nephew."

The other partisan, having regained his footing, stood rubbing his butt regretfully and eyeing Tadek. He came to look

Tadek over for himself, bending down and squinting at him in the moonlight. "It's all right," he allowed. "I know who he is. He lives in Liaski."

"Chopin...I don't know if you call him that..."

"Of course we know Chopin. If it's who you mean."

"He's been executed by the NKVD."

The man gave a visceral grunt, as if he'd just been gut-punched.

"Did you hear that? Chopin's been killed."

"I heard it."

They both stood staring at Tadek. Momentarily he felt queerly responsible for Chopin's death and felt that they might feel he was too.

They shook themselves. One finally said, "All right. Come along then." He followed the first man into the woods. The second man followed him. For a few minutes they seemed to thrash blindly through underbrush, but then a trail resolved itself out of the murk and they could move faster with smoother footing. They walked at a rapid even pace for a long time before they came to a clearing with two horses tied to a tree. The leader hurried to untie them both and swung himself into the saddle of one. "Get up behind me," he said to Tadek, and Tadek scrambled to get up as the horse began to move. They were now in a wider trail, an old road, overgrown with saplings chest-high to the horses, but with good footing. The moon shone down upon them between the trees. Tadek felt the vast high darkness of the forest enclosing them like a strange ocean under which they traveled, and he felt in his gut that the partisans would triumph, that no matter how long they were chased and oppressed, the forest would breed and protect generation after generation of partisans who would never surrender. The final leg of their journey took them on a winding trail through a frozen swamp.

After less than an hour, the two men halted and slid off their horses, followed by Tadek. One gave a loud three-noted whistle, which was answered by the inky woods ahead. They walked a hundred meters and three men stepped out of the bushes.

"Dzien dobry."

"Who's this?"

"Kazimierz's nephew. He has news."

"Good news?"

"Since when do you expect good news?"

They walked over a hill to where Tadek could make out a dozen low, sullen campfires scattered through the woods. The two men led him to a circle of men around a fire and Tadek was joyous to see Kazimierz's face, lit orange by the fire, break into a smile. He leapt up and hugged his nephew.

"You're a man now, Tadek. I don't see you in, what? Seven, eight months, and you were a kid, and now you're a man."

"I'm growing," Tadek said modestly.

"That you are. Come and sit down. Why do you honor us with this visit?"

"I have bad news."

Kazimierz looked at Tadek, his mouth still smiling but his eyes gone serious.

"Chopin's dead."

"Dead?"

"They executed him and two others in the market square at Liaski."

The entire camp seemed to go quiet.

"That's the worst news in a long time. Who ordered the execution?"

"Captain Orbatov. The short one with glasses and a face all pitted." Tadek described him as best he could. Kazimierz nodded, thinking for a moment.

"Tell us about it."

Tadek stood by the fire and summarized the events as the men from the other fires gathered around him. Distracted and exhausted as he was, he still noted Kazimierz's hollowed cheeks and blood-shot eyes. Kazimierz's shoulders sagged as Tadek told his story, but after a moment he stirred into action, gathering himself, taking command, and starting across the camp with a brisk stride, Tadek beside him.

"Is Orbatov stationed in Liaski?"

"No. He's not there so much anymore. He comes and goes from Grodno."

"When?"

"I don't know. It seems to vary. Sometimes he stays the night."

"Kozel! Where's Kozel?"

Kozel stepped forward from the cluster of men trailing behind Kazimierz.

"Take six men and stake out the road to Grodno tonight, the curve where it nears the river. We'll count on Orbatov returning to Liaski tomorrow to deal with the consequences of his murders. They'll slow down by that curve. Maybe we'll get lucky and give them a surprise. If you don't see Orbatov, don't let them see you. Just lie low."

Kozel just nodded and walked away, pointing at men and calling names in his grating, bass voice.

His uncle put an arm over Tadek's shoulders and pulled him close, saying again, "It's late now. You need to eat and sleep and we'll talk more in the morning. Bleashka, get my nephew something to eat." Kozel had gathered a small group of men shouldering rifles and holding horses on the edge of the clearing, and Kazimierz crossed to talk to them, having turned Tadek over to a big blonde man in a leather vest, who looked over Tadek skeptically. "Come with me, Kowal's nephew," he said. He had a drooping mustache and the start of a beard. He turned and walked toward another campfire. Despite his size, he walked with a quick, athletic stride.

"My name's Tadek," Tadek said at his back.

The man laughed. The sound reminded Tadek of normal life, and reassured him that if only people could remember what it was like, people might someday return to such a life.

Bleashka got Tadek a plate of onions and boiled potatoes and they sat around the campfire with a few other men. They were ill-clothed, ill-shaven, ill-washed, and looked tough but sympathetic, some with pistols jammed into their belts. They asked him about Chopin and the execution, listening to him with judicious eyes. Their voices were low, as if the shadows of the forests might overhear them and betray them. They discussed the possible identities of the other executed partisans, if that's what they were. Tadek realized how cold he was, and tried to thaw out his hands and feet by the fire, while he listened to the men, drawing confidence from their voices: bitter, but with growing resolve. He was handed a tin cup that surprised him with the clear vile taste of vodka. He almost spit it out, and the man who'd handed him the cup laughed. "Not a drinker yet, huh? Want something else?"

"No, it's okay. I didn't know what it was."

He took a deeper draft of the vodka and felt it shoot to his head behind his eyes, working on a black knot of anxiety that he hadn't been aware of. The man tapped his cup with the tilted neck of the bottle. Tadek lifted his eyebrows and nodded—yes. With a few more drinks, the vodka began to untangle the knot. He watched as steam rose from his fire-warmed boots.

After a while Tadek noticed that a man who sat across from him was looking steadily at him, unnerving him. The man's face was blazed orange by the fire. Finally the man said, "Let me say this about Chopin. Some say he thought he was better than everyone else, some sort of intellectual full of prissy, precious ideas. But I don't care, dammit! He was reliable for us and risked his life many times for Poland, against the Nazis and the Soviets, and that's all that counts. Now it's over. To Chopin!" He lifted his cup.

"Chopin!" they all echoed. Though the Chopin described bore little resemblance to the austere, steady man Tadek had come to know, he drank deep in the man's honor. This time he felt the vodka spinning through his head, churning down to his hot gut and shooting down his legs.

"Poor Wladislaw," a slight man next to Tadek said softly.

"Wladislaw?" Tadek asked.

"His real name was Wladislaw Walsinski."

It surprised Tadek that Chopin had had another name.

A man at another campfire began playing the accordion and someone sang along with him in a grave, tender voice. It was a bittersweet song about a boy who loved a beautiful girl, a girl he left behind to fight for Poland, only to return to find that the girl had married another.

When the tune ended, the chords drifted away through the ceiling of high pines, and a circle of quiet grew, like a mysterious smooth spot on a lake's surface—into which came the call of an owl from the woods, answered by another, more distant, faint, and hesitant. Everyone crossed himself to exorcise the omen. They all sat still a moment as if expecting something to happen. A few men started to reminisce about the battle of Wilno, when 10,000 AK members had driven out the Nazis and the Polish red-and-white flag had flown in triumph from Giedymin Tower for a few days before the Soviets had marched in, promptly arrested the AK officers, and conscripted the rank-and-file that they could corral into the Soviet army. Only Kowal and a few others had anticipated the Soviets' move and slipped away with their troops the night before.

Bleashka nudged Tadek's shoulder. "Come on. I'll show you where to sleep."

When Tadek stood up, he realized the vodka had not only dissolved that black knot of anxiety, but had slid like silver eels down his limbs, loosening them and making his legs wobble and flip as he steered himself behind the man toward a hut. He was relieved to duck into the dark entrance, find a platform covered in straw, and collapse into sleep.

* * *

Tadek blinked his eyes open, gazing on needles of light that split the hut where its cowhide lining was incomplete. He got up and stumbled outside, trying to orient himself. He inhaled deeply the smell of the forest, the mist that hung about the ground, full of the odor of frost and pine needles. There was also the smell of coffee and frying sausages as breakfast began. Spears of light broke through the woods to shoot across the camp at a low angle from the morning sun.

The partisans had formed their camp in a shallow, bowl-like depression on top of a gradual rise in the land, under a canopy of old-growth pines. Tadek was surprised to see, all around him, dug into the ground and buried in the snow, filling the bowl, hut after hut like the one where he'd slept, half-burrow, half-cabin. From twenty meters each looked like little more than a pile of sticks and brush, yet a thin column of smoke rose from each of them.

There were maybe eighty men scattered through the forest, standing around fires or crouched at the entrances of the dugouts. A young man walked up to Tadek, gazing at him with a steady grin that seemed amused, but still more friendly than mocking. He wore a thin beard and was not much older than Tadek, maybe twenty-one or twenty-two. "So you're Tadek. I'm Hipolit Lebed."

They shook hands in a friendly fashion, as if they'd just met at a cotillion. "Come on. Kowal said to take care of you."

A group of men played cards on a stump and glanced up indifferently at Hipolit and Tadek as they passed. One man was shaving another man with a straight razor. He paused to take in Tadek.

Hipolit led him across the camp to a hut larger than the rest, where a kitchen was set up outside, and they waited in line for a plate of sausage and potatoes and a cup of coffee. Hipolit turned away from the entrance of a nearby hut where some other men had taken their food. "We can eat outside. It's foul in there and not bad out today." They sat by a fire with half a dozen men. Tadek wolfed down the meal and listened to the men talk. They were giving one man, who evidently used to be the camp cook but had been demoted, a rough time about his cooking.

After breakfast Hipolit led him over to Kazimierz's hut. The morning light revealed to Tadek that the years in the woods were taking their toll on Kazimierz. His beard had gone completely gray and he seemed to have lost much weight. His eyes seemed to have shrunk into the dry sockets of his skull. He looked like an old man, though he couldn't've been much more than forty. Yet when he saw Tadek he smiled his old confident smile and squeezed his nephew's shoulder.

"I heard you enjoyed our vodka last night! I hope you aren't ruined now. Your mother wouldn't forgive quickly. Listen, you're going with Lebed here to find us some food. We'll give you the full picture of our luxurious life here! You'll be back in the afternoon, and you can rest some and we can talk. We have some plans for you. But we'll talk about that later. Anyway, you better wait until dark and then go back tonight."

Tadek found himself walking in the center of a line of five men

229

making their way across a stream and then down a forest path. He proudly held a rifle, which Hipolit had acquainted him with before they'd left. They made their way for a long time along a narrow path surrounded by frozen swampland on either side before the ground rose and the forest thickened about them again. They emerged into a field and walked across it, through another strip of woods into another field, crusty and firm under a thin layer of snow. Across the field lay a small farmhouse with smoke rising from the chimney. The leader of their group was a solid, pop-eyed man named Matelski, who said, "I don't feel that these people are our supporters, but they must pay our taxes anyway," and the men chuckled or grinned sarcastically at a meaning Tadek didn't get. The men walked across the field and up to the door of the house. A boy chopping wood at a stump beside the barn stopped and watched them. A wide-hipped, red-faced woman, wearing an apron over her dress and a blue babushka, came and stood in the doorway. She squinted at Matelski in an unfriendly fashion. They bartered for a time, she shaking her head no and Matelski shaking yes, till finally she called over the boy, who hadn't moved from the stump, and sent him running to the henhouse where he came out grasping a chicken upside down, squawking and flapping its wings. He lay it on a second stump, lacquered with blood from previous use, fit its neck in a notch, and made three ugly, short chops at the squirming bird before its head flew off and it ran a few feet and then collapsed.

The men took their booty and continued on through the fields. "There's another place up here where they like us better." So they made their rounds to two more farmhouses. "We have to keep our movements unpredictable. We vary which houses we go to and in which direction," Matelski explained.

Walking free and easy through the fields with the armed men, Tadek felt an exhilaration creeping into his mood. It was so different here than in the village, where the Russian soldiers and the NKVD always lurked, hedging them in, watching them, acting as an actual physical fence around them. And free and easy, too, was the way Hipolit walked among these men, one of them, his rifle over one shoulder and a bandolier over the other, his laugh open and loose and generous. Tadek unconsciously mimicked his loping stride and the way he turned his head about, scanning the countryside constantly for information. Hipolit and Tadek lagged behind the group and talked.

"How long have you been here?" Tadek asked. "Why did you join the Home Army?"

Hipolit stopped and looked at Tadek with his startling blue eyes. "You want to know? Okay." He started walking again. "I'll tell you."

Hipolit was from Grodno and neither of his parents had made it through the war. His father had died in the Germans' bombardment of 1941, and his mother had been raped and killed by the Russians on their way back through Grodno, pursuing the Germans. He spoke of these events matter-of-factly, and his ever-present smile did not entirely fade. "It's not that I even hate the Russians. I know they all didn't rape and kill my mother. That was two men. But they give me no choice. I had nowhere else to go. I wasn't going to join a kolkhoz!"

"It's our land," Tadek agreed. This was the one true fact he had grown up knowing. This was truer than anything else had ever been and ever could be.

"What are they doing here?" Hipolit said, his voice rising as if someone was arguing with him. "They're just banditos. They can go home. We are home."

"Right."

They came to the edge of a field. Matelski, in the lead, held them back with a gesture of one hand. He waved to Tadek to move up to him and keep low. They both lay on the frozen ground. "Let me show you something," he said. He scanned across the field with binoculars and then handed them to Tadek, who fiddled with them until everything came sharply into focus. He could see across several vast fields of the kolkhoz, where all hedgerows had been removed, to where a line of Russian troop carriers had parked. Beyond the vehicles, blocks of Soviet troops were moving down the road, perhaps two hundred men.

"They're out of Grodno. They use these fields to train sometimes. They have their little parades. Don't worry. They have no idea we're here. Oh, they know we're somewhere in the woods, but it's all a mystery to them. Sometimes we take a shot at them from the other side, just to confuse them and give them something to think about. With the Russian troops there, I assure you there will be their Byelorussian playmates to play with them. But what can we do? There are too many of them for us to do anything. We have to separate them and then pick them off, one by one by one by one . . . . Come, we're late now."

They walked deeper back in the woods, where a deer bolted from the underbrush and sprang away, angling first one direction, then the other. Matelski leveled his gun, took aim, and shot: the tawny doe tumbled to the ground thirty meters away, and all the men cheered. This unexpected good fortune would mean meat tonight.

They returned to the camp mid-afternoon, with Hipolit carrying the slain deer over his shoulders, displaying it to the hungry men. Tadek, exhausted from the night's skate and the day's walk, slumped down near a campfire and took a tin cup of coffee one of the men gave him.

In a clatter of hooves and groaning of leather, the men who

had gone to lay an ambush for the NKVD captain the night before rode into the camp and dismounted, relinquishing their horses to two men who gathered the reins and led the horses away. A group of men gathered around Kozel and his men as they walked to the front of a hut where Kazimierz stood. A few of them went inside. A minute later a man who had been on the mission walked over and shook his head to the inquiring gazes from the campfire: "No luck. That assassin wouldn't show his head all day. After a while, it seemed too dangerous to stay, so Kozel called off the wait. We'll get that bastard yet!"

Tadek helped Hipolit clean and butcher the deer on a rough table set outside the kitchen. The cook stood watching them and giving directions, grabbing the choice cuts as they made them. As they finished, Tadek saw Jan sitting with Kazimierz in front of a fire across the clearing and went over to them. Only now did Tadek think about how Jan's lameness hindered not only him, but also the cause, especially in the winter when Jan couldn't travel by boat to the outcropping of rocks to relay messages. He nodded to Jan. Jan gave him a sour look. "You should have stopped by my place with the news, Tadek," he said.

"Okay."

"I need to know as soon as possible what's going on. I relay the orders and information."

"All right."

Jan spit into the fire. He poured some vodka into a coffee cup by his side.

"Tadek did what seemed right to him," Kazimierz said. "It worked out all right. Tadek, get something to eat and then come back here."

Outside Tadek found Hipolit and lined up with him to get their plates filled: onions and boiled potatoes again. The cook announced to groans that the venison would be cooked tomorrow.

They searched for a place at a fire to eat, but for some reason, no one moved over to make room at a nearby fire. One man who refused to budge said over his shoulder as they walked away, "What's the kid doing here, anyway? We don't need a fucking mascot!"

"Shut up!" Hipolit called back at him.

"Leave him alone," someone else said. "He's worth more than your miserable fat ass! All you do is eat!"

Tadek and Hipolit walked away to a friendlier circle as the men continued their argument.

"Don't let him bother you," Hipolit said. "He's like that with everyone. From him, that was like a big sloppy kiss! Also, he's angry because your uncle demoted him for falling asleep on guard duty. Twice he fell asleep. That could ruin us."

It was already twilight when Tadek took two steps down into the hut where Kazimierz, Kozel, Jan, and two other men stood or sat around a scarred wooden table. One man was peeling apart a package with a knife. The package was similar to those Tadek carried. He thought he recognized it as the one he'd given to Jan over a week before, and wondered why it had taken Jan so long to deliver it. Inside was a short-barreled machinegun, dismantled, all the parts packed in thick, yellowish grease. He admired the way they'd broken down the gun to package it so tightly.

The room was crowded and murky, lit only by a single lantern hanging from a rafter, and smelling of kerosene, woodfire, grease from the gun, and unwashed flesh. Tadek stood in front of them as if facing an examination.

"These are my lieutenants, Tadek," Kazimierz said. "We need to have a discussion before you return."

"Sure."

"Get him something to sit on at least."

One of the men slid over a chair, the back of which had been broken off, and without preliminaries Jan took the lead in his usual brusque style.

"We need more from you, Tadek. You're in Liaski. You should see everything. We need more."

"Now with Chopin gone, we've lost one source of information," Kazimierz explained. "We hate to bring you further into this than you already are."

"He's been under-utilized!" Jan said.

"Anyway, don't take any chances," Kazimierz said. "Just count the Soviets, both the regular army and the NKVD, in Liaski. Find out for us where they are staying, if they stay in Liaski. Otherwise, when they come and go. We know they move around some and aren't sure how up-to-date our information is. We need to know when they go to bed, what they do at night, if they have any girlfriends. We know way too little about them."

"We want to know when they shit and when they just fart, okay?" Kozel added with his crooked smirk.

"Okay."

"They've decided to come live with us poor Poles in this part of the world, and we've never given them a proper welcome," Kazimierz said.

"Okay," Tadek said, a bit confused but not wanting to ask questions.

"You can do that, right? Without jeopardizing yourself?"

"I think so. I see them around. Most of the NKVD stay in the station on the square, but some officers are posted around the village. I can find out where they stay. I know a few by sight. Others go into Grodno every night."

"Okay. Tell us everything you can think of now, all right? Write this down, Kozel. And you, Jan," Kazimierz said to his brother, "take it easy on the vodka."

"I'm all right. I'll sleep in the morning."

Tadek told them what he could remember, but even as he talked he realized that he hadn't been paying enough attention. He'd let the Soviets become just the background that he tried to avoid.

"We need more specific information. This is too vague," Kazimierz said.

"I can get more. Who will contact me now with Chopin gone?"

"The people in Grodno will have to arrange something," Kazimierz said. "They'll let you and Krystyna know and you will tell us. It's difficult now for us to contact Krystyna or anyone in Grodno on our own without running a risk. That's why we need you."

"Right"

"There are spies out there, Tadek. Don't think that there aren't," Jan said. "You can't trust anyone besides your mother."

"But everyone in Liaski hates the Russians!"

"They hate them but some are expedient and keep their self-interest in mind. Jan's right," Kazimierz emphasized. "We've talked about this before. No one can know about your missions. Not your best friend, not your girlfriend, no one."

"I'm careful!" he said, genuinely insulted. He'd been keeping his secrets now for years.

"I know you are, but it's easy to get careless. You have to protect yourself," Kazimierz said, "If you ever hear anything about when the NKVD are going into Grodno, tell us as soon as you can. Especially the officers. Especially Orbatov!"

"They go different times. Every day. Sometimes just two in a staff car, other times trucks full of them. It's hard to predict."

"Well, we want to know."

"How can I find out? They don't tell me."

"Don't be smart. Listen to him! He's turned into a smart-aleck," Jan complained. "Listen, if you hear anything specific, let us know immediately."

Kazimierz ignored his brother. "What else we really want to hear about is any movement of guns. That's what we need, their guns. We're killing them off, one here, one there, but we get one gun here and one gun there and it's not enough. It's never enough. There are too many of them. We lost a third of our soldiers in the false amnesty!"

For the first time Tadek saw frustration approaching despair in Kazimierz's face. The spring before, Stalin had announced that all the partisan soldiers still fighting would receive an amnesty if they came out of the forests and turned in their weapons. Thousands across Poland streamed into the towns, turned in their weapons, and were immediately arrested and herded onto trains and shipped to Siberia. Those remaining in the woods had renewed their vows to freedom or death, wishing for one but not blinking at the thought of the other. Things were ratcheting up between the Soviets and the partisans. "For a long time, we and our enemies have both been willing to let things simmer, more like a feud than a war. But this isn't a spat between friends," Kazimierz said.

"So, it's settled," he continued. "Tadek will bring us all the information we need on the NKVD. Grodno will find a way to contact Tadek so we can coordinate. Then I have some ideas I want to act on."

The meeting broke up and most of the men left the cramped hut.

Jan and Tadek were left in the hut together. Tadek noticed that on a table in a corner of the hut sat a radio set, with English lettering on a metal plate in its corner. Several of its vacuum tubes had been disinterred and lay on a table, covered in dust. Jan noticed Tadek's attention to the radio and said, "A gift from London, from years ago. Now it's just a museum piece, from when someone in the rest of the world pretended for a time to care about Polish freedom." He shrugged and filled his cup from the vodka bottle. Tadek could see how drunk Jan was. He'd been filling his glass regularly during the conversation.

"It doesn't work?"

"Not for years. And there's no one left to talk to, anyway."

He sipped his vodka and focused his glare on Tadek. "Remember, I relay the orders and the information. Come to me next time."

"I know that. You said that already."

"We have a chain of command."

"Right."

Jan seemed only somewhat appeased. An idea seemed to come to him and he leaned forward, leering at Tadek across the table in the smoky yellow light of the lantern, and said in a not-nice voice, "Do you want to know something, Tadek? Something you should finally know?"

"What?"

"Your father. Your father, he has been gone a long time now, and I believe your mother misses him. I've seen her shed tears... but she never wanted to marry him. I think maybe she's learned to love him. I don't know. And for her sake and yours, I wish he'd come back. But I never understood the man, myself. You see, your mother, our little Krystyna, she was a wild girl when she was young, and she ran away with a Polish army officer to Krakow when she was seventeen. And such a soldier! Oy-vey. Ha-ha. When we got her back, your grandpapa married her off right away to the timid visiting bookkeeper from Warsaw. Oh, I guess she loves your papa enough now. He's a nice enough guy. Too nice, most people say. He better have toughened up some if he's ever going to get out of the Gulag in one piece!"

"Brother, why are you saying this to him now?" Kazimierz stood in the doorway of the hut. "He doesn't need to know about things that happened so long ago that they're dead to us all. He hasn't seen his father in, what is it? Seven years now? And you. . . ."

"You're right!" Jan looked genuinely contrite, shaking his head at what he'd said. "Sorry, my godson, but I've had too much to drink. Forgive me. I get too emotional sometimes and don't know what I'm saying. Forgive me. We all must pray for forgiveness."

"Are you being sarcastic?" Kazimierz wasn't going to let him off so easily.

"No, brother, I'm not. I'm just drunk and it's not even late." He stood up, bumping his head against a low rafter. "I'm going to bed now." With bruised dignity, he clambered up the two steps and wandered, limping even more heavily than usual, off into the shadows.

"Ignore him," Kazimierz said. "He can't drink. Usually he doesn't."

"I know."

"You have to go now."

"Can't I stay?"

Kazimierz laughed. "No, warrior. You can't. You're more good to us in town."

But Kazimierz settled himself into a seat and just sat there for a while, his face going through various changes in the dim light. "I'm serious about your not coming to the woods. I don't want that for you."

"But I could really fight then. Instead of just being a message boy."

"Ha, is that it? You don't want that. Besides, it's not 1941

anymore. Times are changing. It's too late for us, but not for you."
Tadek didn't really understand what Kazimierz was saying. "Have you seen Helena and my children at all?"

"Not for a while. She doesn't come into Liaski much. My mother went to see her a few weeks ago."

"I haven't seen them for two months. Someday when all of this is over I want to be able to walk down the streets of Shabany and Liaski holding my children, one in each hand, Helena by my side, and not be worried about anything."

"Someday when Poland is Poland again. When we've driven them out."

Kazimierz gave Tadek a long look that seemed to shift between different emotions—pity and sadness, despair and resolve. "Some men just want to drift away, to turn themselves in and live out their days in Siberia." Kazimierz's look finished on resolve. "But I will fight on." He said nothing about their eventual victory. Instead his mind drifted back to his children. "Does Genia still do that thing with her eyes? When she pops them out whenever she thinks hard?"

"Yes. The last time I saw her."

"That worries me. It's funny." He laughed as if to illustrate his statement, but it seemed hollow. "But it still worries me, that she feels so much tension so young that she has to do that."

"She'll outgrow it."

"Yes, she will." The old confident Kazimierz regathered himself. He stood up. "Let's go. I need to get you back to my sister or she'll never forgive me."

On the edge of the clearing, Kazimierz hugged him, hard and long, and Tadek stifled, hard, a sudden urge to cry: hugging Kazimierz reminded him of how much he missed his father. "Remember, notice everything but don't go out of your routine and get conspicuous. We need you. Don't act different from anyone else your age."

"No one knows what I've been doing."

"That's good. Now Hipolit will take you as far as the Niemen. Then you're on your own again. It's good that you know how to get here. Don't forget it. Hipolit, point out our trailmarks so he can find his way back on his own."

"Yes, sir."

Hipolit, Tadek, and two other men, who were going to act as sentries along the Niemen, mounted their horses and began the trek to the river. Tadek was an indifferent horseman, but he'd ridden enough before to keep his seat, though Hipolit turned often to make sure he was all right. Several times he told the other horsemen to slow down. Hipolit pointed out to Tadek what landmarks there were—an uprooted tree, an abrupt gulley—in case he had to find his way back to the camp alone. At the river Hipolit and Tadek nodded goodbye, Hipolit showing again his candid, mocking but friendly grin. Tadek laced up his skates and took off at a steady pace down the center of the river, feeling the power of the blades on his feet, his eyes scanning the banks for any sign of the wolves. Tonight they were gone, and little more than an hour later he was back in Liaski, finding his way to the back of the town through the shortcuts he knew, past the odors of ashpits and outhouses. He let himself through the overgrown back gate into his yard. His mother was sitting at the kitchen table by herself, smoking a cigarette, with a cup of ersatz coffee by her elbow, the kerosene lamp flickering yellow.

He looked at her for a moment through the window: was it true, what Jan said, that she didn't even love his father? How little anybody knows anyone else!

But he didn't believe it. He let himself in the door and the relief on her face and the flurry of kisses with which she covered his face left him no doubt at least as to how she felt about her son, who was the product of her forced marriage to the man from Warsaw.

"I was worried."

"You didn't have to be. Everything went all right."

"I heard about Chopin. You saw them kill him?"

"Yes."

"You'll have to be more careful than ever, Tadek. I've lost my husband and I don't want to lose my son."

"I'm careful. And you haven't lost your husband! He'll be back."

"Good. Yes. He will." She seemed to go within herself for a moment.

"What's in the bag?" Tadek nodded to the paper bag set on the counter. Krystyna seemed grateful that her son had snapped her out of her reverie and back to the present.

"You'll never guess! It's cocoa!"

"Cocoa?"

"Yes. I can make you some."

"Hot cocoa! We have cocoa? Where did you get something like that?"

"In Grodno. At a shop! I wanted to tell you before but didn't have time."

"What a luxury. Do you know, I've never had hot cocoa before!" Tadek laughed at the absurdity.

"Oh, yes you did, when you were younger. Before the war!"

"I don't think so."

"Yes, absolutely. I remember."

"Well, I don't remember it. And you're drinking that slop!" He knew the coffee his mother was drinking was a horrible concoction, made out of barley.

She looked at her cup of phony coffee.

"You're right! I've gotten so used to the miserable life, I can't break out of it. I'll have cocoa with you! Tell me about your journey. How was Kazimierz?"

They were both relieved by his return, but the relief lay on top of a layer of grief and fear fed by the thought of Chopin's fate.

Tadek went to prepare the cocoa, but Krystyna took the process over, as if by this maternal act, she could transform him into a little boy again, just come inside after playing late with friends.

Chapter 23:
Looking Innocent

He went to work as usual the next day, Monday, at the early shift in the factory. And the next day. There was silence for a while from Grodno, with no replacement yet for Chopin, and a similar silence from the partisans in the woods. Life continued for Tadek as if in genuine peacetime. He was comforted by the routine. He even went to the dance with Halinka and Pawel and Sabina, though he felt himself distant, and Halinka kept asking him what was wrong. They'd ended up sharing an awkward, hasty goodbye kiss as a group of others waited impatiently on a street corner in Grodno, since Halinka and Sabina were spending the night at Sabina's cousin's in the city.

A few weeks later he'd managed to get out of work a half hour early and hurried to catch the bus back to Liaski, where he glimpsed Halinka getting out of school. He felt as if she might've forgotten about him, and he had to see her even though he was in work clothes, was sweaty and grimy.

Coming up behind her, he touched her elbow and she turned about in surprise. "Oh, I didn't know who it was!"

"It's me," he said.

"Yes, I can see that." She smiled. Even though the weather had changed, and now and then one felt warm currents of spring in the wind, like the caress of a hand, she was still wearing her familiar black coat, frayed on the sleeves, and hugging several books to her chest. The sight of the coat touched him and made him feel closer to her. He made a silent resolution to someday buy her a better coat, a beautiful coat—a mink coat.

"Can I walk you?"

"Certainly." She had a very precise way of enunciating her words that he liked. It was elegant with a shade of irony. It seemed to offer him a perspective on things that he would like to share but couldn't quite achieve.

They turned down the street. "Where have you been?" she asked. "You disappear for weeks at a time."

"Busy with work in Grodno."

"So, have you given up on school for good?" This picked up on a thread of their conversation from the night of the dance. Tadek felt, since the day of her birthday party, there was much more to say to her than there had been before, but their encounters were too fleeting.

"I think so. I like working better. It's all propaganda now, isn't it?" he continued. "To make us good Soviets."

"Mostly. The Krzaczeks continue their little lessons in Polish, mostly for the younger kids now—the future of Poland, you know—but they have nothing more to teach me, and it's all so futile. My cousins are moving to Poland."

"This is Poland!"

"Well, all right, but they're leaving what the Soviets and their millions of soldiers insist on calling Byelorussia, for Krakow. Krakow, everyone can agree, that's Poland."

"Hm." He was dissatisfied with the conversation. "Well, I

don't want to leave."

"I don't want to either."

"My grandfather would crawl out of his grave to smack me on the ear if he heard me call Liaski Byelorussia instead of Poland!"

They stopped at the corner, needing to decide which way to go. "I really need to be home. To keep peace between my parents. Otherwise, they're ready to strangle each other."

"Just ten minutes." He took a hold of Halinka's hand and pulled her away from her house, beseeching with his eyes. "Five minutes," he said. "We can stroll down by the river."

"Okay."

"I just need a skill. I'll get by," Tadek said, giving himself the luxury of thinking out loud with her. "I can do anything. I'm learning how to repair the sewing machines. They're simple. And leather stamping machines. And the giant looms. They aren't simple, not at all. But I'm a good mechanic. Everyone says I learn fast."

"Well, I need school," Halinka said, almost insistent. "I want to teach children some day. I'm going to move to Grodno. To see what education I can get there. What I really want is to be a doctor, but I know the Soviets will never let me study medicine."

"You aren't going to join Komsomol, are you?" To go to university, one had to join the communist youth organization.

"No!" None of the youths in the village joined, refusing to acknowledge their Soviet rulers' authority, preferring to accept thwarted ambitions. "But maybe I can still scrape together some sort of education anyway, and they'll let me teach on some level, somewhere."

"You'd be good at that."

"Do you think so? I hope so."

"You'd be a good doctor too." She'd always been the best

student in the class, with the possible exception of Pawel.

"Well, that's my dream, but I have to give that up I guess."

"You'd be good at anything you do."

"Oh, don't flatter."

"No, really. You know you're smart! As well as beautiful!"

"Very good! Great!" she said, laughing. "Is that all? Say more!" She beckoned forth his compliments with her hands. "More!"

They walked a few silent, smiling paces. They'd reached the bluff over the river. The river curved away, metallic gray under marbled gray clouds which stretched over the still-leafless forests on the opposite shore.

"No, really, Tadek." She sobered. "Listen, I wanted to talk about what happened after Sabina's . . . . " The phrase "what happened" chilled Tadek. It sounded like something you'd say to someone after a social embarrassment. "I don't mean those executions . . . . " She shuddered. "These are such horrid times. I thought they would end with the war. I mean, that was our childhood! Nothing but war! And they just keep going and going."

"Until we get our land back!"

"Ah, I think it's too late for that. I just hope to live my little life in peace."

"I can take care of you!"

She laughed. "That's what I wanted to talk to you about."

"Go on."

"I just want you to know that you were rushing things a bit the other day."

"But we've known each other since we were children."

"Yes. But things are different now, wouldn't you say? It feels as if we've just met."

"I know what you mean."

"And I don't want you to get the wrong idea about what

sort of girl I am."

"I think I know what sort of girl you are."

"I hope so. I have to go back now."

"No! Can't you stay? We can go down by the river?" He tugged on her hand.

She laughed at his eagerness. She often seemed tense, but sometimes, such as now, she'd let loose a liberated laugh that rang in Tadek's ears later.

"I told you I need to go home to keep the peace. And even if Papa isn't home, I have to do chores. There's always so much to do." Halinka had two younger sisters whom she complained were lazy.

"But we can walk sometime?"

"We just walked."

"I mean longer. More. Can we?"

"Maybe Wednesday evening. Just for a while. Papa wouldn't like it much. But he doesn't have to know."

* * *

Rising at dawn, riding the bus into Grodno, trailing behind Stronski all day as he dismantled, oiled, and reassembled some rebellious machine, then riding the bus home, all wasn't enough to exhaust Tadek that spring; and in the evening maybe once a week, on nights when he couldn't see Halinka, he would bike to Jan's after dinner and would find himself enjoying the silent time on the muddy paths and empty roads by the river. Jan encouraged these trips, to keep the soldiers and NKVD used to seeing him around. He would be free of anything incriminating if stopped. Usually he just brought three or four loaves of bread his mother had baked for the partisans.

At Jan's cabin beyond Shabany, he'd sit and drink kvass for

twenty minutes, and Jadwiga would sometimes give him a slice of black bread with some bacon fat while Tadek told Jan all he had noticed about the NKVD's movements and habits in Liaski. Most of what he observed seemed trivial, but Jan noted in his memory all the details, forcing Tadek to repeat himself until Jan was clear.

"Any action on the NKVD in Liaski has been delayed," Jan told Tadek in the spring. "Kazimierz is in Warsaw now, trying to revive contacts we had during the war. Everything's drifting apart. People would quit, but they follow Kazimierz. He won't quit. And the Russians won't let anyone quit without shipping them to Siberia." Jan made a bitter face, then shrugged. "But your trips here will continue."

After they'd spoken business, Jan would place the chessboard between them, the pieces frozen in place from their previous game. They had time to make only two or three moves each before Tadek headed back to Liaski. Jan almost always won their games, but Tadek had won his first game that winter, and was now more competitive, rather than just a student, and he sometimes made a move that would make Jan grunt and sit back in his chair, stroking his chin, then lean forward, frowning. Jan was getting truly obese, and it was painful to watch him limp about the cabin, but when he slit his eyes in concentration Tadek had to smile at the flicker of fear in his own belly, knowing the depth of Jan's cleverness, his duplicitous pawns, his adroit knights. Jan was kinder to Tadek, too, when they played chess, as they talked over a completed game, reminding Tadek of how he missed his father and Kazimierz.

Chapter 24: A New Friend

At work one day he stood outside a supervisor's office, waiting for Stronski to emerge from a meeting. He sat on the largest of a line of toolboxes that he muled about all day, in the middle of a long, empty hallway, the floors and walls of which had been painted and repainted with the same battleship-gray paint till they seemed lacquered. A woman, whom he'd seen before around the factory, turned a corner and walked simply and quickly up to him. She was a large woman who nevertheless walked fast, her thighs surging under her tight skirt. She had a round, flushed face and small blue eyes.

"Come with me after work, Tadek. This concerns your other work."

Shocked, he could think of no response.

"I—I don't have other work," he stuttered.

"Don't worry," she said. "If I wasn't a friend, you'd be arrested by now." She gave him a gap-toothed smile that seemed both foolish and knowing at once, as if simplicity was a type of wisdom. "We'll meet across the street in the park. I have some onions to give you. And wouldn't you like some bacon?" she smiled.

"Okay."

He found her in the small park on a bench. Even though it was a warm spring day, her babushka was pulled down over her head like a helmet. She winked and, without a word, got up and started down the street, walking faster than he might have imagined possible. She led him across a busy street, down along the flank of the old stone synagogue and then through a quick zigzag of narrowing alleyways before descending a basement stairway and passing down a long hallway, littered with empty paint cans and a mop and bucket, and into a one-room apartment. There was a sink, a cot in one corner, and clothing hanging from a line, female items that made Tadek avert his gaze. She clanked open the door of a stove and roughly shoved in a few logs.

"Close the door, Tadek. Tea?"

"No."

"How about that bacon I promised you?"

"No, I have to hurry."

"Don't hurry too much, dear. You'll miss life. The Russians will wait for us. Believe me, I know. I've been at this since I was younger than you are now."

"I've been at it for over three years." He knew he shouldn't reveal anything about himself, but he couldn't help trusting the woman.

"I know it, dear, I know it."

She sat down at the scuffed-wood table and gestured to him to do the same. Sitting across from him, she surveyed him frankly with her clear blue eyes, and he studied her back, a bit daunted. She dressed with a brutal stylelessness and her hands were reddened and chapped and blunt-fingered, but a sexual force-field followed her about the room, strengthening and weakening by turns but always present. The middle button on her blouse strained heroically to hold its place against the force of her prodigious breasts. She took off her scarf and tossed it on the table.

"This is the old Jewish neighborhood," Tadek said.

"Yes." She shot him a look. "So, you were here before . . . when Jews were here?"

"I used to come to this neighborhood with my grandfather, before the Germans came and made it the ghetto. He had business at a store near the synagogue."

"A few returned after the war," the woman told him, "and wandered around looking lost. No one could believe anyone survived. One or two got beat up."

"Why?"

"People had moved into their apartments and didn't want to give them up. And besides, some people blamed the Jews for these assholes who are in power now. Because the Jews were for them, or some of them were. Or so people said." She gave an ambivalent, slow shrug. "It wasn't fair, maybe. But I didn't make the dirty old world, did I?" She looked at Tadek as if she expected him to think this over and get back to her. "One Jew I know got his apartment back for a while. Then he sold it cheap and went to Palestine. His store had been nationalized, so he really had nothing left. All his relatives were gone. No one had time to deal with the Jews' problems then anyway. During the war, I helped get some food to some Jews I knew in the ghetto. Good Jews. Not like some. But it didn't do any good. They disappeared with the rest. And don't tell anyone! If people think you were Zegota, then they'll assume you were AK and denounce you."

"What should I call you?" Tadek asked, turning with relief away from the topic.

"What do you mean?"

"Do you have a nom de guerre?" The French phrase Lech had used had stuck in his mind.

She laughed, showing again the amiable gap between her

front teeth.

"No, dear, should I?"

"No, it's all right."

"Do you have one?"

"No."

"Well, we both suffer then. Just call me Ewa, the same way everyone else does. Nothing poetic." A reflection crossed her face and she sobered. "Oh, I see. Poor Chopin." But after a moment she was back to business. "But I do have something for you," she reminded herself, "even if you won't let me fry you some bacon." Standing on a chair, she withdrew from a high cupboard one of the compressed, heavy packages that he was used to: either ammunition or a gun. She handed it over to Tadek.

"Put it in your bag, dear, and take it to your uncle Jan. He's told you to locate where all of the NKVD agents are boarding in Liaski?"

"Yes."

"Well, we need to know everything about them. You can report to me as well as to Jan. Be careful. You're a good-looking boy and we'd hate to lose you. There's a new major in charge of the NKVD in Grodno who seems to be ambitious, not like our slovenly butcher Captain Orbatov, but maybe even more trouble. Have you heard of him?"

"Yes."

"Well, he's already disrupted things in Grodno. We'll have to adjust. Anyway you and I will plan to meet again the first Tuesday of next month, just the way you did with our patriot and friend, Chopin. Only now that you're in Grodno, we can just meet here. I'll get word to you if meeting plans change. And no more trips to Gombachy. Lech is in Grodno now and contacts me directly."

"All right."

The next Saturday Tadek took the package Ewa had given him and set off for Shabany. He coasted by the unguarded bridge on the way into town, and when he reached the edge of the village, in order to vary his route, he cut up a steep alley that kept him off the main road and got off his bike to walk.

Halfway up the hill, he saw an old lady turn into the entrance of the alley, look at him, and begin to walk toward him. She was amazingly fat and even more surprisingly fast. She came up to him and leaned a round, red face into his: "I know who you are. Come and see! Leave your bike here for a moment." Puzzled, he followed where she led him, not up the alley but to the end of an even narrower side passageway, with just room for them single file. It slanted up to the main street. From here they could peer through a fence to see a solid line of Soviet troops coming toward them. Some soldiers had already stopped several men who were showing them their papers while the rest of their troop advanced. Tadek shrank back from the fence, not needing to see more.

"Come," said the woman, and he followed her massive butt, shifting beneath a shapeless gray skirt that dragged in the dirt. She led him back down the passageway where he retrieved his bicycle. Then she made her way around a corner, through a long alleyway paralleling the river and up a short pathway to a dead end where there was a small goat pen.

He followed her through the gate and across the pen, the few goats baaing their indifferent protest and eyeing them with their golden eyes. She led Tadek into an unpainted, two-story barn. With a gesture she showed him where to throw his bicycle in a stall. "This way," she gasped, out of breath. She stood by a ladder built into the wall of the goat shed. After a moment's indecision, he took the package from beneath its covering of onions in his basket, thrust it inside his jacket, and scrambled up into a small loft filled with old tools and a few bales of hay. After a minute, he heard Russian voices outside and the vague replies in Polish of the old lady. He made his way to a glassless window that let onto the rooftop of another cabin and let himself down as quietly as he could onto the flat, tarpaper roof, made his way across it, and then dropped down into the alley that ran down to the river. Another alleyway between small hovels paralleled the river, and he ran down this as quickly and as quietly as he could, ducking under a building up on pilings along the edge of the river. He picked his way between the pilings, the mud sucking at his feet, until he came out on the other side. Here he slipped into some weeds and dashed across a fallow field. From there he could find his way unseen into the woods. He made his way down river to his uncle's cabin, which sat atop a little ridge a hundred meters from the river. As he neared the cabin, he heard activity in the backyard and circled around to find Jadwiga taking in laundry off a clothesline.

Inside he described the incident to his aunt and uncle, and Jadwiga made him describe to her again the old lady and precisely what cabin the woman had been in. She headed into the village to see what she could learn. Tadek was still catching his breath when he realized that Jan was limping from window to window, peering out, his breathing louder than Tadek's. "Are you sure you weren't followed? You shouldn't come here if someone's following you. What are we going to do with this?" He gestured to the package Tadek had brought, lying on the table.

"Bury it out back," Tadek suggested. "In case someone comes."

"Right." Jan grabbed the package and headed out the back door. A minute later Tadek could see him through the back window, kicking and shoving a spade into the damp garden soil. Jadwiga returned half an hour later, and only then did Jan calm down. "It's all right. It was old lady Ruscha, as I suspected. She's loyal. She says you can get your bike in a few days. You should walk home today through the back fields."

Taking some old onions in a burlap bag as a pretext for the trip, Tadek started to make his way through the back fields as instructed, but the ground was damp and muddy from rains, and the going was slow. After ten minutes he shrugged and cut back over to the road to Shabany, where he made his way back to the alleyway where the old lady had helped him. He didn't see her around, but he climbed over the fence to the goat pen, where the same two goats skeptically reviewed his actions with their yellow, slit-pupiled eyes. He found his bike where he'd hidden it and a minute later was bicycling back down the main street of Shabany as if nothing had happened. All went well until he reached the bridge out of town. No one had guarded this bridge since the Nazis, but today there were several Soviet soldiers who waved him to stop.

One of them told him: "You can't use this road any more." The soldier spoke Russian but Tadek, with the help of the soldier's waving arms, could decipher most of what he said well enough.

"What do you mean?"

"Don't ask questions. Just do what we say."

"Search him," another said. The soldier put a hand on Tadek's shoulder and turned him around with a steady force. The other, giving up on Tadek's Russian, showed him how they wanted him to stand, hands against the bridge, legs spread. Reluctantly, Tadek did as instructed. The first soldier began running his hands roughly along Tadek's side and up the insides of his legs to his crotch.

"What's going on here, comrades?" Both soldiers whirled about, stood at attention, and saluted. An officer had pulled up with his driver in a staff car. He wore the blue tabs of the NKVD on his shoulders. He jumped out and walked toward them, waving his hand in irritation as his car's dust trail swept over them all.

"Who is this?"

Both the soldiers stepped back in deference to the officer.

"Comrade Major, he appears to be just a kid," one of soldiers said.

"A Pole?"

"Yes."

The officer scrutinized Tadek. This was the new major of whom Ewa had spoken. He was a handsome man, with an angular face, his lanky body lean as a greyhound's but strong looking. When he took off his cap, he ran a hand through close-cropped gray hair. His face was unwrinkled but drawn into a hard, worried look that did not change as he studied Tadek.

"You searched him?"

"Yes, comrade."

"Do you have any reason to suspect him?"

"No. He said he was just was bringing onions from his uncle." The officer lifted the lid on the basket on the front of Tadek's bicycle to reveal the unimpressive cargo of yellow onions. The major looked at them awhile, as if he was waiting for them to change into something more interesting. Then he again studied Tadek, who felt a curious wave of sympathy pass between them, as if, circumstances being different, they would be friendly.

"Onions from his uncle," the officer echoed the soldier. "Are there no onions in Liaski?" he asked Tadek, this time in Polish.

"Yes. But their garden always does better than ours."

"I see." The major's eyes strayed down to Tadek's shoes, which were coated with river mud. "And how did your shoes get so filthy?"

"I helped my uncle in the garden. Everything is mud now."

"I see. Yes, the rain. These are last year's onions."

"Yes."

"You came to Shabany for six withered onions from last

year."

"And I brought them some bread my mother had baked."

"I see. I see."

Tadek did not like that this officer seemed to notice everything. The river mud was a light reddish brown, unlike the black mud of the gardens here, and he waited for the major to notice this. Instead he finally said, "Let him go."

Tadek didn't hesitate, but stood on the pedal and swung his leg over the seat as the bike went into motion. The major was explaining something to the soldiers as Tadek rode away, something about how to treat the local populace for the best long-term results.

Chapter 25:
Wildflowers and Mushrooms

In early summer Halinka and Sabina organized, with Pawel and Tadek, a foray into the forest near Gombachy to pick the mushrooms called little foxes, *lisichki*. The plan was to bicycle east through Gombachy and then northwards, on a forest road, to where the river hooked eastward past Shabany, into a sort of no-man's land where the endless forest abutted the restless river, and a flat expanse of pine trees dropped carpets of needles, under which the tender, early *lisichkis* grew. The four youths met a kilometer outside Liaski, to keep their mission secret.

Halinka wore a white blouse and navy blue skirt, and her hair was up in a lighter blue scarf, that pulled it back away from her face in a way that simplified and revealed her face, purified it and accented its clear lines. Small silver and blue-stone earrings swung from her lobes, catching the morning light and attracting Tadek's eyes to her face time and again. Her presence put all his senses on alert.

"I told my parents I was just going with Sabina," Halinka confessed.

"And I said I was going with Halinka."

"So we didn't lie, did we?"

"By omission," Pawel said.

"You really should be a lawyer," Sabina kidded, kissing Pawel on the cheek. He'd spoken of law as one path for his future, an outlet for his increasingly restless mind, but rejected it as impossible with the political situation. Tadek had to admit that Sabina was lovely, too, shorter and curvier than Halinka, wearing today a pink blouse and a narrow-brimmed straw hat that sat on her head at a rakish angle.

"If only we *had* a law here!" Pawel said. "I mean, a *real* law, like when Poland was independent."

They pedaled slowly down the side road, the same one Tadek took on his missions to Gombachy. As if they all wanted to expand the moment, they'd slowed to a wobbly-wheeled crawl. "Look how slowly you're pedaling!" Sabina said. "Let's see how slowly we can pedal." One by one they slowed till they keeled over and caught themselves.

"But wait! What are we doing?" Halinka asked. "We have to get there before all the old babushki of Gombachy pick the forests clean!"

"They're all old there."

"You're right. Let's hurry!" Sabina demonstrated by pedaling ahead. "And what about the trolls and sprites! They love mushrooms too!"

They made quick time then past Gombachy and into the forest on a road that was little more than a dusty path. They pulled off to let a couple of boys pass, prodding along a herd of sheep. Eventually they reached a meadow that ran up to a riverbluff on one side and down to a thicket of brambles on the other. They left the road and let their bikes race down the hill over the bumpy terrain. The dew was still heavy on the grass.

"Look, my shoes are soaked already!" Halinka laughed, pointing. All of their shoes were wet.

Sabina knew the area best so she grabbed a basket and led the way, finding her path through the bushes. The others took their baskets and followed. She stopped and called to them. "Come look at this spider web! It's so geometric."

They gathered around to look at a dew-soaked web hung between two bushes where it caught the sun just right, turning each strand luminous. A black and yellow spider sat in the center of the web, which swayed slightly as if the whole web were breathing.

"I should kill it," Tadek said.

"No, just leave it." Halinka pulled him away by the elbow. "It's part of nature too."

"Right. The part that stings and poisons everything else. Smash it, I say."

"Well, it made the web."

"Oh, a philosophical debate. I'm ready for this," Pawel said, coming up behind them. "Is nature benign or vicious? Let me first tell you what Rousseau said. Then, I will give you Marx, who never saw a tree in his life, except in the form of the paper for his books."

Soon they were out of the thick grass and the maze of bushes and were poring over the pine needle strewn ground for mushrooms. The air in the forest smelled of flowers and pine needles, making them all a bit giddy as they walked along.

"The partisans are near here, I bet," Pawel said.

"Maybe," Tadek said, knowing the truth of the statement.

"In Gombachy, you know," Sabina elaborated on her theme of the day, "they don't have anything else to eat, besides mushrooms, and the people here are all just like they were a hundred, three hundred years ago!"

"And all the babushki live to be three hundred years old!" Pawel said.

"And trolls steal the children who are left playing in their yards when the parents walk to the barn," Halinka added.

Tadek smiled at his friends' banter, thinking of the kid Lech, for whom he used to drop off a message or package once a month. Diabeł! The Gombachy kid *was* odd!

He also smiled because his friends seemed in possession of a carefree spirit that he could only mimic now, but their voices brought that world so close he could almost step into it as if onto a stage where unreal things could happen.

"Come on. No trolls yet, at least," Sabina said.

Sabina was first to cry out, "I found one!" She knelt and pushed aside the needles, revealing a small, fox-colored mushroom poking its tip out from under the tawny pine needles.

"Here's one!" Tadek shouted.

"Over here!" Pawel called.

It seemed as if once one had been glimpsed—once the youths knew the color to look for—the mushrooms were everywhere. The youths bent or knelt and began tugging gently at the fleshy mushrooms. There was another, and another.

The pickers quieted down and each pursued a different course, stepping quietly, bending, filling the baskets, eyes focused on the ground, picking on their own, their fingertips turning rusty, drifting apart in the stillness under the looming pines.

When their baskets were full they gathered again back by their bicycles, comparing their hauls of mushrooms. The sun had dried the long grass, and Halinka took a quilt out of her bicycle basket and unfolded it. The grass made a spongy cushion underneath the quilt when they sat down. The girls unpacked their picnic: the blackbread sandwiches they brought, the cheese, cucumbers, kielbasa, *kumpiak*, and more bread, a round loaf of peasant bread.

Tadek had managed to acquire a bottle of wine in Grodno, and after a struggle liberated the cork.

"I only brought two glasses," Sabina said.

"We'll share."

Tadek poured the wine and they toasted to the day and to friendship.

A stork glided low overhead, surprising them, and they followed it with their eyes. Halinka's eyes stayed on the treetops where it had disappeared, and she said, "The bird, as always, glided." She then recited:

> You would not take my hand. The dawn glow
> Made the world alter.
> At that moment your brother called to you.
> For a moment you faltered.

Pawel and Sabina chimed in with Halinka:

> You ran to him and came back. He was dead.
> Fate, for the clouds, shone golden.
> "Now I belong only to you," you said.
> Your voice broke, and rolled on.

Only when they got to the last stanza would Tadek reluctantly admit that he, too, had had the poem incised into his memory by Mrs. Krzaczek, and he joined in:

> Without a glance at you I asked: "Did he know?"
> "Yes," you replied.
> Outside, giving thoughts distance, aslant, aflow,
> The bird, as always, glided.

"Oh, good God! What was that?" Tadek mocked. "You three are such bookworms!"

"Oh, you remembered it too!" Sabina said.

He remembered Mrs. Krzaczek reciting Lesmian's "Brother" in her quavering tones, in the basement with the floor joists full of cobwebs where he'd sat behind Halinka and her thick braid for hours and for days and for weeks. Those times seemed so close he could touch them. Yet it was as though it was forbidden. He was different now.

"Do you remember this?" Halinka said. "'The Poet and the Peasant Bride'?"

> Poet: You could pay the whole world a visit
> and watch it grow and grow
> but Poland you'd never find.

"I remember," Pawel said. And they finished together, Halinka taking the part of the bride and Pawel taking the part of the poet.

> Bride: It can't be very big.

> Poet: Put, Jugusia, your hand
> —for there is a cage, a twig
> under your breast.

> Bride: Right.
> It's the dart in my bodice
> sewn up a bit too tight.

> Poet: And what do you feel beat?

> Bride: This isn't much of a lesson:

my heart in all this heat.

Poet: And that is your Poland.

They were all silent a moment, as if embarrassed. Only Tadek grew angry at his friends, thinking, if you want Poland back so bad, then fight for it!

"What's the matter?" Halinka said, putting her hand on his.

"Nothing."

"Let's see if we can find some more mushrooms before we head back," Pawel said.

"There's a good spot the other side of that birch grove," Sabina said.

They all stood up, tired of poetry, and entered again the maze of bushes, through the pines and then past the birches to one side, following Sabina deeper into the woods. There were plenty more mushrooms. The pickers kept crying out their discoveries of hidden patches of mushrooms lurking beneath the musty needles. Gradually the two couples drifted apart. Sabina and Pawel disappeared into the woods.

Tadek felt as if they'd wandered into a story told by an ancient babushka over a sleepy child, with the high-arching canopy of pine branches overhead, the path padded with needles, the occasional fine stripes of birches across the darker trees. In one spot the forest floor was covered—from where they stood and on into the shadows—in calve-deep white flowers. Halinka picked a small bouquet, smiling silently up at Tadek as she bent to pick the flowers, silently smiling as she lifted the bouquet to his face for approval. They walked onward through the flowers as if through a shallow white lake. They came to a spot under lofty trees filled with ferns, tremulously parting and brushing against their calves and thighs as they walked through them.

"Let's not go too far," Halinka said, slowing down. "We don't want to get lost."

It was true: They could easily wander away into the woods and find themselves disoriented and unable to return. It happened every couple of years: they would hear about a child in a neighboring village wandering off and disappearing as irrevocably as if they'd slid off a cliff into the ocean, or been pulled away by the relentless Niemen, an event which also occurred every few years either in Liaski or in a village up or downstream.

Tadek and Halinka found a clearing with heavy, dusty lilacs past their blooming, along one side.

"Whew!" Halinka wiped her brow. The day was growing warm.

"Let's sit down here for a while and rest," Tadek said.

They both knelt to the ground. Bees rose from the flowers and hovered about them. He reached out and took Halinka's hand. She stopped and turned toward him with a questioning look. He turned her hand over, examining it, the intricate mechanism of bones, veins, and muscles. A bit of a breeze came from inside the forest and lifted Halinka's hair from her temples. "That feels good," she said. She smiled her cryptic, withdrawn smile, and that made him need to kiss that smile. He lifted away a strand of her hair that had fallen free from her scarf and across her cheek and kissed her. That wasn't enough. She smiled again and he felt driven to find out what lay behind that smile, driven to unearth her secrets, to know her completely.

"You're wearing earrings," he said, trembling with the effort to restrain himself, to move carefully.

"I didn't think you'd notice."

"I noticed. They look like fishing lures."

"Fishing lures!"

"Yes." He kissed her smiling mouth, which lost its smile

and became quite serious. There was a tiny smudge of wine-stain blurring her upper lip, the flaw that focused her perfection. They kissed for a long time.

When Tadek would float on the river he'd let his arms and legs dangle and would breathe deeply so he was buoyant, the sun warm and pink on his closed eyelids, water muffling his ears and carrying him away. Then he felt like this, so lost in the sensations that it was a sort of hypnosis. Only now it was Halinka's lips and breathing and hair that buoyed him up and surrounded him. He slid her blouse up and was shocked that she let him, stunned by the sight of her unashamed breasts as she lay back in the grass sighing deeply. They kissed some more. He kissed her breasts till he became impatient for more and moved his hand up past her knees to her thighs.

"No. No," she finally said, a firm grip on his wrist. "Not that. We have to go now."

He stirred up out of his daze as if he'd been dreaming on the river, drifting out to the ocean while he basked, dissolving into the water and the current, as if time had been turning in a slow circle. It took them both a while to recover their senses.

Halinka repaired her hair and clothing and she and Tadek made their way back through the ferns. As Halinka and Tadek neared the clearing where they'd left their food, they could hear Sabina angrily scolding Pawel. They entered the clearing to see both Sabina and Pawel kneeling on the blanket, trying to gather the food. Crows hung about nearby and Sabina jumped up and ran at them, waving her arms. They flew a few feet and then settled back to the ground, cawing sardonically as she turned away and walked back, reverting to her tirade at Pawel. Evidently it had been his responsibility to cover all the food and secure the lid with a rock or a branch. Sabina was not at all abashed by the presence of

Halinka and Tadek, and rained down her judgments upon Pawel: he was lazy, he was distracted, he had his head in the clouds, he was selfish, he never paid attention!

He didn't respond, just quietly finished cleaning up, acknowledging Tadek and Halinka with a wry lift of his eyebrows.

And then Sabina stopped. She turned herself to folding up the blanket as if nothing had happened. Even started humming a bit. Everyone packed away the paraphernalia on their bikes, subdued and chastened. They were ready to lean into their pedals when Sabina burst out, "I'm sorry!" and went to hug Pawel. "I'm so sorry! I just got frustrated." Halinka and Tadek watched awhile as the other couple hugged, and then began to kiss, and as the kisses continued, Halinka and Tadek started down through the forest path toward the lane.

They both laughed when they got out of earshot. "What a temper!" Halinka said.

"Yes."

"You always know what she's feeling!"

"Even when you don't want to know." Tadek marveled a bit at the scene, though he'd seen Sabina's temper before, and he wondered what it would be like to be with a girlfriend like her. He was falling in love with Halinka, but he often had to guess at what she was thinking or feeling—yet that was the fascination.

They all four gathered together near the lane and pedaled lazily back to Liaski as the sun grew higher and warmer, with Halinka seeming to retreat into herself with a distant smile, Tadek letting his mind wander back to his partisan work, and Sabina and Pawel trying clumsily to ride their bikes while holding hands, stopping now and again to kiss some more.

By the time they reached the village, the weather seemed to have shifted once more for Sabina and Pawel. She sailed off on her bike with a cavalier wave, and Pawel, who seemed to be brooding, turned the other way absent-mindedly with a muttered farewell. Halinka and Tadek got off and walked their bikes through the village, dragging out their goodbye. They reached Halinka's little cottage, immersed now in the foliage of the mulberry trees, in the middle of a row of similar cottages.

"Do any of those NKVD agents board on your street?" Tadek asked, his mind jogged back to reality.

"There's their secretary who lives down at the end of our lane, across from the fields. Why do you care?"

"They just bother me. Does she rent from...?"

"From the Bleashkas. From what I hear, they commandeered it from them. My Papa rants about it all the time. But it's all hopeless . . . . "

"Here, you take these." Tadek handed Halinka two small wicker baskets. He had a burlap sack full of his share of the mushrooms ensconced in the basket on front of his bike.

He stopped in the alley behind Halinka's house to avoid being seen by her father. His disapproval was generalized, not focused specifically on Tadek, but it still made them wish to keep him ignorant of their relationship. From the alley they could just see a corner of the garden.

"What's that? In the garden?" Tadek said, pointing to a rumpled pile of blue and gray cloth beneath a bush.

"Oh my God," Halinka put a hand to her mouth. "It's my father!"

As Tadek walked closer he could see Mr. Nowak sprawled out on his back in a path between two patches of vegetables.

"Should we call someone?" Tadek said.

"No. It's been happening. He's just drunk. Usually he has the decency to wait until dark."

"You should've told me," Tadek said.

"I'm too ashamed."

"Don't be," Tadek said. "What could you ever have to be ashamed of?" The thought that she could ever be anything but proudly ideal was a surprise to him.

"You can see for yourself."

"But that's not you."

She gave a bitter shrug. "He's not usually this bad. But it seems to be getting worse."

"Do you need help?" Tadek said.

"I'll get my mother. Let me see if we can get him up. You wait here. No, back there." She shooed him away with her hands to behind the rabbit hutch at the end of their garden. She was retreating into herself. "He'd hate you if he knew you saw him like this."

Tadek backed around the corner of the hutch and watched as Halinka ran to the pile of cloth—now more recognizably a large man, curled up as if in bed. His mouth was open wide, his eyes closed. He was snoring. She shook him and he raised himself on one elbow. Tadek tried to discern in his slack, florid face the lineaments of Halinka's sensitive nostrils and fine-drawn chin.

She said some consoling words to him and then ran to the backdoor of her house. After a few moments, her mother and two younger sisters tumbled out of the door into the garden behind her. Tadek moved further behind the hutch. Together the family roused Mr. Nowak. He lifted his head, let them sling his arms around their shoulders, and let all four together lift him, tottering, to his feet. He seemed to be awake now and stumbled along with them as they walked him up the steps and to the door. Pacing an alleyway, Tadek waited for a long time for Halinka to return to him. A lazy dog lying in the shade of a water barrel lifted his head to eye Tadek and then went back to sleep. Tadek smoked several cigarettes, a new habit he'd picked up, but that day Halinka never did return.

Chapter 26:
An Evening Stroll

During the summer Halinka was working two evenings a week in a yarn shop off the square, and her walk home gave them a chance to meet. Tadek waited for her to get out of work, walking up and down the street, feeling privileged to be able to cast his eyes inside where he could see her, in a purple blouse with a purple band in her blond hair, sitting behind the counter or jumping up to climb a ladder to fetch yarn for a customer. She smiled when she left the shop and turned to find him waiting for her.

"How much time do we have?" he asked.

"Maybe half an hour before Papa starts getting suspicious."

It had been raining earlier and a mist remained over the village, full of the scent of river and woods. The night had turned cool. Halinka wore a light jacket over her purple blouse. The purple band in her hair accented the pure structure of her face. For Tadek, she transformed everything she wore into something charged with her essence.

Tadek had a new leather cap he'd bought with his pay from the factory.

"New cap!" she noted, laughing at his self-consciousness.

"Yes." But he was glad she'd noticed.

She leaned back judiciously to take him in. "I like it. It makes you look rugged, but cultivated."

Tadek just chuckled at her precise observation. She had a knack for setting everyday things in a fresh light for him. She put her arm through his and they smiled at each other as they walked, reluctantly turning away to watch where they stepped.

They passed through the square where two NKVD agents were talking to several soldiers in front of a recently opened inn, The Blue Swan. Each light in the square created an aura of mist.

The NKVD had not been inconspicuous in the village. They all dressed in the same drab gray jackets. The light blue tabs on their shoulders were such a familiar sight around town that they were called "the blue tabs" as a shorthand. The sound of their Russian voices was something the entire town had been forced to get used to. It seemed almost worse to the citizens of Liaski when some of the Soviets erupted in a few Polish words, barbarously transformed by their accents. The town was almost all Polish and almost all of them supported the partisans, though a trickle of immigrants, Russians and Byelorussians, had followed the triumphant Soviet army into the area, putting the Poles on guard and stirring their resentment.

The Soviets stilled their conversation as Tadek and Halinka passed: it was a long time since Tadek as a boy had run the envelope across the square for a Russian officer. Now Tadek and one agent, a short stocky man with a broken nose, eyed each other. Tadek tried to keep his face neutral, even mildly amiable, a skill he had worked on. For some reason, the agent grinned and said something to one of his friends, who laughed. Tadek kept his neutral look and kept walking. His Russian was starting to become decent, but he hadn't caught the remark.

"They make me so uncomfortable," Halinka said. "Why don't they leave?"

"Maybe someday they will."

"What do you mean?"

"I mean the partisans will win."

Halinka shot him a surprised, skeptical look. "What's left of them. It looks worse and worse all the time."

"I know. But they have to fight."

"Do they? Why?"

"Because it's right."

"Of course it's right, but . . . .Let's not talk about this. It upsets me too much."

"All right." They had turned off the main street. A crooked wooden bench sat next to a house in a niche half-concealed by a shrub, and they sat for a time and kissed, bundled in their jackets against the mist. He kissed up and down her sculpted face. Her lips were open and pulpy and giving. They unbuttoned their jackets, pressing their warmth into each other, brushing each other up and down through their clothing. Tadek slid his hand up under her dress and Halinka gasped and bit the side of his jaw.

"I have to go," Halinka broke away. "It's getting late. And I'm soaked from the mist."

"Me too. I don't want you to go."

"I don't want to, either."

"I wish there was somewhere we could go. I love you."

"I love you too."

They stood as if something had been settled.

"Don't walk me. I don't want to run into my father. I have to get out of that house." She sighed and shook her head, then turned and dashed around the corner out of sight.

Tadek made his way slowly back through the misty village, feeling a bit as if he were emerging from another realm, from a forest or an ocean. He shook himself and tried to be alert. He had a job to do now.

He returned through the square in case he might see anything of interest. The two NKVD agents he'd walked by earlier were both just leaving the square, the one streetlight gleaming off the rain-slickened shoulders of their long coats. Tadek decided to follow them. The street immediately darkened off the square, but after a few moments his eyes adjusted.

There was a little light from the moon through a thinning of the clouds. A wind seemed to be brushing aside the mist. He could see the two men walking ahead of him and heard fragments of Russian. They didn't turn. They laughed at some shared joke. They turned by the railroad station and walked toward it. There was a guard on duty there, sitting inside under the glare of the station lights. When the two NKVD officers entered, he sprang to attention and saluted. Tadek found a pathway between two houses where he could hide and still watch the Russians. They talked for what seemed like a long time. Finally the two officers left, calling a few words of advice over their shoulders to the guard. They shook hands beneath the wide eaves of the station and went separate ways. Tadek followed the short man with the broken nose, since he was headed away from the square and the other headed back to the police station.

The lights from the train station quickly faded, but Tadek could still discern the dark silhouette ahead of him. At the edge of town he turned to walk alongside the huge, darkened potato fields of the kolkhoz. The rain had awakened the odor of the freshly tilled dirt and the mist carried the crunching sound of the officer's footsteps back to Tadek. Tadek lagged back. The street was deserted. It would be just as easy for the man to hear Tadek's footsteps as for him to hear the man's. The man stopped. Tadek crouched down next to the field. He watched as the man tried several times to light a cigarette, finally succeeding and walking on. Tadek let him get about fifty meters ahead. The man turned into a side street. Tadek hurried to catch up, careful when he approached the corner, stopping there. He could smell the man's cigarette smoke. He heard voices and laughter. He peered around the corner, low, from behind a hedge. Shockingly close, the officer stood in a shaft of light from an open doorway, talking to a woman. Tadek leaned back behind the corner. More laughter. They hadn't seen him. He peered out again. He couldn't see the woman, but saw the man standing back jauntily, smiling, rolling his cigarette between his thumb and forefinger, gesturing with it in what seemed an urbane manner. The woman laughed again, and an arm reached out to grab his sleeve and pull him inside.

Tadek stood outside across the street in an alcove till the lights went out inside the house.

* * *

It was the first Tuesday of June when Tadek got out of work and made his way out of the factory in a throng with hundreds of others. He crossed the busy street and gradually separated himself as he filed down narrower and narrower lanes to a dead end clogged with garbage cans, where he descended concrete stairs into the basement hallway, still lined with empty cans of paint, and tapped on Ewa's door. She greeted him with her gap-toothed smile and let him in. He was surprised to find Kozel and his Uncle Janusz sitting at her scarred wooden table, full of damp rings from beer glasses. Smoke turned round the bare bulb hanging from the ceiling.

Kozel and Jan both nodded, businesslike, almost unfriendly. He'd interrupted a conversation.

"Here's the expert," Jan said.

"Right," Ewa agreed.

"What about the sergeant?" Kozel, in his low, growly voice, started up where he'd left off. "That little prick."

"He is living with the Pivovars, and is eating all of their food," Tadek said. "He's the one children call squint-eye. He killed their dog when he moved in. Shot him in the yard. He is the worst."

"Because of a dog? There are worse things to do than to kill a dog," Kozel said.

"You said they are near the square?" Ewa followed up. She sat down and leaned her big, reddened arms on the table, her breasts again almost ready to break free from her blouse. Both Jan and Kozel listened to her when she spoke as if she held an equal or greater authority.

"Yes."

"That puts him one street over from the police station. The streets are lighted there. There's always someone around. That's just stupid."

"Kazimierz has decided that an attack directly on the station is too dangerous. We would make a lot of noise, but there would be casualties we can't afford, maybe civilian casualties too, and unless we were incredibly lucky, we would get few arms, which is what we need more than anything. But what about the big shot? The major. That would be best."

"No. He's all right," Tadek said. "After that sergeant shot the Pivovar's dog, he bought them a new one."

Kozel looked around the table as if taking in an audience much larger than these three men with his wide, sardonic eyes. "Oh, is he 'all right' then?"

Jan leaned forward and made to slap Tadek on the back of the head with his hefty hand, but Tadek, older now and less helpless to such blows than before, parried this one with his forearm.

"No, I just meant . . . . I mean, I know he's NKVD, but compared to the others. You see, he stopped me once, and he seemed decent."

"Decent!" Kozel sneered. "Jan, can you explain to your nephew the facts of life?"

"It doesn't matter what he's like," Jan recited in a dead voice, as if any emotion would be inappropriate at this time. "It doesn't matter if he's Jesus. He's on the wrong side. He is our enemy."

"Where's he live?"

"He comes from Grodno about twice a week," Tadek said, repenting his comments, angry at himself. "Often in the same staff car as the captain, Orbatov. They have bodyguards. Even if he is our enemy, he would be the most difficult target."

"I want to shoot Orbatov myself," Kozel muttered. "I'll take care of him. I want him."

"Tadek is right about the major," Ewa said. "His driver is always by his side. And he lives in the Soviet compound here, in Grodno. It's well guarded. It would be suicidal to attack him there."

"If we could get them both together, that would be perfect."

"The timing of the trips is unpredictable. Sometimes they're with other troops," Tadek said.

Tadek knew that the others were right: an enemy was an enemy. And yet he still harbored a sympathy for the major. He knew that he liked to make surprise visits to Liaski and was often driven in a staff car late at night, but Tadek suspected that there was a timing to the major's return trips to Grodno: often but not always, he'd noticed, these trips took place around ten, just after a report was made over the radio at the police station.

"The major is a problem," Ewa meditated. "He's smarter than Orbatov. He's cracking down and trying to make friends at the same time. He brings Polish conscripts from the area with him when he talks to people. It confuses people."

"A traitor's a traitor," Kozel said. "They are traitors for helping him. There's another Soviet two houses down from the train station."

"Toward the square?" Ewa asked.

"Away from it. I'm not sure who lives there but it's a little house with a metal fence around it and a wind vane on top of a bear." Tadek was amazed at how they had all been memorizing everything he'd been telling them about the Soviets' movements. Kozel also seemed to have other sources of information.

"The Pivovar's," Tadek said.

"The Pivovar's? Who are they? That's not even Polish."

"They've been here for generations, I think," Tadek said.

"That's right," Jan agreed. "Their grandfather was Czech." Three generations in Liaski was not quite enough to remove suspicion. "They were always different," Jan continued. "Always looking out for themselves."

"It may not be of their own volition," Ewa cautioned.

"I never trusted them!" Jan said.

"Their rooms have been commandeered," Tadek said. "That's what the neighbors say."

"And the fat one, where is he?" Kozel said.

"He is with the Lebinowski's," Tadek said, after giving a pause to see whether Kozel knew. Tadek noticed Kozel observing him carefully, his fixed, unpleasant grin on his face. He had a way of staring in silence that always unnerved Tadek.

"By the road toward Minsk?"

"Yes. But a street away, toward the river."

"Still too close to the square. We need to get in and get out." Kozel shrugged dismissively.

"There's one who has a girlfriend," Tadek said. "The short

one who looks like a boxer. With a broken nose. He goes to visit her sometimes. A lot, actually. Three, four times a week. Sometimes he spends the night there."

"Why didn't you tell us about this before?" Jan asked sharply.

"I just figured out his pattern recently. His girlfriend lives on the last street of town, and he walks along the northern edge of town, by the kolkhoz, the potato fields . . . . " Everyone had become quiet and was leaning forward. An air of dark, fascinating possibilities curled about the room. "When he goes to her house, first he stops by the train station, then he continues by the potato fields."

"What time?"

"Ten-thirty. After they gather at the police station. They make a report on the radio. Then they go their separate ways."

"Alone by the potato fields?" Kozel asked.

"Yes, he walks there alone."

"About 10:30?"

"Yes. Not always, but regularly. At least a few times a week."

Kozel leaned back in his chair, hefted a knee up to the tabletop to prop him, and squinted at Tadek through the smoke of the cigarette in his mouth. Jan turned his glass of beer around on the tabletop, gave it a philosophical sip, and began audibly swishing the liquid back and forth between his teeth. Ewa leaned forward and said, "That's enough for today. Tadek, we'll make a decision. You can go now."

"When will it be?" Tadek asked.

"We'll decide," she said. "It's best if you don't know anything more."

* * *

Tadek had stayed at work late, working with Stronski on a tangle of fabric stuck deep in the innards of a loom. He ended up catching a late bus home from Grodno, arriving at Liaski at dusk. Krystyna wasn't home. Often she too stayed late at work, now as a secretary for the head of the state university's agricultural department. Tadek went out back to do his chores: checking on the bees, feeding the chickens and the two sheep that they now had, and bringing in water from the well. He hooked the tin bucket over the spout of the well and held it there with his left hand. With his right he gave the handle a few laborious, dry, groaning pumps. Finally the water gushed forth and into the bucket. One more pump and it was full. He set it down and fit another bucket on the spout, but before he could fill it, he heard a faint, "Hey! Hey!" from the gate underneath the grape arbor. He left the water and walked down the gate to see Halinka standing there, a questioning smile on her face. She hadn't stopped by his house since they were kids, when she and the gang would swing by to roust him out for a game of tag or Go Hide.

"Was I wrong to come?" She smiled her secretive smile, though there seemed to be a different cast to it tonight, a shared something between them.

"No."

"I finished my chores and put my little sisters to bed. My papa is drunk and asleep, snoring like a black bear, and my mother's too worried to follow what I do, so I just left! Just like that! I had to get out of that house!"

"I'm glad you came."

"Is your mother home?"

"She will be soon."

"Then shall we walk?"

"Let me just bring the water in." He let her into the gate. She followed him to the back, where he filled the second bucket and lifted them both, declining her help. Without a word, she held the door for him as he carried the water inside. It felt illicit, with her in his family's house, both of them alone together. "Let's go," he said.

"Yes."

They headed on to the village streets away from the bus stop to avoid Krystyna.

Holding hands, they walked along the bluff above the river, where a few night fishermen tended their lines below, at river's edge. They stopped and kissed. There seemed to be an urgency in this meeting, as if something had to happen soon or else it would be too late, and whatever option had briefly revealed itself would be forever closed from them.

"Where can we go?" Tadek asked.

"We can go into Mrs. Witcowicz's garden, if you like."

"The widow?"

"Yes. I've been taking care of her garden for her. She never goes back there. Especially not at night."

"All right."

"I know it well."

"Take me there." He held her hand.

She opened a rickety wooden gate under a vine-laden arch and led him down a path. There was a row of apple trees with fresh new leaves, and through them occasionally, over the rooftops of the village, Tadek could see the crescent of the first quarter moon, low in the west. They stepped carefully over uneven ground along the row of trees. Tadek tightened his grip on her hand and stopped in one shadow. She turned, and he leaned into her face that seemed luminous in the shadows, and he kissed her, feeling her lips slicken, feeling her breath. Beneath his lips she gave her restrained smile, pulling back, and he was driven to force through that smile, to see what lay behind its calm aloofness. He felt driven almost to hurt her, almost even to destroy her if necessary to reveal her secret.

"There's a bench down here." She ducked into an arbor formed by some shrubs and they pressed together on a wooden bench. He was filled with the memory of her breasts from the day in the forest and soon slid his hands under her blouse and she gasped and gave a long sigh. Moments later they tumbled to the uncropped grass together, their laughter mixed with panting. He rolled on top of her, his thigh pressed against her warm thigh.

Slowly he inched his hands up her dress, expecting her to stop him at any moment. With her dress hiked up to her hips, she pulled at his pants as he slid them down to his knees. He touched her, surrounded by the scents of the garden and her scent, his head swimming. He lay on top of her then, but this was so new to him, to her, and it seemed as if she were sealed tight, there was just a tiny crevice—and then it all opened for him, and he was inside her. Her smile was gone and she gasped in pain: She looked at him with utter seriousness, deeper than anyone, closer, as the shadows, the garden, and the stars swam around them. Her gasp turned into a long moan, then many stifled gasps as they moved into each other, beyond smiles, beyond lips, beyond eyes.

He rolled off of her and they lay together on the grass, looking up at the stars, hugging as if comforting each other for some sorrow. They were screened in the garden by the thick shrubbery, but could hear someone passing in the alley, a man's footsteps crunching in the dirt, the sound seeming physically close but quite irrelevant, as if it took place on a different plane altogether, on a radio or stage somewhere. They could smell the trail of his pipe smoke after he'd passed. Minutes turned with the stars.

There came the sound of voices, then the sudden abrupt laughter of several men, not far away in the alley, awakening Tadek and Halinka from their daze. They'd tried to be quiet, not altogether successfully, and now Tadek wondered at the chance they'd taken. They sat up and began slowly to gather their clothes around them.

"Did it hurt?" He saw a dark spot on her dress, blood, that she tried to hide.

"A little."

"I love you."

"Yes, me too. I mean, I love you too."

They separated in a daze and Tadek walked home in the same state. He had to focus his thoughts as he passed the police station and made his way across the village square, beneath the massive sycamores. There was just one soldier out front now. He yawned as Tadek passed, looking pointedly over his head, a subtle snub. Tadek reminded himself that he had to focus on the danger of these people. But he wanted just to dream about Halinka's slick lips, the look she gave him as he lay on top of her.

* * *

When he arrived home, he was surprised to see his mother waiting for him, sitting on the steps of their house. He couldn't believe she'd waited for him, tonight of all nights. It was as if she knew. But she couldn't know.

"It's late," she said.

"Not so late."

"I was just sitting here, looking at the stars. Some nights it seems as if there are more of them. Have you noticed that?"

"Yes."

"And tonight they seem so close."

Tadek sat down next to her. He felt the familiar bowing of the tired, unpainted wooden steps beneath him. Home.

"Papa used to teach them to me." It felt strange to use that childish name for someone he hadn't seen for years.

285

"Yes, it seemed he knew all of their names, like they were his friends," she laughed. "Are you hungry?"

"A little."

"Come on inside. I've made borscht. I was out checking on the bees."

"You? Check on the bees? What do you know about bees?" he teased. "You'd better leave that to me."

"You do a good job. But I'm my father's daughter, so you'd be surprised how much I know!"

They went inside and she put out a bowl of borscht, put in a dollop of sour cream. Tadek had to smile. There was something stilted about her concern for his appetite that seemed suspicious.

"Well, mother, what's on your mind exactly?"

She smiled too. "Ah, you've figured me out. It's just this . . . . I have to ask, Tadek what are you doing with Halinka?" Krystyna asked.

"What do you mean?"

How could she read his mind this way?

"What are your plans?"

"I'm in love with her."

She pursed her lips and nodded to herself as if to say, I knew it. "You're too young for that."

"I'm old enough to run messages for the resistance!"

"Shush. That's something different," Krystyna looked pained. "Everyone does what they can."

"Hardly everyone!"

"Should I have not got you involved with the partisans?" This was the first time a question like this had been raised since Kazimierz visited them almost four years before.

Tadek waved the thought away with a hand. "I was born involved. I'll see Stalin eat dirt!"

"You're talking like your uncles now. You needn't talk that

way."

"I'm not a child anymore! That's the way I feel!"

"Well, you're still too young to get involved with that girl."

"I'm already involved there too."

"What do you mean? You'd better not mean what I think you mean!"

"I'm serious about her," he said more calmly. "That's all there is to it."

He stood up, abandoning his meal.

"I don't want you to make the mistakes that I made."

He almost said then, mistakes like marrying father?

Instead he just said, "What mistakes?"

"The usual mistakes."

"Well, I want to make the usual ones, too. I don't want to miss out on any! Thanks for the borscht, mother. Now I'm going for a walk."

"So late?" It was a rare disagreement between the two, and Krystyna was reluctant to let him go this way.

"Yes, so late."

Tadek stepped out onto the enclosed porch, finding himself also reluctant to leave matters this way between them. Yet he was angry that she would pry. He needed Halinka more than anything. She was the thread he would follow to his future, the only way he knew to one. He stood calming himself, breathing in the odors of the stacks of firewood and of the baskets of potatoes and onions shoved beneath the plank bench.

A rattle of machine gun fire ripped across the night. It was muffled and distant, from the other side of town, but he had heard the sound often enough to know it. Another, shorter rattle of fire punctuated the first. A few pops of handguns seemed like an afterthought. Then there was nothing but stunned silence, as if there was nothing more to be said. The silence seemed shaped into a negative configuration of the shots, as if each one had poked a hole in the night. Then all the dogs of the village began to bark at once.

Krystyna came and stood on the porch with him.

"Was that it? What we've been expecting?" Krystyna asked.

"Yes. That must have been it."

Soon the distinctive yodeling Soviet sirens took up deep in the night and seemed to converge on Liaski from all points of the compass.

Chapter 27:
Swimming, Plotting

After the shooting, the Soviets increased their presence in Liaski, while the partisans seemed to vanish from the area. Little rumors about them getting food from peasants in Shabany or taking pot shots at guards, the typical susurration of their invisible presence, came to a sharp end. At work Ewa pointedly, absolutely ignored Tadek when they would pass each other. It was more difficult now to get to and from Shabany, so Tadek seldom biked to see his uncle, though he noted that the troops ignored him on the weekends when he went by. For a time Orbatov made daily harangues over the loud speakers in the town square to the captured audience of Poles. They clustered in surly knots and turned the other way and waited for him to leave.

Still Tadek and Halinka would walk at night, though it seemed more and more difficult to find a place or a time alone. Halinka had come out of her house the night of the attack to see the body of the NKVD agent lying in the street a hundred meters from her house and was frightened by the closeness of the violence.

When Tadek finally went to Ewa's apartment on the first

Tuesday of the month, he was told that they were going after Orbatov. It was too much disruption in their movements to go after lower-level Soviet army or NKVD. Again she wouldn't tell him details of the planned attack, but he gave her what information he had about the comings and goings of Captain Orbatov and Major Rostov.

Tadek and Pawel sometimes took a boat that belonged to one of Pawel's cousins out fishing, and today was perfect, because the sun shone in full summer warmth, yet the fish were biting because the water was still cool. They took off their shirts and drifted downstream, pulling in fish and talking about their futures. Tadek held within him the knowledge of his new tie to Halinka, nursing it, unsure whether he should share. They drifted down past Shabany, rowing across the river and back from spot to shady spot. They thought they'd never caught so many fish—perch, pike, zander, and bream. With the boat, they could catch three times the fish they would in a day fishing from the bank in Liaski. Engrossed in fishing and forgetful of where they were, Tadek was astonished to look up to see themselves floating downstream toward the rocky outcrop where he'd met the partisans on that winter night.

"There are rumors that there are banditos here," Pawel mused, reading his mind the way of longtime friends. The area had an ambiguous reputation of being lawless and intimidating.

"Not banditos, partisans," Tadek corrected.

"How do you know?"

"Maybe banditos too."

Pawel shouted: "Hey!" His voice echoed off the riverbank.

"Cut it out! It's not funny!"

"Why? What's the matter?" He gave a few strong pulls on the oars as they neared the outcropping of rocks. It was unusual for Pawel to tease Tadek, who was usually the teaser, but Tadek's reaction inspired him to take a new role. "Partisans, come out!"

"Quiet!" Tadek snapped.

"Home Army! Where are you?"

The two boys watched the silent wall of trees facing the water's edge. In the spring, the trees dragged their branches in the swollen current like girls bending over to wash their hair, but now, the water was low and the trees were dry.

"The partisans are not the same as banditos," Tadek lectured.

"You're right," Pawel said, looking at Tadek a bit oddly, letting the oars drag in the water. "I'm for the partisans as much as anyone. But what can we do?"

"We can do something! Not sit out here taunting them!"

"You're right. I apologize."

"Apology accepted. Now let's row back."

Tadek feared that they were being watched from behind several rows of silent trees, and that one of the partisans would recognize him, and reveal himself, thinking it was important. He regretted letting their boat drift downstream this far. The everyday outing had turned into something treacherous. He grabbed the oars from Pawel and began vigorously rowing up stream.

"They'll never win, you know," Pawel said.

"Yes, they will."

"Be realistic, Tadek. We are abandoned by the world. The war is long over."

"The war will never be over as long as Poland's split in two and Stalin's troops walk the streets of Liaski."

Pawel gave his friend a searching look, as if puzzling something out. He turned away and was quiet as Tadek rowed.

Back at the village, they were both soaked with sweat from battling the current. They beached the boat and walked upstream to their usual swimming spot, secluded from the village by a bend in the river and a small thicket of birch. From here, off a narrow ledge of grass that ran alongside the small creek entering the river, it was an easy low dive into the water. Today they made their way along the dusty path on the top of the bluff, but when they reached the top and looked down, there were a half-dozen men already there, swimming naked in their spot. The sound of Russian voices floated up to them.

"Look at them!" Pawel said, disgusted. "I can't believe this."

"This is our spot!" Tadek agreed.

"What are we going to do?"

"Not swim with them!"

"Look. The twins are on the other side of the creek."

A few of the other village boys had faced the same dilemma and made a decision. Tadek and Pawel followed their example, passing without a word within several yards of the Soviets, who were sunbathing on the sand or splashing in the shallow water. The Soviets quieted down for a moment before picking up their conversation again. They had hardly forgotten that someone, someone Polish, had assassinated one of their own just two weeks before. But one among them passed a bottle of vodka, they drank, and picked up again their mood of momentary escape.

Tadek and Pawel crossed the stream on a makeshift plank bridge. On the other side, they stripped in the woods and made their way out onto small grassy bluff where they looked down on the sandbank where the twins lay. A few other Liaski kids swam in the shallow water.

From here Tadek could survey the two groups of young men thirty meters away from each other, swimming like pale frogs in the clear greenish water. From this distance, they looked almost identical, not like people who hated each other and might kill each other if the occasion arose.

"They were here when we got here," explained one of the

twins apologetically.

"Someone must've told them about this spot," the other grumbled.

"Oh, they could figure it out themselves," Tadek said bitterly. "It's the best spot around."

"We could steal their clothes," one of the twins suggested.

"Better not," Pawel said. "They don't have much tolerance for anything now."

"Hmph," Tadek replied, little more than a grunt, contemptuous of how much or little his enemies could tolerate. He ran to the river's edge and on into the river, wading until it was thigh-deep, then diving. The crashing immersion washed away thoughts of the Soviets.

The water was cool and the sun was warm. He swam out toward the center of the river. The water was cool and the sun was warm, and Halinka! Halinka! She was his. He smiled to himself at his delicious secret. Immersed himself again. Burst up from the water.

Pawel and Tadek treaded water off the sandbank where it deepened quickly. They could feel themselves being pulled downstream by the current. Alternating cool then mild tentacles of water slithered along their legs and curled around their waists.

The young Soviet soldiers—not NKVD, Tadek judged—were splashing each other and laughing. After a while, hearing their Russian voices poisoned his moment of escape, and he felt that mood slipping away: whatever happened in his personal life, they were still here. He swam to shore, now in a darkening state of mind. Pawel followed to lie beside him, both naked to the sun. A few more village boys arrived and the twins swam into the river with them. The day was so still, they could hear scraps of the conversation of the Soviets.

"What are they saying?" Tadek asked Pawel. Though Tadek

was picking up Russian, he resented everything he learned. Pawel now attended school in Russian, and his grandfather, after all, had spoken Byelorussian, a closely related language, so he'd picked it up quickly and was already fluent. Either the Russians assumed the ignorance of the Poles, or the influence of the vodka and the sun and the water made them incautious.

"They're talking about going into Grodno. To pick up some officers and guns."

"When?"

"Why do you care?"

"Just tell me what they say."

"It seems on Thursday night.

"Did they say what time?"

Pawel stopped and looked very closely at Tadek. "You are so interested in their comings and goings? Why?"

"Just tell me!"

"Yes. They're saying that they will be home by ten and can play cards then."

"This Thursday?"

"Yes."

"Okay. Let's go in again."

"You shouldn't get involved in anything to do with them. It's none of our business," Pawel warned.

"I know. I'm not. I'll race you across!" Tadek sprung up and ran across the sandbar to dive into the shallow water, stroking as he emerged. He could hear Pawel following him. He knew that Pawel would take him up on the challenge. It was not an easy swim across. The river was their gift, bringing them fish all year round, saving them from starvation in the past when towns less blessed than Liaski ate bark, but it was also treacherous. It demanded its sacrifices. One boy whom Tadek had grown up with had drowned during spring floods. A boy from Shabany had become paralyzed from diving into a shallow spot further downstream.

As they swam the river took them downstream. This downward tug was as relentless as time, day and night, summer and winter. When they reached the other side, they were fifty meters downstream from where they'd started. Here the woods pushed close to the bank. Tadek and Pawel sat on a dead tree that lay a bit out of the water, its trunk dry and smooth as an ancient bone.

"When we get back, you know we're going to be way down there!" Pawel pointed downstream. "Then we're going to have to walk back naked past the Russians."

"I know it! I don't care!"

"You're crazy!"

"What are they going to do to me? Arrest me and my cock for un-Soviet-like behavior?"

Pawel laughed. "Maybe just your cock!"

They were silent awhile, sitting side by side on the log, their feet dangling in the water. Across the river they could see the two groups of naked men, swimming and splashing on either side of the stream's entrance. The Russians were only a few years older than the village boys whom Tadek and Pawel had known their whole lives. Again they looked like two identical groups of pale frogs in the greenish water.

"Why don't they just go away!" Tadek said.

Pawel shrugged. "Because the Kremlin tells them what to do. Because the Russians won the war!"

"Well, we won it too!"

"Did we?"

"Poles fought the Nazis too!"

"Why are you arguing with me? I know this as well as you do! What can anyone do?"

"We can do something."

"What? It just is. I'm just going to live my life. Find a girl, get married, have kids."

"Not Sabina?"

"I don't know. We'll both be in Grodno next year, working and going to school. First we're together, then we're not. She's not really happy if she isn't fighting. But if we can find a way to get along, we'll marry maybe, and after we marry we'll move to Warsaw. If the government will let us. Maybe I could go to university there. It's easier to be a Pole there, anyway."

"But you're only part Polish!"

"I'm Polish! Don't say that." Pawel's face revealed the wound Tadek had struck, and he felt guilty for his gibe. He wasn't sure why he said such a thing to his friend. He never had before.

"You're right. I'm sorry."

It took Pawel a few moments of silence to cover over his pain. He said, "And you? Are you going to marry Halinka?"

"Yes. Absolutely."

"Really? When did you decide?"

"I've been thinking about it."

"But she doesn't know yet?"

"Not really."

Pawel laughed delightedly. "You're funny! But I'm happy. When are you going to do it?"

"I don't know yet. Soon, maybe.

"Really?"

"Yes. I think so. Remember when we fought over her?"

"Ha! When we were kids? You mean, you fought over her. That was puppy love on my part. How long were we together? Two weeks? I love Sabina. I just never know what she'll want or do next."

"Have you two had sex?" Tadek asked.

"No!" Pawel looked shocked. "She's too...proud for that.

Independent. How about you?"

Tadek was silent, and then he nodded, the gravity of their action overcoming him. "Yes. Yes, we have."

"Really?"

"Yes."

"I can't believe it. Halinka? We used to call her the ice princess! That's a serious step."

"I know. I can't believe it happened. It just happened. But it's as though we're almost married, now. We're going to be married," Tadek reiterated, feeling that saying this to Pawel brought the event very close. He looked away. As they'd been talking, the Russians had gotten dressed and were now making their way back to the village in a line along the top of the ridge, still playfully shoving each other and laughing loudly. One by one they disappeared over the ridge. A stork drifted overhead, from the forest to the village, where it disappeared amid the trees.

"I'll be best man, right?" Pawel asked.

"Of course. Best man." After a moment, both sensing from long familiarity that the conversation was done, they shoved themselves off the branch into the water.

"Race back!" Pawel called.

Chapter 28:
Doves in the Rafters

That night Tadek went to Jan's, taking a new roundabout route that took him twice as long as the route through Shabany. He knew that Kazimierz would want to know immediately of the arms convoy. The planned attempt on Orbatov's life would likely cause a cancellation of the convoy, and the partisans' opportunity to get their hands on some serious armaments would be botched. Jan agreed and said he would see Kazimierz the next morning. Tadek told Jan he'd pass the word to Ewa at work. When he approached her directly at her sewing machine, she shooed him away, whispering over the throbbing rattle of the room for him to come to her apartment after work. There he told her all that he knew, and he could tell that she was in accord with the plan to switch targets from the captain to the arms shipment. She gave him a note to deliver to Jan and left him with the directions that had become a refrain for her. "You don't need to know what we're going to do. The less you know, the safer we are and the safer you are. Just live your life."

That was the goal Pawel had mentioned. To just live his life.

Tadek's life now meant Halinka, though with both their jobs and her father's vigilance, they struggled to find occasion to be together for more than a brief walk around the village. What had happened between them had not been fully talked about, and after bringing them closer, it now threatened to push them apart. Around sunset of the Saturday before the planned attack on the convoy, they walked arm in arm above the river. They were both in a serious mood and Tadek wondered if they shared the reasons.

"I wish there was somewhere we could go where we could be together," Tadek said.

"Well, I told my parents I'd be with Sabina, so we shouldn't be out here where people can see us and gossip. But I have a plan, if it's not too bold."

"What's that?"

"I told you about old lady Witcowicz."

"Yes?"

"Well, she's visiting her sister in Grodno this weekend, and wanted me to look in on her place. But even if she was home, nobody ever comes out to her little barn. So we can go there. Everyone's used to seeing me come and go."

He squeezed her hand. They walked along the river's edge toward the edge of town till they approached the Witcowicz's buildings. Her house was on the last street of the town and her yard sprawled into the fields behind it.

"I'll go in first. You wait here and follow in a few minutes, okay?"

He watched her disappear and turned and walked back up the lane overlooking the river and then back down it, passing fishermen and two kids kicking a football back and forth as they walked, the way he and Pawel used to.

He made his way down a side alley and through a gap in the fence to the Witcowicz's yard, around a new garden to the small,

300

ramshackle barn where her husband had stored straw and hay when he was alive and still kept a horse.

It was still twilight when he stepped into the complete darkness of the barn as Halinka pulled the door shut behind them. "I can't see a thing," Tadek said. Pigeons stirred and cooed in the rafters and the scent of straw filled his nostrils. He turned to kiss her.

"No. Let's find a place."

As his eyes adjusted he could see shadowy forms of the haymow looming above them. They picked their way further along, past several stalls, hay up to their ankles, loose like snow but pricking them, its odor filling their heads. "Here." She took a blanket off the railing and spread it out, and they sunk to their knees and kissed.

This time everything seemed to move with slow delectation as they kissed and tugged and plucked and slid off their clothing. He could feel her but could hardly see her in the dark. Her long slender limbs and smooth stomach were cool and warm at once. Then all semblance of shapes disappeared and time divided itself into smaller and smaller moments and finer perceptions until it collapsed into itself and disappeared too.

Afterwards they lay naked on the blanket side by side. The barn held the heat of the day still but they could feel the coolness of the evening prying its way through the loose boarding around them. They let their fingertips play over the length of their arms, legs, bellies.

"You'll never desert me?" she asked.

"No. We'll be married."

"We'll be married?" A wonder filled her voice.

"Yes. I feel married to you already."

"I do too. But really married?"

"Yes, I'll go to the town hall and see what has to be done."

"Have you told your mother?"

"No, not yet."

She laughed. "See, you aren't so brave after all, are you?"

"I'll do it," he protested, a bit miffed.

"When we were growing up, I always thought you were the bravest boy in the world. The way you tried to save that dog on the ice. The way you let that pig loose with 'Hitler' written on it."

"That wasn't brave; that was just stupid!"

"Maybe both!"

Both smiling in the dark, they let the past wash over them and then recede, revealing again the outlines of the present, its options and dangers.

"After they murdered that man..." Halinka said.

"Executed."

"Yes. I ran outside and saw him down the street, lying there. His girlfriend was kneeling over him."

"Yes, it's a tough business. You want them to let us be Poland again, don't you?"

"Yes. Of course. But...you're Home Army, aren't you?"

Tadek felt stunned. This was something he'd lived with for years but had never imagined anyone discovering.

"Why do you say that?"

"Everything. It just fits. The last couple of years."

"I'm not saying anything."

"Well . . . . Just be careful. I want a husband, not another dead Polish patriot. I was frightened when that shooting took place. It was just down the street from me. It showed me how real the fight is, how it's always close."

"I know."

"So, you'll be careful?"

"Yes."

He ran his fingertips over her face like a blind man, over her closed eyes, along her nose and mouth, down over her chin and along her throat, and she was already shuddering. Along her breasts and down her belly and between her legs. He rolled on top of her again and she gasped, and the doves in the rafters stirred and cooed, stirred and cooed.

Chapter 29: Ambush

Despite the warnings to stay as ignorant as possible of the partisan plans, Tadek knew when the convoy of armaments was coming from Grodno, so on Thursday night he and his mother sat waiting at the kitchen table drinking tea, waiting for the sounds of guns. Nine-thirty came. Ten passed. Then ten-thirty. Krystyna said, "Something hasn't evolved the way we expected."

"Maybe it was cancelled."

"Maybe they decided…"

"Did you hear that?" Tadek said.

"I didn't hear anything."

"I think I heard something."

"No. It was nothing."

But it wasn't nothing. It was the sound of gunfire two kilometers away towards Grodno. Tadek heard more of the distant, muffled shots. After a few minutes the sirens from the town's center started up.

"They did it," Tadek said, standing abruptly and running to peer out the window into the darkened garden, as if he could see through the trees and houses to the Grodno road.

"I think so."

"I want to go see."

"No, that's just stupid." She moved between him and the door as if ready to block him from leaving with her body if necessary.

"No, it's natural. Everyone will go to see."

"It's too far."

"I want to see what they do here in Liaski. How they react. Kazimierz would want to know. Don't try to stop me."

She saw that he was determined, saw, perhaps for the first time, that he was no longer a boy, and stepped aside.

"Don't make yourself conspicuous. What good does that do?"

"I just have to see."

"Don't go too close."

The night swarmed with sirens as he walked the dark streets. Other villagers were standing in their doorways, asking their neighbors what they knew. When he came to the square, he saw a truck already arriving, filled with the dead and wounded. He joined a crowd of villagers, keeping himself near the back.

The Soviet soldiers leaped from the trucks and took a run at the crowd of Poles, jabbing at them with their guns as if ready to shoot, blaming their unspoken allegiances for the attack. Other soldiers unloaded six stretchers and lined them up in front of the police station in a row under the trees. On three of them the men were still alive, and a doctor came and knelt beside one of these, ordered them moved into the police station. The other three of them had sheets stretched over their full lengths, covering their faces. Out of one flopped an arm, the sleeve of the shirt dark with blood, rivulets of red mapping the hand.

The soldiers formed a ring around their fallen comrades and began more methodically to chase the crowd of onlookers, spreading out and jabbing again with their rifles, barking in Russian.

Tadek backed up with the rest of the crowd to the edge of the square. He turned to head home when he saw Halinka just a few meters away walking toward him, clasping an unbuttoned jacket at her throat with one hand. She came up to him and grabbed his arm and pulled him aside to whisper, "Did you know about this?"

"Don't ask me questions about it."

"I hate them too, you know. But I'm sick of war. It's all I've ever known."

"I know," Tadek said. "I'm sick of it too." It was the first time he realized this. "But it's what I have to do. I just will never accept them. To do that would be like killing myself." They walked together quickly down an alleyway, heads lowered, whispering.

"I'm worried that you'll get hurt, or worse."

Tadek scoffed, "There's no danger. I'm just a messenger boy. Besides, the Russians are stupid. Now, we can't talk about this anymore."

"I know. I understand. Let's walk a bit. Just a bit. My mother will be worried."

They wandered down another alleyway in the general direction of Halinka's house but immediately pressed up against a wall to kiss.

"Let's sneak away somewhere," he said.

"Tadek! No! You're treating me too lightly! This isn't a normal situation!"

"We'll get married."

"Please, Tadek. That would make me so happy."

"Me too. We will."

"I have to go."

She turned, her hand still at her throat, glancing over her shoulder, once, twice. The distant light from the square just limned the perfect, anxious profile of her face as she turned a corner and disappeared into the shadow of a bush. That was the image of her that he would have to keep for years, until they would finally see each other again, after the passing years had made both of their lives unrecognizable, even to themselves.

* * *

The word on the street the next day was that the partisans had gotten away with one truck full of armaments. Three Russians had been killed, including the hated Captain Orbatov, the killer of Chopin and the other resistors. The Poles of Liaski clustered in twos and threes and whispered in muted pride to each other the events of the night before, and for a few days it seemed as if the triumph of a moment could matter.

Tadek found out later that day from Krystyna, who had spoken to a partisan in Grodno, she would not tell him whom, that the actual events weren't as clear cut as the Poles rumored to themselves. The partisans had set explosives in the road to disable the lead vehicle, but they'd gone off too late, leaving the first truck to drive out of range where their guards could dismount and return to aid their trapped comrades. Three partisans had been killed, matching the three Soviets, though the partisans had managed to unload half the truck-full of armaments and munitions and had scattered with them into the woods, on horseback, before Soviet reinforcements arrived from Liaski and Grodno.

The Soviet reaction came a few days later, announced with the dusty rumble of two troop carriers, filled with gray clad soldiers, into the Liaski town square. Tadek passed the troop carriers as he rode the bus to work in the morning. When he returned home that evening, he walked to the main square where Pawel was also huddled with a group of friends. Pawel took him aside.

"Listen," he whispered intently. "I know that you had something to do with that ambush!"

"What are you talking about?" He looked away from his friend, unsure how to react.

"I'm not stupid, Tadek!" Pawel threw a cigarette in the dirt and ground it with his heel. He'd just started smoking. It was part of a new intellectual image he'd been cultivating in Grodno recently, hanging out with people whom Tadek didn't know well and didn't particularly like. Tadek would get out of work late in the day and walk by the cafés, where he would see Pawel's new friends, who drank coffee and talked nonsense all day, and looked down on him because he was from Liaski and did something besides reading books constantly. "We heard the Russians talking when they were swimming."

"And so? If we heard them, other people did too."

"So? Just be careful, is all."

"I am careful."

"I want the Russians gone as much as anyone."

"Then just let me do my job!"

"All right!" The two friends seemed angry about something, but neither was sure what it was.

The troops now stood triple-guard at the police station entrance and walked the perimeter of the town five-abreast, trying to stare down the contempt of the villagers.

* * *

Tadek was in the back with the bees when he saw someone at the gate. He replaced the shelf of honey he'd been about to harvest and walked across the orchard to the gate, more and more astonished as he realized who it was. It was Lech, the gangly, wall-eyed boy from Gombachy, who wanted to be called Diabeł. Tadek hadn't seen him in almost a year. Surprised, he just stood and looked at him across the gate.

"Let me in."

Tadek still just didn't like the boy and instinctively had been willing to let him stand on the street, but he could see he was in a panic about something. He'd been running and was sweating. Also, Tadek remembered all the times he'd met Lech at the fallen tree outside Gombachy. The kid had never been late. He'd always done his duty. Even when they'd fought, Lech had fought to protect the Gombachy partisans as Tadek had fought to fulfill his duty to Chopin.

Lech walked quickly through the gate and under the grape arbor, hunching the way he did, looking suspiciously at the window, peering into the yard with his crooked eye.

"Listen, you. Tadek. I just came from Grodno where I was meeting Ewa. You know Ewa?"

"Yes, of course."

"As soon as I left, the NKVD rolled up in a lorry and rushed into her building. I watched from across the park as they hauled her away."

"They arrested her?"

"Yes, that's what I'm telling you! But that's not what's important. I went into Grodno to tell her that there is a caravan of troop carriers full of soldiers that pulled into Gombachy last night. Russians and Byelorussian troops. The government troops. They were attempting to hide away from Grodno overnight. Ewa knew about this. But we weren't sure what their plans were. Now they've all headed out of Grodno on the other side of the Niemen toward the Liaski partisans' camp. That's what she wanted me to tell you. You need to warn them. They're coming full force with about ten troop carriers full of soldiers. Even two tanks."

"Tanks! They can't get through the forest."

"They can get near enough! And the troops can. They have mortars."

"I'll leave now. They'll have hard going through the forest. Maybe I'll have an hour or two."

They turned away from each other without goodbyes and hurried in opposite directions. Krystyna wasn't home for him to consult or bid farewell, and he snatched his bike from its spot against the house and let himself out of the gate. He ran a few steps before stepping on one pedal and swinging his other leg over the bike.

In his haste, he headed down his usual route, through several fields and away from the river, but then approaching the river near Shabany, emerging from a field just feet away from two NKVD guards standing by a small bridge.

"Halt!"

For half a pedal, Tadek considered trying to flee them, but they both raised their rifles: "We'll shoot!" That was a Russian phrase he could understand. He came to a stop. They leapt upon him, roughly grabbing him by the shoulder.

"I've got this one!" He watched them sling his bicycle into the ditch alongside the road and wondered how he could ever retrieve it.

They spoke to someone over a walkie-talkie, and a few minutes later, a truck drove up. Three more soldiers in the truck placed him in the back and drove him into Shabany. Here he was told with gestures to sit with three other prisoners on a long bench before the police station, not much more than a low shack with a roofed porch running its width.

One soldier paced up and down in front of the prisoners. He looked Asiatic, perhaps Kazakh, and wasn't much older than Tadek. He gripped a rifle in one hand and a cigarette in the other as he paced up the length of the porch, continually peering down the street, evidently expecting the appearance of someone. The other prisoners on the bench, three older men who looked like farmers, slumped with their heads in their hands. Tadek thought he had seen two of them around before. The NKVD were taking no chances and rounding up anyone who was on the roads that day.

Tadek inched down the bench a bit when the guard's back was turned, and slumped in imitation of the others when the guard turned and paced back along the length of the porch. Again, he slid down a few more inches. The guard returned slowly, smoking, perhaps nervously, not looking at the prisoners. When the guard passed a third time, smoking, craning his head to peer down the street, his back turned, Tadek slipped around the corner as silently as possible, running instinctively toward the river, which lay at the end of a brief alley. He heard a shout behind him.

He remembered the route he'd used through this edge of Shabany before, when he was helped by the old lady. Cutting down an alley, he found the goat pen he'd hid in before, and retraced his route up to the loft and then out the window, across a roof, and down to another alley. From here he slipped under the pilings of a building that lay above the river, weaving his way through the forest of wooden pilings to the other side, the river mud now dry, hearing shouts behind him from the alley he'd left behind. He ran past the rear of several buildings above the riverbank, then across a field with waist-high wheat, then into a forest of reeds, twice his height, along the river. Here they wouldn't follow easily. He ran through a maze of tiny paths, trying to edge the river, and on the other side of the reeds he made his way back through a thicket of birches, across a gravel road, and through an open oak grove. He ran along the river and then cut up the bank and through the scrim of black poplars that always told him it was time to cut up the bank to his uncle's. A raucous flock of crows rose and voiced their harsh complaints as he passed their nests in the trees, until he finally reached his uncle's house.

At Jan's he found Jadwiga slumped at the kitchen table. She sat up at the sight of Tadek but seemed as if stunned.

"What is it?"

He told her about the Soviet troops pouring out of Grodno.

"But Jan's not here."

"Where is he?"

"He went into Gombachy." She seemed unspeakably weary, speaking the words. "At dawn. To buy a calf."

"To buy a calf!" Tadek scoffed, dumbfounded.

"Well, he didn't know!" She grew more animated and stood up from the table as if just now fully grasping what he'd been saying. "You'll have to go yourself. Take the boat. Take fishing gear, in case they're out on the river. You know the way. Hurry."

He cut at an angle back to the river, ending up near the birches where he headed north fifty meters to find his uncle's boat pulled up on shore, one among half a dozen. He flipped it over, shoved the oars under the seat, and dragged it over the grass and sand into the water where he jumped in, rocking it in a near-capsize before it settled, and he managed to fit the oars in their locks and start rowing. He could fell the pull of the current lending its strength.

For half an hour he rowed hard. Finally he glanced over his shoulder to see the remembered outcropping of rocks at the river's wide bend. He angled his bow toward it, having to fight the current that wanted to keep him mid-river. Unable to find a decent beaching spot, he crashed into some of the smaller rocks, managing to wedge his bow between them, and he leapt over the bow waist-deep into the water and then onto the rocks, tugging the boat roughly behind him.

"Hey!" he called into the forest. "Hey! It's me! Tadek

Gradinski!" He pulled the boat further onshore, awaiting a response. Tentatively, he began to retrace his route from that winter, trying to remember what inconspicuous landmarks the forest yielded. Every once in a while he shouted again. He found his way to a small clearing and called again. Three men with raised rifles came at him out of the woods from different sides. One man wore a leather vest and hat and carried a machine gun instead of a rifle. It had a red bandanna wrapped around its barrel like a ribbon. His lean, unshaven, lupine face was familiar. "It's him," the man said.

"Yes," another agreed. And then angrily to Tadek. "What are you shouting for?"

The three men surrounded him and listened as he explained what he knew of the Soviet forces, and he watched their faces grow tense. They turned and led him at a trot to their horses. Tadek clambered on behind one of the partisans, and they were off through the forest, now opening up into huge, widely separated oaks and occasional pines that let them travel at a rapid pace. There was nothing but the sound of the slap of leather and the horses' husky breathing for a time. Then they were single-file on the path through the swamp; on either side stretched algae-covered water and trees that seemed to have been dead since the beginning of time. Twice the horses had to splash through chest-high water. A man called out into the woods: "White eagle!" and got an answering call: "Eagle rising!" as they hurried past the sentries and on into the camp.

Again the camp surprised him as he gradually realized that he was surrounded by huts, half-sunk into the ground, their roofs covered with branches, a few campfires going, and the men, dropping their tasks and moving towards him, were also earth- and bark-colored, and seemed to arise out of the forest itself.

Kazimierz strode over to meet the horses. He was gray and

thin. He looked sick. But seeing Tadek, he flushed, his eyes charged with energy, as if he immediately sensed urgency. He seemed more excited than panicked. He grabbed the horse's reins and held them while Tadek slid off.

"Tell me what's happened!"

Again Tadek repeated what little he knew.

"All right. This is it," Kazimierz said, breathing deeply as if in relief. He began shouting orders and walking toward the cluster of his men, fifty at the most. When he was done, he grabbed Tadek by the shoulders, and they walked back toward his dugout. He talked as he walked. "Good work on the convoy! We made away with arms and sent them south and north to partisans. And if they come after us today, we're ready to take them with us!" Inside the hut he grabbed a rifle and strapped a bandolier of cartridges across his chest.

They stepped outside again. There was a single gunshot in the distance: a signal. Both of their heads snapped around and for a moment the clearing full of partisans was quiet.

"You have to get out of here!" Kazimierz snapped.

"Let me stay!"

"No! This isn't for you. You'll slow us down. Hipolit!" Kazimierz gestured across the clearing to the young man Tadek remembered, who now sprinted toward them, a pistol in his hand as if ready to shoot someone at Kazimierz's order. "Take Tadek back to the river," Kazimierz said. He saw Hipolit and Tadek both hesitate, drawing their breath to protest. "You both take orders from me!" his uncle snapped angrily. Then: "Come here." He hugged Tadek, the rows of bullets hard against Tadek's chest, Tadek realizing he was now almost as tall as his uncle. "Tell your mother—and Helena—that I love them. Now go!"

"Come on," Hipolit said tersely. Machine guns were rattling away, still distant. Kazimierz ran toward one edge of the shallow depression that held the camp, shouting orders. Hipolit led the way to the horses where he fastened a bridle and put the bit in the fretful, pacing horse's mouth. He threw on a blanket and a saddle and cinched it tight. More gunfire in the distance. Hipolit leaped on the horse, followed by Tadek. Just as they were climbing the ridge out of the camp, an explosion blasted on the far edge of the camp. The horse reared and danced but Tadek held on and then they were galloping away from the camp just as a chaos of shooting and explosions ripped through the air behind them. Hipolit swore but they continued on unimpeded, reaching the edge of the swamp where the horse picked its way carefully, a different route than the men had used before. For a while they rode in silence through the mixed pine and oak. At one point Hipolit slowed his horse to a walk and veered off into thicker underbrush, pointing with his hand. Maybe a hundred meters away, a line of clay-clad Russian soldiers was advancing through the woods toward the camp, their guns at ready. Hipolit kept his horse pacing straight ahead through the brush. At the river Tadek slid off the horse. "You aren't going back there, are you?"

Hipolit looked at him with the contempt of the soldier for the civilian.

"Of course!" Without a word more, he urged his horse around and back into the woods.

Tadek found his boat. Just as he began tugging it off shore into the water, he heard the throbbing, thrumming sound of a boat's motor coming from upstream. He pulled the rowboat as far back behind the rocks as he could before he saw the lean, wolf-gray prow of a Soviet patrol-boat emerging from around the bend, turning toward him. A machine-gun at its bow lit up and sprayed the water in front of him. Tadek dashed back into the woods and kept running. He could hear the machine gun bullets ripping through the trees on either side of him. Some came so close to his head that he could hear little popping noises as they passed by.

Safely hidden again by the forest, he made his way downstream for what seemed like a long time, trying to stay just within sight of the river so as not to get lost. The boat was gone, either upstream or waiting for him, but silent anyway. The going was difficult, marshy, reedy, tangled now and again with briars. He heard the thump, thump, thump of cannon and mortar fire in the distance, sounds he recognized from the invasions of his childhood. After a while, when the sounds were muffled and more infrequent, he found a spot underneath a low-branching tree where he could sit and catch his breath. He had a view from here of a slice of the river. He could feel the throbbing of the boats' engines through the ground before he could quite hear it. He watched as the gray, wolfish patrol boat passed with sluggish patience, its engines throbbing, throbbing. The sound of the engines faded downstream, and then began to grow again when the boat returned, menacing and methodical in its search. He could hear the voices of the crewmembers as he watched an officer, a blue-tabbed NKVD, scanning with binoculars across the patch of forest where Tadek sat hidden.

He was on the move all day, dodging under the many hemlocks and then, when brambles grew thick, moving inland and jogging under a high canopy of pines, still loosely following the river. The artillery that had once pounded the day was now silent, and that silence grew like a tense, swelling bubble to fill the rest of the day. He could hear the boat returning several times, prowling up and down the river. It began to rain. At dusk, having not heard the boat for a time, Tadek made his way down to the river. A fog had filled the river, seeping into the woods, and a slow drizzle maintained. He could not return to where his boat had been. He was certain it was gone or destroyed. He took off his shoes, pants, and shirt and, with the laces and his belt, attempted to make a bundle and fasten it to his shoulders. Amid some reeds, he eased himself into the water up to his waist and then up to his chest. He stood still, watching the water swirl ceaselessly past him. Around the reeds came a swan, two swans, followed by two gray cygnets, all coasting silently toward him at an angle, just a few meters away, oblivious and intact in their serene beauty.

The lead swan somehow sensed him and turned toward him, recoiled, hissing at him, and the others flapped away, startled, to give him a wide berth. Safely away, they settled back into their peaceful line and disappeared into the fog, swept along by the current.

He slipped into the twilight-colored water and began to swim across. His clothes around his neck dragged him down, but at least his legs and arms were free, and soon he felt the powerful midstream current pulling him rapidly downstream. He fought his way through it at an angle to where the current weakened close to the other bank. Finally he glimpsed a small felled tree lying half in the water and pulled hard for it, catching onto a limb and pulling himself, hand over hand, onto shore, where he lay on the muddy bank and must have passed out for a while before coming to and forcing himself to rise and to wring out his clothes, which were only half-soaked. He put them on wet and stumbled inland through the underbrush. He found a fisherman's path paralleling the river and his progress improved. After half an hour, he came into a small clearing with a hut. A kerosene lantern lit one window. He went to knock on the door. A small bearded old man, wearing a leather vest, swung open the door and peered suspiciously out at him under eye brows so long they looked like wings. "My boat capsized," Tadek pleaded. "I almost drowned."

"Hm," the man said, and swung back the door by way of invitation. The cottage smelled thickly of wood fire and fried fat. The man gave Tadek a blanket and hung out his clothes to dry over a rail by the fire. Tadek sat on a chair with its back broken off of it and pulled up to a rough wooden table, wrapping a small rug wrapped around himself. He remembered the old lady who had dried his clothes after he'd fallen in the frozen river and he thought, everything in life must happen twice. If you live long enough. The man gave Tadek a bowl of *kasha* and a slice of pork fat. He sat across from Tadek in the flickering light, peeling an apple with a stubby knife. The man spoke Polish well, but Tadek judged him to have a Lithuanian accent. Tadek was unsure how this would affect his attitude to the Polish partisans. After a time, the man said, "I heard gunfire across the river."

"I heard something too."

"Hm." He went over to the fire where he poked at the coals while eating his apple. "You should be more careful in your boat."

"Yes."

The man peered at him, bit into the apple again, wiped his mouth on his shirtsleeve.

"I know who you're with."

"What? What do you mean?"

"Don't think I'm stupid, kid." He poked at the fire as if getting the winking coals just right. "It's all right with me."

Tadek didn't say anything, but wondered if that was an admission of sorts and was about to insist on his capsized boat again when the man burst out, "I was in the Czar's army! I was in the Polish army! I'm an old man! I just want to fish until I die! Then I'll have them throw me in the river and the fish can eat me for a change!"

"All right."

"All right? All right? Hm." He poked at the fire again with ferocious concentration. "Did the Russians destroy the partisans?"

"I don't know."

"Where you from? Shabany?"

"No. Liaski." Tadek didn't know why he told the truth.

"Well, well. Listen, the Russians are bastards, that's true. But the partisans will never win."

"They *will* win."

The man gave Tadek a sharp look under his wing-like brows and smiled slightly to himself. "So, you hope so. You hope so. Maybe your grandchildren will live free. But this land soaks up blood like a sponge and it isn't full yet. Do you want your blood to add to the mess?" He stood abruptly. "Well anyway," he gestured to the floor to the side of the fireplace, "you can lie down over there! I'm sleeping." The man pulled a ladder away from the wall and leaned it against a loft. Precariously, slowly, miraculously, he climbed up the ladder, which was made of mismatched boards and split half-logs, up to the loft where, with a loud groan, he grabbed an overhead timber and swung himself like an arthritic acrobat into the dark. Tadek made so bold as to put another log on the fireplace and, wrapping the carpet around him, curled up on the floor.

Next morning the old man gave Tadek a cup of bitter tea before sending him on his way. Tadek tried to stick to back roads and wasn't stopped by Russians along the way—he didn't even see any. Most of them were on the other side of the river, he figured. He gave Shabany a wide berth. When he let himself into the front gate and walked up the little rise under the grape arbor, the sun was already lowering, shooting its setting rays through the sides of the arbor and the leaves of the apple trees beyond. His mother wasn't there. He figured she must be out looking for him. He fell onto his cot and slept.

Chapter 30: Arrest

Tadek awoke in a panic, gasping and lifting himself on his elbows. But he had no memory of a nightmare. And it was so quiet. Still dark. He got up and took a drink of water from the bucket in the kitchen, drinking directly from the dipper, a liberty he'd never take with his mother around. "Mama?" he called, and went to look in her bedroom. She still wasn't there. The bed was neatly made.

He wanted to go looking for her, but it was too early yet, and he was so exhausted that he lay down for a moment and dozed.

Again he awoke. The first light of dawn had come. But the light hadn't awakened him. He'd heard something. A tentative bird trilled. Yet it was something else he'd heard. Or dreamt that he had.

There it was again. A light clink of metal. The scuffing of feet. Whispers.

Before he was well awake, there was a crash at the door and the pounding of many feet on the floor as men rushed into the house. He leaped out of bed and sprang into the kitchen. Russian soldiers filled the room, their clay-green khaki, their guns, their barking Russian voices; they bumped against walls, tables, each other, and more men poured in. It seemed they would burst the walls. What were they trying to prove? They surrounded him. Gun barrels prodded his ribs, shoved him first one way, then another. Baffled, dazed, he didn't even try to answer the questions they were shouting at him in Russian.

An officer entered the room and silenced them with a few words. It was Major Rostov. He looked Tadek over, then spoke a few quiet words, and all the soldiers but a few filed out of the house. In his precise, Russian-accented Polish, Rostov told Tadek to get dressed. Then, in Russian, he ordered a soldier to make them coffee.

The major was awaiting Tadek in the front room of the house, sitting much at his ease. He waved a hand, inviting Tadek to sit opposite him, where a cup of the awful phony coffee awaited.

"Drink your coffee, Tadeusz," he said. "You're going to need to be awake."

"What's going on?"

"I think you know very well." He was quite cordial. He was as Tadek remembered him from their previous encounter, with short grizzled hair on his narrow head and a thin, handsome face that seemed more focused than worried. "Sit down. We'll have a pleasant talk." A soldier stood at the door looking at Tadek with venom in his eyes.

Major Rostov stood up and walked about the front room, a spare but clean room with lace on the windows and a credenza from Zygmunt's epoch, with a few pieces of glass and crystal. There were a few books on a shelf and the major removed one. Tadek recognized it.

"Piłsudski," the major said. The book was a biography of the Polish military hero. "Are you an admirer?" the major asked.

"Everyone is," Tadek said, finally picking up his coffee and gulping half the cup down. Some Poles criticized Piłsudski for his coup d'etat of '26, but Tadek had always heard everyone agree that if he'd been alive when the Germans had invaded, he could have at least bloodied their nose.

"In certain circles," the major said, thumbing through the book, stopping now and again to scan a passage, nodding his head as if his expectations were being confirmed. He lowered the book and turned to look at Tadek. "I remember you. The bike rider. Always on his red bike, pedaling, pedaling, pedaling, going somewhere. Somewhere more important than you let on, I suspect? You've been busy, haven't you?"

"Not especially."

"Yes, especially. The captain told me you've been around for years. The captain, my colleague, whose body we put on a train two days ago. He'd said he'd seen you. We'd talked about you. Always on your bike, riding, riding, riding. Always on the go."

Tadek shrugged.

"How old are you now?"

"Seventeen. Where is my mother?"

"She has been arrested, Tadeusz, for aiding the terrorists. You probably know something about that, don't you?"

"No. Can I see her?"

"No, Tadeusz, you can't. As I said, she has been arrested. I don't know what will happen to her now. The district troika will deal with her in an appropriate manner."

"I can't see her?"

"No. I understand your father is in the system as well, is that right?"

"I don't know where my father is. No one will say."

"Well, many people are in your position now. You have no reason to feel special."

"I need to see my mother."

"We've been through this, Tadeusz. I've told you the situation already. You Poles are stubborn, aren't you?"

"This is our land. You people are just bandits."

"Ah-ha. It comes out." The major smiled. He had a nice smile, full of white, even teeth, a gentle, disappointed smile. "Now we're making progress."

He still held the book in his hands, which he now silently closed. He took a few steps to replace it carefully in the bookcase.

"Piłsudski. He had a good military mind. He knew when to retreat, when to regroup. When to wait. We Russians, we retreated and he thought he'd defeated us. But we were merely regrouping for a few decades. Now it's our time to advance. Perhaps it's time for you to retreat, Tadeusz. Your side has lost. You can get away from here, start a new life. The Soviet Union is a huge country, Tadeusz. It's a whole universe east of here, where we're building a new society, based on new principles. It's an exciting time. We can take you away from this little town. We can send you to the best schools. In Moscow or Leningrad. Whatever you want. We are always looking for talented people. You just need to give us a little cooperation."

He paused, giving Tadek a chance to speak. Tadek, having recovered from his comment about bandits, looked steadily at the major with a slight smile on his face and his eyes vacant, allowing no rancor or rebellion to enter them. His mouth was open a bit and he knew this made him look a bit foolish and that was how he wanted to look, as if he had no idea what the major was talking about. "No? No?" the major continued. "Ah, I can see you're playing a little game, Tadeusz. Now I see you very clearly. But you don't see what position you're in. You're making a grand strategic error, Tadeusz. Not for your side. That doesn't matter anymore. History has taken that out of everyone's hands. But for yourself. For your own life. It's time to think about your own life. Just tell us everything you know."

"I don't know anything. Just what everyone else knows."

The major breathed out slowly through his nostrils and,

closing his eyes as if in pain, pinched the bridge of his nose. When he removed his hand, he gave Tadek a long look. His blue eyes had gone gray, and now they took in Tadek with a neutral gaze as if he was something that had fallen to the floor that he wasn't going to pick up.

"Comrade Bezuhov!" he called into the other room, and a junior officer entered from the kitchen where he'd been waiting. "Arrest this terrorist and take him into Grodno headquarters for interrogation."

The soldier roughly pulled Tadek's hands together behind his back, wrapped a leather strap tightly about his wrists, and pushed him out the door, down beneath the grape arbor and to the street. Here a lorry waited and soldiers stood around smoking cigarettes, turning their faces to the fresh sun. The soldier prodded Tadek to jump into the lorry bed, which was roofed with canvas, but with his hands behind his back, he had to roll onto the bed. There were two guards and four prisoners, also with hands strapped behind their backs, already in the back of the lorry. Two of the prisoners were strangers, farmers, Tadek thought, but two of them he recognized from his uncle's camp. In the forest these men had had a corsair-like gallantry with carbines on their shoulders, bandoliers across their chests, and lean faces with no-nonsense eyes. Now they just looked like miserable peasants, unshaven, with bad teeth. They looked at Tadek. Recognition lit their eyes, and they both looked away to protect both him and themselves. All the same, Tadek was elated to see someone alive from the camp. The presence of the guards on a bench at one end of the lorry stifled conversation. One of them undid one of the straps and fastened Tadek to the rail of the bench.

Tadek spent the day in a separate cell in the basement of the police station in Grodno. There was a straw-stuffed mattress on the floor and a bucket for a toilet in the corner. He paced all day, his mind racing. He hit the walls and paced some more. Time died and there were only the four walls and his racing mind. He was brought nothing to eat. Finally he guessed it must be night by his hunger and fatigue, and he lay down and tried to sleep.

It seemed as soon as he started falling asleep, he was awakened, and two guards jerked him up onto his feet and led him down a corridor into a plain windowless room with three wooden chairs and a plain metal table. They strapped his hands behind his back, through the back of one of the chairs. After a while he fell asleep in the chair.

It seemed very late at night, or maybe early in the morning, when he was awakened by the major flanked by two privates. The major repeated his offer of the previous day of a fresh start in Moscow, if only he would cooperate. Tadek was too tired to feign ignorance or innocence at this point and said, "I will cooperate when you give us back our land and get out of our country!"

A slight smile twitched at the corners of the major's mouth. He shrugged, as if such obtuseness was beyond him. "I'm sorry to hear you insist on that ridiculous stance. You could have had a productive life. None of you Poles know when to quit."

It seemed that Tadek's urbane colloquies with Major Rostov had ended. The major stepped into the hallway and called out, "Private! Fetch Corporal Smerdyakov."

"Yes, comrade major. Smerdyakov!" he called down the corridor.

In a few minutes a very large man entered the room. In truth he looked fat and out of shape to Tadek, unimpressive except for his size. The man had a large, shapeless, mild face, like a giant potato with eyes. Rostov gave Tadek a final look. His long, subtle face lost its neutrality and seemed for a moment genuinely sad, then resigned, then contemptuous. He shrugged and turned his back on Tadek and left him with Corporal Smerdyakov. Smerdyakov closed the door gently behind the major, the tips of his huge fingers sensitively touching the doorknob.

Tadek studied the corporal further. His large head was completely bald and he had several chins. That's what gave Tadek the impression of a potato. He smiled at Tadek with a mouthful of small, gapped teeth. He leaned his face down uncomfortably close to Tadek's, as if inspecting him. Tadek could count the gray and black bristles on his poorly shaven cheek. The smile, the small, gray eyes, the pores on the man's nose, the smell of stale sweat—all these small things made Tadek realize how wrong he'd been about the man and his mild face.

With a slow, steady, almost friendly hand on Tadek's shoulder, Smerdyakov sent his chair toppling backward. Tadek hit his head on the concrete floor. The man casually walked to the side of Tadek before falling with both knees onto his chest. The air rushed from Tadek's lungs and he gasped to fill them. The weight on his chest was huge. Smerdyakov grasped Tadek by the hair with both hands and started pounding his head against the floor. After this must have became monotonous to him, he got off of Tadek and lifted the chair back to an upright position. He leaned down and punched Tadek in the stomach. Then on the side of his head.

After twenty minutes of this treatment, the door opened. The major entered the room and looked at Tadek carefully. "Now, Tadeusz, is there anything more that you can recall about your work with the partisans?"

"I don't know anything."

"You're sure of that?"

"Yes, of course."

"I'm sorry to hear that, Tadeusz. Tell the corporal if you change your mind." The major nodded to the corporal to continue. Again he tipped back Tadek's chair and sent it falling to the floor, fell with his knees onto Tadek's chest, grabbed his head in both hands, almost tenderly, one on either side, and began pounding his head with measured but increasing violence against the concrete floor.

After the first blazing, black and silver shockwaves crashed through Tadek's head, it was as though the man was pounding Tadek further and further into himself, and as if with each bang of his head Tadek's entire self—his memories and emotions and desires—was being compressed into a pea-sized self in the center of his brain, and that center knew beyond anything else that he would die in this room before he told these people anything. Bang, bang, bang went his head against the floor. It was no use to struggle against the man's huge hands. The pounding grew harder and harder. It stopped, and Smerdyakov pried up the chair from the floor, went to wipe his face with a towel, and returned to slug Tadek in the stomach again, then in the face, stepping back afterwards to appraise Tadek the way a painter steps back from a canvas.

* * *

Tadek woke up on the floor of the small room where he'd spent yesterday. What must've been yesterday. A single lightbulb burned above him. He was lying on the thin, straw-stuffed mattress. His head felt like an egg that had been cracked but had not yet fallen asunder, held together by a thin, inner integument. He closed his eyes and lay there a long time. The bare bulb hanging from the ceiling stabbed at his eyes. Some time later—he couldn't guess if it was day or night now—he heard footsteps up and down the hallway outside. He felt too sick to stand up to try to see through a crack in the barred portal at the top of the metal door. The steps faded away, and he heard a door slam and some moaning ensue.

The steps returned, accompanied by the shuffling of another set of feet. This time someone was asking in Polish-accented Russian: "Where are you taking me? Where are you taking me?" Tadek could hear every word quite distinctly.

"Shut up."

"Where are you taking me? Tell me! Where are you taking me?"

"To a pleasant place," came the bored reply. There was a brief silence as the prisoner must have been ruminating this answer, but before he could respond, there came one sharp shot followed by a muffled fall.

Russian voices began a mild, peeved argument. Tadek could smell the acrid scent of gunsmoke seeping under the door. There came vague sounds of several people moving around the hallway, a heavy clomping of steps, then silence. Later, someone with a mop was whistling to himself while he sloshed water back and forth down the hallway. Tadek's grandfather had always told him that whistling indoors invited the devil inside, and now he couldn't help but feel the devil's presence and crossed himself.

It seemed as if he might have closed his eyes for a few moments of sleep before the door was abruptly opened and two soldiers were hauling him to his feet. He tried to walk as they dragged him, one on either side, down the still-damp hallway and around several corners, down a few concrete steps and back into the room where Corporal Smerdyakov and another soldier were waiting for him on either side of a chair. "Sit down," Smerdyakov said. When Tadek did so, the other soldier roughly removed Tadek's shirt and began taping Tadek's arms to the arms of the chair. Smerdyakov watched the procedure while lighting a cigarette. Without even asking whether Tadek had reformed and was ready to give up any helpful information, Smerdyakov touched the coal of the cigarette lightly to the back of Tadek's hand.

The three-man troika was seated behind a wooden table set up in the center of a large room, bare except for a few rows of wooden chairs and large portraits of Lenin and Stalin on the far wall. Large windows lined one wall, and through them Tadek could see the green leaves of an oak tree almost brushing the glass. They must've been on the second floor. Tadek was too confused to remember how he'd gotten there. He walked with difficulty, since on the second day of his torture they'd ended by beating the bottom of his feet with clubs. On the third day, Smerdyakov had hit him so hard in the side of the jaw that one of his side teeth had spurted out in a fountain of blood. There were tracks of cigarette burns up and down his arms. But he had told them nothing, and finally they'd given up on him. For a week he'd been abandoned in his room with no medical care, but had still recovered just enough to stand and move when they came for him that morning.

From a half-open window, the sounds of children's voices drifted in.

Soldiers on either side of Tadek held his upper arms in an iron clench, and they half-carried him to a spot facing the three men, who were deliberating among themselves, ignoring Tadek for a few minutes, alternately nodding and shaking their heads, exchanging sheets of paper.

They eventually looked up at Tadek. On one side was Major Rostov, with his suave, urbane face. When he looked at Tadek, his look said that friendliness, irony, disappointment, and sadness were all now purged away: his look was brief and hard, a look that told Tadek he'd had his chance and now he meant nothing to the major.

In the center was another NKVD officer, with a gray crewcut

and wire-rimmed glasses. He looked at Tadek with red, sodden, dissolute eyes, and seemed preoccupied with something else, some private wrong or inconvenience. On the other side was a corpulent man in a navy blue suit, shiny at the elbows. He had a large mole on one side of his nose and was gazing at Tadek devoid of curiosity, puffing out his cheeks in a meaningless, bored manner. The three men consulted again briefly. Tadek heard the man in the blue suit speak Russian with a Polish accent, a traitor in Tadek's estimation. After their final discussion, the men nodded in unison and turned toward Tadek.

"Tadeusz Gradinski," read the major in a colorless voice. "Twenty-five years hard labor." Only then did he glance again at Tadek with mild curiosity. The crewcutted officer stamped a paper. "Next."

The two soldiers came and gripped Tadek's upper arms again and led him off. As he shuffled down the hallway, stunned and unable to fully comprehend what had just happened, he heard for the next prisoner, a similar quick verdict: "Twenty-five, no correspondence."

PART V:
THE GULAG

THE GULAG

U.S.S.R.

Camp 3

IRKUTSK

Camp 1

OMSK

MT. YAMANTAU

Camp 5

VORKUTA

Camp 2

Caspian Sea

LENINGRAD

Camp 4

MOSCOW

Grodno

Black Sea

Map Drawing: Elliott Grinnell

Chapter 31: On the Train

At dawn two days later Tadek stood in line with about twenty other men and two women to be put on the train in Grodno. The guards guided them ungently with their rifle butts and terse commands, telling them repeatedly, no talking. They stood in the cinders along the tracks. A light mist rose from the Niemen and mixed its odor with coalsmoke from a solitary engine down the tracks. Birds sang their territorial dawn songs in a few trees across from the station. Tadek was so exhausted that he stayed on his feet with difficulty as the line of prisoners was moved from one track to another. They weren't allowed to sit down. Tadek recognized only the two men who had been in the back of the lorry with him. He heard two other men talking before they were silenced by the guards, and he understood that they thought a terrible mistake had been made. Tadek knew very well that no mistake had been made in his case.

They waited a long time. The mist burned off and the dawn birds ceased their singing. It was almost noon when a train of six cattle cars pulled into the station and stopped. Nothing happened for a long time. Tadek felt his impatience and anger crest within him like a wave, and he writhed where he stood, fighting the impulse to run away down the tracks until the guards shot him and he was done with it all, but the wave broke and he let the emotions wash away. The soles of his feet still ached, but in derisory compensation, he could now amuse himself by feeling with his tongue the gap in the side of his mouth where he'd lost a tooth. His shirt material stuck to the open sores of his burns and ripped them open every time he moved. Nevertheless, after a time he seemed to sleep even while he stood waiting in the sun. One man fainted and a guard went to prod him with his foot, but the prisoner refused to stand up. A group of guards stood discussing what to do with the collapsed prisoner, coming to no determination. They ordered the prisoners to kneel in the gravel before opening the doors of the cars, revealing that they were already full of men, who stared out at the new prisoners with listless eyes. Everyone waited some more. Finally the guards separated the Grodno prisoners, scattering them among the six cars.

The men in the car were strangers. It was not, after all, completely full, but had only looked so as men had crowded to the doorway for fresh air to dilute the permeating, wretched odor from the open bucket latrine in a corner. Tadek found a place to sit against a wall. No one spoke to him.

The train sat a long time, heating up in the sun. Several more groups of prisoners were led out into the sun and dispersed throughout the cars. Finally Tadek heard a chain reaction of jolts before the motion reached their car, jerking it forward and backward several times before the car settled into a regular forward motion.

Tadek stuck his eye to a crack between the boards and watched as the train went along the river through Grodno and then out into the countryside. He remembered the Jews that he had seen crowded into cattle cars on these same tracks and how he had stood tossing a football in one hand while his friends mimed the slitting of throats. Now it was his turn.

Though he was a negligent Catholic, still he closed his eyes and began to say ten Hail Marys, and he hoped that this act of penitence might mitigate his sins, but before he was done a fight broke out between two men next to him, so he broke off during the third Hail Mary.

He turned his back on the fight. The tracks were curving toward Liaski. He stood and found again a gap in the boards through which he could peer. His eyes craved the sight of Liaski, as if they could squeeze the memories out of those places and into him for his journey into the Gulag. They were passing a low wall of trees. The tracks turned away from the Grodno road to slice through the eastern part of the village, headed northward, before they turned east. Peering above the low trees, he saw the roofs of Liaski come into view, some thatched, some tin, some tiled. He thought that he could see the roof of his house from the tracks. At least he could make out the tops of the apple trees. He wondered who would take care of the bees. In the distance, perhaps that was the roof of Halinka's house, or at least the row of houses where she lived. The train did not stop at the small Liaski station but rocked on through and even seemed to gather speed as if intent on leaving Tadek's childhood behind. He slumped back down to the floor of the car.

The men around him were talking of how there was a region-wide crackdown, not only on the partisans, but Poles in general. They spoke of how the NKVD had names in their town to arrest. When they ran out of names before their quota was filled, they arrested people on the streets. No one knew where the train was headed. After a while, the men all tired of talking and gave themselves up to the rhythm of the train, the wheels grinding the desire to talk out of the prisoners as the sun heated the car. It seemed to grow hotter even as the sun began to sink.

For no apparent reason, the train began a rapid deceleration and then stopped. Tadek had been dozing and woke to peer through the crack between boards and see that they were in the middle of a forest. He watched idly as two men got off to empty their car's latrine, but was surprised to notice that two different men got back on. He heard one calling his name in a low, grating, familiar voice.

"Over here."

The two men pushed through the car to sit next to him. In the lead was Kozel, followed by a large, knobby-shouldered, silent man, both with puffy, bruised faces from their NKVD beatings. Kozel inspected Tadek's face and grinned his crooked-tooth grin, seeing Tadek's similarly bruised face. "They worked you over, too, huh?" The other man was smiling too, as if they'd pulled some clever prank and just been scolded.

"Yeah." Tadek gingerly touched his fingertips to his face, still tender from the beatings. When in his cell he'd first touched the back of his head, it had felt soft like a baby's skull, and he'd quickly withdrawn his fingers. He hadn't touched it since, and didn't now.

"What'd they do to you?"

"Beat my head against the concrete. Burned me with cigarettes. Punched me in the stomach till I vomited. Beat the soles of my feet with sticks."

"Ha!" Kozel seemed amused. This was all good fun. "They took it easy on you because you're a kid! They started to roast me in a fireplace! They did everything but stick an apple in my mouth! Then they strapped me to a slanted table and poured water over my face instead. It makes you think that you are drowning." Kozel laughed again, but it was a bitter laugh, and Tadek could see the hatred in his eyes: he wanted someone to pay for what they'd done to him. If it took years, he would make someone pay.

Kozel told him about the Russians over-running the partisan camp. "We were returning from a foraging party, and found ourselves walking along with them, the Russians, headed for the camp." Kozel leaned too close to Tadek, his sour breath warm on Tadek's face, and told his story in a gravelly whisper. "We stumbled upon each other. We shot a couple of them. I saw them fall. But then they all turned on us and we had to run. They picked us up the next day in Gombachy trying to pass as civilians."

"And Kazimierz?"

"Kowal? It looked bad for him and everyone in the camp. There were just too many Russians. Our people were surrounded."

Tadek felt gutshot. For a moment he couldn't breathe. Kozel didn't seem to notice and went on. "The shooting went on a for a long time. They had mortars, raining down. Maybe some were arrested and taken prisoner but I doubt . . . . "

"Do you know how my mother was arrested?"

"I didn't know. I don't know anything about that. I heard that in Grodno they had lists of names of people they were rounding up and taking away."

"Who are these people?'

So began a discussion with the surrounding prisoners. Some of them, Kozel said, would be good partisans. Others, the politicians and the artists and the intellectuals, were no good to anyone. They would never survive. Others were just thieves and snitches. "That's how they do it. They like the mixture. So be careful. You'll be with other nationalities too. Ukrainians, Kazakhs, Jews, Chechens, the lot. And Russian soldiers who were POWs. You have to figure out which will cooperate with you. We can't fight against them all."

Kozel and the other partisan moved away and got into an argument with some prisoners about room to lie down. The train sat in the forest through the night.

It was dusk the next day when the train stopped again, outside Minsk. The boxcar full of prisoners was given a few pailfuls of water, which they crowded around, pressing, grabbing, spilling. A ladle finally reached Tadek, and he got a few mouthfuls before it was snatched away. A few loaves of bread were torn into pieces and passed around. Two men and a woman were loaded on board. The woman stood framed in the doorway of the car, then stumbled into the darkness, her eyes adjusting, and she somehow caught sight of Tadek. Perhaps because he was her age and less threatening than the others, she came to sit next to him.

"I'm afraid," she said.

He didn't say anything, just stared at her.

"I need someone to protect me." Her voice had a pleading note to it. He wanted to tell her it would all be all right, but he had no confidence in that. But anyway he said, to say something, "It will be all right."

"Can I stay next to you?" she asked. "I'm scared."

"All right."

"I need your help. Please."

"Yes, of course."

"There are men following me. Those men who got on the train with me. They're going to do something bad."

"Don't be silly," he said.

"No. I know it. The guards said there wasn't a woman's car on this train and I had to take my chances. They laughed."

"It will be all right," he said again, less sure even than before.

They leaned shoulder to shoulder with their backs against the side of the car, which started up again, swaying and rocking. Tadek realized after a while that he felt another motion—this girl crying into her hands, at first a slight shaking, finally breaking into sobs and moans. He patted her hand and didn't say anything. After a while she slept, though the rocking of the car, the stench of the latrine, and the moans and curses of the people made it almost impossible for Tadek to sleep, even into the night as the train continued its monotonous motion. There was a gap between two boards where cool night air kept feathering through, relieving the stench somewhat. Moonlight crept in from a barred window at the front of the car. The girl was breathing regularly, and he felt her warmth against his shoulder. He thought of Halinka. What was she doing now? What did she know? Did she think he was dead? He would somehow get out of prison and find his way back to Liaski and marry Halinka as he had promised. He thought of that last time they had lain together, her breasts, her mouth, her breath on his cheek.

Tadek must have dozed, because he awoke when the girl screamed, and he felt her fingers clinging to his shirt as she was pulled away. "Here you are!" someone said. Tadek rolled over and a man hit him in the face, pushed him down with a foot on his chest, and said, "If you make a squeak we'll kill you." He heard other men pulling the girl away, telling her to shut up as she called out.

Tadek stood up and followed. Then he thought and called, "Partisans! Criminals are raping someone! Help!"

"Shut up!" someone said.

"Tadeusz?" He recognized the voice of Kozel.

"Over here!"

Kozel was there with his large friend and another man. "Tadek?"

"Yes."

"Here." Kozel slid a rock into Tadek's hand. The four men followed the girl's calls and her attackers' curses through the pathway that had silently formed for them. She had been thrown on her back in a corner of the car. Three men huddled over her. Without any hesitation Kozel threw himself on one of the men, pounding a rock on his skull with a thick, nauseating sound. The other attackers backed away in the face of Kozel and his friends, and Kozel put a pocketknife to the throat of the man who had already knelt between the girl's knees with a hand over her mouth. He pulled the man away and threw him aside. "Stay away from her or you'll all die!"

Holding their heads and protesting innocence, the three attackers made their way to the opposite corner of the car.

The girl sat up, dazed, and pulled down her skirt and blouse, which had been pushed up. When Tadek knelt beside her, she hid her face in his shoulder. "Thank you," she said in a voice just above a breath.

"You're welcome!" Kozel said gruffly, and nodded to her. He stayed by their side as they all three crouched against the wall. The rest of the car had already turned over and gone back to sleep, but Kozel's friends stayed near.

"Thanks, Kozel," Tadek said. Kozel leaned his face in close to Tadek's and whispered roughly, "You're welcome, Tadeusz. And take the lesson that's here. We need to stick together. Mostly they tried to split us up, but you and I and a few more have been thrown together. We both served Kowal, the captain. You did good work for him and Poland, and so did I. And when we get out of here, we will discover who betrayed us, track them down, and kill them."

"Betrayed us?"

"Of course!" Kozel leaned his face in again toward Tadek and said with sudden intensity, "How do you think the Russians knew where our camp was? The birds told them? They weren't hunting through those woods for us. They lobbed shells down on us like kids throwing snowballs into a rain barrel. They knew exactly where we were."

* * *

At dawn the train stopped. A guard called names and a few men were unloaded. Tadek and the girl moved to a spot with some straw on the floor, further away from the latrine. All day they sat wordless in their corner on the straw, and she rested her head on his shoulder. Tadek wondered whether Halinka would blame him. It was just that the girl's aching need touched him so that he couldn't turn her away. Yet while she rested her head on his shoulder he thought of Halinka. He and the girl hardly spoke at all for another day. At night they lay on the straw next to each other, and he felt her pressing against his back, felt the needy fear in that pressure.

At one stop that day, Kozel's name and several others were called and they left the car, Kozel tossing over his shoulder, "Remember, Tadeusz. We have work to do ahead! Don't trust anyone!" before the guard pulled him roughly down from the doorway. Tadek saw that the girls' attackers had also been pulled off the train.

A pattern established itself over the next few days of a flowing, timeless period, a rocking ride, followed by static periods in which time hit a wall and could no longer move. It was easy to lose track of time altogether. The train rumbled on. During the day the heat in the car grew unbearable. When the train would stop sometimes at night, for inexplicable hours, surrounded by forest, the mosquitoes would find their way through the gaps between the boards and feast on the human cargo. The fetid bucket for defecation in the corner of the car seemed to grow more powerful in its stench by the hour. Only once a day was it emptied and a little food was shoved into the car, and the bucket of water was passed around.

From another corner of the car, with a sort of horror, Tadek heard the shuffling, panting, gasping, tormenting, and tormented sounds of sex. He sat up.

"Are you asleep?" the girl asked. She sat up next to him.

"Who can sleep in this hell?" he said.

"Not me."

"Where are you from?" he asked her.

"Wilno, originally. My name is Jania. Thank you for saving me."

"I helped a bit. But it was my friends who saved you. What did you do in Wilno?"

"I studied the violin." She gave a laugh.

"Were you good?"

"Very. My father thought it would be my career. What did they arrest you for?"

"Aiding the *lesni ludzie*. You?"

"My father had a Polish newspaper in Wilno in '39. When the Russians first came in, it wasn't very safe for Poles anymore there, so we fled to Grodno. Of course I was just a kid. Then after the war we tried to go back. It was just him and me after my mother died. But the Soviets didn't want us back in Wilno. We were arrested, and they transported us to Minsk, for some reason. No one would tell us why. I guess to keep an eye on him. They made him work as a janitor. He made me keep playing the violin, no matter how ridiculous it was. Now this new crackdown. They took him away two weeks ago, and then came after me. I don't know…"

The couple on the other side of the car were going at it again, their breaths rapid and painful. Someone shouted at them. There were curses.

"I was going to be a violinist," Jania said. She told him about her part in a Beethoven string quartet that she'd been working on in the week before her arrest. "The late quartets are so difficult," she said. "But so rewarding."

"Yes?"

"And you? What about you?" What about him? The job in the textile mill? The trips on his bike with the messages and packages?

Tadek told her about Halinka, that they were planning on marriage.

"Is she beautiful?"

"Yes. Very."

"I can hear it in your voice." She told him about her boyfriend, a tenor singer, the best in Minsk. He used to sing Schubert songs. She laughed as she told him. A tenor! Schubert!

In the dawn they could peer together through a crack in the boards and see mountains in the distance: the Urals. They were beautiful with the sun painting the clouds above them from underneath, striping the trainful of zeks making its way east. The clouds were like the quilted, salmon-pink lining of a plush jewelry box.

That morning as they talked, Tadek could not help but realize that despite the dreadful rags she wore, the dirty red scarf tied on her head, she was a breath-catching beauty. Her eyes were large and gleaming, the angles of her face came to a precise rounding of her chin, and her nose was narrow with a slight exquisite curve of the nostrils. She was slender, skinny now from poor diet, but even under the shapeless garments, he could see that she was shapely. All of this the three men who had assaulted her had noticed as well. It was true what she had said: she would need protection. Her beauty was no gift here. How could she survive in the camp on her own? What did the authorities expect to gain by sending her into the Gulag? But as Tadek mulled these questions, he knew the answer. The pointlessness of the punishment was the point: they could do whatever they wanted with you or anyone for whatever reason they cared to invent.

They slowly climbed the Urals and then rushed recklessly down them and were in Siberia, crawling like a stubborn bug across its vast surface.

Chapter 32: Beyond Omsk

The train traveled through vast swamps on what turned out to be the final leg of their journey, over two weeks after they had begun, at least half of that time spent sitting motionless. The last city Tadek had heard mentioned was Omsk, which they had crawled through late at night—nothing but silhouettes of buildings against the stars and the faintest gleam of a river. That was two days earlier. At last the train rocked through the open gates of a work camp. The prisoners had quieted and stood with their eyes pressed to the cracks between the boards. Tadek could see that the perimeter wire stretched along a series of three-meter high poles with crossbars like crucifixes, where the wires formed a horizontal barrier, extending as far as Tadek could see, punctuated by watchtowers—primitive huts atop straddling legs. The wire wasn't necessary. Where would anyone run? It was all a vast wasteland, with nothing more than some knee-high cranberry bushes to hide behind, and all that eternal swampland to slog through.

The prisoners could hear the concatenation of cars jerking to a halt down the line, coming towards them before their own car jerked to a halt. Then came the waiting.

Finally came the sliding crash of doors opening and the

shouts of guards ordering all the prisoners out. "Keep this for me," Jania said, handing him a handkerchief tied into a bundle. "Some sentimental things. Help me if you can."

"I will. Good luck."

Their legs were stiff and deadened from inaction. They all tumbled out of the car, some people collapsing immediately onto their hands and knees on the gravel. They were herded into lines by the guards who were spaced down the tracks, some with dogs which barked with pointless fury. Jania and he stumbled down the tracks together till a guard separated them with a gesture of his hand.

His line was funneled through a wooden hut where he was seated on a chair and his head was shaved in a matter of seconds. He stripped and said goodbye to his filthy civilian clothing and filed through a delicing compound. He was handed a bundle of camp clothing and his name was ticked from a list. They'd given him felt boots and gray underwear and a striped pajama-like top and bottom with numbers on the left thigh and left breast, on the back, and on the cap. Now he was AS1387.

There were ten barracks laid out in two rows of five within the compound of hard-trodden earth, as well as a mess house and a latrine and a guardhouse. More low unpainted wooden buildings lay beyond the wire, which Tadek was soon to learn constituted the industry and administration of this village-prison, including a power plant, a machine shop, and a factory where they made cement blocks. A few kilometers away lay a real village that catered to the needs of the guards and their families.

"Line up. Four to a row!"

The men shuffled in a straggly line, each with his eyes focused on the back and feet of the prisoner in front, until a guard shuttled them into one of the shed-like barracks. Tadek was shuffled to number seven. He recoiled at the vile smell inside, only then realizing how fresh the air had been for those few minutes outdoors. He stumbled forward into the smelly shadows, down a narrow aisle, relentlessly pushed from behind. "There are bunks at the back," someone said. "Everyone move to the back."

He was pushed further into the room, a low-ceilinged place filled with shadowy rows of bunks built of mismatched boards and with sawdust-filled bags for mattresses. To get away from the shoving and the disagreeable sensation of being in constant contact with others' bodies, he clambered up a rickety ladder to an empty bunk and found himself against the corner wall of the dugout, his face a foot from the ceiling.

He lay there craving sleep but the hunger cramping his belly kept him awake. A mosquito buzzed at his ears and he slapped himself on the side of his head. He could hear the mosquito hovering a little further away, then the rising of its buzz as it approached. He slapped himself again. Now that they had found him, there were dozens of them. He rolled over and hid his face in the sawdust mattress.

A brutal call from the doorway snapped him awake: "Prisoners! Parasites and enemies of the people! Wake up! It is time to make amends for the crimes you have committed!" Tadek clambered down from his upper bunk and made his way with the rest of the unshaven, ill-dressed prisoners into the courtyard.

After a latrine trip there was roll call in the courtyard outside and a lengthy recital of rules for the sake of the newcomers. Each zek had to call out his name and number, place and date of birth, offense, and the date of his release: "Tadek Gradinski, AS1387. Born, Liaski, Byelorussia, September 24, 1931. Convicted of sedition against the state. Date of release, August 8, 1974!"

The prisoners were siphoned like a liquid humanity into the mess hall where they had half an hour to eat one bowl of watery kasha—Tadek picked a squirming white grub out of the bowl and tossed it to the floor—and two small potatoes. Discolored water passed for tea.

Tadek was part of a work team that was led outside the compound and over the rough ground for a kilometer to where a factory was being built. He and two others carried bricks on a hod all day from a pile of bricks, across thirty meters of uneven ground, to a wall where ten men worked on scaffolding laying the bricks.

Sometimes he would glance up at the other teams of zeks, clumped along other walls which stretched out into the swampy wasteland in no apparent plan, and they gave the sense that rather than building something, they were excavating ruins of some civilization that had been destroyed and justly forgotten because it had been so deranged to build in such a spot at all.

Men at the brickpile loaded Tadek's hod full. On his first trip he let the load of bricks get off balance and it went crashing to the ground. He had to stop and attempt to replace the bricks by himself, making several runs to the wall with partial loads and receiving the weight of the tongue of the lead worker, another prisoner. The mosquitoes from the surrounding marshland were torment. With both hands occupied, Tadek learned to endure them as they settled on his ears and face.

At a brief break for lunch, exhausted though he was, it was apparent that he still had more energy than the workers who had been longer in the camp. An old hand sat down next to him and muttered with hate in his voice: "You act like a Stakhanovite shock worker! Slow down!"

There were few other words exchanged between him and his fellow zeks that day. By the afternoon, no one had to tell him to slow down, as the weight of the hod against his shoulders and the constant unnatural strain of his arms to balance it had worn him down almost to a standstill, and only the threats of the lead worker kept him and the others going.

The sun was setting as they gathered into a column four zeks wide to begin their hike back to the compound. They were searched before entering the gates and went through another roll call in the yard. "Tadek Gradinski. AS1387. Born, September 24, 1931. Convicted of sedition against the state. Date of release, August 8, 1974!" When the litany was done they filed into the mess hall for a slice of bread and another cup of watery tea.

Tadek crawled up to his bunk. He didn't want to talk to anyone. He didn't know if he could survive this. He wanted only to eat a real meal, to sleep, to see the face of his mother again, of Halinka. He felt something behind his ear and picked it off with his nails—a louse. The delicing had been futile. The louse must have been in the bedding. He had seen lice before on occasion but this one was huge. He held it up and inspected it in the smoky light. It was the Emperor of Lice, the Czar of Lice, the Premier, the General Secretary of the Central Committee of all Lice. It was dark gray with black markings on it and it waggled its legs at him. He crushed it between his nails, an overwhelming repulsion churning in his stomach.

Angry voices came from the front of the room. Three men—zeks, not guards—were making their way through the room, shoving prisoners out of their way and rifling through the goods of the newcomers to see whether there was anything worth stealing. All three of them wore caps pulled low and, under their waistcoats, an untucked blouse. They all walked with small steps and a swaggering sideways motion in their knee boots, as if they'd all had similar training in the army of thieves to walk this way.

Tadek had heard about these thieves, whom the guards employed to harass and punish the political prisoners and who ran the camp at its lowest level. Tadek slid down from his bunk and reached under his sawdust mattress to pull out Jania's bundle and thrust it under his shirt to his armpit, where he held it in place standing up beside his bunk.

A man on a lower bunk near the stove protested to the thieves, hanging onto a leather bag, valuable in itself, and pulling it to his chest with both hands. A thief over him pulled out a small wooden club and began hitting him over the head. Two other thieves hurried over to help. Even after the man gave up the leather bag they struck him, and they pulled him from his bunk onto the floor where they kicked him till they must have grown tired.

The first thief came over to Tadek's bunk. "What do you have for me, pretty boy?" he asked.

"Nothing. Take what you want," he said in Russian.

"Ah, sounds like a Polack. So accommodating." He was a small man with a scruffy black beard on a weak chin and ferocious black brows. Half of one of his ears was missing. Tadek learned later he was called One Ear. "Yes, I will take what I want, thank you so much." One Ear's hands quickly ferreted out Tadek's own bag, but there was nothing in it but a bar of soap and a handkerchief, both of which he put in the canvas bag by his side. "Thank you, young Pole," he said with a chuckle. His hands probed the edges and then quickly disinterred the mattress, thoroughly searching it in a matter of seconds before moving on.

When the thieves had left, Tadek realized that, on a bunk below and opposite his, an old man was weeping into his hands.

"What's wrong, old man?" Tadek asked, realizing the oddness of his question: everything was wrong. What could be more wrong for anyone here?

The man looked up at Tadek as if thinking those same thoughts.

"The thieves. If it wasn't for them, I could die in peace here."

Tadek could see the man's skull in clear outline beneath the waxy flesh. His eyelids drooped, showing a thin pink crescent of inner lid.

"What are you here for?"

The man sat up. Despite his cadaverous condition, he wanted to talk.

"Deviant thought."

"What's that?"

"Thought deviating from the party line. There were disagreements. I didn't understand the dialectic then. And so I deviated. They called it counter-revolutionary Trotskyite thought. I was denounced by people whose deviation was worse than mine! Now, now I understand the dialectic!" This last statement sounded both defiant and hopeful.

"You're a communist?"

"Yes! A good Bolshevik!"

Tadek laughed. "You're crazy!"

"No! I'm just not like those thugs who are running the show now. At least, some of them are thugs. But I was at the Winter Palace! I know what the revolution was meant to be! If I could get my letters to Comrade Stalin, he would understand. But it's so difficult to get paper here. No one has paper here. Do you have any paper?"

"No." Tadek wondered momentarily whether he was in a Corrective Camp or an insane asylum.

"How long have you been in?"

"Since 1936. Thirteen years. It's all a trivial mistake. On my part, yes, but also on the part of some bureaucrat, some nonentity who doesn't understand what I've done for the revolution! Sometime I will explain the dialectic to you in detail. You will see my point of view. I understand the General Secretary. One cannot make an omelet without breaking eggs."

"And if you're the egg?"

"It's a historical necessity."

Without a word more, Tadek turned away from the ancient prisoner in pity and disgust. He clambered back into his bunk. A brief period of darkness flitted by before he heard again the brutal call of the guards to rouse them to work.

Again the same round. Roll call again. "Tadeusz Gradinski, AS1397. Born September 24, 1931. Convicted of sedition against the state. Date of release, August 8, 1974!" Bread with a little sugar, the supposed tea, a long hike over the rough, barren ground to the workplace. The repeated trips back and forth between the brick pile and the scaffolding along the wall. His hands blistered and bleeding from the splintered hod-pole. No words exchanged with his fellow prisoners. A bowl of notional borscht. A cup of theoretical tea.

Back at his barracks, Tadek was shocked to see Jania waiting for him outside. Usually movement of women was restricted to the area immediately surrounding their barracks, which was encircled by an extra wire fence.

"I didn't know you could come here," he said.

"I have special permission."

She'd rebounded somewhat from her dismal state on the train. He realized once more how stunningly beautiful she was, just a rarity of nature, even in her camp uniform. Her brows were arched and delicate, giving her a surprised air, and her jawline was clean and pure, as was the slightest swaying in the line of her nose, the slight equine curve of her nostrils, and her precise, slightly childish chin. She seemed embarrassed about something and they stood in silence.

"Can I have my bundle back?" she asked abruptly.

"Of course." Tadek went to retrieve it. He'd been lucky not to have it stolen already.

He handed it to her.

"Thanks," she said, and stood there again in silence. They looked at each other only glancingly, staring instead out over the low buildings where a few zeks hung about. The perimeter lights went on, bathing the moonscape of hard-trodden ground in an eerie light. She tried to finally say something just as an announcement came over the loudspeakers.

"What?"

"I said, 'I have to find someone to protect me.'"

"Sure."

"You can't really do it."

"No."

"So...all right then. Good-bye."

"Good-bye."

He watched her walk back toward the woman's compound and saw that there was a large woman who had been waiting for her alongside the next building.

He wished her well. To talk with someone like Jania brought momentary respite from the ugliness that surrounded him, but it was Halinka he loved. Still, as he watched her walk away with her protector, he felt as if he was seeing a loss greater than he could name, a loss to more than just himself.

Chapter 33: A Zek's Day

Autumn began and the nights quickly became colder. The zeks' days were almost indistinguishable one from the other besides the change in the weather. The zeks themselves were almost indistinguishable in their caps and quilted jackets that they wore out to work in the morning, taking them off at the work sites as the sun grew warm.

By October in the evening there were a few minutes when people would gather around the stove in the center of the barracks and talk. No one trusted the other prisoners. Most of them were much older than Tadek, and many like the old communist had been in the Gulag for over a decade, shattered, timid souls, bewildered by history, whom the criminals had accustomed to intimidation and harassment. Also, there were rumored to be snitches scattered among the prisoners, who would report seditious talk to the guards.

Vladislav Nadoz, another elderly man, occupied the bunk across from Tadek, on the side opposite the aging true believer. He confessed himself to be a "bourgeois intellectual" with indifference. He seemed somewhat less insane to Tadek than the rest of the lot. Vladislav had had a wife and two children before his imprisonment. "I used to receive packages from them, but no more. I don't know if they made it through the war. I hope that they did and have just forgotten about me. That would be for the best." As a young man he had wanted to become an ornithologist, before the revolution had spun the country's life out of control. Even now he pointed out migratory birds that would perch momentarily on the barbed wire before continuing on their way. He would get excited at glimpsing a bright one or, even more so, some dun-colored fistful of animated dust, inconspicuous as a shrew, that he knew was extraordinarily rare in these parts. At such times Tadek wondered about Vladislav's sanity as well. But he had tutored Russian in Moscow to the children of aristocrats, and now worked on smoothing out Tadek's uncouth and heavily accented Russian.

The old Bolshevik found a sheet of paper somewhere and a stub of pencil, and sat across from Tadek and Vladislav, composing a letter to Stalin.

"He's been writing for years," Vladislav shrugged. "He never finishes. And besides, who would take his letter for him? We're supposed to receive one package a month and they seldom deliver them. Most are probably stolen along the way. What makes him think a letter would go anywhere?"

"Beware of what you say around him," Vladislav added. "He might be a snitch. At any rate, he's certainly a cretin."

The weeks filled with mid-day warmth passed, and it began to rain, a frigid, relentless shower that soaked through their jackets within minutes as they worked outside. They had no chance to exchange more than an occasional word while they carried hods of bricks back and forth to the wall. The quilted jackets they wore did little to lessen the bite of the wind that swept undeterred by the low bushes and sparse trees of the taiga. When the first snow came, it painted the landscape a white that turned blinding in the mid-day sun, monotonous and hopeless under the endless quilt of gray clouds.

Tadek and Vladislav played chess together on a set made out of dried pieces of bread. Each night they had a chance to make only two or three moves. The bracing order of the pieces and their clear rules held its old fascination for Tadek like an island of sanity in the squalor of his life. Some combinations of moves seemed to have almost a specific flavor in his mind: a certain knight move seemed bold and odd like cinnamon, and a pawn move seemed as forthright as salt. His imagination turned ineluctably toward food, tormenting him, and he shook his head to clear it. He should focus: chess, chess. He could remember specific moves that he'd made in games against Jan, the specific layout of the pieces. Uncle Janusz! Where was he? Where was his mother? Could Kazimierz possibly be still living?

One day was like another, creeping deep into winter. The smallest events had to suffice to make one day different. They had kasha instead of sugar on bread. The tea was slightly better. One day Tadek saw Jania, through the wire that separated the woman's barracks, with a tough-looking woman, different from the first. He heard that she was a Lithuanian thief who ran the women's barracks and was feared by all. One day he found a piece of metal on the ground and hid it up his jacket sleeve. He knew how valuable this could be once he sharpened it. One day he won at chess against Vladislav, who raised his eyebrows in homage. One day they were all punished because a loaf of bread had disappeared from the galley. They had to stand in the courtyard after roll call till someone confessed. Luckily for them, after half an hour the culprit collapsed on the ground holding his stomach and groaning with cramps: he'd eaten the entire loaf and his shrunken stomach rebelled. He was lucky not to die that night. One day a misguided, misbegotten dog from the village caught himself somehow between the two wire fences encircling the camp. It ran frantically back and forth, unable to discover its exit, rhythmically barking, until a guard shot it. It didn't die immediately but lay there whining. Tadek could still hear it when they'd gone inside and the lights were extinguished and he listened in the dark till the brutal call of morning came. The dog's corpse lay between the fences for days until it was buried by snow.

Against the odds, Tadek received some packages. First there was a parcel from Halinka—at least he deduced that it had to be from her: a jar of honey, the preserves she knew he liked, as well as their favorite mushrooms, dried, the little foxes that they'd picked that day. But there was no letter. It could've been lost along the way. That was a common enough occurrence. There was a limit of five kilograms to parcels, and he could tell by its weight, a slipshod rewrapping, and some gaps in the package that someone had looted the parcel. A week later he received another parcel that he thought might be from Pawel, again without a letter. Later, he received a parcel from Jadwiga. She included a note, saying nothing but the safest inanities, which the censors would ignore: hope you're well, no news here, take care.

Zeks came to blows over a bunk closer to the stove, though the fire burned out by midnight. They tried to smuggle in small bits of wood under their quilted jackets when returning from their work sites. The guards were supposed to search them and shake out the wood, but sometimes they were in too much of a hurry to get out of the cold themselves, and a few precious sticks made their way to the fire.

The aging Marxist sat on the edge of his low bunk with his letter to Stalin on his knees, turning over phrases in his head, when a zek casually snatched it out of his hands and walked to the stove and threw it in the fire. "A moment of warmth is worth more than all of your words, old man," he said, warming his hands in the momentary glow. The old man watched slack-jawed before falling back on his bunk. A minute later, Tadek heard sobbing. He didn't let himself look over at the old man.

The cold was cruel to the old man, and each night after his meal, he'd collapse immediately onto his bunk, snoring loudly, his mouth open, his face as gray as winter clouds.

Tadek heard that Jania had become a mistress of one of the guards, and was receiving special privileges and protections from him. Later it was rumored that she'd moved out of the women's lodgings, and now was in housing reserved for the guards' wives and women outside the gate.

Tadek didn't believe this until one day he saw Jania, in civilian clothing, on the arm of an MVD officer (still NKVD to Tadek), being escorted into a building beyond the barbed wire.

Vladislav had seen her too.

"Didn't you know her?" Vladislav asked.

"Yes."

"She's a slut with ambition, isn't she?" commented one of the zeks who watched their chess game.

"No, she isn't!"

"Well, she's screwing every one of the guards now," the prisoner said.

He was a disagreeable little man, who some said was a snitch and ally of the thieves. It was difficult to tell. He was friendly to Tadek in an unfriendly way, standing too close to him and speaking out of the side of his mouth while looking all around the barracks.

"I've heard them talking about her," he continued.

"She's trying to screw her way up the line to Stalin," someone else gibed.

"That can't be true. I know her. She's not like that."

"Don't be naïve, Tadek," Vladislav said. "But here, don't

take it so seriously. She has to eat and she's not your sister. Let's play chess. We have a few more minutes."

One day, after a new shipment of prisoners had settled in, the thieves made their rounds and Jania was with them, giving orders to One Ear, swearing in a way he'd never quite heard anyone swear before. He was appalled and almost fascinated in the manner in which her voice had changed, from the frightened, breathy tones he'd remembered, to shrill and brutal threats, that had an iron authority to them, as if some spirit had possessed her. She didn't look at Tadek and he didn't look at her as she walked by his bunk.

By the end of December, she had truly graduated and was living in a hut next to the lodgings of the camp's commandant. This was a hundred meters away from the barbed wire enclosure, but the zeks had falcon eyes. The commandant had a wife in Moscow, but that was a long way away, and Jania came and went from his lodgings at night.

She didn't show her face within the barbed wire for a few weeks, but soon she was going about the camp with a quirt in her hand, sporting fine leather boots and a sheepskin jacket. She looked beautiful but transformed, with no trace of the fear and vulnerability she'd worn before and which had melted Tadek's heart. Her face was hard, and she took on the work of the guards, some of the cruelest chores, beating zeks about the head and shoulders at slim provocation, as if determined to beat out of herself the last sentimental attachment to the zeks, now that she had flipped sides. She became known for the torrent of imaginative foul language that flowed from her whenever she spoke, as Tadek had heard for himself—obsessively biological, scatological, graphic, sexual, animalistic, perverse, a constant, strenuous feat of swearing, as if through her inventive words she was inverting everything she had once been.

Even the blue-tabs were frightened of her, and spoke to her with downcast eyes. When she stood along his line of prisoners coming back from the work zone, Tadek turned his head away from her, looking at the mud.

One day when the wakeup call broke through Tadek's dreams, he roused himself, slid from his bunk, and noticed that the old Marxist still slept, his gray face slack-mouthed and tilted to one side.

"Hey, get up." Tadek nudged his arm. No response. "Get up." Tadek touched the old man's hand that protruded from the soiled rag that served as a blanket. Cold as metal. At first Tadek didn't know what to do. He stood there thinking of the touch of his grandfather's frozen fingers.

"This man's dead."

The shuffling prisoners paused momentarily to glance over at Tadek, as if he were the one who had caused this diversion, neither interesting nor uninteresting, in their routines. A few idle comments were tossed his way.

"Lucky guy!"

"He's well out of it!"

"May he meet Lenin in hell and explain the dialectic!"

A guard worked his way down the narrow aisle between the bunks, shoving prisoners out of his way. He nudged the old man with his foot; the bunk was barely knee-high off the floor.

"You!" He pointed at Tadek. "And you! Take him to the morgue!"

As they waited until the barracks had cleared out, Tadek recalled that the old man kept a needle in the seam of his pants, and he quickly felt along the man's leg, muttering a quick prayer asking forgiveness at the same time, till his finger was pricked and he worked the needle out and slid it into his own inseam. This was a valuable inheritance from the old communist, since now Tadek could repair his clothes, which had to last him for a year. The other man designated to carry the corpse was a dark Kazakh with a menacing face whom Tadek had seen across the barracks but never spoken to. Now he watched Tadek's actions through blank eyes, grunting once in envy when he saw the needle.

Tadek and the Kazakh picked up the old man, the Kazakh carrying the legs and Tadek gripping the shoulders. With only two men, it was awkward. Though the old man wasn't heavy, neither man could get a good grip. Tadek finally settled his hands into the corpse's armpits, but could feel them slipping as they made their way down the aisle, the Kazakh walking backwards. Outside the barracks Tadek asked, "Where's the morgue? Which way?" The Kazakh said nothing but just turned to one side around the barracks, and Tadek followed his lead. He could look at nothing but the old man's gray face, tossing from side to side as they walked. He asked the Kazakh to stop so he could refind his grip. He didn't know whether the man understood his words, or just the situation, but they stopped and both regripped, then continued, the old man's face flopping from side to side again as if in a terrible negation, a negation of the dialectic, a terrible antithesis he'd finally discovered, certain now never to deviate again.

When they'd reached a small building behind the administration complex—it was the clinic that must've doubled as a morgue—the Kazakh shouted, "Open the door!" So, he could talk. They trundled their floppy bundle inside and the soldier who'd opened the door glanced at their load and waved a hand: "Over there."

As Tadek bent down to lay the body on a table, he remembered the devil's mark on his neck which the znacharka had wanted to cure at his grandfather's funeral. He quickly grabbed the old man's hand and touched its chill fingers to his neck. It was worth a try. On his way out of the building, he rubbed his hands against his sides to rid them of the odor of death and the memory of the man's waxy flesh. He and the Kazakh, wordlessly again, hurried back across the courtyard to the mess hall. He was relieved to see that he wasn't too late for a piece of bread, 500 grams, with a little sugar on it, and a cup of the weak tea that the zeks had dubbed Stalin's urine.

Chapter 34: New Zeks

The administration, for reasons clear only to them, were shifting prison populations around. At the end of January, a trainload of new prisoners came in, and the day after that another. Some of the old intellectuals were being shifted about to other barracks or other camps, but there was no shortage of prisoners coming in by the train. Tadek watched them file in and take their bunks. He could tell at a glance that these men were different from the old-time political prisoners who had been cowed by the thieves since the thirties. He wanted to talk to them and went over by the stove. Some of them told their stories. Many were Ukrainian partisans who had followed a path similar to Kazimierz and had been fighting from the forests for years. Some were Russian veterans who had fought from Stalingrad to Berlin but written indiscreet letters home or let slip a critical phrase in front of the wrong person. Others had been in German prisoner-of-war camps for years. They all shared a proud, reckless look in their eyes that reminded him of Kazmierz's *lesni ludzie*.

Tadek watched as a group of thieves came in and one of them boldly started going through the goods of a Ukrainian partisan, who stood up and shoved the thief. The other thieves hurried over, clubs in hand, and the man backed down and let them take whatever he had.

"Who are they?" a man asked Tadek.

"They are the thieves. They run the show here," Tadek said.

"Why?"

"Because we let them."

"We'll see about that."

Tadek and the man talked, and other new prisoners circled round.

Tadek was heartened by their presence. The natural leader was a Russian officer, Kuznetzov, a short, solid man with a square jaw and deliberate movements, as if every step and gesture was considered. He talked to the Ukrainians and reached a pact: they would put their differences aside here. Many Ukrainians, during the years of all-against-all, had fought with the Germans against the Russians, or as partisans against the Poles, attacking hundreds of Polish villages ruthlessly. Many more had fought on the side of the Russians, but were later considered enemies of the state. Here, no one asked. Outside, they said, we are enemies. In here, we are allies. The same pledge was made among the other groups.

"What shall we do when the thieves come back?"

"Can we make any weapons of our own?"

There was little spare material in the barracks, but it was discovered that one could take bracing boards off the bunks and replace them later so they looked the same. Usually the thieves came with the arrival of a new transport, but sometimes they would sweep through just on a whim, and it was this that happened a few days later. Five thieves, led by One Ear, strode through the hut between the rows, their hands everywhere, under mattresses, prodding through bedding and giving quick shoves to the political zeks. A sharp whistle sliced the air.

They paused, One Ear still grinning with pleasure, but a

niggling puzzlement slowing him down. The thieves paused and watched the slow movement of many zeks around them, gradually realizing that they were encircled by twenty zeks with makeshift clubs. Kuznetzov stepped forward. He was backed up by a huge Ukrainian called Bhodan. Kuznetzov stood inches away from One Ear, who had taken out his club and held it up, brandishing it, expecting it to work its power.

"No more thieving here. Leave us alone!" Kuznetzov said, and before One Ear could respond, he smashed a bedpost club into the side of his head, knocking him down between the bunks. Tadek jumped in too, trying to get a good shot at a thief. Four or five prisoners swarmed each thief.

The thieves began crying for help. "We're being attacked by fascists! We're being attacked by fascist gangsters!"

The zeks continued beating the thieves. "Shut up!" they told them, continuing to pummel them in a steady, methodical style, beating them down to the ground between the bunks, continuing to beat them until they quieted. Finally, out of boredom or fatigue, they turned away and let the thieves struggle to their feet and stagger out the door.

Tadek was elated, but knowing the nature of the thieves, he mistrusted the moment and went over to Kuznetzov. "They'll be back, you know," he said.

"And we'll be ready for them." Tadek was astounded that, even in prison, one could act like a free man.

When the thieves returned, twenty of them came rushing into Barracks No. 7, clubbing and beating zeks as they made their way toward Kuznetzov. The surprise worked in their favor for a few minutes, but none of these new zeks had endured years in the forests or in POW camps or on the battlefield to capitulate in the face of a few scrawny thieves with clubs. The cowed prisoners from the 1930s, the aging intellectuals whose sins had been verbal or mental, hid under their bunks, while the new prisoners grabbed their clubs and went after the thieves, attacking them with a viciousness that surprised even Tadek. After a battle that lasted only fifteen minutes, but on which seemed to pivot the fate of characters, they drove the thieves from the barracks.

In the aftermath, the thieves were still reluctant to admit their defeat. Every time they passed No. 7, they called in: "I smell dead meat! You already stink!" but they tossed their words from a distance, steering clear of the prisoners, even outside in the courtyard.

The success of the rebellion faded quickly. The thieves were an arm of the administration of the camp, used to punish, weaken, and demoralize the political prisoners, and to go against the thieves was to go against the administration. So it was anticipated when a week later, the prisoners from No. 7 were led before a trio of camp administrators one by one. When it was Tadek's turn, he wasn't surprised to see One Ear standing behind the table of his judges, and only moderately so to see Jania there as well, in the background against a wall.

As he neared the front of the line, he saw that she was terribly changed. When their eyes caught, a crimson flush spread over her face and down her neck, as the thought of all she had done to survive must have rushed through her mind. A moment after her flush passed, a terrible, jeering rictus took possession of her mouth, and her eyes blazed defiance at Tadek.

The commandant, whom Tadek had only seen a few times from a distance, was a tall, narrow-shouldered man. He had a small, round head, and his face seemed frozen in an expression of tense calculation. Only every once in a while did a pained smile twist his lips in a sort of spasm. This was the man, if the rumors were true, with whom Jania was sharing her beauty.

Some of the zeks from No. 7 were having years added to their sentences, others were being sentenced to the cooler, others were being transferred. The administration was determined to break up the dangerous combinations that had mixed in the barracks.

As soon as Tadek approached the desk, One Ear began to point and exclaim: "He was one of them! He was one of them! He hit me in the head! The fascist!"

Tadek restrained the urge to smile at One Ear from the fond memory of hitting him in the side of the head with a club. Jania stepped from behind the table and bent over to say something into the commandant's ear.

The commandant nodded curtly. "Twenty-five year sentence, concurrent. Date of release, February 6, 1975. To be transferred to Yamantau," he said, and stamped the paper in front of him by way of dismissal.

Tadek was stunned that he'd received a concurrent sentence, almost nothing. He turned and made his way out of the building, accompanied by a guard, making his way back to his barracks. He felt a tug on his elbow. It was Jania. She dismissed the guard.

But she seemed at a loss for words. Her face had hardened and was distorted by a writhing anger and even torment that lay just beneath the surface, as if part of her had had its spine broken, like an animal run over along a roadside, that still couldn't help twisting helplessly because it couldn't quite die yet. The lines of her face were as beautiful as ever, but it was a different character of beauty now. A tightening at the ends of her mouth and a farouche glare in her eyes created a cynical cast over her beauty now, a beauty that hated its own inescapable power and what it brought upon itself, and there was something slightly repellant even about its attraction now. Then, in a rush of furious words, she said: "Yes, I remember you, Tadek. And I'll be glad not to have you looking at me anymore with those big stupid eyes of yours. Durok the Fool!

You don't understand how things work here. You still haven't figured it out!"

When Tadek didn't respond, having rid herself of her anger, she seemed to change her mind about something. All the pain of her position rushed back into her eyes for a moment, and she added in a tense whisper, "Don't let them do this to you, too," before she turned away and strode in her glistening black leather boots back into the building.

The next morning, twenty soldiers trotted into the No. 7 barracks, and an MVD officer read off the names of twenty zeks. Without even their usual pan of slops for breakfast, they were marched to the rail line where they were dispersed among eight red cars, already half-full with other men being dredged out of the Gulag for transfer. This time the train was headed back west.

Chapter 35:
Mt. Yamantau, *Gorlag*

On this trip, Tadek rode in a red-painted Stolypin car, custom-made for the transportation of zeks, a former passenger car with all the seats and partitions removed and replaced by a series of cages, each filled with six or eight prisoners. With this setup a guard at each end of the car could see his way to the other end with a clear view. Tadek found a patch on the floor as close as possible to a pitifully small stove in the aisle of the car, crossed his arms over his knees, lay his head down, and tried to sleep. Thus began their journey that strung out, day after day, with only a little water and food each day. A half-boarded window strung with barbed wire gave them a slice of the countryside sliding past beyond their cages. The suffering intensified when they stopped and sat at a siding for five hours, ten hours a day, when the minutes and hours wasted in nothingness accumulated in their boredom, reminding them of how their lives were wasting away. It was possible to resist, at least internally, a cruel guard or a grueling work assignment, but it was impossible to resist the crushing emptiness and pointlessness of these journeys. Then Tadek felt that he and the other zeks had given up entirely.

One Asiatic-looking zek babbled in a corner of the cage in a language foreign to all, sealed in its pointless complexity. He seemed to be asking pointed and wry questions of himself, and then giving himself fulminating answers. Finally he leapt to his feet and threw himself face-first against the wall again and again until even the impassive guards took notice and hauled him by the arms out of the cage and away. A little while later, there was a shot. Still the car sat. No one looked at anyone else.

It took them days to cross the interminable flat stretch of Siberia, from somewhere between Novosibirsk and Omsk, westward past Omsk, continuing onward till finally they could see the snow-topped Urals in the distance. When they hit the mountains, the train slowed to a crawl, climbing for two days, beyond any vegetation, and then speeding down on the western slopes, flattening out again until they hit the Ukraine, and everyone wondered where in the world they could be going.

They passed dozens of deserted villages, without so much as a dog in the streets, often with abandoned, weed-filled gardens and burnt-out houses with broken windows and loose doors flapping in the wind. Almost twenty years after the collectivization and mass starvations of the thirties, no one had returned to rebuild these wastelands.

Tadek and the others were herded out at a transit station. Someone said they had been traveling for twenty-two days. He had abandoned all attempts to discern a logic to this itinerary. Here they spent a week in a lice-infested barracks before being separated according to the logic of the great mind in Moscow, or some minor, distorted imitation of that mentality, and they were packed again into Stolypin cars. This time Tadek was headed back east, and he could well imagine spending the rest of his life hunched on the floor of a railroad car, traveling back and forth across the expanses of

Europe and Asia.

After a few days of heading back east, undoing much of the progress they'd made before, the train was finally halted and the zeks were disembarked into a camp. The zeks found themselves back in the Urals, in a Gorlag, a forest camp. Under bright spotlights, in an eerily silent night, Tadek and the others were shunted from the train between two lines of guards into a barracks, where they scrambled for bunks in a sepia stench before collapsing in sleep.

* * *

The zeks stood the next morning, before dawn, in ranks on the frozen turf of the courtyard for roll call, and the freshness of the piney air was a tonic. Tadek had already discovered that here the barracks were not locked up at night and there were no bars on the windows, so that the prisoners could go to the latrine outside rather than being forced to use the overflowing bucket in a corner of the barracks.

Their meal that morning was a slice of black bread with sugar and a cup of soup, which, though not thick, had a few vegetables in it. He marveled at the improvements of his status and wondered whether Jania had steered his sentencing in a lenient direction.

Still, he soon realized that the work could be hard and dangerous here. A trustee, the head of their brigade, put him on a detail of quarry work, and he followed the other zeks out of the gate to walk ten kilometers over uneven, frozen ground where there was the beginning of a limestone quarry. They wore felt boots and quilted jackets and mittens that offered only slight protection against the cold, so that they huddled around the weak fire in the center of the work camp whenever possible, constantly chased away by the guards. In the distance, Tadek could see through the haze of morning, through the forests, the snowy peak of Mt. Yormantau rising in the distance.

The trustee set explosives to blast away at the blocks of stone. A large, bearded, Russian zek, who was obsessed with productivity, he would often give a shout to clear the area just seconds before the explosives went off, strafing the workers with rocks. Then Tadek and the others would dust themselves off and walk through a cloud of chalky dust to shovel up the gravel into large bins to be put on carts, which donkeys would carry away. On the larger rocks, Tadek and another zek would find a narrow split into which they could work progressively wider wedges, taking turns pounding away till the rock gave way. That first day they worked for sixteen hours, leaving and returning in the dark. A zek told him that their labor each day depended on how close they were to the quota for the week.

A few days later, on some whim of the trustee, Tadek was shifted to a detail shoveling the gravel onto a road that was being built between the camp and the quarry. While they waited for loads of gravel, they shoveled out a level area for the road, often having to cut down trees or sledgehammer rocks into gravel. Though this job was less dangerous than the quarry work, even so he could feel his strength wasting away day by day. The food, though better than in Siberia, was never sufficient to replenish his lost energy from each day's work. In a few weeks he felt himself falling further and further behind as he worked. He watched other zeks holding on as best they could, but gradually, inevitably collapsing to the ground. Zeks checked their feet and fingers each night for the telltale blue-gray signs of frostbite, which could easily progress to amputation and death.

One day at roll call a guard asked their barracks if any of them knew how to repair motors. Half of the zeks jumped forward, shouting their credentials, Tadek among them. The guard walked through the barracks, choosing half a dozen to quiz further, but Tadek was not among them, and another zek was given the choice inside job. Tadek trudged again out through the forest to the quarry, and for the rest of February he did his stone-splitting, or gravel-tossing, twelve hours a day, six days a week. The attitude that trickled all the way through the chain of command, down from the commandant of the camp, was that punishment or rehabilitation was not the point here, only productivity.

The first machine-expert, who had been recommended by a zek trustee to the guard, turned out to be a fake, and was eventually ejected from the machine-shop in humiliation. This time the guard in charge of the shop, the warder, quizzed the volunteers more carefully.

The guard came up to Tadek and said, "Do you really know about machines?"

"Yes, I repaired fabric machines, weaving machines, leather-stamping machines and worked some with small electric motors."

"Not with gasoline engines?"

"A little."

"We'll see if you really do know anything."

The next day Tadek watched the other zeks trudge through the muddy snow and out the gates toward the quarry, with pickaxes and sledge hammers slung over their shoulders while he was following a guard to the machine shop. Here two other zeks sat (sat!), each at a large table scattered with machine parts. They maintained the small electrical motors and generators for the camp, as well as for the guards and the dependent village down the hill.

The machine shop was ill-lit and dusty and heated by a pot-bellied stove in the center of the room that would burn through the allotted wood by noon, leaving them working with blue fingers and in clouds of their frosty breath, but the shop looked a lot like paradise to Tadek. An older zek named Vasilenko was in charge. He was quite different from Tadek's old boss, Stronski, even though Tadek couldn't help feeling the same way toward him, treating him with the respect due someone who knew something that he needed to learn. Vasilenko was a tall, haggard zek, with an aquiline nose and suspicious eyes. Despite his zek rags, a shaved head, and a constant, lung-shredding cough, he managed to keep an air of proud disdain about him that lifted him from his surroundings. The third machinist was named Ullmanis, a small and laconic Latvian who liked to sit off in a corner, work by himself, and pretend he didn't understand Russian unless asked a pointed question.

* * *

Tadek settled into the routine of this camp's life as winter passed into spring. There were thieves in this camp too, whom Tadek found strangely reminiscent of those in his first camp. He realized their dress and even their walk was the same—kneeboots and an awkward swagger—as if they adhered to a strict, unwritten rulebook for thieves. But these thieves were not nearly as powerful as the others, and if a zek just lay low, they would ignore him, especially if he had nothing for them to steal. Though the food here was better than at his previous camp, it still was never quite enough. Five hundred grams of bread, a few cubes of sugar with hot water at dawn. A watery bowl of soup at night. At holidays there might be a slice of pork fat.

Tadek was not being treated as a '58er, a political offender, but was in with a confusing medley of ethnicities and offenders. Some zeks, those who had them, even wore civilian clothes, and different ethnic groups wore their colorful costumes, the Turcomen, Uzbeks, and Khirgiz. There was a group of the

Raskolniki, the Old Believers, an Orthodox sect who were ignored by the administration, which was aware that these people would die before taking an order or cooperating with the government of the Great Satan in any way.

There were few of the defiant partisans and veterans Tadek had admired at his previous camp. Many of the zeks here were older, resigned products of the purges of the 1930s. The Gulag was a home, a way of life, a place to wait for death. One of these old timers discovered that his sentence had been changed to exile in the surrounding *oblast*. He grabbed his meager bag of belongings and trudged out the gate and down the muddy lane. There was nothing out that gate besides towering pines and steep mountains, except some housing for guards and the small village a kilometer away. Within a week he'd made his way back to the camp, begging to be let back inside. To the jeers of the other zeks, he shrugged. "At least there's a little food here. Outside, there's nothing an old zek can do."

* * *

The zek in charge of the machine shop, Vasilenko, spoke nothing beyond curt orders to Tadek. Throughout the spring Tadek was regaining his strength and learning about the new machines, grateful to be away from the quarry. Summer passed and autumn, and they were into another winter. There were only a few other Poles in the Gorlag, and they knew as little as he did of the outside world or of their distant homeland. He received no packages and heard no word from Liaski: not from his mother or father, not from Jan or Yadwiga, not from Pawel or Halinka. He felt as if the Gulag was a great sea which had submerged him, and its depth and vastness, and absolute foreignness from all that he had known, could destroy him if he let his thoughts dwell on the people he loved.

Still, Tadek remembered the first camp, and the quarry-work in this one, and he was grateful for the routine in the machine shop, for the small pot bellied stove, and for the crystalline logic of electrical generators.

For hours, days, months, and seasons, Vasilenko and Tadek worked in silence across from each other, with Ullmanis in his silent corner. Occasionally other zeks would come for a week or two before fully proving their uselessness and being moved on. Gradually Vasilenko realized that Tadek actually knew something about machines and wasn't going to be a similar fraud.

Gradually, Vasilenko's vigilance, suspicion, and privacy slackened somewhat, and he let drop a few phrases here and there that let Tadek piece together his history. Vasilenko had been an engineer in Leningrad, and was swept up in a general purging of the profession, prompted by some velleity or shadow that had crossed the mind of the great leader in Moscow. He'd fulfilled his ten-year sentence already, but no one had bothered to release him, and every time he petitioned for release, he only received threats. He had a wife and daughter, who sent him occasional packages, yet he seemed without illusion or hope. He'd been transformed by imprisonment from an engineer to a poet, and eventually, he began to recite the massive amount of poetry that he'd committed to memory. "We used to have access to books, back in the old days. We even had a library at one camp. And I memorized as much as I could, to keep me sane when they'd throw me in isolation for days."

Vasilenko became Tadek's second Russian teacher of the camps. He corrected Tadek's pronunciation and used words that stretched Tadek's vocabulary. Mostly they were left alone by the guard in charge, who had other duties, and would come and look at their work a few times each day with an undiscerning eye. Tadek learned more than words from Vasilenko. Despite the old man's obsession with poetry, he was a veteran zek, adept at survival. He taught Tadek how to make needles out of fishbones and matches, how to unravel scraps of worn-out socks to make thread and trade the thread and needles for food. He taught him how to make buttons out of dried bread to keep his pants from falling down.

"You have to size up people right away here. No time for mistakes. Stay away from Kirilenko," he said, referring to someone in Tadek's barracks whose bunk was near his. "He's a snitch. A bitch."

"He seems friendly."

"That's the sign of a snitch. Why would anyone be friendly here unless they want something from you?"

"But you're friendly."

This observation seemed to sour Vasilenko, who didn't like to think of himself that way. "That's different. I've studied you almost a year. We don't have anything to gain from each other."

"What about Ullmanis?"

"He's okay. Just unfriendly. I like that."

It didn't bother Tadek that Vasilenko never asked him anything about who he was, where he came from, what his life had been like before the Gulag. He evidently assumed that he, Vasilenko, was not only older and better educated than Tadek, but much more interesting, and so he talked while Tadek listened.

As they worked, Vasilenko recited poetry.

"'The heavy-hanging chains will fall,
The walls will crumble at a word;
And Freedom greet you in the light
And brothers give you back the sword.'

That's Pushkin."

"Yes!" Tadek shouted, inspired by the words of freedom. Then more quietly, as Ullmanis glanced over at them. "That's it! It will happen!"

"Listen to this one," Vasilenko said.

'I had bread from the wives of the village
And the lads saw me right for makhorka [tobacco].'

"In the old days of the czars, the peasants in the countryside used to help the escaped zeks on their way."

"Escaped zeks!" Tadek couldn't quite conceive the idea. "How could anyone escape from here?"

"That was in the old days, mind you. Don't get ideas. Now a peasant will get a twenty-five slammed on him for aiding fugitives! But if your mind is free, you are free," the old poet said.

Tadek knew little enough about poetry beyond the patriotic Polish lines drummed into him by Mrs. Krzaczek, but the hundreds of lines which Vasilenko had memorized could transfix him for much of the twelve hours of the day during which they worked together. Tadek could return the favor by reciting the Polish poems that still lingered in the recesses of his head, and Vasilenko, who knew some Polish already, would frown with concentration and then nod in approval and widen his eyes at a singing line.

One poem Vasilenko recited chilled Tadek's blood.

"Listen to this, young Pole. You should remember this. Alexander Blok, "The Scythians." This is what we Russians are really like," Vasilenko said, slitting his eyes at Tadek theatrically.

You are but millions. Our unnumbered nations
Are as the sands upon the sounding shore.
We are the Scythians! We are the slit-eyed Asians!
Try to wage war with us—you'll try no more!

His cough interrupted him, a frequent event, but when he regained his breath his voice captured a singsongy rhythm, his eyes diffused with distant, inner sights, and he seemed to fall under a hypnotic spell that had its effect on Tadek.

> You've had whole centuries. We—a single hour.
> Like serfs obedient to their feudal lord,
> We've held the shield between two hostile powers—
> Old Europe and the barbarous Mongol horde.

* * *

> O Ancient World, before your culture dies,
> Whilst failing life within you breathes and sinks,
> Pause and be wise, as Oedipus was wise,
> And solve the age-old riddle of the Sphinx.

> That Sphinx is Russia. Grieving and exulting,
> And weeping black and bloody tears enough,
> She stares at you, adoring and insulting,
> With love that turns to hate, and hate—to love.

* * *

> But if you spurn us, then we shall not mourn.
> We too can reckon perfidy no crime,
> And countless generations yet unborn
> Shall curse your memory till the end of time.

> We shall abandon Europe and her charm.
> We shall resort to Scythian craft and guile.

Swift to the woods and forests we shall swarm,
And then look back, and smile our slit-eyed smile.

Away to the Urals, all! Quick, leave the land,
And clear the field for trial by blood and sword,
Where steel machines that have no soul must stand
And face the fury of the Mongol horde.

But we ourselves, henceforth, we shall not serve
As henchmen holding up the trusty shield.
We'll keep our distance and, slit-eyed, observe
The deadly conflict raging on the field.

We shall not stir, even though the frenzied Huns
Plunder the corpses of the slain in battle, drive
Their cattle into shrines, burn cities down,
And roast their white-skinned fellow men alive!

When he finished, a cadenza of his lung-tearing coughs possessed him.

"That's what you're really like?" Tadek asked, when he'd recovered.

"Yes!" Vasilenko said emphatically. "It's part of our Russian character! And what's more, my young Pole, I've seen enough of human nature to tell you that it's part of everyone's character."

Tadek didn't say anything. He shivered to think that someone could put something so primal into words. Was the hatred between people so instinctive and so unavoidable? "Don't worry, Tadeusz," Vasilenko let out a rare laugh at Tadek's disillusioned stare. "I'm on the other side now. Besides, I'm not really Russian. Or only half. I'm Jewish."

"You? Jewish? No!"

"Yes. At least my mother was Jewish, so they say that makes me Jewish. I would have been Jewish enough for Hitler!"

Tadek felt the old, crisp categories of Liaski crumbling in ways like this day by day.

* * *

During Tadek's second winter under Vasilenko's tutelage, it became clear that his mentor had tuberculosis. Vasilenko struggled to keep going throughout the day, and Tadek took up more and more of his work, covering for him when the guard nominally in charge of the shop would walk through.

It might have finally been his worsening health that brought Vasilenko to confide to Tadek that he was working on his own poem. He'd composed it and memorized it during the long years in prison.

"I don't care if I die here," he said. He always said this.

"You'll get out!" Tadek protested, as he always did. "You've already served your sentence!"

He waved an agitated hand at this. "I said I don't care if I die here!" He calmed himself. "That's all right. But my poem is 10,000 lines long, and it only exists here." He tapped his head. "And it will die with me. Fuck the world!" His curse disintegrated into a long series of dry coughs.

"Tell it to me. Let me hear it."

"All right. I began it when I was in prison for a year, before I was sent to work in the Gulag. Much of that time was in solitary, and I figured if I could think and compose and memorize, it would keep my mind from drifting away. I recite a section of it to myself every day of the week. It takes me two weeks to get through it all. Then I start at the beginning. I constantly have to go back and repair parts of it. These are the first four lines:

'Across Siberia's vasty plains
the knifey winds do blow.
I fought against the new czar's reign,
refusing to bow so low.'

The poem was the saga of his conviction and imprisonment, an earnest diatribe against Stalin and his henchmen, as well as a reminiscence of zeks he'd known, brave and craven, all told in contorted, archaic rhymes, not without a stiff dignity.

One day Vasilenko said, "I'm dying, Tadeusz. I want you to memorize my poem and write it down for me when you get out of here."

"I'm never getting out of here, Yuri! I have twenty-five years! They'll give me another five if I sneeze! You know that."

"You'll get out. You will get out. I know that."

"And anyway, I can't remember your poems."

"Poem. Just one. Ten-thousand lines."

"That's what I mean."

"You have to try."

The old man started to cough again.

"I've been working on it for years!"

Tadek could see the insistence in the old man's eyes, and they began that afternoon, as they dismantled a water pump, the memorization.

"Across Siberia's vasty plains . . . '"

Vasilenko made Tadek repeat the first stanza by memory before he'd go on to the next stanza. Then he made Tadek repeat the two stanzas together before they went on to the third. "Repeat!"

He did his best to memorize the lines for the old man while they worked. Ullmanis the solitary Latvian just shook his head at their deranged project and worked by himself in silence.

One day the old man, who lived in a different barracks from Tadek, was taken to the infirmary. But two days later he was back, defiant. "Tadeusz, you must pay attention! We'll start from the beginning."

Tadek looked at the old man: he knew Vasilenko's thought that the poem would survive him was the only slim tether connecting him to life. "All right, I'll try." The old man nodded in satisfaction, and went through the first two quatrains. He repeated after the old man. "Pass me that oil."

"Here.

'The tyrant rides his saddle high,
he sweeps his saber low,
but the peasants know the time is nigh,
their strength will surely grow.'"

Again Tadek was struck with the awkward dignity of the old-fashioned lines, though he knew, as Vasilenko often enough said, "They're not Pushkin." But more than the lines' anachronisms and pride, Tadek was struck by the discipline of Vasilenko's mind to have created and stored these thousands of lines as a barrier against the anarchy and degradation of the Gulag.

Tadek repeated each quatrain twice before Vasilenko would go on to the next. After three stanzas, Tadek would go back and try to reconstruct all three, and after nine, all nine. In this way they continued, as with another part of their brains they dismantled, cleaned, and greased the parts of a small engine. Sometimes

Vasilenko would stop and rephrase a quatrain, turning over the words again and again. Tadek saw that passing on his work to someone else pleased Vasilenko. Perhaps he had hopes that Tadek could write it down someday, that someday his words would be on the lips of schoolboys.

* * *

Sometimes when the workload in the machine shop was light, they would be put to work outside on a loading dock behind the galley. Trucks pulled in with provisions and he and the other machinists carried burlap bags full of potatoes, onions, or flour inside to the storeroom, where a cook directed them. On one of the first thawing days of his second spring in the Gorlag, Tadek noticed that several of the galley workers had set their galvanized tubs full of potatoes outside on the dock, so they could sit in the sun while peeling the potatoes. Tadek kept passing them on his way to the truck and back, and he noticed one of them, her bare forearms scalded red from the hot water. She laughed with another worker, showing a row of small white teeth, like baby teeth, and plunged her arms in the tub again, looking at Tadek and still laughing as if they'd been passing in the streets on a Friday night in a free city square. She had straight, black hair and a round face with high cheekbones. Her eyes were narrow and her skin was the tint of burnt clay. She seemed to come half from Europe and half from Asia.

After that, he began to notice her again and again, as if she'd been flitting in the background of his life here all along. Who could think about such things in such a place? A tug of guilt pulled his thoughts back to Halinka. Halinka! A thousand or two thousand kilometers away, he didn't even know how far! And twenty-five years away! He could not possibly live that long, not in here.

Every once in a while there was a lag in the work, when one

truck would pull away and they would wait while another truck was cleared through the distant camp gate. Sometimes Vasilenko and Ullmanis would pick their way through the half-frozen puddles back to the machine shop to catch up on some work, while Tadek shared the rare luxury of a homemade cigarette, made of dried cowberry or black currant leaves, with the galley girls. They struggled to find a common language.

The girl he'd noted had a tender, wispy voice and shy eyes, but a sudden bold laugh that showed those small white teeth as she turned her gaze full upon him, and what had seemed shy was revealed as full of warmth and possibilities. Once when a truck delivered a load of loose beets, the girls were ordered to help the men unload them onto the dock, and he and she passed back and forth near each other for an hour. Once he was passing her cans of food, and their hands brushed, and he saw her cheek glow as she stood beside him, looking away.

He tried to put thoughts of the girl away, but discovered that it wasn't easily done. He discovered that the girl was a Chechen. A Chechen! That meant that she was Moslem, of course, and a member of the most fiercely independent tribe in the Gulag. Other groups might eventually break under the system, but the reputation of the Chechens was that nothing could dent their will to resist. This was a quality that everything in Tadek had learned to admire.

An astonishing event overtook the camp the next week. In the middle of the day, a Black Raven van had arrived at the gates of the camp and driven up to the administration building, and in full view of everyone, the camp director and the subdirector had been handcuffed by the MVD, loaded into the back of the Black Raven, and driven out the gates and away into the forest. No one bothered to explain anything to his startled staff, who huddled and wandered in confusion the rest of the day, with no orders or plan.

Camp directors seldom gained much popularity, even with their staff, who, although relieved not to have been arrested themselves, were still uncertain whether another Black Raven might arrive at any moment. The guards seemed to not care what the zeks did that day. The zeks savored the irony of the events. That evening some of them lingered in the dining hall, ignored by the guards, who clustered about the camp in worried groups. An impromptu party began.

One man started beating a tambourine. From somewhere emerged an accordion, handled with surprising vigor by an emaciated old man with a long beard and fiercely strong fingers. Two sinister-looking Ukrainians dropped their menacing glares and started clapping and singing a song in Ukrainian, their faces lit with smiles. A fat woman stood up and started a hip-waggling dance, lifting her skirts high up her thighs and laughing with her gapped teeth. The dance was raunchy but good-humored and Tadek couldn't help clapping his hands to the music and laughing with the rest of the room. The music seemed to go round in circles and spin the room with it.

He caught a set of dark eyes looking at him from across the room. It was Lamaara—he'd learned her name—the Chechen girl who worked in the kitchen. He tried to make his way toward her around the edge of the room. Other dancers had joined the fat woman and the center of the room was a chaos of bumping bodies. Just as he approached the girl, the music ended and he stood next to her in stupefied silence. She smiled up at him and another song began. He found her hand and together they moved to dance. This was a song he recognized, a Ukrainian folk tune to which they attempted to dance the polka. He suspected she'd never danced before in her life, but she followed him with enthusiasm, smiling up into his face, bumping her breasts casually against his chest, crowded by the other dancers. He remembered dancing with

Halinka and with Sabina. Another song began. Her breath smelled sweet so close to his face. Her face was round and flushed, her smile constant.

He led her away by her hand. He tried to speak to her in Russian, in Polish. She just smiled up at him, nodding, lifting her face like a present, bumping against him as they made their way down a brief hallway where, already kissing, they found the door to an empty storage room unlocked. They knelt on some wooden pallets stacked with empty flour bags.

As they took off their clothes, the dry, acrid smell of ill-washed flesh only excited him more. Her skin was rough-smooth and her dry lips chafed against the skin of his shoulder. The moonlight from a high window—even in the Gulag, there was a moon!—caught eyes opened wide to accept him and whatever he'd bring. Her hands too were smooth-rough and cool-hot on him. She was short and taut, with wide hips and small breasts. Between her legs he touched with awe her slick, pure, silk purse and she was on top of him, still in her voluminous skirts, moving slowly and then more quickly. She shivered and swayed. She leaned her head forward and her black hair covered her high cheekbones and her mysterious lynx-eyes, but he could see them still gleaming down at him.

* * *

A few days later, the machinists were pulled from their shop to unload a truck into the galley, where Lamaara and her friends were swabbing down the floor. Tadek and Lamaara at first smiled bashfully at each other and then looked away. With each trip that Tadek took into the galley, they caught each other's eyes briefly. Others were around. There was work to be done. A guard stood nearby. After they unloaded the truck, the machinists were ushered back into their machine shed. It wasn't until the end of the week that he found a moment when they were alone on the loading dock and they moved behind a concrete pillar and he kissed her. She pressed herself against him. In her halting Russian, "*Zaftra*," she said. "Tomorrow. Maybe."

It wasn't tomorrow, or the next day. But the time came when they snuck into the back storeroom paradise and lay on piles of burlap bags behind stacks of oil drums, and for the next few weeks, they managed now and then to find a way to sneak away together. They seldom had more than twenty minutes before one of their names would be called by another zek. He wondered whether anyone had ever been married in the Gulag and what she would say if he asked her. If he even could ask her! They pointed, and smiled, and caressed, and kissed, and laughed, but struggled to find more than a dozen words between them.

Also, she was Moslem and he was Catholic. If he ever got out of here, with her, if such a thing was even imaginable, could he ever bring her back to Liaski? He didn't care what anyone thought. He clung to the thought of being with her as the lifeline that would somehow lead him out of the Gulag.

The other zeks knew of their rendezvous and smiled or teased or chided them, but secretly helped them by keeping a watch out for wandering guards. Only Vasilenko did not approve. At first he was angry at Tadek for his involvement with her and said, "If you're caught, I disavow you." Later he let it drop. He had other things to worry about. His cough was worsening day by day, sometimes causing him to double over while coughing for five minutes at a stretch, waving away Tadek's offer of help with irritation.

Tadek waited for the next chance to see Lamaara. Circumstances had to be just right: the right time of day, the right supervisors in the galley. And their meetings were hasty. He tried to talk to her. He asked her to marry him in Polish, in Russian. She smiled and looked uncomprehending, shaking her head. Did she even begin to understand how he felt? She had a few words of Russian, such as yes, no, I want, I don't like. He would have to get a translator to clear things up between them as soon as possible. Then she lowered her head. He could barely see her face in the dim light. Her shoulders were shaking and he thought she was laughing at him. But when he lifted her face, he saw it was wet with tears, which he kissed away, with no idea why she was crying. Then she started nodding, yes, yes, yes, but he still was unsure whether she had understood him.

But it was just the next week, before they could meet again, that a co-worker of Lamaara's was standing on the loading dock in the sun, waiting for Tadek. She was a homely Russian girl whom he recognized but never spoke to.

"Where is Lamaara?"

"She's gone, Tadek. I'm sorry."

"What do you mean, gone?"

"They transported all the Chechen women out of here last night. It's rumored they're going to Archangelsk."

"But why?"

She gave him a pitying look: how could he ask such a question? She just shook her head. Stunned, eviscerated, he walked back to the machine shop, answering Vasilenko's questions with monosyllables. Roll call. The evening meal. After which he curled up into his bunk and stared at the wall, ignoring the voices behind him. Exhausted as he was, his torment kept his mind racing all night with images of Lamaara, above him on the burlap sacks, Lamaara, whom he had dreamt of marrying, now crouched in a train somewhere making its way steadily northward.

He no longer made an effort to memorize the old man's epic, but just listened, a bit stupefied, as the words rolled over him.

But their task was never to be completed. Just a week after Lamaara's disappearance, Vasilenko didn't have the strength to make it out of his bunk and was carried on a stretcher to the infirmary. Tadek heard that the medical orderly had pronounced him a *dokhodyaga*, a goner.

With Vasilenko dying, just three weeks after Lamaara's disappearance, without warning Tadek was told at roll call not to report for work, but to grab his light canvas sack of possessions and follow the warder: he was being shipped out with a gleaning of other zeks, to other camps for reasons discernible only within the vast, opaque bureaucracy of the MVD. In an hour Tadek was on another red-painted Stolypin car, headed east again, leaving behind in this vale high in the Urals his dreams of a life with Lamaara, together with the old man whose epic poem was fated to die within him.

Chapter 36:
Irkutsk Oblast

For days the train went east, always east. Some zeks tried to keep track of the days, lost count, and argued, but Tadek ceased to care. He spent the days slumped in depression, thinking not of his future but only of Lamaara, and occasionally of Vasilenko, and then of Liaski and all that former life. At one of the many stops, Tadek stood and stared through the bars of the small high windows at three camels tethered alongside the tracks. The bizarre, ill-shapen creatures, double-humped and laden high with parcels and boxes, made him think he must be hallucinating. They were complacently chewing and squinting through the dust as the train started up, turning their heads in slow unison as it crept away. One gave him a satiric smile.

Later that day Tadek thought that the camels must've been a sign, because their car was shunted to a siding, where it sat closed for over twenty-four hours, with no water, without even the sound of guards. The zeks were certain they'd been forgotten. As the sun heated the car to sweltering temperatures, they all become certain that they would die of thirst before they ever reached their destination. They wouldn't be the first zeks to have met such a fate.

Finally they heard a train backing up to them, coupling with their car in a clanging jolt, and guards came in and passed around a few pails of water from which each man managed to gulp down a few mouthfuls. For days no one could rouse himself out of his misery to even speak.

There were frequent and lengthy stops, during which Tadek's hunger and thirst seemed to intensify as the prisoner cars were connected and disconnected according to the inscrutable plan and logic of some distant bureaucrat. He was still numb and and lost in a reverie of dreams, too stunned by events to even be aware of his pain and hunger as something separate from his loss and confusion. In the midst of an endless, rocking trek through the day and into the night, one man began to moan, as if he'd been selected to voice their communal emotions, though once he began, his voice was intolerable, and the carful of zeks rained down abuse upon him. Holding his side, he shouted and writhed all night as the train rattled onward. Near dawn he was quiet. When the train stopped and the door rattled open for the guards to pass in a bucket of water and another of moldy breadrolls, the man was dead. Appendicitis, was the muttered word. His body was shuffled out the door, and he was forgotten.

They traveled past Omsk, near his first camp, but then on relentlessly past Novosibirsk, past Krasnoyarsk, past Taishet, and finally northward past Irkutsk, along the Angara River, then through the endless taiga, the flat, swampy forests of larch, spruce, and pine, north of the treeless steppes, south of the treeless tundra, not seeing a city or even a cabin in the woods for entire days.

When they finally reached their destination, the zeks disembarked into a pelting rain, between two lines of soldiers with barking dogs, and hustled through several lines of barbed wire, across a muddy courtyard, and into a long wooden building where the prisoners' heads were shaved, after which they were walked through a shower and sprayed with a delousing chemical. At the end of the shower, Tadek was handed the striped uniform of a '58er, a political prisoner, sentenced to *katorga*, hard labor—again. He could see lice still crawling on the collar of the uniform as he put it on, scarcely annoyed by their own chemical bath.

Beyond the shower building, Tadek saw that most of the buildings, the zeks' barracks, were nothing but dugouts with boards and sod thrown over the top as a roof. He stepped down into the makeshift barracks as into a fetid pool and the odor met him in a rippling wave that stopped him cold. Zeks were shoving at his back and he had to force himself to enter. More shoves and shouts kept him moving forward further into the smoky darkness. Gradually he could see that the bunks closest to the central stove were all taken—even in summer the zeks were planning for the winter—but Tadek found one mid-way, against a wall. He crawled in and hugged his knees and prayed for sleep.

Instead of the brutal voice at the door as a wakeup call, here they had a ferocious klaxon that sounded the alarm, as if each morning were a recurrent disaster. Outside they lined up for roll call. Now the new zeks could see what they'd missed the night before in the darkness and rain. At one end of the muddy yard was a scaffold where three bodies swung on nooses. Crows kept flapping down to peck at the eyes of the corpses and then flapping away at any loud sound, but never flying far, returning quickly to their feast. Nobody told the new zeks anything about the three hanged men, as if this was in the normal course of affairs. Tadek found out later that they had been caught stealing food from the kitchen, and that their bodies had already hung in the yard for two days and would be removed, as was standard, on the third day.

As usual each zek was required to go through his name, date and place of birth, offense against the state, and date of release.

The mosquitoes had seemed to rouse themselves with the zeks and began biting while the zeks stood for roll call. The brigadier, or trustee, of their barracks, a hulking Russian with a flushed face, called Tadek's number for a lumberjack job. Many worked laying railroad tracks here, and the lumberjack job was considered even worse. Tadek tried to tell the trustee that he had a skill, he was an electrician, but the man just laughed at him. "Everyone says that. You're just a general worker here and you'll do whatever I tell you to do."

Tadek was given a saw to carry and, under the watchful eyes of guards, he began the trek with the others deep into the forest. Here the mosquitoes swarmed in multitudes. They crawled up Tadek's sleeves and down his collar. Tadek felt his face puffing up from the bites. At lunch a team of zeks brought porridge, and the forest crew crouched where they were to eat. Mosquitoes filled up the porridge bowl like rice. They flew up the zeks' noses and down their mouths and fringed their eyes. The zeks plucked ferns to stick into their collars to whisk about their faces and tried to ignore the torment.

He worked one side of a two-man saw, and within minutes his hands were raw with blisters, his shoulders and arms weak and aching. He knew he'd gone quite soft from years as an electrician in the Urals. That first day his arhythmic flailing made the zek on the other side of the saw more than once stomp away, cursing at Tadek. They had a quota to fill. If they failed to fill it, their food portions would suffer and that could mean death. These scenes attracted unwanted attention from the guards, who would prowl over and scatter additional threats over their heads. "I'll never work with him again! Put me on the splitting team!" his partner complained to the trustee, who ignored him.

When they returned in the evening, the three convicts still swung from their nooses at the end of the courtyard. Gradually

Tadek was recovering from his emotional stupor, becoming aware of his surroundings, and realizing that he had to regain his senses, become alert to the threats around him, or he could not survive long in this camp, where everything conspired to destroy the drifting, despairing zeks. He brutally resolved to put away dreams of Liaski or Lamaara or friendship as if they were the enemies that threatened his life.

The evening meal was nothing but a colored water they called soup and one slice of bread. It was clear to Tadek that just getting enough to eat here would be difficult. With the work demanded of him during the day and the little food given him, eventually he would starve to death. The Stakhanovite workers sat at a separate table and got extra helpings, as did the thieves, who, here again, were the unofficial administrators inside the camp. One scrawny, boney zek with bright black eyes and a shaved head haunted this camp like a crow, avoided by everyone. Tadek learned that this was Krytslov, who was rumored to have escaped from another camp with a friend. When they ran out of food in the tundra, Krytslov had murdered his friend with a rock to the back of his head and then eaten him, managing to extend his escape in this way for another week. Though he would never admit to the crime, after one look at his glittering black eyes and boney hands, no one doubted the truth of the story.

The thieves were the same as at other camps, walking with the same short steps and side-to-side movement, wearing the same informal uniform of untucked blouse and knee boots. Among them was the brigadier of their barracks, who wielded power by choosing the work teams. He was named Yurik the Red, both because his closely shaved hair had a reddish tinge and because he'd retained his communist faith. Back in the dugout barracks, one of Yurik's cohorts came to rifle through Tadek's possessions that evening. "Let's see what you've got here, young Polack," he said, smiling his malice. He had an evil-looking face with a wide, slick scar running up from one side of his mouth to his cheekbone. He picked up Tadek's bag and emptied the contents on the bunk as Tadek watched him. "Not much here," he shrugged, snatching up a bar of soap and a clean rag. And then, not unkindly, he said, "You're in the meat grinder now, punk. Don't fool yourself. If you want to survive, you better not look at anyone funny."

Another man was walking down the aisle toward Tadek, who viewed him suspiciously, ready for more trouble. He was a lean, gray-faced man, with narrowed eyes and a thin, bitter grin, as if he'd just pulled a prank on someone. "*Dzień dobry*," he said, to Tadek's great relief: a fellow Pole! "I'm from Krakow. There are a handful of us here with you. Get your stuff. We've a bunk for you in the corner where they've shunted us Poles." Tadek saw beneath the man's wry smirk the possibility of friendliness. Now if the thieves came after him, he wouldn't be completely alone.

The next morning when the blood-curdling klaxon went off, jolting Tadek out of his dreams and back into the nightmare, he stumbled out into the yard and was relieved to see that the three, crow-ridden corpses were no longer swinging against the sky, though the scaffold itself still stood, ready for its future tasks.

One night there was a poker game in the center of the barracks, five zeks leaning over a table using greasy homemade cards. Because money was scarce, the zeks played with matchsticks standing for food or favors, but the lack of money made the games no less serious, and Tadek had heard stories of unlucky players being killed for running up large debts. Tonight as Tadek turned toward the wall, trying to sleep, the game got more and more raucous. Finally, a deathly stillness came over the barracks. Tadek turned back to see. One player had just lost a big hand to Yurik and was so far in debt that he could no longer conceivably pay back his debt. Now he had his hand stretched out on the tabletop, really just a stump. Zeks on each side gripped an arm. Yurik himself was lining up a hatchet carefully over the zek's hand. "Just one! Just one!" the zek kept saying to Yurik, his face sweating and distorted, his voice desperate but almost inaudible. And chop! Down went the hatchet! The zek shrieked. Everyone laughed. Yurik laughed and plucked up the severed little finger, holding it above him for the others to see, blood riveling down his wrist. Howling, the man jerked away his hand and pressed it under his arm and curled over it, slowly slumping to the floor with a sustained, muffled groan. Tadek turned back and waited for the tumult to subside so that he could try to sleep.

* * *

Tadek attempted to question the administration about why he'd been shifted here, but they had no interest in talking to him. He pointed out that he'd been sentenced when he was only seventeen years old, when he shouldn't've been punished as an adult, a fine legal point that Vasilenko had raised in one of their final conversations. This technicality was waved off. When he insisted that they look up his file, to prove that the birthdate and date of sentencing he recited at every roll call was both true and illegal, they told him that they'd lost his file, they had no record of him whatsoever. He saw his name misspelled on the one official form they had and tried to tell them of the error, but the clerk just looked up at him and smiled appreciatively as if such humor was a rare and subtle thing. With a misspelled name, he gave up all hope of ever proving the illegality of this sentence or ever receiving any packages from Halinka or Pawel or anyone from home. He tried not to think about any of them, or Liaski, or his mother or father, or Kazimierz. He had to stay focused on the moment, where the right decision could extend his life a little longer, and the wrong one could end it.

Here the guards were as corrupt as the thieves. While walking to the worksite once, a guard told a zek to climb the hill to fetch a log for firewood. He shook his head. He wouldn't do it, no matter how much the guard threatened. "What was going on there?" Tadek asked, as they continued their trek through the path in the woods.

"They receive bonuses for stopping escapes," the man ahead of him in line said. "If they ask you to get out of line, or to go near the warning fence at camp, don't do it! They'll shoot you and pocket the bonus!"

Tadek was sharing his bunk with another zek and they had to sleep feet to face, to crowd together, so one night he had crawled up into his cot early, for a few moments without his bunkmate. The one dim light in the center of the barracks flickered and went out. A silence descended as sudden and complete as the darkness. Someone ran to the door and threw it open, looking out into only more blackness. "The lights are out all over the camp!" Gone were the spotlights that usually probed into every nook of darkness. A few random confused shouts and questions rose around the bunkroom. After a few minutes, there were shouts and the sounds of a rushing crowd outside. Tadek climbed down from his bunk and rushed with the others to the door of the barracks. Outside by the light of a low half moon, he could see a crowd of thieves tossing long boards against the barbed wire along one side of the camp— but this did not separate the thieves from freedom, but from a small barracks where the few women of the lager slept. Now the thieves scaled their makeshift ladders and rushed toward the women's barracks. The guards stayed in their towers and in their barracks outside the wires, playing over the crowd with electric torches without urgency as screams from the women's barracks ripped through the night. Tadek stood with the rest, listening to the screams of the women. They went on a long time, until finally, out of exhaustion or hopelessness, they ceased.

The next day it was discovered that two of the women had been murdered and the rest had been raped. The commandant of the lager came to address the zeks at roll call, an unprecedented event. He was a large, fat man who always wore long, imposing coats, and lived at a villa several kilometers away, visiting the camp no more than once a week or so. He explained that because of the dark, no one knew who the malefactors were, but the women were comrades too, and the prisoners must understand that someday, all of them would be in the free world together as comrades, building the Soviet future together. After this edifying speech, he got back into his staff car with his driver, and headed back to his villa.

Chapter 37:
The *Dokhodyaga*

Tadek managed to survive through that summer and autumn, his hands forming calluses where there had been blisters, his muscles hardening and learning the rhythm of the two-man saw, how to adjust to minute signals from the other person transmitted down the blade, the two prisoners bobbing back and forth like clockwork men. The Poles had managed to shift about until most of them were on one work team, so he was surrounded by the welcomed sound of his childhood language.

Yet the other Poles could not save him from the situation. Despite his growing skill and the growing hardness of his muscles, he knew he had to get out of this job or he wouldn't last very long. The trustee marked the trees, mostly tall pines, for felling, while four other zeks worked with hammers and saws to bring them down, and the rest sawed the trees into three-meter lengths and dragged them to the sledge. Sawing the trees once they were felled was arduous but safe. But Tadek also had to take his turn in bringing down the towering pines, the wind whipping snow horizontally past his face, the high crown of the tree swaying arhythmically to and fro, a constant threat to those working below to bring the tree down.

Even as he toughened and escaped any accidents, his anxiety did not lessen, as everywhere he looked he saw the longtime zeks with missing teeth from scurvy that caved in their mouths and gave them the look of a jesting image of death whenever they smiled.

He applied some of the lessons Vasilenko had given him about unraveling socks for thread and making needles out of fishbones and matches, trading the yarn and needles for a little extra food when he could. He saw the other zeks who were wasting away, the half-dead goners, the *dokhodyaga*, who stumbled to and from work until they collapsed or refused to move in the morning. Still the guards drove them outdoors during the day. They were standing corpses, their skin like parchment, their eyes with an eerie gleam. Once at the end of roll call a man collapsed and he was stripped of his mittens, rubber-tire-soled boots, and quilted jacket within moments. As the other zeks hurried away with his clothes, he raised his head and said, "It's so cold," then lowered his head again and said nothing more. He was allowed to lie there a few minutes more before a guard ordered two zeks to carry him away to the morgue.

With the help of his fellow Poles, sticking together at work and in the barracks, together they made it through the winter and into the next spring and summer. Tadek avoided any major injury, but was gradually losing weight and strength.

When the next winter came, it was abrupt and total, and immediately so cold that to stop moving outside in the wind became dangerous. Even during roll call Tadek would dance in place with the rest of the zeks, slapping his arms against his legs, sticking his hands under his armpits, even though they all knew they were burning up the energy they needed to keep them alive.

Near Tadek's bunk was that of a man, a disagreeable Muscovite who'd never adjusted to life in the camps and who complained and cried every morning as they prepared to head out to work. No one—not the camp commandant, who lived in his comfortable villa, or the guards who shot zeks for no reason, or the thieves who stole from everyone, or even Krytslov the cannibal—no one in the camp was more hated than this man.

If only he could keep his mouth shut! Everyone suffered here, but he moaned and cried every morning and most of the day. Tadek thanked God that he was not on the same work team as this man. He was said to be an alcoholic professor who had been swept up into the Gulag for no apparent reason, perhaps to fill a quota. A small man, with little but bones left of him, he had a narrow, twisted nose and almost no lips. Some scabrous, red skin disease had spread over his chest and neck and up one side of his face. Tadek was amazed that he had enough energy to complain all day long and still to do the work. His complaints, which began as soon as the morning klaxon went off, were a dreaded way to start the day, and were regularly greeted with curses from all corners of the barracks. At night after the lights were put out, the old man's moans and sobs continued in the darkness as if the misery of every zek in the compound had been collected and made audible in this man's voice, so that it could not be evaded even for a moment of sleep.

The second winter hit them with storm after storm, interrupted only by periods of shocking cold. As the snow fell, traversing deep into the wood to take down trees consumed more and more of the zeks' energy. Soon the snow was a half-meter deep and the footing treacherous. Tadek's ragged mittens, quilted jacket, and rag-wrapped boots did little to cut the cold. The zeks' workday was twelve hours, starting in the dark and ending in the dark as they made their trek back to the triple square of barbed wire. Snowflakes swarmed in the blazing cones of light that illuminated the prison yard. The next day was the same, and the day after that.

One day a tree came down with a twisting motion and caught a zek as he tried to run away through the deep snow. It slapped diagonally across his legs and back, swatting him to the ground like a fly. When they removed the tree, they saw that the man had a broken femur, a shard of white and bloody bone speared through his pants legs—a certain death sentence here. The other zeks were grateful for a few minutes of rest by a small fire while the screaming prisoner was put on a sledge and hauled away.

It became so cold that even to venture out into the wind for a few minutes was painful, let alone to work in the wind and snow for twelve hours a day, as they did. At sixty degrees below zero, spit froze before it hit the ground. The zeks gathered moss when they could find it to stuff between the cracks of the logs for insulation, but it continually had to be replaced as it dried up and blew away. Frostbite was common, and most of the zeks knew that they were slowly starving to death.

Every morning began with the same piercing, mawkish, whining complaints from the Muscovite. He'd lift his hands and show them to everyone: he'd lost a finger on one hand and two on another to frostbite. "What good am I?" he'd wail. "I've lost toes! I cannot even walk!"

Curses rained down upon him.

"Shut up, old man!"

"We've all got problems here!"

Tadek felt that here, beyond any doubt, he was every bit as much in the hands of the Soviets as when Ivan had held both sides of his head with both hands and had smashed it against the concrete again and again as Tadek had withdrawn further and further into himself. He was still in that same grip, and though its technique for smashing him had changed, it was no less relentless, and it would not stop until he was dead.

One day Tadek was curled in his bunk, eyes staring straight ahead of him at the wall where the dugout earth met the helter-skelter roof of tarpaper, branches, and moss. The gnawing pain in his stomach was the source of his strange, dream-like state, in which he was awake and yet felt asleep. The dim, sulfurous light in the center of the barracks created shifting shadows against the gray planks. He sensed a movement before he saw it: a mouse on a plank a few feet from his face. He didn't move. He'd become intensely alert. Everything took on an unreal clarity and movements seemed to slow down, as if Tadek could suddenly see every action broken down into a thousand slight motions. He noted the mouse's tiny scaly claws, its pinkish nose. It skittered with timid movements out onto the plank a few inches, then turned and disappeared into a hole in a rotten log. A moment later, it ran out a few more inches before pausing, twitching its whiskers. Tadek focused his entire being on the small gray sack of life. When it skittered up near his hand, then turned away and paused, his hand shot out and grabbed the mouse. He smashed its biting face against the log, and then thoroughly crushed its head between his thumb and forefinger. It was dead. Without a pause he put the entire mouse into his mouth, chewing and sucking on the guts and muscles, craving its tiny bit of strength, feeling it fill him, separating the bones with his tongue, finally spitting out the pelt and splintered bones against the wall.

* * *

For three mornings in a row the scrawny old Muscovite cried real tears as he rose in the morning, almost too exhausted to move. He chanted, "I'm not going, I'm not going." He sobbed unselfconsciously to himself, tears glistening down his filthy face. Tadek could scarcely look at him, whether from disgust or pity, he wasn't sure himself.

Finally the Muscovite would get up and stagger along with the rest of them outside to roll call and to breakfast, and from there to the worksite, where they were exposed in the flat-out Siberian wind that seemed to suck all heat from one's body. The old man was on a mortar-mixing job erecting a new administrative building outside the perimeter of the camp, so Tadek did not have to see him during the day.

Yet he made it through that day like everyone else. So the next morning when he began to sob and chant, "I'm not going. I can't do this any longer," Tadek looked away as usual. As he swung himself out of the bunk, he realized that the entire barracks had gone silent except for a rhythmic thump, thump, thump. He looked up and followed everyone's gaze back to the old man. He couldn't see what he was doing, backlit and cast into shadow from the doorway behind him. Tadek moved closer. Thump, thump, thump. The man held a brick in his hand and was pounding it into the bench between his legs where he sat. Tadek moved closer. The barracks full of men, unmoving, under some deranged spell, stood watching the man. The man was pounding a nail into his scrotum, nailing his bloody sack of skin to the bench, weeping as he lifted and lowered the brick that he used for a hammer. "I'm not going!" Someone finally lunged at the man, cursing him, and grabbed the brick out of his hand. Others called for the guards.

Tadek was certain that he was in the bottom pit of hell, lost beyond all redemption.

Chapter 38: Typhus

It was still early in Tadek's second winter in Irkutsk Oblast that the typhus began. The guards marched the zeks through weekly baths, which the zeks despised. Here anything they had was stolen, including time they might've spent resting and recuperating for the next day. They were given a small bowl of hot water with which to wash (cooled with as many icicles as you wished). The delousing process was considered a sour joke, fulfilling some Moscow order but only seeming to invigorate the parasites. Further, if you had a coat that fit you and offered a little insulation against the cold, you could count on ending up with one that was too small and useless after you fell upon the pile of clothing following your futile, ritualistic stripping and wetting of your hands and armpits.

It was here that Tadek first noticed red spots on the arms and back of the man in front of him. Once he saw the spots, then he saw them on another man, and another. He wondered what the spots meant, and within a week a hundred men were down with typhus.

The disease began with a slight fever and reddish spots over your back and chest and arms. Later came the delirium and the coughing and the joint pain so severe that you could not stand.

his grandfather who came and put a hand behind his back and fed him spoonfuls of soup, his grandfather, the badger.

In a week the fever broke. He awoke from the torment, lucid and hungry. The little badger man, a zek, an orderly, came and knelt by his side. "Ah, I knew you'd make it!" he said. "I can always tell." The man brought Tadek a cup of water.

"Thank you," Tadek said. It seemed like months since he'd tasted water.

"Not too fast."

"I thought you were a badger," Tadek said.

"Ha-ha! Maybe on my papa's side!" He gave him some more water. "Slowly, slowly. That Moscow doctor, you know, called you dokhodyaga, he did, but I knew you could do it!" His shrewd wrinkled face smiled widely, as if proving the Moscow doctor wrong was a feather in his cap, perhaps as important in its way as Tadek's actual survival.

Later he brought Tadek a bowlful of soup with large chunks of potatoes floating in it. Over the next few days Tadek learned that his name was Lev Kostrapov and that he was from near Leningrad and had been in the system ten years. Tadek talked to him and watched him as he tended on the twenty patients lying in the barn, astounded at his energy and patience. Lev was an uneducated peasant who seemed to divine what his patients needed through scents and intuitions, visions and megrims. He made various teas with bark and herbs, going from zek to prostrate zek, kneeling down and cajoling them to drink. His long intelligent nose was always sniffing, wrinkling, judging. All the while as he walked up and down the line of patients, his shrewd face bore a secretive smile, and he hummed folk tunes to himself. He'd been given authority in the barn, with no formal doctor assigned to the camp, and three or four zeks working under him treated him as the master alchemist. As Tadek lay in the barn, regaining his strength, he studied the man, wishing to decipher the hidden life-secret Lev had discerned for himself, but eventually Tadek decided that whatever the secret was, it wasn't for the telling, but was in the very spry step and wrinkled nose of the man himself.

Within five days Tadek was standing up. Two days later he was sent back into the woods. A week later at roll call he was told to get his sack of belongings: he was being transferred again.

Chapter 39: An Old Friend

With twenty other zeks, Tadek was trucked out of the camp through the taiga, and then along the Angara River to a transit camp, where they waited a week before being boarded into a plain freight car and shipped past the city of Irkutsk and then west, west, and further west. They reversed Tadek's route across Siberia from almost two years earlier: Irkutsk, Taishet, Krasnoyarsk, Novosibirsk, Omsk.

Finally they crossed the Urals and then traveled through the heart of Russia, skirting Moscow, and then northwest, deeper into the end of winter, across flat plains filled with dark pines, streaked with occasional birches. The train trip lasted almost three weeks, during which the doors were opened once a day to give each zek a lump of bread, empty the latrine pail, and pass around a bucket of water with a dipper for them to fight over. There was a central stove, which only sporadically had a few scraps of wood to burn, so Tadek spent those days as close to it as he could get, huddling on a scrap of straw, shuddering with the cold, incurious about anything, certain for some reason that if he was going to die in the Gulag, it wouldn't be on one of these interminable, pointless train trips during which he lacked a life vivid enough to lose; no, he would die by the slash of a sudden knife blade while he stood in line at the mess hall, or under a toppling tree in the forest, an incidental event barely rippling the tedium of another featureless camp's routine.

Finally they were unloaded at night into a camp which Tadek discovered was located at another far edge of the Soviet universe, somewhere in Leningrad Oblast, past Luga. They were surrounded by forests and under a dark gray sky, which crumbled upon them a slow, gray, constant, mealy snow, as if the sky itself were gradually disintegrating and flaking down.

Lined up for evening mess later that week, Tadek felt a nudge on his elbow behind him. "Hey! Is that you?" A grating, bass voice, a voice familiar from another life. "Gradinski?"

He turned slowly to see a wiry man in a camp uniform, smirking at him as if they'd just met up in a tavern.

Besides a sleek, nasty scar under his eye, the Gulag hadn't changed Kozel. They sat down across from each other at the long, greasy table for their fifteen minutes of mealtime. Kozel gestured to his scar and said, "A snitch!" He smiled. "But he'll never rat on anyone again. The little bitch!"

"Any word from Liaski?" Tadek asked. "Do you know anything about what happened to my mother?"

"Nothing about your mother. She's still in prison I assume. They've wiped out the partisans in that area."

"And Kazimierz?"

"Kowal? Yes, he's dead." Kozel was matter of fact. His eyes were cold and hawk-eyed, as if he'd never loved or lost anyone.

So it was done. All of the sacrifices of Kazimierz and the others. Finally they'd sacrificed their lives. What had they gained? Stalin had won.

And all of his own actions, what were they for? Four years of his running messages. The arrest. The beatings at the hands of the NKVD. Now the Gulag. Till 1975.

"But I do have other news," Kozel said, smirking still as he spooned the horrible gray soup into his mouth. He leaned forward to whisper. "That girl of yours, that Nowak girl. She got married. Right away. To that friend of yours, that Karposowich kid."

"What?" Tadek asked, tormenting himself by needing to hear it again.

"That girl. Halinka Norwick. She married Pawel Karposovich."

The clinking and scraping of tin spoons on tin bowls continued. Kozel still grinned. Tadek could still hear the sounds. He could see Kozel's grin. Maybe Kozel was lying, inventing this just to torture him for whatever opaque motivations his obscure soul might breed. Maybe it wasn't true. And how could Kozel know all this? But Tadek felt that it was true.

Tadek seemed to have been disconnected from things and swam somewhere behind himself, disembodied, behind a sheet of ice. He couldn't connect. Whatever he tried to hold onto just let him slip away.

"Hey, Gradinski! Don't take it so hard! Pussy's everywhere. Even in the Gulag!"

Tadek stood up and stumbled away, turning in his bowl at the window, moving outside into the continuous snow. Between the buildings lay shoveled paths heaped with snow on either side. For a moment he couldn't remember his new barracks, didn't know what path to take. He heard Kozel behind him, "Hey! Hey, Tadek!" but he wandered the courtyard until he found his way back to his barracks where he stumbled to his bunk and curled up, waiting for the brutal call of the next morning, when he would rise to stand in line for roll call, just as he had a thousand other mornings. Only now he wasn't sure why he should bother trying to make it through another dangerous day. He looked out over the brutish landscape

419

of the courtyard, nothing but churned mud and ridges of ice, and felt he saw the underlying essence of existence.

It was as though there was no love or loyalty left in the world. Always, despite everything, he had rested his hope on the memories of life in Liaski, on the friendship of Pawel, and finally on the love of Halinka. Pawel and Halinka, married!

Over the next few days, he decided that he must resolve to trust no one and nothing, to no longer give in to the illusions that he'd needed in his youth. He also resolved to keep himself alive for himself, if for no other reason but to spite the rest of the world. His existence would be a spit in their faces.

* * *

A few days later Kozel approached him as he left the mess hall.

"We have something going on in my barracks I want to get you in on."

"What is it?"

"I can't tell you now. We have to get you transferred to my barracks."

Tadek was suspicious. "I'm all right where I am. What difference does it make?"

"It makes a difference."

"Maybe."

"Believe me. I'm trying to do you a favor as Kowal's nephew."

"All right."

There were other zeks who could have asked for a transfer to Kozel's barracks, including snitches and foremen whom the administration favored and who had more pull than Tadek, who was a nobody, but Kozel had a few brief, persuasive conversations with these other candidates for transfer and they decided to pass on their opportunity. This was the first sense Tadek had of how widely feared Kozel was in the camp.

So Tadek transferred into barracks No. 11, a Finnish-designed hut, different from the rest at the camp, which were regulation army, and not the squalid burrows he'd faced elsewhere. This hut had been intended for free workers but was built accidentally inside the barbed wire. It was divided into four rooms instead of the one large room typical of barracks. It was here Tadek arrived, carrying his small bundle of possessions after dinner one night. Kozel introduced him. There were eleven other zeks there who occupied the six bunks in one of the rear rooms.

"Well?" Kozel asked. "Notice anything?"

"No."

"Look around. See what you can discover. Look closely."

"All right."

What was there to notice? It was a perfectly regular barracks besides the different room layout. He walked around shaking his head while the others watched. He inspected the floor carefully. He knew something was being plotted, but he didn't know what he should look for. He sensed a certain tension from the other prisoners as they watched him inspect the pot-bellied, cast-iron stove at the rear of the room, but even with that clue, looking twice as closely, he could find nothing.

When everyone was satisfied that he was unable to discover their secret, they showed him. He followed Kozel up a bunk by the stove, and through a loose board into the attic of the barracks, where Tadek saw mounds of dirt spread throughout the attic. Kozel crawled across some boards, with Tadek following, and then swung himself down in a gap beside the rear wall. There had been a recess in the wall to give extra space for the stove, and here a false wall had been built. It was behind this false wall that Kozel now climbed down a makeshift ladder, into a hole in the ground that gave just enough room for one man to move about. Kozel disappeared from that small area and Tadek followed him down the ladder. Here at the bottom was a dugout space giving enough room for Kozel and Tadek to crouch and turn around. The black mouth of a tunnel, less than a meter high, gaped before them. Kozel flipped a switch and a long string of lights lit up, stretching into the distance down the tunnel.

"How?"

"It took us months, but we stole wire and lightbulbs from the camp's stores and then hooked up to our barrack's lights."

Tadek was dumbfounded. He'd never heard or dreamt of such a wonder coming to be in the Gulag. Later Kozel explained the plan. They had started the tunnel the previous summer and planned to finish in the early summer. They had continued only haltingly during the winter months, because they needed to wait for the thaw to put in more airshafts. Without adequate ventilation at the furthest reaches of the tunnel, no one could work more than a brief period. An elaborate pulley system allowed them to bring a wooden boxload of dirt up to the attic where they scattered it along the flimsy floorboards.

They would all escape to the free workers' camp a few kilometers away, steal a few trucks, and scatter into the forest. Eventually they would abandon the trucks and head over the taiga either north for Leningrad, to blend in with the masses, or west for the Bay of Finland, with the hope of escaping the Soviet empire entirely.

Tadek had seen people shot down just for straying too close to the fence, let alone attempting escape. He wondered whether the whole plan weren't more of an elaborate fantasy than anything practical. Kozel saw his hesitation.

"What other plan do you have? Are you going to stay here until 1975?" This last argument was one that Tadek couldn't get around.

He'd been in the Gulag three and a half years now and it was the end of February, 1953. He was twenty-one years old and would be forty-three when his sentence was up, an age he could scarcely imagine: the better part of his life would be gone, if, indeed, he lived to see freedom.

When he thought of Kazimierz's death and the marriage of Halinka and Pawel, any remaining caution turned to ash and blew away. Unsure whether he aimed to run away from the Gulag, or away from the thoughts of Pawel and Halinka that tormented him, he nodded and said, "All right. I'll go."

Kozel smirked. "I knew you would. I've got you figured out, kid. I always have."

Ilya Marchenko, a thickset Russian with a pockmarked face, spoke up. He'd become the de facto leader of the group. Tadek knew he'd been a captain in the army and had fought his way on foot across Russia, Ukraine, Byelorussia, and Poland into the heart of Berlin. Though Tadek mistrusted Russians as a rule, he felt he knew what to expect from Marchenko's straightforward style. He reminded Tadek of someone he'd known before who had been trustworthy, even though he couldn't remember whom. Besides, Kozel was the only other Pole in the group, and one of only a few scattered through the camp. As elsewhere in the camps, groups here that were enemies on the other side of the barbed wire formed alliances against their common enemies. Another Russian, an architect from Moscow named Rostropovich, was also a leader. It was he who had planned the tunnel and plotted its course.

Tadek was still regaining his strength from his bout of typhus and was nagged by a heavy cough, but he looked forward to his own chance to work on the tunnel. The prospect of lying on his belly in the dirt two meters under the ground, digging with a spoon stolen from the mess hall, was the only reason he could see to live.

*   *   *

"Follow me." Kozel nudged Tadek's arm. Lights had been out inside the barracks for a time and he'd been drifting off to sleep.

"Where?"

"We have a job to do. Just follow me."

Tadek climbed down, slipped on his boots and jacket, and caught up with Kozel, who was already down the hallway to the barracks door. The door was locked every night and there were bars on the windows, but these barriers were indifferently maintained, and Kozel went without hesitation to open one of the side windows, and, sliding a knife through a crack, flipped open one side of the bars. He quickly squeezed through the narrow space and dropped down to the ground outside. "Hurry!"

Tadek neither particularly liked nor trusted Kozel, but his respect for Kozel's resourcefulness and courage was considerable, and he felt he owed him in several ways. He followed him through the space. "Where are we going?"

"Better if you don't ask questions."

The campgrounds, brightly lit until eleven, were now darkened except for the perimeter lights on the guard towers and the spotlights that probed the interior. The guards made only infrequent rounds within the barbed wire this late, and the widely spaced towers afforded only a limited view of the yard. It was a moonlit night, but still Kozel and Tadek slipped with little exposure from one shadow to the next. The footing was tricky with the frozen ridges of mud and trampled snow, but they managed to quickly dodge from barracks to barracks to the other side of the camp. Kozel stopped at a corner of another barracks. "Wait here and tap if anyone comes by. One tap, danger. Two taps, all clear." Kozel had evidently worked out his plan ahead of time. He slid around the corner. Tadek could hear him climbing onto a rain barrel and making his way through a window to the inside of the barracks.

Tadek stood waiting in the shadows, growing colder and more in doubt. He could see the edge of one guardhouse and the end of the mess hall down a long alleyway between the barracks. A spotlight swept over the courtyard, blanching it a deathly white, but when it was gone, Tadek felt hidden in the moon shadow of the barracks.

Confident Russian voices rang through the clear night, startlingly close. Footsteps crunched on frozen turf. Two guards came into view, shadowy figures walking down the center of the clearing between the rows of barracks. Tadek pressed himself against the wall. He heard Kozel scraping to open the window around the corner. Ever so slightly, he tapped on the window on his side of the building. The scraping at the window stilled. The Russians continued their casual inspection of the night, disappearing down the lane between the barracks. He tapped again, twice this time. He heard Kozel drop to the ground around the corner, and then he was beside Tadek, grinning, stooping to wipe his knife blade in some dirty snow.

"Let's go." Kozel ran quickly, with a sort of bow-legged lope, to the shadow of the next barracks. "Wait a moment." Kozel ran between the ranks of barracks, where the guards had just passed, and stooped down. When he ran back to Tadek's side, he was dragging deeply on the cigarette butt the guard had tossed. "Ahh," Kozel sighed, luxuriously, "this is real tobacco! No dried cowberry shit!" The long scar under his eye looked particularly sinister in the shadows. "It's good to be alive, even in prison." Just the smell of decent tobacco made Tadek's head swim.

The next day at mess came the news that a snitch from barracks No. 18 had been knifed during the night. It turned out that this war against the snitches had been building gradually. This was the second one killed. The thieves had never been as big a problem in this camp as in Irkutsk, but the zeks here were just as defiant and rebellious, so they'd focused their attention on the snitches, who were the administration's main source of information. Kozel and a few others scattered throughout the camp volunteered to be the enforcers for all the zeks.

Tadek could scarcely believe the arrogant manner in which Kozel had used him. That was his manner—boldfaced, defying you to do anything about it.

"I'm not helping you again," Tadek said. "You don't need me."

"I do need you. I needed you last night. We'll put it to the room." Some of the tunnelers thought that it was too risky for Kozel to continue his role of commissioned snitch-assassin when their tunnel was so far advanced, but others were persuasive that it served a larger cause for the whole camp to get rid of snitches. Only the recent space created by snitches being in fear had allowed them to get this far, and since the camp would be stuck with a crackdown once they'd escaped, they owed their fellow zeks some help. Besides, it would be the snitches who would be most likely to uncover any rumors of the tunnel. They needed to be kept watching over their shoulders. And there were a few particularly damaging snitches still operating. A vote was taken among the tunnel-diggers, and it was determined that it was Tadek's job to continue helping Kozel when he needed it.

At the spring thaw, their progress improved. By autumn they had already dug one airshaft under the neighboring barracks, and this had allowed some work during the winter. Now they added another one directly under the guard tower. The first breath of fresh air far in the tunnel was like the scent of freedom for the prisoners. Rostropovich calculated their position with precision, scratching figures with a pencil stub on a piece of wood, which he would then sand down.

The tunnel itself was only about forty centimeters high and had now reached almost thirty meters in length, so the work entailed shimmying oneself over that distance on one's elbows, forwards and backwards. As the tunnel lengthened, their work slowed. The tunnel was now over halfway towards its endpoint of a drainage trench that ran along one side of the camp, where the prisoners could emerge shielded from the sight of the watchtowers and the sweep of the searchlights. From the trench it was a short run to a thicket of trees. They hoped to finish by the first warm weather.

They worked in three shifts of four men each after their twelve hour workday: one at the end of the tunnel, a second behind him to drag back the excavated dirt, and a third to scatter the dirt over the loft. The fourth served as a lookout: there was a simple system to tell the tunnel workers whether to lie low (one knock) or to evacuate (two knocks). When the workers' shifts were done, they changed in the attic into extra uniforms stolen from the bath house, so that no muddied clothes could reveal their underground work.

* * *

"Come on," Kozel said. He was standing next to Tadek's bunk in the dark. Tadek realized he'd been nudging his shoulder for a time.

"What is it?"

"A job to do. Come on."

Half nauseated at the trap he was in, he dropped to the floor, and, feeling his way in the dark, followed Kozel out into the hallway, out the side window and into the night. Searchlights swept their cold ellipses over the rows of barracks and moved on with a predatory swiftness, leaving the darkness intensified.

"Who is it?"

"You want to know who? What difference does that make? We've been over this with the whole group. This is your job! Here. Just in case." He handed Tadek a three-inch blade with a wooden handle wrapped in black tape. Tadek stuck it in his waist and followed Kozel as he crossed to the next barracks. They timed their flight from barracks to barracks a few seconds after the spotlight swept by. Sometimes the guards would get bored and start zigzagging the lights about the camp, but usually they followed a set progression. Tadek and Kozel crossed to a barracks halfway across the camp, where they both pressed against the side of the building.

Kozel evidently had an accomplice inside the barracks who had informed him of a way in and had loosened a latch for him, because without pause he stepped around the corner of the barracks, climbed onto a couple of wooden crates, pried a window open with his knife, and pulled away a loosened bar.

"Follow me," he said.

"I'm going in?"

"Yes. This guy may have been tipped."

"Then let's wait."

"Probably he knows nothing." Kozel gave Tadek no more time for debate, but slipped around the bar and through the window.

Tadek followed him, slumping onto the floor of the barracks as quietly as possible. Kozel was already conferring in whispers with someone crouched next to him in a corner. He reached back and plucked at Tadek's sleeve. Tadek followed him as he hurried down three rows of bunks and without hesitation stabbed a sleeper in the bottom bunk. The man groaned and curled up on himself. Tadek turned to flee and immediately felt someone throw an arm around his throat. Before he could resist, the strong arm threw him backwards onto the floor. In the dark he felt two knees bounce on his chest, thrusting the breath out of his lungs and leaving him gasping. Someone's hands were at his throat, thumbs pressing into his windpipe. He struggled, but his efforts seemed to make the thumbs press down harder in a grip he could not break. He felt a black wave sliding over his consciousness as he groped for the knife in his belt. A sort of apathy overcame him, as if it didn't really matter one way or the other what he did. The man shifted and loosened his grip, and that moment of fresh air was enough for Tadek to come to himself, grasp his knife, and jab it into the man's side, slipping it under the ribcage. The man grunted and Tadek felt him jerk with surprise. His hands loosened and warm blood flowed down over Tadek's hand and wrist. The man let go his grip and Tadek rolled him off and slid free, scurrying on all fours down the aisle. Shouts were now coming from the room in general. Tadek found the open window and dove through it. He saw Kozel, already across the courtyard, pressed against the neighboring barracks.

"What took you so long?"

"Someone jumped me. Didn't you see?"

"No. Did you kill him?"

"I don't know. I had to stab him."

"Good."

"Good?"

"One less snitch. Give me your knife and follow me."

He followed Kozel to the latrines, beside which was a tank of water. Kozel broke through the surface layer of ice and they washed their hands quickly and then made their way back to their own barracks. No sooner had they slipped through the window than sirens filled the night and the spotlights began going haywire, moving in fluid ovals over the black barracks and grounds. Tadek crawled into his bunk and waited out the commotion.

Tadek's racing mind kept him awake all night, afraid to move in dread that even his tossing and turning would reveal him. Somehow he must've dozed, or slipped away into a state of timeless, unaware, paranoid fantasy, because when he opened his eyes, minutes before the klaxon, Kozel's face was six inches from his, watching him.

"Here." Kozel thrust a new prisoner's shirt and trousers at Tadek. "Get rid of your shirt. It has blood on it."

Tadek changed and stuffed the bloody uniform behind a wallboard on his way out of the barracks.

There was going to be a special inspection that morning. The administration announced that one man had been murdered, another severely wounded in an attack during the night. Tadek had no way of knowing whether the man he'd stabbed had lived or died. Guards went up and down the line inspecting each zek, one standing for what seemed like a long time in front of Tadek, studying his uniform, his hands, his face, before moving on.

"I'm not going to go with you anymore," Tadek told Kozel. He had no idea whom he had stabbed or even why that person had jumped him: had he been an ally of the supposed snitch? Or just someone who didn't like intruders in his barracks?

"That's okay," Kozel shrugged. "We've decided to hold off on the snitches for a while anyway." Kozel seemed to feel that he'd accomplished something through implicating Tadek in his assassinations, though Tadek had no idea what it could be.

Chapter 40: He is No More

Before evening roll call, an extraordinary event took place which distracted the guards from the attack of the night before. Tadek and his brigade had just returned from their forest work and were milling about in front of the mess hall. Over the loud speakers came, to everyone's astonishment, strains of somber, solemn music. Everyone stood still. They'd never had music played over the speakers before. Why this sudden desire to entertain or elevate the squalid groups of half-dead prisoners?

The music became vehement in its pointless pouring forth of beauty upon the mud and stench of the compound. Tadek heard some scrawny zek, still clinging to a pointless rag of culture, mutter that it was a Beethoven Overture, *Egmont*. Apart from that, no one moved or spoke or even whispered.

In about ten minutes, the piece came to an end. The zeks stood in apprehension. After a few moments, a color guard of soldiers, not regular guards, came out into the courtyard and lowered the flags, replacing them with black-trimmed flags. Yet no explanation came.

Finally there came a voice over the loud speakers: "Comrade Joseph Stalin, The Premier of the Soviet Union, The General

Secretary of The General Committee, is no more." The voice continued, leaden, implacable, laying out each word as a monument for history, explaining how such a calamity could befall the Union and right-thinking people worldwide.

Tadek labored fully to understand the first words. Stalin was no more! How could this be? He wasn't a person; he was a principle of physics, an evil foundation stone of the universe.

Gradually the zeks bestirred themselves and turned about in aimless circles. From one corner came a weak cheer. But mostly there was just confusion. Tadek wondered if others suspected, as he did, that this announcement was some trick to force zeks to betray themselves. How could Stalin be dead? The thought was absurd.

People whispered in more fear than ever. Perhaps the world would collapse onto itself now, the stars fall like leaves, the moon spin off into darkness, the oceans wither, and the mountains crumble and blow away.

But no, he was just a person, and now he was so much manure to be thrown under the ground. Tadek smiled grimly to himself. The courtyard was silent. Funeral music began once more. Finally the zeks were permitted to eat, and did so still in that strange silence, and afterwards, they stood about in small groups, as if no one knew what to do anymore, now that the mainspring of the Soviet clockwork had wound down.

In the barracks they discussed the event. Some thought that their release was imminent. Stalin had been the architect of the system. With him dead, it was all pointless. Others argued that he was just one of many, and that the entire system was built on ideas that no one would disavow now, having dedicated their lives to affirming them.

They decided to keep digging and wait to see what happened. After a month more of digging, as they approached the fence itself in April, it was clear that nothing had changed. The system created by The Mustache continued without him. Beria, the spiritual guide of the Gulag, was in charge of the whole USSR now. Their plans to escape were still on.

Every night a different team worked on the tunnel, reinvigorated now. Easter came and went. Shoots of green lit up the trees that their brigade was sent to cut every day, and small ferns began to uncurl themselves in the woods.

In the second week of May, Rostropovich did his final calculations. They had a three-meter string that they used to measure their progress, pinning it, then stretching it forward again and again, matching these measurements with those paced out and estimated above ground. They were beyond the fences, underneath the drainage ditch dug along one side of the camp. Here they could surface unseen, crawl along its length, and time the movements of the spotlights until they could make a run to the woods at its nearest point. They stopped digging a meter beneath the surface and fashioned a camouflaged cover for the hole. The plan was to escape on Saturday night, after lights out, so that they would have time to put some landscape between themselves and the searchers during the night.

* * *

Tadek was on watch when he saw through the window an unusual crowd of guards and MVD officers walking through the well-lit main camp street and then turning in toward their barracks. He knocked on the wall three times, the highest alert—get out now!

"Betrayers of the state! Awake! Awake! Parasites and traitors, awake!" The calls came from the front of the barracks. The lights glared on in their room. One, two of the tunnel-crew dropped from the loft. Tadek could imagine the two men in the tunnel crawling back as quickly as possible. The lead tunneler had been signaled by three pulls of a string on his ankle. "Everyone up and out! We're going to search your barracks!" A third zek dropped from the loft and slid back the entryway boards. He crawled into bed and rolled over as if asleep. MVD officials and regular camp guards were stomping through the front hall, shouting orders. An MVD official threw open the door to their room and stood in the doorway. "Everyone out now!"

Since everyone always slept fully clothed, there was nothing out of the ordinary to be seen as the zeks tumbled out of their bunks, feigning that they were just waking. All of them filed out into the night. An indecisive rain, half mist, fell softly through the halos of the guard tower lights. Guards with German shepherds in tow pressed past the zeks and down the corridor of the oddly configured, Finnish barracks. More guards passed them gripping crowbars. Though the whole building was emptied and searched, the MVD seemed most interested in the rear room of the building.

The tunnelers huddled together in the mist and said nothing. They looked at the thawing ground, kicked at stones, and avoided each other's glances. Tadek looked around and counted. One of their group was missing, somewhere back in the tunnel or behind the stove wall or in the loft.

They stood there for over an hour. An MVD officer emerged and called the zeks from the front room back to their barracks. The search continued, but the warders seemed not to pay any attention to the zeks. No roll call!

Two other rooms were called back into the barracks. Still the guards searched in the rear room.

Finally, the officer emerged, and without any explanation said, "The rest of you, back to your bunks!"

The dogs trailed away, the guards left with their crowbars. Back in the room, floorboards had been pried and left up in every corner of the room. But the false wall behind the stove, the incriminating dirt in the loft, remained undiscovered. Why should they search the loft? Would the prisoners fly away?

After a half hour, the zeks gave the all-clear tap, and in a few moments Misha, a skinny, goofy peasant lad, not much older than Tadek, dropped from the loft, grinning sheepishly. "What happened? They found nothing?" The other zeks hugged him as if he were their relative, their friend, their loved one. This was the only time Tadek saw anyone show such feelings in the Gulag.

As the zeks turned to their job of trying to replace the floorboards as well as they could without hammers, they all suddenly sobered, working quietly and without words, left with their thoughts of their continued peril.

Chapter 41: Into the Tunnel

They delayed their escape until the next Saturday night, since morning roll call was an hour later than usual on Sundays. Also, it was hoped that the guards would be distracted or imbibing at night. That Friday night, the whisper went around the darkened barracks: "We broke through!"

"Already?"

"The drainage ditch was deeper than I thought," Rostropovich said.

"Well, is the cover in place?"

"Yes. Kozel looked out. We're right in the ditch. No one will go there."

All day Saturday it was raining. There were furtive discussions about how this would affect their escape. Would it slow them? Would it make it easier for them to be tracked? Or more difficult? Either way, no one was willing to wait. After lights out, they waited an hour, and then Marchenko rose from his bunk and said, "Let's go."

The plan was to leave in three groups of four, each ten minutes apart, so that there would be no backup in the tunnel. They had drawn straws to determine their groups, and Tadek was in the second group, with Marchenko, Misha, the young peasant, and Sasha, a taciturn Kazakh, whom Tadek scarcely knew.

Tadek stood lookout at the barred window while waiting. Rain dribbled down the glass pane and puddled in the courtyard mud. The first group of four had left five minutes before. Perhaps they were out of the moat by now, into the woods. There had been no shouts from the guards, no alarms, no barking dogs or converging searchlights.

Once out they were to wait for the others outside the free workers' settlement, two kilometers away, where all three groups would attempt to steal a truck.

Tadek had no idea where he would end up after that night. Once they had made their way beyond the barbed wire, a route every inch of which was microscopically known and imagined and covered, the zeks' plans seemed to dissolve into a haze of dreamy options. Neither the group which planned to head into Leningrad and blend in with the crowds, nor Tadek's group, headed toward the Bay of Finland to be quit of the Soviet Empire altogether, had a clear sense of either its route or conveyance to its goal. The zeks all indulged in schemes about making their way back to their hometowns, getting false papers, or stowing away on a boat to Finland. And from there to Paris! Or maybe even America! Tadek dreamt he could eventually make his way back to Liaski and try to repair his life. He would search for his mother and father. He would confront Pawel and Halinka and discover why they had betrayed him.

Of course he feared he would never make it back to Liaski. He feared he would lead a miserable life of exile in some foreign hut—or more likely, that he would be shot within the next few days. But he couldn't stay in this Gulag death-in-life forever.

"It's time, Tadek. Come on." Marchenko nudged his elbow.

Tadek had learned to trust his round, ugly, impassive face and calm eyes. "You go first. I'll be last out."

Tadek lifted himself up through the loft and then climbed down the makeshift ladder. He crouched to fit his frame through the entrance of the tunnel and began the long rough crawl on hands and knees. It was about seventy meters and took a long time. Towards the end water was dripping into the tunnel, turning the dirt to slippery mud. Past the final light it was dark and Tadek had to feel his way.

"Everyone here?" he asked over his shoulder, keeping his voice low. He could half stand up here, right beneath the lid. Water was pouring in all around the wooden circle that held up a layer of dirt and leaves.

Voices came from behind him.

"Wait."

"Let's go."

"Keep it down."

"Remember to wait till a searchlight passes," Marchenko said. "You should be able to see it against the trees."

Tadek lifted the lid and waited. "I don't think I can see beyond the moat. I can't see any trees."

"Wait."

"I'll wait a little longer. I don't think you can see out of the moat."

"Okay, just stay low. Don't stand up. Just lie down in the moat. We'll wait for the searchlight there."

"I'm going," Tadek said. When he lifted the lid, water poured down. The rain had been steady for hours and the moat acted as a drainage ditch. Tadek pried himself up by his elbows and shimmied out and away from the hole. He lay down in the mud. Just then the searchlight skimmed over the moat, revealing a skeletal bush on its edge. He could see scars in the turf where the others had gone before them and hoped that the searchlights wouldn't pick up these marks in the rain. He could hear the other prisoners gathering beside him in the dark, lying along the center of the moat.

"Did you replace the lid?" someone asked.

"Yes," Marchenko said. "After the next sweep of the spotlight, as soon as it's past, we'll go." It was just a few minutes between each sweep of the light, but now, the time ballooned in the dark, and became a vast empty room in which they were lost and groping. "Wait. Wait for the word. Wait." Then it swept by. "Wait a second more. Okay, now!"

All four of them were up and running in the dark. In moments Tadek saw the dark wall of underbrush and crashed into it, hearing others nearby. After the first tangle of underbrush there was a sudden gully down which he and the others tumbled. Someone cried in pain.

"What happened?"

"Ow-ow-ow. My ankle!" He let out a string of curses.

"Quiet!"

It was Misha. He'd leapt through the bushes and straight into the gully where he'd landed badly.

They all gathered around him in the dark. He tried to take a step but collapsed. The lights swept over their heads, broken up by the woods.

"Come on! Let's go!"

"It might be broken!"

Already there was the urge to abandon him, to take off running as fast as they could into the night. Tadek felt it in himself, as well as in the other dark shapes clumped together in the rainy woods. But Marchenko made a decision.

"We'll take turns helping you," he said. "Come on, we have to go!"

The four of them scrambled up out of the gully and into the woods, Misha with his arm around Marchenko's shoulder, limping along as best he could. It was rough going through the underbrush, with uneven footing. After a few minutes they found the road, where they would be more exposed, but could move faster. Misha and Marchenko were falling behind. Tadek slowed a bit, whether through a sense of concern or with the thought that it wouldn't do to separate himself from Marchenko, he didn't know.

"Here, I'll take over." Tadek slung an arm around Misha. "But don't leave me!"

"We'll both do it." With one man on each side, they carried Misha along.

Sasha had disappeared into the dark road ahead. The road was a slippery clay, and Misha's wounded leg kept getting tangled up in Tadek's legs. They toiled along in the rain. Tadek wondered how much farther it could be to the trucks. It was difficult to tell in the dark how far they'd gone already.

An alarm siren began behind them. They hastened their steps, sliding on the slick road, cursing, and breathing hoarsely. The siren fell low and then lifted itself like a nightmarish tower of sound that would then collapse in the dark to rise again. They could see the settlement lights in the dark, and Tadek attempted to will the space between them and the lights to vanish, but it was one clumsy step at a time before they reached the edge of a line of trucks parked in a field. The engine of one truck choked, spit, and died, and they turned their steps that way.

"It's us!"

"Hurry!"

"What happened?"

"What went wrong?"

"We don't know."

"The last group...."

"We can't wait."

"They may be caught already."

"Puncture their tires, Tadek, Sasha." Marchenko handed a knife to Tadek and he began to run from truck to truck, jamming the knife blade into the side of at least one tire of each truck. Each puncture was a concussive blast of air, more violent than loud, and muffled enough by the rain so that Tadek could hope it would not be heard.

The engine choked and died again. Kozel was in charge of touching the ignition wires together, in the dark and the rain.

"Come on!" an urgent half-whisper, half-call came in the dark. Tadek heard the engine catch, heard the truck's wheels grinding impatiently in the gravel.

"Wait!" Tadek ran to the most distant two trucks. He jammed the blade in a tire. The air exploded out. He heard the truck rolling in the dark. He ran to the next and jammed in the blade.

"Come on!"

He ran across the lot and, grabbing a hand stretched out from the truck bed, threw himself onto the back.

They drove out of the parking lot, and up a small rise where the tires spun for a moment before catching. The truck turned down the only street of the settlement, beneath the one dim, grainy streetlight, and out the other side into the dark again where Kozel turned on the headlights. From the rear of the truck, Tadek could lean forward to peer through the back window into the rain-filled cone of headlights, or out the back at the receding dim streetlight, soon eclipsed in the distance.

A few kilometers away from the camp, they paused for a moment and threw a rope over some telephone wires and pulled them to the ground, ripping them from the poles and cutting them all. They drove on again. Misha was lying on his back and moaning in the dark bed of the truck.

"His ankle is broken," Marchenko announced. He was knelt beside Misha. Tadek crab-walked over beside the two, thrown about by the wild motions of the truck. "Here. Feel." Marchenko had removed Misha's boot and now guided Tadek's hand to the ankle, where he felt the sharp, unnatural thrust of the shattered bone beneath the fabric of Misha's trousers.

"What can we do?"

"Don't leave me," Misha said.

"We'll think of something."

But one by one they slumped with their backs against the sides of the truck bed, put their heads in their arms, and attempted to gather their wits and rest if they could against the background of Misha's moaning after each bump in the road.

They passed no one on the desolate way. They drove for hours. It was still dark when the engine began to cough and choke and then died. They were out of gas. Everyone save Misha climbed out of the truck and clustered together beside the road.

"Don't leave me!" Misha called, to no one and everyone.

One zek with a bit of medical knowledge attempted to set the bone. They searched with their hands in the back of the truck and found some scraps of wood with which they could fashion a splint. Misha groaned and cursed as they tried to straighten his leg before wrapping rags tight around the wood.

The rain had stopped and a swollen moon hung low in the west, silvering the landscape. They could see that they were in a sparse woodland of birch and cedar, interspersed with clearings of knee-high weeds, which would probably have soggy, swampy patches. They walked away from the truck, ignoring Misha's shouts, talking quietly about his fate.

"What do we do?"

Marchenko shook his head. "We can't take him."

"We can't." The others agreed.

"I'll tell him," Marchenko said, and climbed into the back of the truck. The others could hear his low voice. Misha shouted and pounded against the wooden bed of the truck. They gave him a share of the food they had been saving, and set off down the road.

Misha was unrelenting. "If you leave me, they'll kill me! I'll be eaten by wolves! You aren't men, you're dogs!" It was gruesome to see him transformed from the happy-go-lucky peasant into little more than a writhing creature—but one with the terrible gift of speech.

His voice carried after them for what seemed a long time, full of curses and moans. Eventually it was swallowed up by the intense stillness of the night, but it seemed to have entered the men, echoing inside them. They were in an angry mood, as if their escape had become pointless, as if their brilliant tunnel itself had been the point.

"What else were we to do?" Tadek asked.

"It's not fair of Misha," someone said.

"Shut up. It's over," Marchenko said darkly. "I'll tear out the gullet of the next person who talks about him!"

They trudged on in silence. They had to get as far away from the truck as they could before the day was truly up, and then find somewhere to hide. After a half hour walk they left the road and cut into the pathless woods. The two remaining teams of diggers, seven men now out of the original twelve, all nodded and wished a terse good luck to each other before starting off at two different angles. The North Star made it easy enough for them to get their bearings, one group of zeks headed north toward Leningrad, Tadek's group headed due west toward the Gulf of Finland.

Chapter 42: Flight

Tadek, Sasha, and Marchenko hiked wordlessly for a few hours over the flat terrain. Marchenko had a fast choppy walk and Tadek followed his steps. The zeks sought out the higher patches of ground between the sparse trees. Occasionally they bogged down ankle deep in the sodden turf. Already their thirst was growing, but they resisted the pools of stagnant water they passed. After a time the trees thinned and they were hiking over higher, drier ground. They made a wide detour away from a village. A pale blue glow began growing in the east. On a distant rise they saw silhouetted a boy with a stick in his hand leading a cow along a path. They decided to find a safe place to spend the day, but it was fully light before they settled on a dry spot of ground in a berry patch to lie down and try to sleep. They awoke midday and stayed hunkered in the shadows, eating the stale bread that they had, waiting for night.

"Do you think they're still after us?" Tadek asked.

Marchenko gave him a look of mute scorn, and then softened. "Tadek, there are dogs on our trail right now. When labor camp zeks escape into the swamps, they just write it off as the cost of doing business, but when '58s disappear—and we're all politicals—they turn the countryside upside down and shake it until the '58s fall out." He chewed on a chunk of bread and rolled back into a red bandana the little food that was left. "It's our job not to be there when they shake."

At dusk they set off again.

Soon they saw a hut in a patch of woods and decided to see if there was a well near it. It was a dark night, with the moon under the clouds, but as they crept close to the hut, a dog started barking, the door slapped open, and a woman's voice came out of the dark: "Who's there?"

They said nothing but tried to recede into the shadows of the woods. They turned and kept walking, and not long after, they stumbled upon the shores of a lake where they drank their full. Along the lakeshore nestled a cabin. Here they managed to creep closer and found some clothes drying on nearby bushes. They absconded with the clothes and at a safe distance changed what clothes they could. For Tadek, ridding himself of his prisoner garb allowed him to leave behind his angry mood, flinging away untold humiliations with the ragged, striped, and numbered zek uniform.

They came upon a whitewashed cabin with a prosperous-looking barn next to it. They decided to be bold. It was early. They were civilians now! Though their clothes were an ill-matched assortment of baggy pants and traditional garb, they walked up to the entrance. Before they'd reached it, the door swung open and a young man stood peering out, backlit by a oil lamp. "Go away!"

"We are surveyors from Leningrad," Marchenko tried. "On government business! We ran out of gas and need food!"

"Get out of here!" The man reached behind him into the doorway and retrieved a rifle, which he pointed at the zeks. He could get a twenty-fiver for helping an escaped prisoner. Everyone knew that.

They backed away, Marchenko repeating his story, the man

continually grunting his disapproval until they were out of speech range, if not rifle range.

A low, unlighted shack—or several shacks sprawled together—lay ahead of them down in a shallow hollow, seeming to grow out of the swampy land like some shapeless fungus. Marchenko walked up to the door. Tadek and Sasha held back. "Hello!" He knocked on the door.

From inside there came a shuffling, and the flicker of a kerosene lantern. The flimsy wooden door flung open and an old man stood there holding the lantern. He was a tiny old man, wearing a shapeless hat even though indoors, which he'd pulled down to his brows. Beneath the brim of the hat, his bright eyes peered out into the night, not without some curiosity. Once more Marchenko tried out his story about being surveyors from Leningrad. He had an air of gravitas that might breathe some credence into the fable.

The old man smiled and, miraculously, stepped back from the doorway and gestured them inside. He spoke Russian with an accent that Tadek couldn't place. They sat on stools around the lantern while the old man brought them cheese and some black bread which they made short work of, always beneath the amused smile of their host. Their host asked Marchenko to repeat his story about how they were important government surveyors, smiling and nodding as Marchenko talked, as if the tale gave him great pleasure.

Now in the smoky light of the kerosene lamp, they could see how ridiculous they looked with the clothing that they'd stolen from the hut in the dark. Tadek wore a baggy pair of pants and a woman's blouse. He still had on his felt boots from camp. Marchenko wore a black coat that he'd pulled tight to cover his bare chest, but he still wore his striped prison pants. Sasha hugged what had turned out to be a small rug around his shoulders as a makeshift shawl. The old man's floppy hat made him seem part of the mismatched team, as if together they constituted some allegory of the wages of folly.

After they'd eaten, they thanked the old man and stood to leave. He shook his head. He gestured for them to come look in a trunk against the wall. He opened it to reveal that it brimmed with neatly folded men's clothing. The zeks were astonished; it might as well have sparkled with gold and jewels. He pulled out folded shirts and pants, a pair of boots, a cap, a coat. "Take them! Take them! You need them!" He laughed, scanning their clothing again. "They were my son's!" Now he sobered. But he explained: "They arrested him last year for hunting on government land. They had his friend and him stand up against a wall for hours, facing the wall. They told me it was an accident. A soldier went to take a piss and leaned his gun against the wall. It slipped and went off. Hit a rock just so, and shot my son in the neck." He shook his head. "His friend couldn't really see what happened. They let him go with my son's body. So take the clothes. I have no need of them. I didn't know what to do with them." They sorted through the clothing and found what they needed. The man saw them to the door, shaking his head at their thanks as if it were misguided. They all stood at the door. "A man should die before his son," he said. "That's the natural order of things." They all stepped out into the night. "Head straight west and in a few hours you'll hit the Luga River, and it will take you to the Gulf of Finland." They didn't respond to that. Why would he think government surveyors would want to find the Gulf of Finland, or would not know where they were in the first place?

"That's the government," he called after them as they left. "They're always just taking a piss when their guns go off."

With new hope, the zeks walked on.

True to the old man's word, they came upon marshy, reedy land, still by the light of the near-full moon. They looked for a place to hide during the day and settled on a relatively dry patch in the reeds. The reeds were taller than a man, concealing the zeks completely. Here they slept as well as they could during the day, the reeds bending and swaying above them, making a whisking and clacking sound in the breeze. At dusk the men hiked out of the marshy ground till they could see the tarnished silver Luga rippling northwards.

They hiked along its banks until they found a dinghy half-hidden in deep grasses. It was tied with a thick rope to a stake, but after failing to pull out the stake, Marchenko took a knife and sawed away diligently for a quarter hour until he'd cut the rope. They dragged the boat to the river and cast off. Tadek took the oars and felt himself truly free now for the first time, just as he'd always felt free on the Niemen with a boat rocking under him, the waves making a crisp sound against the bow, slapping it like a kindly uncle chucking the chin of his nephew. He said to Marchenko: "I'm not going to Finland." He'd started to imagine where he was on the map and had suddenly seen a possibility.

"What? Why not? What are you talking about?"

"I'm going to row south to the mouth of the Niemen and then up the river to my hometown."

"Is that possible?"

"Theoretically."

"Shouldn't we stay together?"

"It's all right. I'll find another good boat. Or do you two want to come with me?"

"No. We'd stick out like Chinamen." Sasha shook his head in agreement.

The two Russians settled back and let Tadek row. The

current carried them swiftly northwards with scarcely any effort on his part. The moon was rising to light their way. Tadek could close his eyes and believe himself hurrying to a favorite fishing spot with Pawel. By the time Tadek had tired and turned the rowing over to Sasha, they'd already put many kilometers between them and the dogs that they still imagined were on their trail.

Near dawn they were getting into more settled territory. The huts along the river were more frequent. They passed several fishermen, anchored along the shore, casting small hand nets out into the waters as Tadek had done on the Niemen, but they were distant enough that no words were exchanged. A morning mist was gathering so it was difficult to see what the shore held. Marchenko had rowed his turn and Tadek took over. As the mist thickened, Tadek steered near one bank so that they could search for somewhere to hide during the day. Finally a slight bluff revealed itself right beside them. It held a copse of birches, lined with underbrush, and so was less exposed than anything they'd seen in an hour. Tadek pulled hard on his starboard oar and cut across the current to the bluff. As soon as they'd pulled the boat onto the bank and wedged it under some bushes, things started to go wrong. They climbed the bank together and there, not twenty feet away, was a man standing with an ax in his hand and a pile of firewood at his feet. Everyone jumped back.

"Who are you?" the man demanded.

Marchenko responded, "We're from the government. Department of Geological Resources. We're doing a survey in this area."

"But where, where are you from?" He was backing away now, his ax held across his chest.

"From Leningrad." Marchenko adopted a mollifying voice and kept walking toward the man, his hands out, palms up, as if carrying some invisible offering.

"Yuri! Ivan! Come quick!" the man called, and, a moment later, two men emerged from the woods behind him, one walking purposefully with an ax and the other with a rifle in his hands.

Without a word, the three zeks turned and ran to their boat. It was wedged deeply into the bushes, so it took a moment to rip it out and pull it to the water. Tadek grabbed the oars again. Sasha jumped in and the boat wedged on a rock. Tadek tried to shove it off with an oar, to pry it loose. Marchenko came running into the water and shoved the boat forward before belly-flopping over its stern as Tadek rowed as hard as he could. Someone on shore shot at them, and the bullet sizzled past them into the mist, which slowly, slowly gathered around them, concealing them from the shore.

Full daylight was rapidly coming now, and the mist was burning off, leaving them with nowhere to hide. There were many shacks along the banks, and the banks themselves were barren of trees, with few hiding places. Indecisively they discussed their next move: whether to settle on an imperfect hiding place and risk detection, or keep on rowing in the bright of day. They had just settled on pulling over when they rounded a broad turn in the river to discover about a dozen boats full of armed men, strung across the river, waiting for them.

They were caught. Tadek didn't even try to flee, but put up his oars and let the current take them until the boats closed about them, surrounding them with angry, unshaven faces. Why should they be angry? The zeks had never done anything to these villagers or even to their local authorities. But their momentary freedom had stirred a deep resentment in these men, who shouted and grabbed them by the shoulders, legs, and arms, pulling them roughly out of their boat and flinging them face-first into the bilge water of the other boats.

The three escaped zeks were thrown in a small log cabin prison where they spent much of the day, until MVD officers, with their sky-blue shoulder-boards, roared into town in a military cortege. The officers interrogated each zek one by one, and then threw them to a few specialized guards, who beat them and kicked them as they lay on the floor of their cells with their hands and feet bound.

That evening they took the prisoners, chained them to each other, and slung them in the back of a truck. The truck started up. Tadek could taste the hot coppery blood still flowing in his mouth. He wondered why the guards took their jobs so seriously. Didn't they have friends and relatives who were also in the Gulag? Were they personal friends of Beria? He chuckled to himself, and the guard riding in the truck bed cursed him and shoved his head with the heel of his boot. Tadek turned on his back and found a patch of straw to soften the ride under his head. He wiggled a loosened side tooth with his tongue. Well, they could do their damnedest. They'd done it before and he'd taken it, and he'd take it again.

His eyes searched the constellations overhead. He picked out the polestar and determined they were traveling due east, back to camp. He remembered his father naming the stars to him when he was a child—Altair, Deneb, Vega—like Adam naming the plants and animals in paradise. He remembered how he felt when that phosphorescent chaos of stars began to crystallize into recognizable forms. He tried to look over the edge of the rattling truck for Pegasus. It seemed important to him now to find the Great Square of Pegasus, as if it would orient his life in a way that was needed now, but he could not find it.

He began to shiver with the cold. He thought of the old peasant sitting across from the escaped zeks, obviously still in their prison outfits, and began laughing. The guard cursed him and kicked him, this time in the ribs. Again he wondered, why this devotion to his job? He laughed again, and the guard kicked him again.

When he kept laughing the guard gave up and, after giving him a departing kick, settled down on an empty ammo box as a seat. His face resting on that handful of straw, Tadek remembered his friend Vasilyenko, the engineer poet zek, reciting to him as they dismantled a small gas motor on the table between them:

I had bread from the wives of the village
And the lads saw me right for makhorka.

Chapter 43: Vorkuta

Tadek was thrown into a solitary disciplinary cell where he stayed a week. All of the escapees had been captured and now sat in similar cells awaiting their fates. Kozel's group had been picked up trying to steal clothes from a farm, still far from Leningrad. The last group had never made it into the tunnel when a random check had been made on the barracks. Tadek learned that another twenty-five years was to be added to his sentence, so that he would be released in 2000, when he would be sixty-eight years old. By now, these were just empty ciphers to him, like the distance to the sun in meters. He was also to be transferred once again. Before his swollen face had recovered from the beating he'd received, he was rousted up at dawn and thrown into a Stolypin car headed west and west and then north and north and north. On the third day, Tadek could peer through the gap between the ill-fitting boards covering a window and see that they were beyond the tree line. There was nothing but barren tundra as far as he could see, like the scraped hide of some long-dead animal. Beneath his weariness and misery, there surfaced a sense of awe that earth held such a desolate spot. There was nothing in any direction. No tree, no shrub taller than knee-high, no sign of a bird or a rabbit. Nothing was human-sized, like the gentle bend of the Niemen around Liaski, or the mild flow of the fields into the forests, which surrounded the village like protective spirits.

The word passed around the train: they were headed to Vorkuta.

When the train finally slowed a few days later, the zeks crowded to the barred windows. Vorkuta seemed more like a separate planet than a simple camp. As the train continued for hours, Tadek was astounded to see how they passed *lagerpunkt* after *lagerpunkt*, labor camp after labor camp, stretching one after the other into the treeless distance. The combination of barbed wire punctuated by the gangly towers surrounding the characterless barracks repeated near and far. Each camp had its mining tower too, with its wheels spinning. Fifteen years ago there had been nothing but tundra. Now they could see in the distance a city built by the zeks where civilian workers lived. He heard that there were almost 100,000 prisoners in the complex of camps. These zeks were not meant to be indoctrinated, rehabilitated, or even punished, but simply to produce coal. The only way in or out was by train, or plane, or, only in the zeks' crazed fantasies, on foot.

Many of zeks on the trains were ex-POWs, who'd been contaminated, in the eyes of the state, by their time as German prisoners and had entered the system upon their return. There were also Ukrainian and Polish partisans still rattling around the system. Together all of these prisoners were like those in Tadek's time in Irkutsk, and he liked their reckless attitude. They cared little for the authority of the guards. When the train finally came to a shrieking, clanging, bit-by-bit halt, and the zeks started filing out between the lines of guards, a beefy young guard began abusing the prisoners: "Hurry up, parasites! Step lively, you enemies of the state! You're going to pay for your crimes now!"

These zeks would have none of it, and as one they began throwing back at him: "You cheeky whelp! I saved your mother from being raped by the Krauts!" "I fought from Stalingrad to Berlin and I'm not going to take any shit from an overgrown cream-fed fop like you!" "I've killed a dozen like you with my bare hands!" "May Eisenhower drop an atom bomb on your head!"

The guard's face paled. Wordlessly, he swallowed once or twice, turned, and walked away.

The sign in an arc above the *lagerpunkt* where Tadek and his group were herded read: "Work in the U.S.S.R. means Honor and Glory." The zeks wise-cracked, "Well, that settles that!" "Yes, I'd been wondering what exactly it meant!"

After the usual disinfection and registration process, Tadek found himself in a barracks with a majority of Poles, flanked on either side by Ukrainian barracks. Here as elsewhere, the Ukrainians and Poles, deadly enemies during the war, had sworn an alliance against the Soviets for their time inside. Tadek went around the barracks before lights out, delighted to be hearing Polish on all sides. He was smiling as if at a party. The others began to call him "the happy boy," as if he was a bit insane. He kept swapping information with the other Poles about their hometowns and the political improprieties that had brought each of them to this fate, and he kept searching for some scrap of information about Liaski.

The next day he stood for roll call in the middle of a vast muddy plain that seemed filled with an infinite number of barracks, an infinite number of zeks, like some newly added circle of hell, and his initial relief at being among fellow Poles was replaced with misgivings.

After a day's work in the coal mine, his misgivings grew. They hiked his work brigade to the nearby coal pit where, six at a time, they rode a rattling cage down and down into the earth. Sinking down into the ground was like sinking into a hot, dusty, clammy ocean, which closed over Tadek giving him a drowning sensation. Then they climbed aboard a coal car, squatting down and ducking their heads, and began their bone-rattling trip, hauled by a donkey, through a kilometer of fetid blackness. Finally unloaded in a room where he could just stand upright, Tadek and the others put in twelve hours in the flickering dark, slamming their pickaxes into a wall of coal, shoveling it into a metal cart to be hauled by the donkey back to the lift. Water dripped from the ceiling all day long, and sometimes he stood ankle-deep in the water, which burned his flesh raw after a few hours. Coal dust filled the air like a mist.

Later, despite the work, as he gauged the feeling of the other zeks, he still felt that there was a different mood here. The angry veterans and ex-partisans set the tenor. He was astonished when, as he sat drinking his grim soup in the mess hall—no spoons were deemed necessary in Vorkuta—someone passed around a sheet of blurry newsprint. It was titled "Camp News" and listed various outrages that guards and administrators had committed over the past month, and it called for the release of prisoners in isolation. It also had items of news from overseas: not only was there a *samizdat* printing press running somehow, somewhere in the camp or perhaps in the town, but there was a radio receiving foreign news reports. He'd never encountered anything similar in all his travels through the Gulag.

After a week at Vorkuta, he'd hardly had time to adjust to this strange new world before the news came: Beria was out! He'd been denounced and deposed!

Stalin had died, and nothing had changed. But Beria was the soul of the Gulag. Now he was called an enemy of the revolution. Tadek felt as if this time the planets really would spin out into darkness, the mountains fly overhead, the oceans transform themselves into stairways to the sky. Everything had flipped over in a moment.

Going to work the next day, the zeks jeered at the guards. "Beria was a saboteur and a running dog! Maybe you are one too! You've been his lackey for years!" The guards had no answers. Sullen, with their faces turned away from the wind, they led the zeks to their mine without a word. Maybe they would be denounced, and the zeks would soon be guarding them. No one knew anymore.

Then over the clandestine camp radio more news: East German workers had rebelled!

Every zek in the system had had enough. The samizdat press circulated with one word across its top: "STRIKE!"

The Ukrainians in barracks No. 7 were the first to refuse to work. They sat down in the courtyard and wouldn't move. Word spread quickly. Even those in distant outlying lagerpunkts could see that it was true because the wheels to the mine lifts were not spinning.

Other prisoners refused to go to work. Tadek and those on his work team from pit 29 joined the strikers and sat in the courtyard between barracks. They elected a leader to confer with the other barracks and ended up electing a strike committee representing all the nationalities. They told the warders to leave the camp precincts, since the zeks would act as their own policemen now, and the warders didn't have to be told twice, trotting for the gates shouting, "Don't shoot!" to the sentries. They tore down the fences between different parts of the camps. The guards in the watchtowers looked on but didn't react. They were used to being able to shoot a zek with no cause whatsoever, but now—who knew?—they might be tried as a counterrevolutionary ally of Beria.

The first day passed, with no reaction from the authorities except some hectoring over the loudspeakers. Another day passed.

Still, little reaction.

The zeks organized communication between lagerpunkts. They organized strike committees. They drew up lists of demands. They demanded that the bars be removed from their barracks, their doors remain open. They were against the work norms that the warders had been imposing. They wanted eight-hour days, they wanted to be paid for their time. They wanted to receive more than two packages a month. They wanted to talk to a representative of the Politiburo directly. They wanted their cases reviewed. The more they talked, the longer their list of demands grew. They wanted a release of all political prisoners! They wanted free elections!

They put up cleverly worded posters over their barracks: "Long Live the Revolution! Down with the Allies of Beria!" The women made huge black flags that the zeks hung from their barracks as signs of mourning for their fellow prisoners who had died.

A train run by the zeks connected the widespread lagerpunkts, each connected to its own mine, almost a hundred scattered throughout the Vorkuta countryside. Now the train ran between the camps spreading the news: Strike! Written on its side in crude red letters were the words: "To Hell With Your Coal! We Want Freedom!"

Within days, tens of thousands of zeks throughout the Vorkuta camp complex were on strike.

The strikers delegated jobs and formed a council with representatives of all ethnicities: Russians and Poles, Lithuanians and Ukrainians, Jews, Estonians, Kazakhs, Koreans, Chechens, Georgians, and a dozen other nationalities. They all mingled together in the June sun. No more rasping voices waking them up at dawn! No more breathing in coal dust for twelve-hour days!

The strike dragged on for days of negotiations. The strike committees clung to their demand that they speak directly with

Moscow.

The strikers had access to the mess hall and food supplies within the barbed wire. They volunteered to clean the mess hall and kept it spotlessly clean, though usually it was slovenly, the floor slippery with water and broken plates tossed in corners. The warders, disoriented and indecisive, continued to supply food to the camps. The mess hall staff stopped stealing, so the food improved.

Electricity had been cut off as soon as the strike began, but engineers managed to develop a dynamo that ran off the water supply, keeping loud speakers and radios going. They broke down the barbed wire that cut off the woman's section, freeing them, but unlike elsewhere in the Gulag, there was no molestation of the women. They mingled freely. Romances blossomed. It wasn't difficult to find priests among the zeks willing to marry couples who had either fallen in love in the heady days of rebellion or, like Tadek and Lamaara, had found a way to nurture a covert love in the gaps in the system. Tadek stood as best man for a fellow Pole, a young man named Michal from Lodz, who had fallen in love with a Russian girl from Omsk.

Someone found a battered balalaika and played before and after the priest intoned the ceremony from memory. Later that night, inspired zeks became poets and composed songs. One began

We will not, we will not be slaves.
We will no longer bear the yoke...

Their songs were quickly translated into a dozen tongues.

One beautiful Kazakh woman took the balalaika and sang to the listening crowd, seated in groups in the yard. A Polish count started up a restaurant, putting out tables and chairs made from food crates, serving ersatz coffee he'd somehow concocted. Ragged zeks sat on the makeshift chairs in the sun, watching the other zeks walk by like flaneurs on the streets of Paris.

A zeks' court was set up to settle disputes that might arise between the different ethnicities, but they had little to do. A few suspected snitches were tried, but punishment was deferred until the strike was settled, and other zeks were forbidden from killing the snitches.

No one was afraid to speak his mind; everyone was on the same side, unafraid of snitches. This was the way life should be, Tadek thought, but never was!

Then news came that the representatives from Moscow had come. Now the strikers finally had the attention of those with power.

General Derevyanko headed the commission of notables from the capital. He harangued the gathered zeks in the courtyard while they stood unmoved. "You will get more food," he said. "You can have your grievances addressed one by one. Now go back to work. You must work first." After he was done, they shouted at him: "Take down the barbed wire! Release the politicals!" The commission turned and left the courtyard without a word more. They got in their black cars and drove to the next camp.

A few days later another Soviet General, Maslennikov, came with more concessions. He told them that they could have their numbers removed from their uniforms. Their workday would be reduced to nine hours. They would have permission to receive letters from home.

His words fell onto the crowd and sunk into their silence. Then, starting as a mutter and building into a chant and then a full-throated cry came the words, "Amnesty! Amnesty! Amnesty!" The words seemed to thrust the General across the courtyard and out of the gates.

Weeks dragged on and the flywheels on the towers remained still. The trains which had departed day and night full of coal now sat idly in the sidings. The warders with their tommy guns, dubbed balalaikas by the zeks, patrolled outside the perimeter of barbed wire. No medicine was allowed into the camp. One day a truck drove past the different camps one by one, announcing through a loudspeaker that there would be no more negotiations. The zeks should be prepared to walk out of their camp peacefully when the time came.

They met to discuss their options.

"Should we surrender?" No one agreed. They argued late into the night. But the next morning was greeted with the sounds of trucks. It would be the next camp over, several hundred meters away, that would have to decide first. Tadek and his fellow zeks rushed to the fence to stare down the shallow incline of barren ground to see as several fire trucks pulled up near the camp's gate.

There were maybe three hundred men in the *lagerpunkt* and fifty women. Together they gathered in the center of the courtyard. One fire truck began to roll through the gate, headed at the crowd of zeks, but before it could get settled and the firemen could turn the hoses on the crowd, with a guttural cry the whole crowd rushed the truck, hit it like a wave shaking a dingy, rolled back, rolled around it, and slowly, slowly, they lifted the truck and then tipped it over, chasing its crew back to the gates. They cheered each other, shaking their arms over their heads as if threatening the heavens and Moscow. Everyone in Tadek's camp leapt and cheered along with them.

Before the cheering had quite settled, there came the sound of more trucks rolling past their camp toward the next, which had been a spearhead in the strike. Tadek counted eleven trucks—troop carriers, their beds hooded in canvas. The trucks pulled up in a line outside the camp gates. Shouted orders brought the metal clanging of the bed gates dropping down, and waves of troops, rifles in hand, came jumping out and trotting in rows to line up outside the camp gates.

The crowd of strikers clustered closer together in the center of the campgrounds. A loudspeaker announced that the strikers would have one last chance to walk out of the gates. After a few seconds, two men broke ranks and ran across the space between them and the soldiers. They kept running until they were behind the trucks. From his angle, Tadek could see soldiers grab the two zeks and start beating them, kicking them on the ground. The troops marched in through the gates and lined up and raised their rifles. Tadek watched the crowd of zeks all join arms in a giant U-shape.

Time dilated, warped, and seemed ready to buckle. Nothing happened. There were no orders. The few wispy, distant clouds in the sky didn't move.

Someone must have given an order, because first came the puffs of smoke from the rifles and a moment later the clapping of the shots. None of the prisoners dropped. At first it seemed miraculous. Then Tadek could see that prisoners who had been shot were being held up by those who had joined their arms. Another round of shots came, and the line broke, some tumbling to the ground, mortally wounded, others running for the barracks. A machine gun that had been set up beside the troops began firing steadily, and the cries of the wounded filled the air.

In moments no one was left in the courtyard except the wounded and dying and dead. The soldiers moved without urgency now, fanning out through the camp and closing in on the barracks. They were followed by troops who picked up the wounded and dead and placed them helter-skelter in the back of another set of trucks. Some of the soldiers were drinking vodka, leaning against the trucks, turning their faces to the brief summer sun of Vorkuta.

Chapter 44: Release

When the troops came to Tadek's camp a few hours later, he and the others docilely walked out of the gates to surrender en masse. They were all made to lie down on the ground with their hands behind their heads. They were searched and casually beaten before being boarded on the trucks. Waiting in the trucks, the prisoners discussed their fate, many assuming that they were simply to be shot. Instead they were driven to another camp nearby and pushed into empty barracks to await their fate. But there were too many strikers for the system to easily grind them all up into dust, and those in charge were still uncertain of their direction. The leaders of the rebellion disappeared into the hidden depths of the system. Tadek was moved to another *lagerpunkt*, assigned to a new work brigade, and he went back to work as if nothing had changed. But every zek who had taken part in the revolt had witnessed something—the trembling of a system that had seemed set on eternal foundations, the vacillation of the authorities, the sweat on the brows of generals and the indecisive eyes of the warders. They'd seen people of all nations for a few weeks cooperate in harmony, and they knew their own inner freedom and their oppressors' vulnerability in a new way.

Two months after the uprising was put down, in small numbers, various ethnic groups were given amnesty. With no explanation whatsoever, the word came: an amnesty for most of the Poles of Vorkuta. Tadek had twenty-four hours before his release.

Yet he didn't believe it, even as the processing began. He was given a token handful of rubles and managed to purchase a pair of baggy black pants and a gray blouse. The released zeks were told that they must go immediately to their hometowns, but were given no directions as to how they might get there. There were not even roads out of Vorkuta, the city of camps built in a wilderness by slaves. There were only the railroad cars full of coal. There were rumors that the government would run trains south especially for the released zeks, but this would not be confirmed by the warders who only wanted the zeks out of their charge. With twenty other freedom-dazed Poles, he was marched out of the gate. With a few others he hitched a ride on a vegetable delivery truck into the city of free Vorkuta ten kilometers away. This city was one long main street with a few eruptions of concrete apartment buildings, trailing off into hovels where the streets ended and the tundra began. The camps scattered over the nearby countryside held almost 100,000 workers, but fewer than 20,000 free workers lived in the city.

Tadek and his countrymen released with him walked through the streets with no idea how they would get home or what they could do.

"Where are you going?" asked Michal. He and his new wife walked alongside. He had been arrested just a year ago for painting an anti-Stalin slogan on the side of the factory where he'd worked. He was a brawny-shouldered youth with a cocky smile. His new wife was a short, plump young woman with a round face, and even though Sabina was none of those, for some reason she reminded him of his childhood friend.

"I don't know."

Gradually his freedom became real. He thought, Stalin's dead! Beria's arrested! And I, Tadek Gradinski, am free! I'm twenty-two years old, and free! They didn't kill me, they didn't break my spirit or even my bones! Their lice couldn't kill me! Their typhus couldn't kill me! Their Stalin-piss soup couldn't kill me!

He breathed in the free air. He jumped up and hit his heels together.

"Let's go get a drink!" Tadek urged Michal.

"No," his new wife had him by one elbow, pulling him away. "We have to find a place to stay tonight. We have to find new clothes. Look at us! We have to . . . . "

Tadek laughed. "You're lucky. You have a woman who has sense to save you from your friends!" He hugged them goodbye, but continued with about half a dozen other Poles, looking for vodka and a celebration.

They found a backroom of a store run by a fellow Pole where, with three other compatriots released that day, he drank shot after shot of vodka, toast after toast. They talked about how they would find their way home. They sang together *Boze cos Polske* and the national anthem, "Poland is Not Yet Lost."

> Poland is not yet lost
> as long as we remain,
> what the foe has seized by force,
> sword in hand we'll gain!

Most of the Poles were leaving the Soviet Union for Poland itself. Tadek received sympathy for going to what was now Byelorussia, but he was in no mood to look on the darker complexion of things.

"Come, we must find something to eat, and a place to sleep," one of the drinkers said. They all stood up. Tadek thought of the zek he'd known—it seemed like lifetimes ago—who had been exiled into the town, nominally free, and had come back to prison after three weeks, where at least he could find a regular scrap of black bread. He'd be damned if that would happen to him.

Outside the second shift of factory workers was just being released. Tadek and his three friends plowed through the crowd of gray-clad men and women. He was unaccustomed now to seeing women and men mingling this way. His eyes searched the faces of the civilians. He brushed past a woman and a split second later her face seemed to flash again in his mind. He turned. Surely it was impossible...but yes! She had stopped and stood against the push of the crowd and stared at him. He elbowed his way to her and embraced his mother. The gray crowd streamed, bumping and complaining, around them. They leaned away to look at each other and laugh, their eyes filled with tears. Krystyna was not given to crying. He could not remember seeing her cry since the day of her father's death, the day that the Germans had invaded. In the jostle and din, they tried to talk. He waved his friends away, calling that he would meet them later. They made their way out of the crowd, as if fighting a high current in the Niemen, until they leaned against an unpainted plank wall, their feet in a mucky puddle.

Krystyna wore an olive green canvas blouse and pants for work-clothes, obviously weary from a shift in, she told Tadek, a fence-making factory. She also wore a black scarf about her head, drawing back her hair, isolating her face in all its vulnerability, a face more lined, more crinkled, and yet still his beautiful mother. They looked at each other a long time, tapping those subterranean reservoirs of emotions that only a mother and son share.

"They freed me today!" he finally said.

"That's wonderful! I had no idea you were here! I got out

months ago in Beria's amnesty! I have a job here!"

"You can't stay here! Now we can go back to Liaski!"

"Tadek, I live here now."

"You can't!"

"I'll explain everything. It's good, Tadek. We've survived!"

"Yes!"

"We can go to my place and talk. I live near here. Are you drunk?"

"I don't know. Maybe a little."

She looked at him.

"Yes, I am," he confessed. "Everything seems strange anyway. I don't have any place to stay."

"You can stay with me and Uri."

"Uri?"

"Let's get away from this crowd."

She took him by the hand and led him down a dirt alley with a stream of dirty water running down its center. She turned several times to smile at him and shake her head. "You look wonderful," she said. "Awful, but it's just so wonderful to see you. You're still my little Tadek, my hero."

"I'm nobody's hero."

"Shh! You're mine." She skipped over another stream and started up an outside set of swaybacked, poorly nailed wooden steps. At the top of the stairs she opened a door into a small room with a stove on one side of it and a small bed on the other behind a curtain. There were some large heavy boots next to the door. His mother pulled open the stove door handle, but it was broken and came off in her hand. She held it up to show him and made a wry face. Tadek helped her with the kindling and fixing the handle. To start your own fire when you wanted to start it! He could hardly yet quite comprehend such luxury.

There was a plate of three greenish apples in the center of

the table. Tadek reached out to touch one. "I haven't had an apple in four years," he said.

"I know what you mean! You must feel like you're dreaming."

"Or insane."

"Go ahead! Go ahead! Eat the apple!"

He grasped the apple and held it in his hand for a moment before biting into it. It seemed charged with kaleidoscopic flavors he had never imagined. He chewed on the bite slowly, letting its juices fill his mouth.

"Do you remember," he said, "the white apples in our orchard in Liaski?"

"Of course. Your grandfather thought he invented apples." She laughed. "He *knew* he invented honey!"

She filled a pan with water and put it on the stove.

"We still have ersatz coffee only," she apologized. "No tea."

"That's fine. Everything's wonderful, now that I'm out. Now that I'm out and with you!" They hugged and she framed his face in her hands, looking at him, quickly covering his face with kisses till he pulled away in embarrassment.

"Enough! Now, how long have you been out?" he asked.

"I told you, before the uprising. That was incredible!"

"It was. To think that we could fight them that way!"

"But it turned out the way everything seems to turn out."

"It's a moral victory on the way to the real victory."

"How many times have I heard that?"

"But even the Russians hate the Bolsheviks. I never knew that before the Gulag."

"Some of them do, yes. But it's such a long struggle and I'm not so young now."

She took off her scarf and shook out her hair, which was shorter and darker than he remembered, and he studied the side of her face as she stirred her coffee musingly: it was true, she had aged. Not only was there the new craquelure about her eyes, but, more painful to him, also around her mouth, giving it a puckery look. Her fair skin had darkened and the lines around her eyes hinted at a steady, internal concern that would not let her alone. She turned her gaze to his and it went milder and less inward. He'd grown up in that gaze.

"Have you heard anything from Papa?" he asked.

"No. I still don't know what's happened to him."

"He could still be alive. So many survived and wandered for years. Maybe now that Beria's out . . . . "

"Yes, it's possible. Don't be angry at me, Tadek. Try to understand."

"Angry? Why should I be angry?"

"I told you I'm not going back to Liaski."

"Not going back? What do you mean? Why not?" Then he remembered. "Who's Uri?"

"Yes, Uri." Her mouth made a sidelong, wry smile at Tadek's sudden recall of the name that had seemed unimportant before. "He'll be home any minute now."

"Home?"

"Yes. I'm living with a man."

"But...what about Papa?"

She looked away. "I said you must try to understand. That was all a part of my life, but it's been broken in two. This is another part."

"Part of your life? You're living with a man?"

"Yes. He's Latvian. And anyway, I love him."

Tadek had nothing to say to that. He stood up and grabbed his jacket, but stood there holding it, not wanting to leave but feeling the need for some gesture.

"No! You can't do this!" he protested.. "After everything.

We need to find Papa and be together now."

She put her hands on his upper arms and he felt the calm pressure of her grasp.

"Yes, I can do this. Everything's different now. We can't put things back together. Life has moved on too far. We don't even know if Papa is alive, Tadek! I need something for myself now. Now, sit down, Tadek."

She pressed his arms. He twisted in her grasp, finally letting her hands on his chest guide him back to his chair. He let his jacket slide to the floor.

"I don't want to hear about it," he said sullenly.

"All right. You won't."

They turned in their hands the cups of suspicious liquid that passed for coffee. Heavy steps came up the outside doorway, there was a stamping on the final steps, and a strapping, handsome man came into the room. He frowned when he saw Tadek, instinctively viewing him as a threat, until Krystyna explained, "This is Tadek, my son." Tadek stood to shake hands, studying the man with all the skills he'd developed in the Gulag. Yes, he was both a good and strong man, his eyes neither evasive nor overbearing. He was surprisingly young, though, not much older than Tadek. His handsomeness reminded Tadek of Pawel, though he also had a placidity reminiscent of his hulking friend Bolek. Tadek thought that he might even be friends with Uri, were circumstances different, but he couldn't help but resent him as he went to stand beside his mother and kiss her on the cheek. Krystyna's face, shapely but careworn, glowed beneath its harsh tan.

"We have a little food, Tadek. We have to try to find a way to celebrate."

"I have a few rubles they gave me. As wages for four years!"

Krystyna and Tadek went out together. It was just starting to snow. It was the beginning of October and the Vorkuta summer was gone. Fat, amalgamated flakes wandered down and lay lightly on the ground. "Where shall we go first?" Krystyna asked. Tadek hesitated answering that question, letting the luxury of choice fill him completely.

"Where can we go?"

It turned out there were few options. They had to stand in line outside the butchershop for a long time, during which a silence descended on them, pressing down with the weight of their separate lives, the four years, the accumulation of experiences that could never be recounted. They turned about in line and were silent, smiled and looked away again.

They found eventually a little pork fat and black bread. "I know someone we can buy some vodka from," Krystyna said. As they walked back through the street, she put her arm through his. "Don't be angry," Tadek, she pleaded. "I haven't seen your father in years!"

"I know. But still . . . ." Yet he could feel part of himself relenting. She sensed this and stopped to hug him.

"I'm so glad to see you! We can be happy now!"

"I want you to be happy."

"I know you do."

Back at the room Uri had tidied himself up and prepared some more coffee, but he gladly made way for the vodka. They toasted, with soft voices, to the eternal death of Stalin. May he die again and again! Who knew someone so evil could ever die? What a gift death could be! And Beria would be next; they knew it! May he go rocketing down to the vile depths of hell! And a toast to a free Poland! A free Latvia! Someday! Without the Marxist lackeys now in charge. To eastern Poland—Liaski—free from the bandits in Minsk!

Uri too had been through the Gulag and ended up in the coalmines of Vorkuta, but he had been young and strong enough to survive vigorous and intact, except for the loss of two fingers on his left hand. Krystyna had spent over three years making boots in a factory near Minsk, and over another year as a laundress for a compound in Vorkuta. Tadek shook his head as he tried again to comprehend her desire to stay in such a wretched place. For him Liaski was the center of the world and the perfect home. He would be content nowhere until he was back in Liaski. Yet watching Uri slice bread for his mother or listening to him talk about his day as a tram operator, he had to admit that Uri was a decent man who might help to keep his mother safe. They looked at each other with a tenderness he could remember only rarely between his mother and father.

After Uri had mumbled something and then crawled into the bed behind a sheet that served as a curtain, Krystyna said, "Let me tell you a story, Tadek. When I was a young girl, seventeen, I visited a friend in Grodno, and there I met a young Polish army officer, from Krakow. Very dashing, with romantic big-city ways. We had an opportunity to see each other a few times and, in short, we fell in love and eloped to get married. His parents were as outraged as Papa, your grandfather. You see, he was Jewish. He wasn't like the Grodno Jews. He was totally assimilated. It was a minor detail, really, his religion. Others had done it. A few. But still, the outrage was there. So we ran away and it was all a scandal. We did nothing but hold hands all night. But you can't explain that to people. Who believes that? Who wants to believe that? Holding hands ruins the whole story! And so I was dragged home and he was dragged back to Krakow, and my heart was broken. Papa found Roman for me, practical Papa. He found a substitute for me, to marry me off and shut the wagging mouths, and I was so depressed I just let it happen. But I was lucky it was Roman. He was patient, and I learned to love him even though at first I must've looked at him as if he was a strange fish that had flopped up out of the Niemen into

474

my life. That young officer, I found out recently, he was killed in the war. Not because he was Jewish, but because he was a Polish officer. The Russians killed him at Katyn Woods. Everybody knows it was the Russians. That's what his friends think anyway. He disappeared, and it seems like the unavoidable conclusion. But no one knows for sure."

They were both silent a long time as the past invaded the present with its swirls of neglected emotions and confusion of familiar people cast in strange roles. Krystyna continued.

"I respect your father. Something I never told you is that when he was working as a supervisor in the granary for the Soviets, he received a lot of criticism for working with them, but all that time he was giving information to me that I would pass on to Kazimierz, and he would pass on to those early partisans. He learned about grain shipments, the Soviets' transportation plans, quotas, and so forth, before everyone else. And he pushed hard sometimes to learn more. He diverted grain to those who could bake for the partisans, a real risk. So he did his part for Poland, even though people resented him because they didn't know. They just tolerated him because he'd married into the Belyawski family. Not that they felt he was collaborating. People had to work. But that he was accommodating, let's say. And he took that resentment and did his small part without a complaint."

Tadek pondered this hidden aspect of his father wonderingly, certain that no matter how many layers he peeled back, he'd never understand even the person closest to him. His father had always seemed apolitical, detached, reading his calculus book at the dinner table for pleasure. How like him to keep his partisan work hidden from his own son.

"I counted the years. It's been almost ten years since I've seen Roman," Krystyna said, casting a glance toward the curtain behind which Uri lay snoring, to show the pertinence of her remark.

"I know. But he's still my papa."

* * *

For a week Tadek slept on the floor of the small room next to the stove. In moments of self-pity, he'd ask himself whether things had improved from the week previous in the Gulag. But then despite himself, he'd smile, and curl up closer to the stove, and fall asleep as content as a cat.

He couldn't remain on his mother's floor, eating her food. During the days he walked around the rough frontier town of Vorkuta, trying to find a way south. Everyone said it was almost impossible to find train tickets. The streets were clogged with confused and demoralized ex-zeks. Tadek was determined not to be like them. When he heard a rumor that there was a freight train with a few empty cars leaving that day for Moscow, he dashed back to his mother's and left a note for her, then dashed again through the streets to the railroad station.

Part VI:
The Return

Chapter 45: Liaski

Tadek had had countless rides in these gaunt, bucking freight cars with a sloshing bucket of excrement in a corner and one futile stove in the center. He had been lucky to find this one heading for Grodno, after a two day layover in Moscow, sleeping on a concrete platform behind the train station with the other ex-zeks and detritus of society. The railcar was almost empty, with a trio of menacing-looking Kazakhs monopolizing the stove and, shoved to the side, a dejected Pole with whom Tadek talked. He said he had been the editor of a small newspaper in Lublin when Stalin first invaded and had been arrested within a week of the arrival of Soviet troops. He considered it a whimsical oversight of the system not to have had him immediately shot, the way most of his staff, friends, family, and competitors had been. He had been in the Gulag for the past fourteen years. Tadek was disconcerted to hear that he was only forty-three years old: this ancient-looking ruin, with a face as deeply seamed with unforgotten torments as if someone had laid into it with a gouger. His hair, growing back now from the zek's shaved look, was paper-white. His mouth wore an old man's permanent frown. Tadek wondered whether his Gulag years had worn as roughly on himself. He'd glimpsed a mirror at his mother's apartment and turned away in mistrust from the intense, wary stranger eyeing him.

This train took a roundabout path through Lithuania—what they now called Lithuania—and so it did not go through Liaski but ended up leaving Tadek off on the western edge of Grodno. From there he hitched a ride on a truck. When he walked up the lane toward his old house, he noticed how the trees had grown in the years that he had been gone. It was autumn. The winter that was already in Vorkuta would be here in a few weeks. The leaves of the trees and bushes had gone brown and yellow and begun to fall. Yet everything seemed overgrown. The shrubs overflowed the fence of each plot of land and crested over the small gables that peered out at the street. The village seemed to have suffered abandonment, in peril of being submerged entirely by vegetation in a year or two more. Had it always been this modest, this inconspicuous and vulnerable? It had been his universe once. Yet here a skinny horse nodded as it pulled a cart full of firewood, an old man all in gray driving the cart, nodding along with the horse, nodding at Tadek as he passed. And there an old woman and what must be her granddaughter, a child hardly tall enough to wield the tool, worked their way across a field of grass with rhythmic scythes. Two boys ran across the street and ducked into an alley followed by a black dog. The scent of Liaski filled his nostrils, welcoming him home. It was a combination of river and woods, fields, ancient wooden houses, and ripe and rotting apples.

He wasn't yet ready to talk to anyone and was grateful he didn't meet someone he knew as he made his way across the edge of town. As he approached his parents' old house, his steps slowed with trepidation. At the gate he stopped and looked down the grape-vine-covered path toward the house. Peering through the tunnel of shadows, he saw an old man raking leaves in the yard, his thatch of gray hair bowed as he raked. Tadek fiddled with the trick lock on the gate, still so familiar. The Russians had broken it when they'd passed through and stolen the chickens. He'd never been able to fix it, but someone had and now it worked fine. He swung open the gate.

As Tadek approached down the grape-arbor, he thought the shape of the man's narrow shoulders was familiar. But the stoop was different. Tadek broke into a run.

"Papa!" The man looked up and dropped his rake.

"Tadek!"

His father ran to meet him too, but he moved in a new, painfully stiff way. They hugged each other hard. Tadek kissed his father's rough cheeks and felt tears rolling down them. They finally let go while pounding each others' backs for emphasis, then leaned back, still holding each other, and stared to confirm their sight. The last time Tadek had seen him was almost a decade before, disappearing down the street in the back of a German truck.

"I can't believe...I never thought . . . . "

"Me too."

"So many times . . . . "

"Yes!"

"So good to see you, son!"

"You too!"

"Where are you coming from?"

"Vorkuta."

"Come inside." Roman turned and put an arm around his son as they walked through the leaves toward the house. "I heard you were in the Gulag, but no one knew where. So good . . . . " He stopped and they hugged again.

They sat in the kitchen. There was more to say than could be said, so they sat for a time in awkward silence. Things had changed, both inside and outside. Someone had cut down a number of the apple trees, and most of their furniture was gone. An inferior table had replaced a stalwart oak one that Zygmunt had bequeathed them. The rickety thing was covered in a red grease cloth and it rocked when Roman placed the teapot on it. Roman tilted the table and lifted a wry eyebrow to Tadek. "If only this were all that had changed!" he said.

Tadek couldn't contradict his father, who had become an old man during his absence, even though he was only in his mid-forties. The actual shape of his face had changed, his mouth itself having crumpled inward. When he smiled Tadek saw that there was a gap on the side where a tooth was missing. His hair was still full but had gone steel gray. It was long and he combed it straight back in a severe fashion. His eyes looked at Tadek from a nest of new wrinkles with a permanent, distracted anxiety, though they still focused on Tadek and softened from time to time. "Good to see you," he repeated softly, reaching across the table and grabbing Tadek's forearm with both his hands. "We're lucky. We're alive. We even have our house."

"Yes, we're lucky," Tadek agreed. Their eyes caught, and they both began to laugh. Their laughter caught fire and for a moment they roared, wiping their eyes and pounding their thighs. Lucky! It was true. But such a wretched truth. Just as quickly their laughter was stifled and they sobered.

"Shit," Roman said. "It's all shit, isn't it?" Tadek realized he'd never heard him swear before.

"Maybe not."

"I hope not."

"Where were you?" Tadek asked. "We didn't hear anything about you."

"Outside Ravensbruck, working. Mostly building and repairing roads. They hoped we Poles would be blown up first when the bombers hit the roads. When the Russians came in, they arrested all us Poles and shipped us east. Mostly I was outside Omsk in a *minlag*. I've been home about a month now. Where is your mother, Tadek? No one seems to know."

This is what he feared. He looked closely into his father's face. Their eyes shared the same blue shade. The eyes Tadek looked into were vulnerable, but as he searched them, he saw something hard rise from their depths that said, tell me the truth.

"Where is she?" he asked again, seeing Tadek's thoughts turning.

"She's still in Vorkuta."

"So then she wasn't released."

"No, she was released...she was released."

"Then?"

"I'm sorry, father. She's staying there."

"Staying? In the camp?"

"In the city."

"But why?"

"She's with a man."

"What do you mean? With a man?"

"With a man."

Roman, who had been leaning forward as if to catch the words from his son's mouth that much sooner, now slumped back in his chair and expelled his breath in a whoosh. He eyes held an undeniably stupid, glazed look for minutes, as he worked on the knowledge within himself. But he had been through too much to be broken even by this. He sat up and shook himself like a dog and refocused his look on his son.

"Tell me everything," he said.

So Tadek began. They sat there until the room turned dark around them, talking, forgetting to put on a light. Finally Tadek got up to feed the fire when the room grew cold, and he stuffed a rag under the misfitted casement that had always sighed and whistled all winter, every winter.

"I got a couple of chickens," Roman said.

"That's good." It was a relief to Tadek to hear his father return to gritty necessity. Neither liked mucking in emotional swamps.

"It's a start."

"We're almost out of kerosene." Tadek shook the tin container.

"I know. I was going to pick some up before you came home. I've been trying to find a job at the textile factory in Grodno, but I'm still suspect politically."

"For being abducted by the Germans!"

"Yes, I guess if I'd been a better communist, they wouldn't've taken me."

"You would've fought them off single-handed. By the way . . . . " He suddenly realized his father had been away so long that he didn't even know of Tadek's job at the factory. "I used to work at the textile factory."

"Did you? Maybe you can return."

"I doubt it." Speaking of that time, Tadek was struck not only with how long his father had been away, but how long he'd been away too. That time itself, when he'd worked with old man Stronski fixing the machines, seemed submerged beneath murky fathoms of experiences, events, emotions. Who could even remember back to then? In what meaningful way could he even be considered the same person that he used to be? He suddenly felt a heavy tide of fatigue dragging on his consciousness, realizing the dark tide had been rising for a long time before he was aware of it.

"Are there beds left?"

"Yes, a friend of Kazimierz's, and Jan's, watched after the house. The father of one of the partisans. We can't blame him for the missing furniture. Scavengers had cleared out most of our old furniture by the time he realized what had happened and got the tenant. But they left your old cot. It's been dragged into the other room."

"My old bed! It wasn't worth their taking!" They both laughed. It was just a wooden frame strung with cords, with a few folded blankets for a mattress.

Tadek went to sleep listening to the whistle of the wind through the loose casement above the kitchen sink, though he woke several times at night, dreaming he was still in some camp in the Gulag and that he had to get up to stand in the middle of a vast muddy plain that stretched to the horizon without a tree in sight, only row upon faded row of prisoners.

The next day he and his father walked past the church, which lay a bit out of town, and on into the cemetery, a place of towering pine trees and of overgrown plots. Each plot was, in the familiar fashion that Tadek found reassuring as ever, separated from the next by bristling fences, like the houses in the village, acknowledging that even in death these people could only coexist so long and in such slight space with constant territorial assertion. Tadek recognized the steel-spiked fences around some of the family plots as a type of fencing that had been made in Vorkuta, in the factory where his mother had worked. He'd seen train cars loaded high with the fencing, being shipped out to all corners of the Soviet Union. Now he saw that the steel was already corroding, typical of the poor materials that had been used. They can't make anything good in this soviet utopia, he thought, not even good enough for the dead. He kicked a pinecone down the dusty path.

They found their family plot with a new, unfamiliar headstone for Kazimierz. They'd brought a scythe, and cleared away the weeds from the plot. They lit candles for the graves and stood in silence a moment. "Who put up the stone?"

"Janusz."

"Still no stone for Grandfather."

"No."

The cross that Kazimierz had emblazoned in the tree trunk as a substitute headstone for Zygmunt Belyawski was still visible, a wound that the tree had healed and made permanent. There was nothing comforting for either of them to say, no sense of a peaceful rest or a gentle rounding off of life.

Back home they walked through the back garden together. Everything was overgrown with weeds. The fence had been beaten down in several spots. Two of the apple trees had been felled for firewood and their raw stumps marred the rows of trees. The tree with the white apples still stood though, a few apples left.

"I've been picking the apples. I hauled them in the front room. There are rats in the barn."

"How are the bees?" Tadek asked.

"Don't ask. There isn't much left," his father warned him. They walked through the vegetable garden. "I got some potatoes and turnips. But look." He pointed at the three rows of beehives, which had all been overturned and smashed. They made their way through the ruins. Tadek knelt beside one hive. The slats that would contain the honey had all been kicked in, one by one, a work of systematic destruction. Tadek picked up a loose board and carried it with him as if looking to fit it in its proper place. The next hive had also been tipped over, but some slats were intact.

"I don't even know who did this," his father said. "Armies came through here, and they left the bees alone. Probably some kids."

Tadek's great-grandfather had built the first of these hives with his own hands. His grandfather had added to them. The sight of their ruins dismayed him more than many worse things he had seen and endured.

Yet he realized that he'd been hearing bees all along, and when he looked for them they were everywhere, moving about amid the blossoms.

"Hitler and Stalin didn't manage to kill all the bees," he said, pointing to the small purple flowers where bees hovered and spun circles in the air.

When he got to the end of the garden, he saw the old log that his great grandfather had dragged home from the woods, transporting the hive with him. Here it swarmed with bees, coming and going, drawing their transparent trajectories in the air. Here there was a swarm.

"In the spring I can split the hive," he said.

"First frost," his father said, "the bees will be gone. Any day now."

"Yes."

They walked back toward the house. "Someone stole the honey separator."

"I can build another one. Or find out who stole it. Someone must know."

"People have changed here, Tadek. They aren't so friendly. Strangers have moved in and pass through all the time. No one trusts anyone anymore."

Tadek shrugged. "What's trust got to do with it? We have to live together." He tossed away the board from the hive.

"Right. You'll do all right. You have skills. I can see no one killed your spirit."

"As Grandfather used to say, good and goddamn right. Hitler is not my father and Stalin is not my mother. And they're both dead and in their graves anyway."

"Good. You'll be fine. But I was thinking last night. I couldn't sleep. I hardly sleep at all anymore . . . . My thoughts raced like going too fast downhill on a bicycle. I couldn't catch up with them . . . . What I'm trying to get at is, I'm going to Vorkuta."

"Vorkuta? That's like choosing to go to hell."

"I'm going to bring back your mother."

Tadek stopped walking as a hopeless anguish washed over him. He had thought that he'd been so long without a father that he'd ceased to miss one, but waking up in the morning with this thin, battered stranger under the same roof as him, he felt the old bond between them, the cord that couldn't break. He wanted his father to stay. He wanted to have a father again.

Yet though he understood that his father felt the same way about him, for Roman there was the other cord running to Krystyna.

They exchanged a look and he saw his father's determination. They began walking again through the calf-length grass.

"All right, Father. Go ahead. But it won't be easy."

"I know that. But I love her more than any part of myself and even if I can just be near her, I'll be happier there than here."

The white wave of hopeless anguish washed over Tadek again.

"I hate to leave you now, after all these years of not being with you."

"It wasn't your fault."

"No, but I wasn't able to be the father I wanted to be."

"That's all right. I turned out all right." Tadek laughed.

"Yes, you did," his father said. "I'm leaving tomorrow."

"Tomorrow?"

"Or the next day. Before winter's really here."

"It's already there in Vorkuta."

"Anyway, I'm leaving as soon as I can. No one has really figured out how to keep track of who's coming and going here yet. I was supposed to report to authorities in Grodno, but I never did. As far as they know, I'm still in the Gulag."

Chapter 46:
A Soldier's Home

Tadek saw Roman to the train station two days later and said goodbye to him once more. Afterwards, though he had little desire to see anyone, he walked downtown to buy a loaf of bread and a few supplies and to inquire about work. It was a chilly day, even in the sun. The central square looked shabby and unkempt. A few old men sat on the benches with their dogs at their feet. An old lady on one bench stretched out a leg to rock a baby carriage. As Tadek approached, someone called, "Tadek! Tadek Gradinski!" He didn't recognize the old man. He studied his face. Slowly the memory of another face resolved itself under the old man's face, a face without a name, but one that he'd seen for years in Liaski. At the sound of his name, the square seemed to animate itself, all the old men, all with faces that were both familiar and strange, like half-wrong memories, surrounded him. Women came from out of doors. Shops emptied. In a moment he was the center of a crowd, everyone talking at once, touching him—they seemed to need to touch him—hugging him, kissing his cheeks with tear-stained faces as if they were all his father, all his mother, laughing and shouting and asking him questions.

For over an hour Tadek stood in the square answering questions, greeting half-familiar faces, moved by their welcome and acceptance. He was a hero to them, though the war was lost, the cause shattered. Eventually he pulled himself away.

A loaf of bread under his arm, Tadek made his way to the stonemason's on the edge of town. He found the mason in a back workshop amid a litter of tools and half-finished gravestones. Krzaczek, a tall, round-shouldered man, was a cousin of the couple who used to run the Polish school in their basement. He had a long-nosed, morose face. From wielding the hammer and chisel all day, his forearms were swollen with muscle, their hair coated with stone-dust like flour. He wore an equally dusty apron and nodded gravely to Tadek.

"I need to have a monument for my grandfather, Zygmunt Belyawski."

"I knew your grandfather. He's been dead for years!"

"Yes. His funeral was interrupted by some German bombs."

"Rude Fritz."

"Yes. So we never got a chance to put anything up. Can I pay you in installments?"

"Do you have a job already?"

"No, but I will."

"I believe you. You aren't going to run away to some Russian prison again, are you?"

"No."

"Then all right." The mason pulled a scrap of paper from his pocket and a pencil stub from behind his ear and scrawled down a few notes as he and Tadek settled on specifics. "Your uncle, he was a brave man," he said while he wrote.

"I know it. He'll never get a statue."

"No. You won't either, but people know what you did. Your

uncle from Shabany, he put down a stone for Kazimierz."

"I know. I saw it."

"Gave him a break on the price, seeing who it was for. Wish it had been that statue."

"Me too."

Next day Tadek was out back cleaning up the mess of the beehives when, from the silence of the crickets behind him, he sensed a presence. He turned to see Kozel, in a long dark coat and a leather cap, standing motionless next to the bushes that covered the back gate. "Kozel! Don't sneak up on me like that!" Kozel was grinning his disreputable grin. Tadek didn't like that he knew the hidden back way into the yard. They stood ten meters apart looking at each other for a time.

"Aren't you going to invite your old friend into your house for a cup of tea?" Kozel said at last. "You do finally have some tea now, don't you?"

"Sure. Genuine tea. Come on."

Inside Tadek began to prepare tea while Kozel watched him with a mocking grin. "Don't you have anything stronger?" Kozel asked.

"No, I don't."

Kozel pulled a battered tin flask out of his coat pocket, tilting it toward Tadek with a hospitable lift of his brows.

"No thanks, I've got work to do."

"Suit yourself. Hope you don't mind...." Kozel twisted a cork from the bottle and took a swig. "Listen, my friend, I come with an offer. I've gone into trade. I've been involved in running goods between Byelorussia, Poland, Lithuania, and beyond. There's always a profit to be had, for the enterprising man."

"Isn't it dangerous?"

Kozel gave his wide grin. Tadek wondered why he should be

holding Kozel's vile grin against him. What had Kozel ever done to him? He remembered him saving that girl on the train from being raped. It seemed the world needed people like Kozel to keep spinning. Kazimierz had depended on him.

"Dangerous? It's a game of Go Hide with the neighborhood kids. I've got some skills; I might as well use them. Who knows the land and especially the forest around here like I do? If there were any fighters left in the forest, I'd go with them again. But there's no one. Oh, scattered groups here and there, but not enough to cause the government any pain and make it worthwhile. Mostly people just hiding out. Some north of here in Lithuania."

"I'd go with them too."

"It's no use. That time is over. You have to change with the times and take care of yourself."

"Yeah, I've come to the same conclusion."

"Do you want to join me? We go through the back woods. We never see a border guard. It's free money."

"I don't think so. I just want a regular job."

"Working for the state?"

Tadek shrugged. "Working for myself."

"Suit yourself. I know you don't like me, but I served Kowal well."

"I know you did. I respect that."

"I guess I'll skip the tea, Tadek." Kozel turned to the door as the teakettle whistled and Tadek removed it from the stove.

"Oh," Kozel said. "You heard about the bike-runner from Gombachy? The one you had the run-in with once?"

"Twice," Tadek laughed. "We fought like roosters! Before I knew he was with us. Lech was his name but he wanted me to call him Diabeł." Tadek had an urge to see the kid and compare experiences. That had been so long ago! "No, I didn't hear anything. What about him?"

"He never made it out of the system. Dead at twenty-two. Kolyma. Typhus."

Tadek's mood soured. "Could've been me. Everytime I met him at first, we wanted to fight each other. But he ended up being the one to warn me that the Soviets were headed out of Grodno toward Kazimierz's group."

"Too bad it was too late. But that reminds me that we have some unfinished business."

"What's that?"

"Remember what I said to you four years ago when we were just setting out on our little vacation to the east? In that boxcar. Do you remember?"

"I remember everything."

"Well, someone betrayed us. The Soviets knew exactly where they were headed the day they surrounded our camp. It wasn't as if some peasant had just waved an arm in our direction. The forest is vast, but there was no guesswork. Their artillery had the coordinates. They had that range down exactly. They were raining shells on our camp like tossing potatoes in a basket. I cut back through the camp after it was over. They didn't miss once. They surrounded us and then obliterated us."

"So. What can we do?"

"We find out who it was, we track them down, and we kill them. There are certain things that can't be left unavenged."

He felt the horror of the camps returning now with Kozel's presence, the nights sneaking into other barracks, the wrestling with that faceless zek that night in the dark, finding his knife and stabbing him, the man slumping over, the blood rolling in hot rivulets over Tadek's hand and wrist.

"I want to put all that behind me now."

"Sure you do. But, you see, Tadek...." Kozel leaned forward and put a hand on Tadek's shoulder and gave it an unpleasant squeeze. "I'm not going to let you do that." He held his shoulder for a moment more before releasing him. "Someone betrayed us. It was treason. They have to pay. Simple."

Tadek didn't say anything. It wasn't only the horror of the camps Kozel brought with him. It was also the code of the forest, of the *lesni*, and he knew that Kozel was right.

"If you figure out who it is, I'll help you."

"Good. Just like old times."

"Sure."

"I haven't figured it out. How about you? Any idea who could have sold us out?"

"No. None."

With ironic deliberation, Kozel uncorked and took another pull on his flask and leaned toward Tadek, taking him in with a squinty, sideways look for a few moments before he said, "Sorry, Tadeusz. It's not that simple. I'll share my thoughts with you. Because I had time to think in the Gulag. This is what I'm thinking. I'm thinking nobody could've followed Janusz. He just had an easy row downstream at night across the river. We would be on the lookout for him and would give him a ride by horseback to the camp. His cottage is isolated. How could someone follow him in a boat without being noticed? I'm thinking you let it slip somehow to someone."

"You're blaming me?"

"Not blaming you. Just thinking. No one knew what you were doing?"

"No. No one."

Kozel took another thoughtful pull on his flask before replacing the cork with a little thump of his palm.

"Okay, Tadek. I respected your uncle, Kowal. He kept alive a dream of a free Poland. Of this land being Poland again. His determination made us think we could win. Nobody else could do that then. Even if we didn't win, he pointed us the way. And someday we will."

"I know it."

"And because I respected your uncle, I helped you out in the camp. Remember?"

"I remember." Tadek wasn't sure that anything Kozel did was uncontaminated by his own murky motives.

"And you did a good job for us, even though you were just a kid," Kozel continued. "So I've helped you out."

Tadek just nodded.

"But this is serious business now. There are others behind me, who will help me. But people remember what happened. Some things, no matter how long ago it was, you can't let them slide. I said I could take care of it. But I figured you could help me. Just like in the camps."

Tadek shrugged.

"And I don't need you holding out on me."

"I don't know anything. If I think of anything, I'll tell you."

"I know you will, kid." Kozel smiled his louche smile. "Listen, if you need money, you can make a run with me. It's all black market now, anyway. Fine beef, first class whiskey, Turkish tobacco smooth as silk. All for the high muckety-mucks. Everybody gets his slice all the way up the line. It's safer than being legal!"

"I'll keep it in mind."

Without another word, Kozel slipped out the door and turned the corner of the house back toward the orchard.

On Saturday Tadek went to the public baths as he'd been doing since he could remember. He used to stand in line waiting for a shower with his father, watching in horror and awe as the men young and old of the village stripped and took a bar of soap to bathe at one of the five hot-water taps. Now after he stripped, some youths horseplaying behind him bumped into him, almost knocking him over. He whirled and hit one on the side of face before he even felt his anger, hitting the flat, vulnerable side of his face again as the boy fell. A circle of men backed away from him. The boy—he couldn't've been more than seventeen, the age Tadek was when he'd been arrested—lifted himself on one arm and groaned, holding the side of his head.

"Tadek! Is that you? What the hell are you doing?" It was Bolek Kosokovski, his old friend. He stepped into the middle of the circle of men and helped up the boy. "They were just playing around!"

Tadek realized Bolek was right. "Sorry. I don't know what happened."

He apologized and shook hands with the boy, who was still holding the side of his head. He would only look at Tadek with fearful, sidelong glances.

Tadek took his bath and met Bolek outside. Bolek had kept on growing and filled out and loomed over Tadek. Bolek's face was built out of a series of ovals culminating in his thick and droopy lower lip that Tadek remembered from childhood, that spoke to him of Bolek's essence. Though his friend could've passed as a forty-year-old, when Bolek smiled his old good humor shone through and the slightly goofy impression created by the droopy lip disappeared, and he was a kid again. He was as amiable and untroubled as ever, and now he laughed at the fight. "I'm always getting you out of trouble! Remember when you were fighting Pawel?"

"Sure. There were some times I could've used you to get me out of trouble when you weren't around!"

"Yeah, I heard you had a hard time of it."

Bolek and Tadek found a table in the square where they could smoke and talk in the October sun. One of the twins, Yanek, had drowned in the Niemen, just washed away as if a tentacle had grabbed him by the ankle and pulled him under. Tadek's thoughts resisted getting around this information. "And his brother seems lost now. No more music. He's a waiter in Grodno. He still seems to be waiting for his brother to return." Yanek had been the quiet, worried twin, and all his worries had materialized. Franek had now assumed his brother's more pensive personality, abandoning his chatty self, as if by absorbing his brother's traits he kept him living.

Bolek was driving a cab in Grodno. Everyone was being drafted into the Byelorussian army. "You have to serve your time, whether you want to or not. They put you in the reserves after training and then leave you alone."

Tadek knew of this but hadn't yet decided how he was going to deal with it.

"And Pawel and Halinka, you heard?"

"Yes, I heard."

"They live across the Nieman in Grodno, right across from the castle. That old square with the fountain." He described the specific building where he'd visited the couple. Tadek realized that this information was something he'd been waiting to discover.

The next Monday, Tadek went to the police station in Grodno and reported his return from Vorkuta, as required. The Gulag may have been shaken by rebellion, but in the outside world, the grip of the Soviets was as leaden as ever. The police station was on the first floor of the same building where the NKVD's, then the MGB's, offices had been. He didn't know if they were still there. He didn't want to find out. He remembered how he'd been kept in the basement and beaten for three days. He remembered how the corporal's huge hands had gripped his head, how his knees had crushed his chest as he'd pounded Tadek into a tiny hard pellet within himself, a place and way of being he'd withdrawn to frequently in the Gulag and still felt inside him. How later he'd heard someone walking down the hallway and then a shot. Now the place still made him shudder, but the yawning clerk with whom he dealt scarcely looked at him through the smudged lenses of his wire-rimmed glasses as Tadek filled out pages of forms in triplicate.

The clerk sent him on a futile round of looking for work. Grinding his teeth, he started where he knew he must—at the Communist Party headquarters. He wasted the next three days reporting to their list of jobs, before on his own initiative he went to the textile factory where he'd worked before. People looked at him blankly when he asked for Jan Stronski, the old man who'd been the wizard of the looms and stamping machines and dye vats five years before. When they finally figured out that he wanted to work on the machinery, they told him, "Talk to Bella Gurskaya," and gestured toward a large man in the distance, at the end of a seemingly infinite row of huge, clicking, whirring, black and silver looms.

With a torch and a frown, this Gurskaya was peering into the innards of a now motionless loom. He turned on Tadek as if he was responsible for the breakdown of the machinery. "What do you want?" he snapped in Russian.

He was a young Byelorussian, not much older than Tadek. He wore a fierce black mustache that reminded Tadek of Stalin. Tadek explained what had brought him to the factory as the man continued his ill-tempered probing of the giant loom.

"If you lift the paten that keeps the cloth straight, you'll see where it always snags," Tadek suggested.

"What's a paten?"

Tadek leaned inside the machine, reaching, smelling the odor, nostalgic for him, of hot oil and cloth and metal. He flipped up a long curved piece of metal.

"Hm. That goes up?"

"See there, the shuttle's snagged. This feeding wire is bent.

That will set the spindle akilter so it won't turn freely."

"Yeah." The man pulled out the offending rat's nest of thread and then a snagged triangle of fabric. He turned on Tadek with a surly look, while Tadek was careful to keep his face as innocent and clear as it had been when he'd answered the questions of the NKVD major over four years before.

Tadek waited for Gurskaya to speak.

"So, you've worked on these before, you say?"

"Yes, with Jan Stronski."

"Stronski, huh? He was on his way out when I came. A real old timer. He showed me around for a couple of days, but I had to tell him how we were going to do things differently, you know?"

"I bet."

"You're from Grodno?"

"Liaski."

"Where have you been all these years?"

"Can't you guess?"

"I can guess all right. A lot of you worn-out Polish zeks are coming home now. We can't give you all jobs. You've all been living at our expense for years."

Tadek didn't say anything.

"You aren't a murderer they let out by mistake, are you?"

"Just a Polish kid who was in the wrong place."

"Come for a walk."

They walked through a couple of rooms and Tadek talked about some of the temperamental problems of the machines and what he'd learned from the old man about fixing them. He recognized all the same machines, like his old classmates from Liaski, a little older but with intractable characters.

"At least you know Russian all right. Not like some of your compatriots."

"I know Russian," Tadek said. "Years of practice."

501

"I'll have to check with the factory council. We have procedures. Come back next week and we'll see."

Tadek left Mustache, as he dubbed him, expecting to get the job. It was apparent that he'd be both an inferior assistant, and a teacher, a tricky position to be in, but he'd been in tricky positions before. Further, he felt the old draw of the machines, the hard, clicking puzzles that worked with a logic and precision not found in the world of human affairs and that were so satisfying to him. Part of him felt that he'd been let out of the Gulag for the vaster prison of the Soviet Union, with the ceaseless pressure of a government which he had fought against still weighing him down, but he also felt that he had kept his integrity through it all and lived to cheer at Stalin's death. If he could not bend history, at least he could pick his fights and live his life in what pockets of freedom he could find.

Outside it was a cool autumn afternoon. His steps led him up to the old castle overlooking the Niemen. The sun weaved between thick cumulus clouds that coasted over the city and the river and headed east. He watched cloud shadows gliding over the rooftops of the houses across the river. The restlessness of the sky stirred him and he headed down the hill and across the river on the bridge. He felt he was walking aimlessly, but in a little while found himself in the neighborhood where Bolek had told him that Pawel and Halinka were living now with their two children. As he realized where his steps had led him, he wanted to leave, but, despising himself, couldn't pull himself away.

They lived in a three-story apartment building facing a small, pebbled park with a few benches, a few bare linden trees, and a dry, leaf-choked fountain. He sat on one of the benches, his head slumped in his hands, letting half-formed thoughts and memories churn within him. Time passed and people were headed home from

502

work. He knew he should go.

Before he could rise he heard crunching footsteps on the pebbles and light voices as a couple with a child between them cut diagonally in front of him not ten meters away. They didn't glance up. "If you don't make trouble, he won't bother you . . . . " the woman was saying. The man responded in a lower voice.

"Papa," the boy said, turning up to the man. "Can you meet me after school tomorrow?" They didn't see him. They kept walking, a tall, handsome couple receding across the park. Pawel, Halinka, and their son. He'd caught a glimpse of their profiles, each as familiar to him as his own, lovely Halinka, noble Pawel. Pawel wore a pair of wire-rimmed glasses now, giving him, Tadek felt, an introspective, insulated look. He still walked with his oiled, loose-limbed, boyish grace that used to carry him gliding across the football field with deceptive speed. Halinka had a purple scarf around her face, framing it, clarifying it, setting off in delicate profile the lines of her nose and chin that Tadek had had imprinted on his memory.

At any moment they could still turn their heads to see him. But no. They kept walking, eyes on the pebbles at their feet, engrossed in their talk. Tadek felt as if he were under some malevolent spell that made him invisible to them and froze him. He might as well still be in the Gulag somewhere thousands of kilometers away. He might as well be surrounded by three rows of barbed wire and German shepherds and freezing boys his age with machine guns trained on him. He just sat there and watched them go. The boy broke into a skipping run between the couple. In tandem they both ran a few steps to catch up and reached to grab a hand, and they all slowed to let pass a teen on a wavering bike. They disappeared into the three-story row house across the park. The veils of dusk fell almost imperceptibly while Tadek sat. Only when it was fully dark did he wake from his daze.

He began work the next week and occupied himself on off hours trying to repair the beehives and clean up the orchard and prepare for winter. He wrote his mother a long letter, wondering whether she would receive it and how she would react when she saw his father, her husband, again. He wished he could see them both, but wanted to see no one else. When he ran into acquaintances, when they welcomed him back, and even when they praised his sacrifices for Poland, there was always a light bitter taste in his mouth as he heard their words. It wasn't resentment at the well-meaning villagers. It was more a sense of irony at the contrast between the idea in people's minds, the words on people's mouths, and the years he felt weighing heavily within him.

He felt different when he ran into Sabina. He'd begun to take his lunches in a park along with the other workers from the textile mill, and then as it grew colder, he was left almost alone in the chilly sunlight, with a few trees that looked as if they were made of iron and a couple of impoverished pigeons at his feet. Across the square he'd half-noticed a woman in a navy blue wool coat and a blue scarf, day after day, until one day they were the only ones in the park and they looked up at each other. With slow smiles of recognition they both rose. Sabina! They walked to hug each other—a restrained, adult hug, with a bit of extra pressure to acknowledge they'd been close once.

"I didn't know that was you!" he said.

"Me neither! I mean, you."

Sabina's childhood high spirits seemed subdued, but she still had the pinkness on the edges of her nostrils and the plump lower lip that he remembered kissing when crouched in the bushes during Go Hide. She had a heart-shaped face, more curved and sensuous than the chiseled edges of Halinka's face.

504

"You live in Grodno now?"

"Yes, everyone does. It's so predictable and boring! I'd heard you were back. You look different. Leaner."

"Prison diet."

"I need to try that!"

It was true she'd put on a kilo or two, but now he saw that she was still fresh-faced even in the harsh, early winter light, and as they talked, the flickering glint in her eyes returned. So did the mocking smile that seemed to scorn all obstacles.

"Listen, I have to go, but let's talk."

He vacillated, unsure if this was just politeness, unsure if he was even fit for company: he felt like one raw open wound, uncertain how to talk to civilians, knowing only how to conspire and calculate to stay alive another day.

She saw his hesitation. "I mean it!" she tugged at his sleeve and laughed. "I'm so glad to see you!" He was surprised to see tears illuminate her eyes. "You're still the same, Tadek!"

He was glad she thought so, but he wasn't so sure.

They met in the park after work and talked till it emptied of workers hurrying home, then moved to an inexpensive restaurant to warm up. Tadek slowly let himself relax in Sabina's presence, even though she was as sarcastic as ever. He wanted to just close his eyes and listen to her talk, but he was too uncertain of anything he felt to say much about his four years away. Her sarcasm was actually reassuring to him. He could share her cynicism, and beneath it he felt an ally. Their talk turned to Halinka and Pawel.

"I don't care that they got married," she said. "But you think I wasn't shocked? I was shocked, I'm glad to tell you. Halinka and I fought. I fight with everybody, you know that."

"Me too."

"Anyway, we got over it. Or I did, anyway." She shook

her head and puffed a lock of hair from her face. "I guess part of me had always thought Pawel and I would marry, despite our problems. But we'd been apart for a while, before they got married. Still, I didn't know whether he really loved Halinka all along, or whether he was trying to be a saint or something. But I know he loves her now. We're friends again. But he's not a very good saint. He bumbles through life like the rest of us. But looking back, I can see how Pawel and I hadn't been right, had been forcing things. But you...." Her dark eyes went quizzing up and down his face. "You and Halinka were serious. I'm sorry . . . . "

"I was shocked. I heard about it in camp."

"I can't imagine."

"What do you mean, trying to be a saint?"

"Oh, you know. But you should talk to Halinka."

"I don't want to see either of them again. They're traitors to me. Worse."

"I still think you should talk to Halinka."

"Why?"

"And Pawel's not bad. You know him. He's the kindest person in the world."

"Not to his best friend! I was in prison!"

"You had a twenty-five year sentence."

"Don't defend them."

"All right. I don't blame you for feeling the way you do. But they're still my friends. Halinka said she wanted to talk to you."

"Shit! They betrayed me! He was my closest friend!"

He realized he'd turned ugly and calmed himself.

It wasn't so much that he still loved Halinka—he didn't think he did—but it was the memory of how much he had loved her, and how Pawel had known that, and how close he had been to both of them, and what the last four years of his life had been like. He wanted them to know somehow.

"Do you remember when we used to play Go Hide?" Sabina asked. Tadek smiled. "And Mr. and Mrs. Krzaczek? That basement cave of theirs?"

"Yes."

"I actually liked school. The world was in flames, but we still had to be kids. Do you feel cheated?"

"No, we did all right. As far as being kids goes."

"I was jealous when you stole Halinka's cap instead of mine that day we were ice-skating."

"You were?"

"Yes. But it was the darkest of dark secrets."

They twisted their tea cups and reminisced, and Sabina smiled her cocky, slanted smile at him in a way he recognized.

They got up to leave and he walked her toward her apartment, one of a half-dozen new ugly high-rises that had been thrown up in a muddy field on the edge of town, someone's idea of a proletarian utopia. They were identical not only by design but also in decay: they'd been built with low-quality concrete, which scaled on the surfaces in patches like eczema and dropped in sheets into the surrounding mud.

He had an impulse to try to kiss her but stifled it. She smiled at him as if reading his mind and then grew more serious. "You need to talk to Halinka."

"I don't know why you keep saying that. I've seen them together. They don't want to see me."

"Anyway, I'll make it on my own from here, Tadek. It was nice catching up."

As he watched her walk away, he felt as if he was seeing the last shred of his childhood walk away from him.

Chapter 47: Old Friends

On Sunday afternoon he found himself again outside Pawel and Halinka's apartment, and when he saw them emerge, this time he set himself walking on a line to meet them. Halinka held their baby and their son walked between them. They looked up, startled at the man walking quickly toward them. Confused recognition swept their faces, along with sadness, some guilt, but also pleasure. They were glad to see him. They both smiled. He held onto his anger and walked up and shoved Pawel in the chest.

"Come on! Don't!" Pawel protested. Tadek shoved him again.

"What do you want from me?"

"Admit you betrayed me."

"Nothing was meant to hurt you!"

Tadek shoved him again. Again. Halinka followed alongside. "Tadek, don't!" The baby began to cry. This was maddening to Tadek. Pawel just lifted his hands, palms out, refusing to defend himself.

"While I was in prison, you stole my girlfriend. You think because you pulled me from the ice once when we were kids…that dog…traitor!" He'd badly rehearsed this, standing in the park, watching their apartment. Now he was forgetting his lines. They'd strayed from theirs from the start.

"It wasn't like that, Tadek," Halinka said.

He turned toward her. "How do you dare look at me?" The baby was squalling. Tadek looked down at the frightened face of their four-year-old boy, a sense of his foolishness overtaking his anger. "I just wanted you to know I'm back!" he said. "And I forgive nothing!"

He walked away. They called him back. "Tadek!" Why should they call him now? So they could all torment him with his lost life even more?

It wasn't right that he should now feel the shame that he'd planned to inflict on them.

In a nasty mood, he stalked to Sabina's apartment building, asking for her of an old woman who was sweeping the walk with a twig broom. Tadek guessed that she kept track of all the comings and goings of the tenants as a favor for what they now called the KGB. She looked him over carefully before informing him that Sabina was out. After walking in circles for a time, he caught a bus to Liaski, trying to escape himself. In Liaski he walked the entire town, past the old houses of Halinka and Pawel, past his own house, unable to settle, and he found himself at a hole-in-the-wall inn, located where Friedlander's general store had been years before. There was still the same battered wooden counter and now a few empty tables in the front half of the building. He was glad he didn't know the man behind the counter or the two men at one table. He ordered a glass of vodka and sat down by himself.

The sky clouded over, and a few flakes of indecisive snow hit against the windows and melted. Tadek was finishing his second glass of vodka when Kozel walked into the inn.

Tadek gave a rough laugh. "You!" He nodded at the chair

and Kozel sat down with his perennial cocky smirk on his face.

At least Kozel knew something of what he'd been through, unlike the civilians in the village, so Tadek felt a certain comfort in his presence now.

"Sure," Kozel said. "Me." He looked at Tadek's now empty glass. "I've got some money. I'll get a bottle."

"Good." Since his release, Tadek had started to develop a taste for alcohol and the oblivion it offered.

Kozel settled himself with the bottle, poured two drinks, and leaned forward to whisper to Tadek: "The bastards will fall some day."

"To the fall of the bastards!"

"To their fall!"

Tadek tossed back the chilled vodka and felt it slip through his veins and creep up behind his eyes where it soothed an ache.

"Did you hear about Ewa?"

"Ewa?"

"Yes, Ewa. Your Grodno contact."

"No. What about her?" Tadek remembered her indomitable breasts pressing against her blouses, her confident, gap-toothed laughter.

"She never made it back either. She was a twenty-fiver, but ran into some bad luck in Magadan and didn't make it to the amnesty. Now *she* was someone you could rely on."

So Ewa too....

Outside the snow fell. Kozel poured another drink. He was back from a run to Poland. He wouldn't say more. But he was flush with cash. He made the job offer again to Tadek, and Tadek pretended to be interested. After a while, the conversation took its inevitable turn.

"Someone betrayed us. Someone told the Soviets where the

camp was. Have you thought about who it might be?"

"No. I don't know. How the hell should I know?" Tadek had other things on his mind.

"How could they follow Janusz? In another boat? That doesn't make sense. But you skated." This idea was upsetting. Tadek realized he was going to have to confront Kozel's problem.

"Just once. No one followed me. Except a few wolves. You're grasping at straws."

Kozel poured another shot. No one stood on ceremony waiting for a toast. They both tossed back their shots and he poured another.

The bar room had been gradually filling up. Tadek found himself searching the faces of the men in the room for the betrayer. Some of them were strangers, some of them familiar since childhood, but all were suddenly cast under a new scrutiny.

"Did anyone know you were a message runner?"

"You asked that before and I said no. I kept the secret."

"You're sure?"

He remembered Kozel had suspected that he was hiding something.

"Someone pointed a finger at your friend. His grandfather's Byelorussian," Kozel added.

Tadek was in no mood to lie or protect.

"Pawel might have suspected."

"Hah! Your friend Karposovich!" Kozel seemed pleased. He poured another shot for them both. They were working their way through the bottle at a good pace.

"He wouldn't betray me."

"Listen to yourself! He did betray you. He stole your girl."

"That's different."

"Well, it worked out fine for him, didn't it?"

"Once, we were fishing," Tadek said. "We were downstream,

by that rocky outcropping, where the pathway began." Tadek lowered his voice and Kozel scuffed his chair forward and leaned on his elbows to listen.

"Sure. That's where we'd meet Janusz."

"I think Pawel guessed something. Then later, after the attack on the convoy, he knew I was working with the partisans."

Kozel drew back in his chair nodding in confirmation. "And with you gone, he had the girl."

"It really wasn't like that."

"Maybe it was. I tell you kid, it's all I've got, and you know I'm not letting go of this."

"Don't get ahead of what we really know." Tadek wished he hadn't said as much as he had. But at the same time, he felt his thoughts veering into parallel with Kozel's. Betrayed! Yes, he'd been betrayed all right. And then his thoughts would veer away. The vodka made them difficult to control. He remembered with masochistic detail what it had been like to lie with Halinka, and the thought of his friend substituting for him could wash like a black wave over his mind in a second.

And Halinka, she had known he'd been running messages, too!

"Let me tell you this, Tadeusz Gradinski." Kozel leaned across the table again, lowering his voice as a nearby table filled with men. "Just because this Karposovich was your friend once won't save him. You know me." His eyes gleamed with a sort of lust as he stared down Tadek. The sleek scar beneath his eye seemed to pulse.

"Sure," Tadek said. "I know you."

"I'm born for the job of killing snitches."

"Right."

"Your uncle," Kozel said. "We should talk to him. He should be in on any decision, anyway."

"All right."

Kozel stood up, corking the bottle and shoving it in his coat pocket.

"You want to go now?"

"Yes, now. We have to take care of this."

They left the inn into the snowy afternoon and started hiking toward Shabany but immediately realized it was too far, too snowy. They turned back to the square where Kozel found a man with a cart that was headed that way, and they hitched a ride, sitting in the back of the cart. As they rode along, their legs dangling out the back of the wagon, Kozel reached into a dirty canvas bag he carried and pulled out a small black revolver. "Here," he said, thrusting it to Tadek. "Take this. You may need it with what's coming up."

"I don't need it."

"No, take it."

"I don't need it."

"Take it I said! You should be aware this is serious."

"All right." Irritated, Tadek took the pistol and thrust it in his jacket pocket.

The ride and the clear, cold air gave Tadek a chance to sober somewhat, but that only made him more confused about where this search for the betrayer was leading. He didn't know how much of it was valid and how much was based on Kozel's inability to leave the past alone and find a peace with the world.

Kozel lay on his back and watched the sky and kept his bottle to himself. Tadek watched the receding lines of the cartwheels filling with snow, watched the parallel Niemen, the color of pewter, where snowflakes struck and melted. At Shabany they got out and started hiking to Janusz's.

"Wait a minute," Kozel said, halfway to Janusz's. "Over this way." He walked down to the riverbank and pointed to the opposite side. "See that old oak? There's where one path used to end, where we'd meet up with Janusz."

"I always met at the rocks."

"That's better. This one's roundabout and too close to the village. But it worked too." Kozel pulled out his whiskey flask. "A toast to the good dead." They each took a sip and spilled a little vodka to the ground in libation to the honored past. The gesture sealed a tacit vow of revenge.

They struggled up the path by the Niemen toward Janusz's place. Through a scrim of trees Tadek could see the cabin in the middle of a clearing, surrounded by a few shack-like outbuildings, a black smoke rising from the central chimney. A large flock of migrating starlings, caught by the snow, had settled in the trees and rippled and cawed in indignation as he and Kozel walked beneath them.

Tadek remembered all the nights he'd bicycled here, carrying the mysterious packages beneath a layer of cucumbers and beets in his front basket.

The sound of a hatchet chopping wood came from behind the cottage, and Kozel and Tadek made their way around to the back where they found Janusz, grown heavier and grayer, splitting firewood atop a stump base. When he first saw them, he seemed exasperated at the intrusion, but he finally grinned, limping around the stump to greet them. He gave Tadek a bear hug. "I heard you were back. Why didn't you come to see me first thing?"

They went inside. Kozel pulled out the bottle and Janusz rinsed out some dusty glasses. "I took care of your house for you, Tadek, before Roman returned. You have me to thank that it's there at all. I found one of the nephews of a Bohatkiewcz from Gombachy to stay in it to keep the looters and drifters and such away from it."

Tadek lifted his glass in a toast to Janusz. "Thanks. It was looted, but nothing that isn't repairable."

Janusz was talkative, and wanted to explain many of the changes that had swept the area in the previous few years to the ex-zeks. Immigrants were coming in from elsewhere in the Soviet Union. The military and government jobs were everything now. The kolkhoz employed hundreds on the huge collective fields, producing a pittance of grain for the labor involved. No one remembered the sacrifices that had been made.

Kozel got to business and told Janusz their mission. "Someone betrayed us."

"Why do you say that?" Janusz seemed surprised. "It couldn't be!"

"They came directly to the camp. Their artillery knew coordinates! You hadn't thought of this?"

"Maybe you're right," Janusz said, nodding his head in agreement, his brow knotting in thought. "The road was crowded with the Soviets that day, streaming out of Grodno, emptying their barracks, trucks full of troops." Janusz shook his head at the memory. He waved a hand. "But that was so long ago. Forget it!"

Kozel gave Janusz a molten stare. "I'll never forget it," he hissed softly. "They're going to pay, whoever they are!"

"Yes, yes." Janusz nodded, reversing himself. "Of course. But who?"

Appeased, Kozel leaned forward and, as if they might be overheard, said softly, "I was thinking this Byelorussian friend of Tadek's."

"He's not really Byelorussian," Tadek protested. "His grandfather's Byelorussian. He's Catholic, not Orthodox. He was born in Liaski!"

"Anyway, he might have suspected our meeting place on the river."

"The rocks?"

"Yes." Janusz nodded, frowning, thinking. Kozel was draining the vodka and Janusz fetched another bottle and opened it for them. "You could be right. That sounds like a possibility."

"But you'll be with us? If we go after him?"

"Of course. Kazimierz must be avenged."

"And Uri, and Zidor, and Hipolit!"

"Yes, all of them."

They began drinking to their fallen comrades. Kozel and Janusz began some serious reminiscing about men Tadek didn't know or had just seen once. He wandered over to study a chess game Janusz had set up on the counter.

"I was just looking over that chess game," Jan said. "Can you help me out?"

"Who are you playing against?"

"Just myself!"

"It looks as if you're losing!"

"And winning, too! That's the way it is. Come visit and we'll have a game some time. Only sober."

"Sure."

"Like old times."

"Yes. I'm better now. I played some in prison."

"And I've gotten old and stupid. Life's not fair. But I've still got a few tricks to show you."

Tadek reached out to touch a piece, considering a move, then thought better of it, deciding he was too drunk now. But he thought he saw something, an innocuous pawn that might swing everything.

Kozel couldn't stay still and soon rose to leave as they laid plans to continue their conversation at a more sober time.

"Where's Jadwiga?" Tadek asked at the door.

Janusz frowned. His face went a dark purple. He seemed not to know what to say and his large frame wavered as he looked at the ceiling. "You won't believe that woman," he finally got out. "She left me!"

"What?" So this was what had been bothering him.

"Yes. After twenty years. She's filled with some crazy ideas."

"Really?"

"Yes. She's living in Shabany by herself now, practically starving to death."

"Well, she'll come back."

"Probably. Probably." They stood at the door and snow swept in. "If I'll have her!"

Chapter 48: A Secret

Tadek awoke uncertain where he was, aware only of the cold. He was still a little drunk. He tried to sit up and his head sloshed with pain. He lay under a quilt on a thick layer of hay in a barn loft. Sunlight slashed in dusty sheets through the gaps between the loosely nailed boards. Someone outside was pumping water. The metal of the pump groaned and clanged and rattled, and then the water gushed.

When Tadek put on his coat, he was surprised to feel the weight of a pistol in its pocket. Then, he remembered Kozel's gift. He found the ladder and made his way down out of the loft. Through the barn door he saw Kozel talking with a stout man beside the well, and Tadek made his way to them. It turned out that they'd been too drunk to make their way back to Liaski and so had bunked in the barn of this farmer, an acquaintance of Kozel's. Tadek couldn't even remember climbing into the loft the night before. While the farmer went about his chores, Kozel and Tadek went inside the cabin and Kozel made himself at home in the kitchen, obviously familiar with it.

"We used to use Mankiewicz's place when we needed a place near Liaski. He's okay."

Head in his hands, Tadek stared down at the black coffee Kozel had put in front of him.

"Is this real coffee?" he asked.

"Of course. I have it from a man in Poland who gets it straight from Turkey."

Tadek nodded his headed admiringly and blew on the liquid, eager to sip it. He couldn't remember the last time he'd had real coffee.

"You held out on me, Tadek," Kozel said. "You knew Pawel suspected the drop site."

Tadek shrugged. He didn't care what Kozel thought of him. "I was just thinking it through. I still don't think he could've done it."

"Don't hold out on me," Kozel said, smiling as steadfastly as ever. He calmly picked up his coat. "I'm going into town, Tadek. You can finish your coffee. I'll come back later and we'll decide what to do with your friend. What I'm afraid of is that you're too soft. You never did have the stomach that it took for our business. I tried to train you, but you were always too soft." He shook his head at Tadek's character flaw. "I'll come back to your place when you've recovered. But remember our business."

After Kozel left, Tadek finished his coffee and then walked the remaining distance to Liaski beneath a clear blue sky. At home he lay down for a while, but though his head was throbbing and he wanted to go back to bed, he knew that he was too agitated to sleep. He washed up, boiled himself a couple of eggs that he ate with black bread and tea, and then took the pistol Kozel had given him and placed it in the pocket of a long, loose coat that his father had left behind. Here it rode against his thigh as he walked to the bus stop where he caught the bus to Grodno.

Pawel worked for the government now, in the agronomy department at the university. Tadek caught him right before he entered the building off of a busy street. Remembering their last meeting, Pawel tensed and looked wary.

"I have to talk to you."

"All right, Tadek. I have ten minutes."

"That's all it will take."

Pawel gestured toward a bench. "Let's sit down here."

"No. We need privacy. I need to talk about sensitive matters."

Pawel looked puzzled, but followed Tadek down an alley, then down another turn, into a blind alley beneath a few boarded-up windows. Tadek sat on concrete steps next to some garbage cans. Pawel laughed a bit nervously, looking around him. The faint smell of garbage hung in the air. But Pawel sat down on the other side of a step.

Tadek turned to his old friend. He could feel the weight of the revolver in his pocket every time he moved his leg. He drew strength from its weight. He felt he needed all the strength he could gather to burst through the knot of possibilities before him.

"Listen," Pawel began. "I never meant to take Halinka away, if that's even what happened . . . . "

"This doesn't have anything to do with Halinka." Tadek cut him off. "There's something else. It involves other people. Old resistance people."

"What are you talking about?"

"Remember when we were swimming that day with the Russians across from us, and they were talking about the convoy into Grodno?"

"Sure. What of it?"

"There was an ambush that week on the convoy."

"Yes."

"And you told me to watch what I was doing, to be careful."

"Yes."

"Earlier that day. You and me. We were fishing upstream, and you ended up talking about that outcropping of rocks and the partisans. As if they might be there."

"I don't remember that."

"You're lying!" Tadek shifted and put his hand in his pocket on the gun. He still felt drunk. Kozel's face seemed to loom in his mind, sneering, voicing his suspicions that needed somehow to be stilled.

"No, really!" Pawel was astonished at the intensity of Tadek. "What's the matter, Tadek? Really, I can't . . . . We used to go fishing down there. There was a felled tree where the fish were in the shade. I remember the outcropping . . . . "

"You knew I was with the partisans." He leaned forward intensely.

"I suspected it, and then you as much as admitted it. I wasn't sure at that time, though."

"You never followed me?"

"No!"

"You didn't betray me? You didn't betray them!"

"No!" Tadek could see that his old friend was shocked at the accusation.

"And Halinka knew, too! Did you ever talk about it?"

"No! Never! Not until after you'd been arrested!"

Pawel's shock deepened at the mention of Halinka. Tadek had always been good at sounding out people, and he had deepened this skill in the Gulag. Now he was certain Pawel had not betrayed him. Pawel was still the same, exactly as he'd always been. Tadek could see that now. This was the same Pawel who would stumble naively toward a train full of Jews, surrounded by Germans, with a cup of water in his hand. Pawel had never had a system put its hands around his neck and pound, pound, pound his head against the concrete for years until he was only a tiny hardened unbreakable speck of himself hidden in blackness. And Tadek was glad for Pawel. Tadek still loved him, his innocence, his kindness, his openness.

Tadek lifted his face and laughed to the sky in relief, leaning away from Pawel, releasing him from his gaze. "You haven't changed, have you?"

Pawel laughed, puzzled. "I think I have! What's all this about, Tadek?"

"Someday I'll tell you. I have to go now. There's something I need to do. I'm sorry I had to ask you these questions. I had to make sure."

"All right. Listen, Halinka and I . . . . "

"No. None of that. I don't want to hear about that now. This has nothing to do with that." Tadek stood up, embarrassed suddenly by the squalid alley down which he'd led his friend, out of the eyesight of any witnesses.

"All right."

Together they walked out of the alleyway. Tadek said goodbye and hurried to a bus stop, waiting until he could get a bus that went through Liaski to Shabany, for he'd suddenly remembered a detail that had been niggling at the back of his mind.

Shabany looked shriveled in the winter glare, low-lying near the river, overgrown with leafless shrubs, gripped by snow. Tadek asked about for Jadwiga's place, which turned out to be a rough-hewn little hovel—there was no other word for it—at the end of a row of houses which ran down to the river's edge.

"Just a minute," came the call when he knocked on the door. Even the door was poorly made, with uneven, unpainted boards you might find on a henhouse. After a moment Jadwiga opened it with a suspicious look on her face that changed to a smile at the sight of him. She stepped forward and embraced him and they kissed. He'd never been very certain that she even liked him much. Her tart tongue spared no one, not even the children about her. But perhaps he'd been wrong about her, or time had changed her. She stroked his face wonderingly a few times, and he hardly recognized, in her trembling tenderness, the sarcastic woman he'd known.

"You were always my favorite, Tadek," she said, again surprising him. She patted his cheeks as if he were a child. He realized how lonely she must be. There were so few people left from the old days. "You look different. A man now. I can see you've been through a lot, but you're still so handsome! Come in!"

He stepped into the dark of the front room and felt his feet on an irregular earthen floor. It took a moment for his eyes to adjust.

"I don't like to burn kerosene if I can save on it," she said, guessing at his thoughts. "And this place is always in shadows. But here, in your honor." She made to light a lantern, but he waved her away from it.

"No? All right. Did you know, I sent you packages, but then they moved you and no one even knew where you were anymore?"

"I did get one. Thank you."

"Only one? Well, I sent more. Someone enjoyed them. We all feared the worst. Why didn't you come see me earlier?"

"I don't know. I needed to be alone, mostly, I guess."

She'd changed physically as well. Her cheeks were furrowed and stretched. Her hair was a yellow gray. She wore a pair of rimless glasses. Her eyes looked watery and vague. But her anger had dissolved. A new gentleness was in her eyes.

"Would you like something to eat? I'll fry you some potatoes."

"That would be great."

She took out some potatoes and began washing them in a

pan.

"Why are you here, Jadwiga? What happened between you and Uncle Janusz?"

"That man, I just couldn't stand it anymore."

She started to slice the potatoes with surprising, heavy, thumping blows of a long-bladed knife against a board. She still had hidden reserves.

"I'm sorry you're here."

"I'm better off here."

"Did he beat you?"

"No. At least no more than some others I could name. I'm just better off here, Tadek. Better we talk about something happier. I saw your father, you know, when he was here. I'd heard he's gone again. I just never get into Liaski anymore. It seems to have grown more distant, as if it's drifting away! But there's always news from there."

"Aunt Jadwiga. I know you don't want to talk about painful things, but I have to ask you some things."

She turned to look at him, searching his face. Her eyes that had seemed vague pinned on him for an intense moment. She set aside the potatoes and sat opposite him, as if she'd seen what she was looking for.

"All right," she said flatly. "Ask me what you want to, Tadek."

"Kozel, you remember Kozel."

"Yes, a brave man. A dangerous man."

"I know. He thinks Pawel, my friend, betrayed us."

"Pawel! How could that be?"

"I know. He suspected I was a partisan runner. He even had a hint where the camp was, or where the partisans met their messengers. His grandfather's Byelorussian." He shook his head. "But he's a Pole to the tips of his fingers. Even though he's gone

525

and married my girl."

"You were gone, Tadek. No one knew if they'd ever see you again. You were a twenty-fiver!"

"I know it, Jadwiga. I can't say I don't hold a grudge, but I can't let that confuse me."

"Of course not."

"But what I need to ask you, Jadwiga, is where was Janusz the day the Soviets annihilated the partisan camp: Grodno, or Gombachy?"

"Why?"

"Because I remember distinctly that you said he was in Gombachy, but yesterday he described how the Soviet troops were filling the roads as they came out of Grodno."

Her eyes fixed on the teacups as if they might be about to start darting about the room. Slowly she covered her hands with her face. For a moment he thought she was crying.

"What's the matter?" He put a hand out to place on her shoulder to comfort her, but before he touched her, she took her hands away from her face, revealing a hard, tearless mask. "Yes," she croaked. "You're right. It was Janusz who betrayed the partisans!"

Though this was what he'd been probing for, he still felt all his thoughts swept away for a light-headed second. He felt disoriented, and his aunt's face seemed to float in front of him.

"Tell me," he said.

"Just that. It was him. They'd arrested him. They knew he was related to Kazimierz, but they were clever and hid their knowledge until they acted. Three NKVD men came and picked him up the night before. He couldn't hold out. He's always been a weak man. They'd questioned him once before. He knew they were circling."

"Why didn't he go into the woods?"

"He wouldn't survive in the woods. Look at him! He was always a coward. The one thing he was good at was secrets."

"He wasn't in Gombachy like you said?"

"No. He went over to the NKVD. I lied for him. They took him away in the middle of night. They came and went the back road around Gombachy. And they threatened me. I was in a panic. Then I kept his secret these past years. I'm ashamed. But I was never really sure. When he returned, he wouldn't look at me. He wouldn't talk. Finally, when I left, I confronted him, and he was so angry that he confessed."

The room was silent save for the crumpling of some coals in the fire.

"That's not all," she continued, shaking her head. "He...he also betrayed those Jews."

"Jews? What Jews?"

"Years before. Under German control. Those Jews your mother hid. Do you remember them, Tadek, or were you too young?"

"Of course I remember."

He remembered Ephraim Reznikoff knocking on his window that night. He remembered trying to get Ephraim to give him a cigarette, and his refusal. He remembered very precisely his mother and himself crossing the back alley with the frightened Reznikoffs, remembered the shadows disappearing behind his mother down the pathway between shrubs and silent houses. He remembered the chill of the night on his face and a dog barking in the distance. He remembered going back home and finding the child's toy left behind and being quizzed by the SS officer. He remembered the smell of the polished German leather of the SS man's boots.

"He was supposed to lead them across the river to a hiding place. They were headed for the Baltic. Krystyna and I waited and waited with that family. They were so frightened. We waited a long time while Janusz rowed across the river and back. He said he had to arrange everything. Then he returned and Krystyna left. They crossed the river, all right. But I heard shots. It was a still night. When I asked him, he said some Germans had shot at them, but they'd all fled into the woods. But he didn't act the way he would, if he'd been shot at. You know, how you can just tell, but not really be sure? So I suspected. But life went on. He'd never admit anything. He could deny, deny, deny until you didn't know if it was day or night. Then, as I said, when I was leaving, we had it all out. He was beyond caring at that point and told me about everything. About the Jews too. He took them across the river, all right. Right into the hands of the Nazis. Just for the money. I didn't want to believe what had really happened with them. Just the thought of it seemed unclean and made me so ashamed."

"And then you moved out?"

"That just made it easier."

* * *

The snowy path to Janusz's house had been churned into a loblolly of mud and ice and snow, and Tadek labored slowly along. A heavy mist stirred above the river and rose from the snow. The clouds were glazed red where the sun lowered over the woods across the Niemen. As he approached Jan's house, he saw that the flock of starlings that had settled there, migrating and caught by the snow, had grown huge overnight. Even from a distance they made a racket, filling every tree with ceaseless motion, nervously shooting out into the sky in waves and then resettling as Tadek approached.

Where the path turned up through the poplars toward the cabin, Tadek stopped and stood thinking, head down at his muddy feet, hands thrust in his pockets, his right hand on the pistol that Kozel had given him. Sober, looking up the hill, he could see how abandoned Janusz's cabin was in a way he hadn't noticed the day before: weeds and saplings had grown out front, a flower-box hung cockeyed and was about to fall from beneath a window, and there was no smoke coming from the chimney.

He wanted to hear Janusz's words. He had to hear it from Janusz's mouth. But he couldn't take care of things Kozel's way. He'd tried that in the camps.

With a brusque movement he took a few steps and flung the pistol as high and as far as he could, over the edge of the slight bluff and down to the river where he saw it splash noiselessly and disappear in the gray water and in a second the ripples were gone. A few birds shot away into the air and then, as if pulled on elastic bands, immediately resettled themselves into the trees. He shrugged and turned up the path toward the cabin, now feeling the absence of the pistol in the lightness of his pocket.

He scraped his muddy feet on a metal ridge for that purpose next to the door. He pounded on the door, the three quick then two spaced knocks he'd always used as a signal. There was what seemed like a long wait, with many shuffling and scuffing sounds coming through the door. Then Janusz slung the door open. "Tadek! Come in, come in, nephew."

Despite efforts at a good-humored welcome, there was a rawness to his voice that hinted at some grievance. The curtains were still drawn in the cabin. Janusz went about opening them, letting in the weak twilight. There was a sour odor of ashes, alcohol, and split wood to the room. "Didn't think I'd see you again so soon."

"There's something I'd like to talk to you about."

"Oh? Sounds serious."

"It is."

"Oh-oh." He feigned a laugh. "You know I like laughing and vodka more than serious conversations. Always did."

"Yes. I know."

"Well, sit down anyway. Vodka?"

"No. Not after yesterday."

"That was a party! Then tea?"

"Sure."

Janusz fussed around getting cups from the cupboard, stoking the fire in the stove. His limp seemed to have grown worse over the years, something else Tadek hadn't noticed in the drunken haze of the day before. Both men were silent. Janusz went to a bucket of fresh water and filled the teakettle with a dipper. He came to slump heavily in his chair across from Tadek and looked at him almost timidly, and Tadek saw that Janusz knew why he'd come.

Janusz lurched up out of his chair and limped with surprising swiftness to the door. "Damn birds!" He slung open the door and went out into the dooryard, from where, with a jerky bend, he picked up a stone and slung it toward the trees by the river. A few birds flew and circled back in their automatic way. Again he executed his fat-man bend and straightened himself to sling another stone at them. He stood and cursed the birds, looking out over the river, framed in the doorway with his back to Tadek. Janusz kept standing there till Tadek wondered whether he was going to come back into the cabin, but then he did turn. His silhouette filled the doorway. "I hate those birds," he said. "Every year it's the same thing."

He limped back to his seat near the stove and gave Tadek that same timid, unhappy look that slipped into Tadek's ribcage like a filthy blade. But his own pity made Tadek hateful.

"That day the camp was raided, where were you? You must remember."

"Oh, yes, I remember. I was in Gombachy. Trading for a pig."

"A pig? Did you buy the pig?"

"Yes, it was a fat one-year sow." He nodded several times to himself as if to confirm the memory.

"Are you sure it wasn't a calf?"

"What do you mean?"

"Jadwiga said it was a calf, that day."

Janusz's slight smile remained but his whole body seemed to have undergone a change, as if he'd been transformed to a material other than flesh and blood, something stiff and clammy to the touch. His movements slowed.

"You were in Grodno," Tadek said. "You saw the government troops leaving! The Soviets must've released you once they were on their way!"

Janusz seemed not to have heard Tadek. His slight smile unchanged, he stared over Tadek's shoulder as if there were someone there who might offer some advise. "Trading for a pig," he repeated as if trying it out to see if it would gather more weight the second time. He shook his head, forcing himself into an effort that he didn't want to make. "Jadwiga, she wouldn't remember. You can't remember, if it was a pig or a calf. No one could." He said this last bit wonderingly.

The water in the teakettle let out a smothered moan.

"You were the one who betrayed us!" Tadek burst out. "The NKVD took you! You told them everything!"

Janusz slowly pushed back his chair and rose to reach high into a cupboard from which he pulled out a greasy piece of cloth that he unwrapped without any haste at all to reveal a large revolver. He held it loosely in both hands as if he wasn't sure how it worked. Tadek's heart began to beat in his throat, but he couldn't stop himself now from saying it all. More softly, he said, "And the Jews. The Reznikoffs. You betrayed them! I used to visit there with Grandfather. Their father was a friend of Grandfather! Of your father."

Janusz shrugged. "Friends with Jews?"

"They were Poles, too!"

Janusz made a wry face, not deigning to respond.

"And they were a family. A mother and her two children."

"It was a war," Janusz said. "Nobody cared."

"I remember those kids' eyes looking at me in the kitchen that first night."

"Well, sure, their eyes." He squirmed and made a sour grimace. "Listen, I wasn't the only one. You were a kid; you didn't know."

They sat in silence. Some coals shifted in the fireplace.

"What do you expect me to do now, nephew?"

"If you harm me, Jadwiga won't keep your secrets for you any more. It's not going to do any good."

"Why couldn't Kazimierz just quit? He thought he'd defeat the entire Soviet Army. I begged him more than once to just quit. It was over, but he and his men just went on and on. That last raid on the armaments convoy, that was suicidal. Why couldn't he quit?"

"Because he wanted freedom."

"Freedom!" Janusz scoffed. "What's freedom? You know, I bought his gravestone for him. No one else was there to do that!"

Tadek had learned from years of practice how to keep his emotions to himself, and he sat still, not showing his disgust now, just holding his uncle's gaze impassively.

"They had me in a vise. How long would I have lasted in prison? It wasn't fair. Kazimierz was out in the woods, and I was here, like a quivering rabbit, waiting to be snatched up in their jaws. Do you know what the NKVD is like, if they want to know something?"

Tadek kept still. He saw the darkening of Janusz's eyes as his uncle recalled what Tadek knew about the NKVD. Then Janusz turned to him a wounded look, which astonished Tadek as he realized that his uncle thought he deserved sympathy and was hurt that Tadek refused it.

"I'm an old man, Tadek. I'm tired of all this." He did look old. There was an ancient fogginess in his eyes.

"I'm going now," Tadek said, almost gently, knowing Janusz wasn't going to shoot him. "I've heard all I need to hear."

"What are you going to do?"

"I don't know."

"Are you going to tell Kozel?"

"He'll figure it out on his own if he has a sober day. He's not stupid. Everyone was arrested except you!"

"If he finds out, he'll kill me."

"I can't control him."

"Tell him I'll be here waiting for him."

Tadek stood as calmly as he could, rising slowly and pulling on his coat. Janusz still held the gun loosely in his hands.

At the door, Tadek looked over the chessboard on the counter. He'd been studying it the day before through the haze of liquor, but that part of his brain had still been working. Black was in a knotted mess, its pieces quarreling with each other in a corner.

Tadek picked up a white knight and moved it into the thick of things. It was all such a tangled mess that Tadek wasn't sure what he'd done. Janusz looked across at the board.

"That's your move?" he asked with a bitter smirk.

"Knight to Queen's bishop three."

"That doesn't change anything."

"No, not much."

"Why didn't you take the side of black?"

"I didn't see any moves for black."

Tadek looked at his uncle and again felt that filthy blade of a look slip under his ribs. He opened the door, feeling the back of his head naked and exposed. He stepped out into the mist and started working his labored way down the slippery hill.

Janusz came to the doorway and called after him. "I never wanted to hurt Kazimierz! They said they just wanted to capture him and stop him!" Tadek didn't turn but just kept walking.

Tadek didn't know where he was going—only away—or what he would do. He walked as fast as he could, but the mud and snow, forming heavy slippers about his boots, slowed him down. The flock of starlings was quieter now at Tadek's approach, greeting him with subdued rippling and chittering. Something froze the starlings. Then as one they all took off above his head in a racket of thousands of wings. They circled the grove of trees in a blossoming dark wave and flew off over the river in a raucous flock, a giant curtain folding and unfolding through itself, then moving over the forest and away. It grew quiet again. Tadek stood in the mud, waiting for his thoughts to catch up to him, until he realized that he'd heard a sound that must have frightened the birds—a muffled bang from the open cottage door.

Chapter 49: Farewells

Tadek had discovered that a better place to wait across from Pawel and Halinka's apartment was on a concrete stairway down to a seldom-used basement doorway. It was littered with scraps of dead leaves that the wind stirred up, but sat kitty-cornered from their doorway, and gave him both a clear view and a low profile. He could go there at dusk after work and usually beat both Halinka and Pawel to the park. Within half an hour Halinka would make her way across the park holding her son's hand and would disappear into her apartment building's entrance. A few minutes later Pawel would come from a slightly different angle. Sometimes if they were late he could recognize them by the shape of their silhouettes. Sometimes men and women whose paths hugged the building where he sat would be startled by his presence but then ignore him, continuing on. After the lights went on in their apartment on the third floor, he would make his own way to the bus stop and thence to Liaski. He was waiting for the words that he needed to say to formulate themselves in his mind, hoping that when he finally said them, he would be released from this potent spell attaching him to the past, and while he waited, he crouched in shame and anger.

He decided that he needed to speak to Halinka alone. From Bolek Kosokovski he'd found out that she worked in the office of the university's biology department. He planned to wait outside, but arrived late from his own work and saw her already cutting across a crowded square. He hurried until he was walking beside her. "Hello, Halinka."

She stared back at the man approaching her in the dusk. Then blanched. "Tadek?"

"Yes, Halinka. Don't run away."

"I'm not running anywhere." She smiled, the old smile that was both winning and distant at the same time, as if covering for some sorrow. "It's good to see you, Tadek."

"I'm not going to assault anyone again." He gave a rueful laugh.

"I can see that."

"I apologize."

"It's fine."

She looked at him a long time. "You're different."

"Yes. Four years."

"But I've got to be home. I can't talk now."

"Can we meet?"

They arranged a meeting, and Tadek turned away, exhausted, feeling that it had taken as much of his courage to confront Halinka again as anything he'd had to do in the Gulag.

Two days later they walked along the river bluff by the old castle, looking down at the river. They found a bench on which to sit. Halinka was wearing a black wool coat, frayed at the cuffs, with a navy blue dress and boots. She seemed armored and hidden, her refined face nestled in a green scarf like a white rosebud.

"I wanted to talk to you, too, you know," she said. "I've got a lot to say. I'm sorry about your uncle."

"Don't be."

Tadek had turned and run back to the cabin after he'd heard the single shot. He had pushed through the half-open door out of the sun and entered into the dark room. The peppery smell of burnt powder was all he sensed as his eyes adjusted. He realized he was walking in blood right before he stumbled over his uncle's body.

"I didn't attend the funeral," he said. "Jadwiga told me about it." Because he was a suicide, the priest had refused Janusz a religious burial, and he was buried in a civic graveyard in Grodno. All of Liaski already knew and accepted the story. Of course, they said, of course he'd done it, as if the knowledge had been hanging over the village like a low cloud that finally broke into rain. Jadwiga had been the only person at the funeral.

"That all must've been awful."

Now Tadek looked at one of his shoes he'd crossed over his knee. There was still a rusty stain of blood on its sole. He placed it flat on the ground, out of his sight.

"It's not so much his death," he said. "It's what he did while he was alive that was awful."

"I heard the story. Was that what you met with Pawel about?"

"Yes. Kozel thought...and had me thinking...that Pawel might have betrayed me."

"You can't be serious!"

"I don't know how serious I was. I was confused and wanted to be sure."

"You've got to know Pawel better than that!"

"I recognize that now. I didn't know how much he might've changed. Anything seemed possible. I just felt betrayed in general and had to talk to him while I thought things through. But he's still the same."

"Yes." She smiled. "He is."

"I don't even feel angry at Janusz anymore. It's grotesque. How could he live like that? He betrayed everyone and everything he touched."

"He must have been so alone."

"Don't feel sorry for him. He's just meaningless."

"All right."

"What I wanted to say to you, to you first, and then to Pawel, is that I don't blame you two. I loved you a lot. You were the only thing I would've left the resistance for. My life would've been different. But that was before the Gulag. Everything has moved on and what happened then is gone. I know that."

"I'm glad you don't hate us."

"No. I hope you're happy."

"Thank you." She made an odd tapping motion with one hand on the back of the other, one Tadek recognized as a sign that she was nervous. "But there's something you should know," she said.

"What's that?"

"You might've guessed it, but I guess you've had other things to deal with. After you left. And I loved you, very much, also, you know. After you left. After just a few weeks...I realized I was pregnant. I was desolate. I was panicked. And Pawel kept me company. And then he offered to marry me. There wasn't much time. I said yes."

"You mean your son...."

"Michal."

"He's mine?"

"Yes. Everybody knows. Or I assume they do. In Liaski, they can count to nine. And they do, they do. So, it's not a great secret. I was the great scandal of Liaski. At least until the next one."

Tadek struggled to take in what she'd just told him. "I'm sorry you had to go through that." He didn't know what to say.

A bus down the street backfired and a flock of pigeons took off from the castle walls, circling over the river in a shifting formation before landing back where it had started. Tadek realized how cold it was in the bleak winter sun. Halinka shivered as if in agreement.

"Say something," Halinka said.

"I don't know what to say."

"Do you want to meet him?"

"Should I? Is it all right?"

"Yes. I told Pawel I hoped you'd come over."

"It won't confuse...Michal?"

"No. But we won't tell him . . . about you. Maybe someday."

"I understand."

They started down the hill in silence. Tadek was afraid that if he tried to talk, it would only make things worse. Finally Halinka said, "When you were arrested, for me anyway, it was as if my life ended then and there. And Pawel was there. A solution for me." He didn't mind her talking and let her go on. It felt comforting to be with her, and he almost felt that old closeness for a while. "I was all alone otherwise. I'm not sure Pawel even loved me when we married. He was just being good. That's what he's like. But he does now. Love me." After a few moments, during which they both looked at their feet pacing in tandem over the granular pavement, she added: "And I grew to love him, too." Tadek nodded. He didn't know what he felt.

"Tadek, you were just on the wrong side of history," she said.

Tadek was disoriented by her comment, as if he were with a stranger, and then his anger flared and he turned toward her, his glare scorching.

"Well then, *history* was on the wrong side!" he hissed.

Her face blanched at his anger. Had he ever been angry at her before? "I...I didn't mean it like that. I know...someday...things may be different. But we have to live our lives."

"You never understood me," Tadek said, not to be bitter, but as if just realizing the truth of the statement.

"Perhaps not, but I loved you."

Feeling remorse at his outburst, he squeezed her hand. "I know. I'm sorry. I know you didn't mean it that way."

They crossed the bridge and turned their steps toward the apartment.

"We've asked for permission to emigrate to Poland," she said. "To Lodz."

"What? Really?" Such an option had never occurred to him, even though the Poles were still encouraged to emigrate by the government, a slow-motion, bureaucratic ethnic cleansing.

"If we go, we'll be back to visit," Halinka hurried to say. "And you can see Michal then."

He nodded numbly again. He followed Halinka up three flights of stairs in a cold stairway smelling of coal dust. When she let them into the apartment, Pawel was seated in a chair with Michal standing by his knee. The little boy, whom Tadek had scarcely glanced at before, was holding an unpainted wooden truck which he ran over Pawel's leg and up his chest and down his arm. Tadek took in the boy, the high cheekbones, the narrow nose. Yes, it could be. Well, it was. He had to understand that. But he also saw Halinka's mouth with its longbow curves and her honey-blonde hair. The boy ducked behind Pawel's knee when the stranger entered the room. Pawel stood, smiling, and went to grasp Tadek's hand with both of his, and they fell into an embrace that, though tentative, felt welcomed and needed to Tadek. It helped ground him even as he began to feel that he'd fallen into a fantasy parallel to his own reality, not quite a dream but something stranger because more real. Everything had a delirious clarity to it that seemed fragile.

"Do you remember the Krzaczek's basement?"

"Sure. Sabina was recalling it just the other day."

"Remember this?" She recited:

> I thought he'd tell his story in the end.
> (Ex-convicts like to speak to an old friend
> About their prison days.) I'd learn the truth,
> The truth that tyrants hide, the Polish truth.
> It flourishes in shadows. Its history
> Lives in Siberia, where its heroes die.

Tadek smiled. "Somehow I knew you'd recite that. But that must've been written by someone who'd never been to Siberia. I don't really want to talk about the Gulag."

"That's all right."

As they all talked, Tadek kept stealing furtive glances at Michal, wanting to get something just from the sight of him, though he wasn't sure what, and each glance seemed unsatisfying. Part of him wanted to stay in this room forever, but another part of him just wanted to get through the next half hour without some disaster happening. He felt that disaster loomed the whole time like a stranger behind a door.

After a while Michal went across the hall to play with a friend. "Come and say goodbye to your uncle Tadek," he said.

"My uncle?"

"He's like family, Michal," Halinka explained. "Like an uncle or a godfather."

Just as with his father, Michal and Tadek began to shake hands and then changed their minds. Tadek went to his knees and they fell into a light embrace. Tadek's eyes followed Michal's slim shoulders as he slipped out the door with Halinka.

With Halinka and Michal gone, Tadek took the opportunity

to wordlessly look over his old friend, as if an intense visual scan might make sense of the recent news. He still felt there was more to say between them.

"How could you marry Halinka?" he whispered.

"But I married her for you," Pawel protested. "At least partly."

"For me!"

"To take care of her for you."

"Not to humiliate me?"

"No, never!"

"Then you didn't love her?"

"I don't know. I saw the possibility of future love. And I was right: I love her now. Sabina and I had been tormenting each other for years. I needed a clean break."

"I don't hold anything against you," Tadek said abruptly. "Either of you. But I'd better go." He stood up. He needed to leave now to beat that disastrous stranger behind the door, waiting to enter—though he still wanted to stay, even with Michal gone, to be with his childhood friends.

But he knew those days had been swept far away like a twig down the Niemen. Pawel gave him a full embrace this time. They met Halinka returning in the hallway and, clumsily, fumbling, he kissed her on her cheek, they hugged, and he left.

Outside twilight was settling in the graveled park. Tadek walked across the river and up by the castle overlooking the Niemen. Sunset still glowed over the forests in the west. He kept walking, plunging into the streets. Streetlights were rare but the darkness was soothing.

He'd escaped the stranger behind the door who'd threatened some unknown disaster, and he no longer blamed Pawel or Halinka. They hadn't planned any of the events that had shaken his life. Instead of feeling betrayed as he had for years, now he felt saddened with the knowledge that the closeness of their childhood was buried beneath a thousand Gulag mornings, beneath the pain of his absent parents, beneath the emptiness created by an uncle who betrayed and killed how many heroes, how many innocents?

He circled through the city and found a stone bench where he could rest. After a time, he came out of his circling thoughts and realized he was gazing on a familiar-looking building. It was a two-story wooden building with chipping white paint that had once been the fabric store of Levy Reznikoff, where his grandfather had taken him along for business meetings. Now it was a plumbing goods store run by the state. The family had lived in the second floor above their business. Tadek remembered the Jewish children playing in the streets here, the adults wearing their odd, somber clothing, and felt the regret you feel after you hear that a longtime acquaintance—with whom you never really became friends, though there were plenty of chances, with whom an unreasonable quarrel had begun—has died, and now everything is too late.

He had heard stories from Ewa and others about a few Jews from Grodno who had come straggling back from the forests, from the camps after the war, to be greeted by their neighbors with cold incomprehension: what are you doing here? They'd wandered around aimlessly for a few days and then left. In other places such as Kielce, their reception had been worse: they had been murdered by a mob. He remembered all the loose talk of his childhood. Always there had been an excuse. The Jewish Bolsheviks wanted to overthrow the government; the Jewish capitalists were causing inflation. The Jews kidnapped and butchered Christian children. He remembered his mother's scorn at the absurdities that people could believe. He knew that if nothing else should have been learned from the war, it was that such thinking was wrong, and yet he was uncertain how many took in this lesson, and how deeply. Nobody wanted to be reminded of what had happened. Nobody wanted to talk about it. Everybody had their own problems to deal with, struggling to survive and to keep some dignity in the new soviet state.

Across the street from the Reznikoff's building, the great stone synagogue still stood, pale and massive in the moonlight. He remembered now that more than once when he was seventeen and had started work in Grodno, he'd walked past the building and up to the castle overlooking the river and not even glanced at the synagogue, not let it trouble his mind. He'd fallen in so easily with the vast silence. It had taken four years in the Gulag to change him enough so that he could see the synagogue and have within him a small echo of the experience needed to try to imagine what had happened there. Before, he had just averted his eyes. Only now was he able to accept the responsibility to look and ponder. It was here that the Nazis had forced the last remaining Jews of Grodno—trembling, praying, crying—to gather before they were shipped to Oświęcim or Treblinka. His uncle had helped to destroy the people who had come here on Shabbat every week for years, for decades, for centuries.

Tadek remembered the gulley full of bodies that Lech had shown him. He remembered the sounds of gunshots at night as he came home from Jan's with his father. By now he had heard enough stories to know that even if Nazis led those hunting parties, too often they'd found some Poles to bring along as helpers, guiding the Nazis to the Jews.

Now the synagogue's doors and windows were boarded over. There was an official notice pasted across the front doors stating in large letters that anyone caught on these premises would be prosecuted. When he'd first been arrested and was headed for the Gulag in the convict train, he had thought—now it was his turn. But he had survived. The Jews were gone.

He could feel the spirits of the Grodno ghetto stir unsettled and unavenged about him in the moonlight. They were gone and he was here. His own story was just a twig floating on a vast river of suffering that had flooded the land, and which, even receding, invisible, had left a litter of destruction, eroding and reshaping the people and the landscape of their memory.

Chapter 50: Life Again

Work back at the textile factory under his young Byelorussian boss was about as he expected it to be, and Tadek fell into the routine, taking the bus to Grodno when it was still dark out and returning likewise in the dark. On weekends when he wasn't repairing the house, he went ice-fishing with Bolek Kosokovski. They seldom spoke, just sat for hours over the lines, bundled up till they were mummies of rags, passing back and forth a bottle of vodka, watching the sun creep its low path across the sky. Sometimes Franek, the remaining Borovski twin, would walk out late afternoons and sit down on a log and pass the bottle with them, no less laconic, though once he'd been the talkative twin. Tadek imagined that both he and Franek took comfort from Bolek's simple, steady good humor.

Tadek still felt himself, his real self, hidden inside this fisherman, like a tough little pellet that had been pounded into shape by the huge hands of the NKVD corporal on the red-painted concrete of the NKVD basement, pounded into him by the hundreds of days awaking in the Gulag barracks to stumble across a frozen yard to a row of open latrines where he would defecate in a row with twenty others, and then stumble to the mess hall only to pick maggots out of the soup before a day of shoveling gravel or sawing logs in the arctic wind. Peeling back those layers wasn't easy to do. He wasn't sure if it was something that he wanted to do or should even try to do. He couldn't do it by himself. An instinct in him still pulled away from everyone, as if pulling him back toward the Gulag.

There was considerable repair work to be done around the house, barn, and orchard. Windows had been broken and chairs smashed. He rehabilitated a workbench in the barn so he could start rebuilding the beehives for next spring. A pot-bellied stove gave his little workroom a bit of heat. He was working here on a Saturday afternoon when he heard an inquisitive "Hello? Hello?" coming from the house. He stepped outside to see Sabina standing at the house door looking puzzled.

"Over here!"

"There you are!"

She ducked her head as if having to forge through an invisible barrier and came down the path between the frozen weeds. When close she looked up and smiled. He remembered her mouth, plush, sensual. She was still fetching in a down-to-earth way that Tadek had always found both appealing yet easy to overlook, not intriguing like Halinka.

"You're just the help I need."

"How so?"

"I have a vise, but I need an extra hand to steady this frame for me while I nail it together."

"Okay."

He showed her how to hold the honey-frame while he tacked it together.

"How many more do you have to do?"

"You see." He nodded to a pile of frames.

"Okay. Let's do it."

"Are you sure?"

"Sure."

They worked in a silent ballet, she stooping to retrieve a cracked and twisted frame from the littered pile on the floor, fitting it in the vise, holding it steady while he squared it and tacked together its joints. A soft light fell into the barn from the doorway, sifted by dust motes. It felt good to be moving, working, doing something that he wanted to do, and to have Sabina, his childhood friend, who understood him, working with him, was quietly elating. Tadek had already measured and sawed extra lengths to replace the pieces completely broken. It was easy with another hand, and soon the piles of damaged frames had been replaced by a stack of solid frames.

They went inside and Tadek poured Sabina a glass of kvass. Without makeup, flushed from the exercise and the winter air, Sabina glowed. Tadek was suddenly aware of their solitude as he stood near her in the empty house. As if reading his mind, or perhaps a lingering gaze, she took one sip from the glass, and when she lowered it, smiled her mocking, sensual smile at him, a smile he was suddenly desperate to kiss.

"I think it's time for me to go!" she laughed.

"No." He was laughing too as he followed her to the door, trying to slide an arm around her waist.

"Yes!"

He managed to pull her to him and to plant a quick kiss only half on her mouth as she twisted out of his grip and went laughing out the door.

His failed kiss confirmed to him that he wasn't fit for society anymore. What was he thinking? When did you kiss a girl? He had no idea. At least she had laughed about it. He walked with her to the gate. "But we haven't had time to talk!"

"I just wanted to make sure you were still alive."

"You won't stay? There's so much to say."

She laughed again, opening the gate herself. She knew the trick: you had to twist the bolt before you slid it. She was always clever that way.

"We'll talk sometime, Tadek. I'm glad you're back." She paused, a hand on the gate. "I knew you'd make it back, out of anybody." She laughed. "You're like a little cork in the ocean that keeps bobbing up no matter what tidal wave it gets swept up in. Just like that day you fell in the ice."

"Sometimes I think you're right."

"You and I," she said, "we're both the scrappy types. We'll always get by. See you later, Tadek."

* * *

Later that week Tadek went to meet Sabina as she emerged from her workplace, a downtown building where she was a secretary in the office of a pesticide factory. Her face lit up at seeing him and he smiled back, relieved. He hadn't been sure whether seeing her was the right thing to do.

She took his arm.

"Hello, Tadek. You came to see me? Shall we walk?"

Sabina walked with a brisk, impatient step that made him hurry to keep up, so different from Halinka's pensive, elegant stride. They headed away from the throngs emptying the offices, down a quieter street where an old lady swept the cobblestone, and Sabina slowed a bit.

"I know you talked to Halinka," she said.

"Yes."

"What are you going to do?"

"What can I do? Pawel is Michal's father now. He's all he's ever known. They didn't think I'd come back. I can't blame them."

"Do you still love her?"

"No." Tadek answered instinctively, but then had to think about his words. "I loved her then, but everything's different now. She's different. I know I'm different. We were swept together and then swept apart. I didn't see her for years." He was thinking of Lamaara. He had dreamt of settling down with her. Halinka had become an idea to him in the Gulag, and he just didn't know what to do back in real life without that idea.

"Pawel received permission for them to move to Lodz. Did you know?"

"It's just as well. I've accepted everything. How are you doing?"

She shrugged. "You grew up with me. You know what it was like. Now, no Nazis, no soldiers, no bombs, no war, no NKVD parked on the doorstep . . . .No friends being hauled away to the Gulag. It's paradise! I keep my head down and go to work and go home."

"That's my plan too."

"No more adventures in the woods with the partisans?"

"No."

"I'm sorry about your uncle."

"I'm not. He finally did the right thing."

"Anyway, it's hard. You've been through so much."

"Thanks for that. Others have been through more. Or didn't make it through at all. I consider myself lucky. Like I said, I just want to try to be normal now."

They walked down a quiet street, meandering toward Sabina's side of town. They leaned briefly against an iron stair railing.

"What did you mean," he asked, "when you said we were both scrappy, getting-by types?"

"I was married, briefly," she said abruptly. "I suppose you

heard."

He had heard this.

"Bolek told me. I wasn't sure if you'd want to talk about it. He didn't say much."

"No, he's a man of few words."

"He'd rather fish than talk."

"Well, I married a mathematics professor at the university. I thought that sounded very sophisticated and impressive, thought that he was some sort of genius. And he was taken with me. But he turned out not to be at all what I expected. He was really quite thoroughly insane. He thought the whole world was a complex trigonometry problem that he'd figured out and everyone else had gotten wrong. He used to follow me through the streets if I went out for bread, hiding behind trees and baby buggies or pretending to read a newspaper. Like in a cartoon strip. It would've been comical if it hadn't been so awful. So I managed to have the marriage annulled after two months of hell."

"Don't take this wrong, and maybe it is small of me, but it makes me feel not so bad, to see that you and Halinka have had to deal with things, even outside the Gulag."

"I don't take it wrong."

"It makes me feel not so alone."

"Well, that's good then. I survived my trial, and a crazed math professor was hardly the Gulag."

They walked on to her apartment building on the edge of town. She made a rueful face looking at the bleak building.

"Not lovely, but I had to leave Liaski."

"I understand."

"Why don't you come up?"

"All right."

They walked past the old babushka, who stood out front with her twig broom scraping the walk as steadiy as a figure on a medieval clock, turning her black gaze on them as they entered the building but continuing to sweep. Inside Sabina laughed. "The old wench! She'd be decadent too if she still could be." The elevator creaked slowly upwards. It was the size of a janitor's closet and swayed from side to side. There was a gap between the lift and the building's walls that let one peer down to the basement and to a receding patch of concrete lit by a bare bulb. That sense of peril invading the everyday prompted a kiss and by the time the elevator stopped on the eighth floor they were gasping.

Inside her apartment door, she looked at him a long time, a bit wide-eyed, with the unselfconscious seriousness of a cat. He felt a rush of gratitude for her presence, feeling without words that he was trading the allure of Halinka's inwardness for the reality of Sabina's candor, a bargain he could now appreciate.

"I don't have time to waste," she said.

"Me neither."

"Both my roommates are gone."

Following her down the hallway to her bed, taking off her clothes, he sensed as if he was walking down a hallway within himself, and door after door flew open spilling light and infinite possibility. When he saw her naked body, he felt that this was finally the balm commensurate to all the pain within him. Nothing was guided by his will: all desires and hopes that flowed unimpeded from within him were equally matched by her, and he needed only not to resist the momentum of all these forces that drove them on.

There was no nuanced, mysterious delicacy such as Tadek had felt with Halinka, just a frank, laughing, sensuality, and Tadek felt that he was finally home from the Gulag.

They were still in bed much later when the winter sun had set and the room had darkened. "Are we ever going to have a chance to be happy?" Sabina asked him. She lay with her palm on his chest, her breasts pressed against his side.

"Are you happy now?" he asked.

"Very."

"Me too. And I didn't go through the camps to give in," Tadek said. "To say we could never be happy is to say that they'd won. Stalin's eating dirt in his grave. I'm here now with you. As far as I'm concerned, I won."

"I feel as if I won too." She drew a circle on his chest with her fingernail. "What happened to that mark on your neck?" she asked.

Surprised, he touched his neck, as if he'd be able to feel it. "You remember that? I guess I got rid of it during the Gulag."

"Sounds like a story."

"All the Gulag stories are gruesome. I want to live forwards, not backwards."

"All right."

"Someday I'll tell you everything that ever happened to me. I want you to know it all. Just not yet."

"All right."

"Listen, tomorrow you can come to Liaski with me and I'll show you what I've done. As soon as spring comes, I want to expand the garden. I need to plant some new apple trees. The ones my grandfather and great-grandfather planted are ancient."

"Yes?"

"The hives are all ready for the spring, thanks to your help. My grandfather built most of them, so fixing them was important to me. He showed me how to take care of bees. He was taking care of them almost until the day he died. In the spring, I'll split the hive that's left and start rebuilding."

"I remember your grandfather from when I was a kid. He was a tall dark man who was always shouting and waving his cane around."

"That's him!"

"He scared all us kids."

"I remember. He could be rough, but he taught me the words I've lived by."

"What were those?"

"'Hitler is not my papa and Stalin is not my mama.'"

Chapter 51:
A Truce with History

His marriage with Sabina was intense and often unhappy. They argued over everything, from proper mealtimes to the way to plant potatoes, from how strong to brew tea, to whether a mist in the air counted as rain. Tadek's settling back into village life and into married life was not a small adjustment. One thing he could be counted on for was to stop and exchange news with any village acquaintances, and to help them deplete whatever vodka bottles were available. More than once Sabina was startled by a knock on the door by a neighbor, come to tell her that she'd stumbled upon Tadek passed out in a neighbor's garden or in a snowdrift with an empty bottle lying next to him. She had to go and trundle him home, reacquainting his groggy consciousness to reality with the lash of her tongue.

Once her tongue had stung him too sharply, and he hit her in the face with a short jab and stomped away, walking around the village three times, sitting alongside the river and finally slipping off his clothes and swimming under the moonlight, feeling the urge to let the river carry him away, the way it had Yanek Borovski.

He did let it carry him away, drifting downstream, feeling the river's tentacles of different temperatures coiling around him. He would let them pull him down to the bottom and have an end to it all. Maybe this was how he'd been meant to end, beneath the ice so many years before, only he and Pawel had thwarted fate unreasonably. His whole life had been a bookkeeping error of destiny: the bicycle messenger years, the Gulag, none of it had been necessary. Now everything was wrong. He could never fit back into his beloved Liaski; he could never make his love for Sabina work after his love for Halinka had been devastated by circumstances. Now he would set things right and just spin away silently like Yanek, never to be seen again.

But rather than pulling him down, the currents only seemed to buoy him up. Well then, he would just keep drifting, down through Lithuania to the Baltic, through the Baltic to the ocean, where he would live in a bubble on the bottom of the...he hit a sandbank a hundred yards downstream, and seemed to come back to himself.

He returned home hours later, sheepishly opening the door, peering in. Sabina sat at the kitchen table, peering through a purple crescent that swelled beneath her left eye. During the week it took the bruise to heal, no one, not one person in the village, spoke to him first, and then only gruffly, and he felt his body tingling with shame that entire time. He never hit her again, though their fights were rhythmic as the cycles of the moon.

Yet they remained fiercely attracted despite their constant fights. The fights even seemed to be part of a deeper dialogue that would bring them even closer together and inevitably to bed, both ruefully admitting this bond despite themselves.

He realized that, after the Gulag, he would never have adjusted to the soul-closeness that he and Halinka had been striving for when they were young, and that he was more comfortable with the daily recriminations, criticisms, and complaints that hedged Sabina and himself apart—until, as if their hostility had been an inverted sign of their attraction, they would surprise themselves in each others' arms in the orchard or the kitchen, hurrying toward the bedroom in a rush of resentful desire.

They had three children in five years, they were busy with the garden and jobs, their house was full of neighbors and friends, and so their marriage was also often happy. It depended on the hour or the minute, on the last word spoken, the last gesture or touch.

During these years, Krystyna and Tadek wrote long letters back and forth between Liaski and Vorkuta. The news of Janusz's betrayal shocked Krystyna more than anyone. She wrote to Tadek, remembering Janusz as a boy and a young man, his kindness and enthusiasm, how close the brothers had been, and she wrote with astonishment that he could have hidden his internal transformation so well. She wrote of her shame and anguish that she had led the trusting Reznikoffs into a trap set by her own brother, who would also lead the Soviets to the forest hideaway of her other brother.

Tadek also read of Krystyna's complaints about Roman, who was renting a room a block away from her and Uri. She constantly saw his hangdog face tagging along behind her in the streets, no matter how many times she told him to leave her alone. For his part Roman wrote Tadek that he was determined to win back his wife, and when Uri and she split two years later, Uri leaving with a woman ten years younger than himself and twenty years younger than Krystyna, Roman succeeded, and Krystyna and he moved back together, and soon, back to Liaski. Tadek and his father built a separate addition onto their house, so the Gradinskis were united after fifteen years spent wandering separately across two continents.

Tadek made such accommodations as were absolutely necessary with the regime. When he was drafted into the Soviet Army reserves, he briefly considered fleeing rather than reporting for training, but decided that his days of open battle with the Soviets were over. He reported as required. Because he was short and adept at machinery, he was trained as a tank commander. He found a hidden hilarity in the responsibility of the position and was determined to transform it into a lark. His crew was from the area and most were Polish like him, viewing the Soviet Army with the same contempt.

A crisis arose in the summer of 1968 when the Soviets were preparing to invade Czechoslovakia. The newspapers and television sets were filled with justifications and calls for good Soviet citizens everywhere to support the battle against capitalist renegades. Tadek scoffed at the news on the radio and went out of his way to pick arguments in the village.

He received the call to muster as a reservist.

"I'm not going," he said immediately.

"Do you want to go back to prison?" Sabina was unimpressed with his defiance. "Did you enjoy it so much?"

"The Gulag's not a prison any more," he scoffed. "It's just a health spa nowadays. They play football all day long and table tennis at night."

"Oh, listen to you!"

"I'm not going to serve those pigs!"

"You have children now. You'd think they'd invited you to a dance and you could just refuse the invitation!"

Tadek went quiet, thinking, developing a plan.

When the time came, he went along with the Soviets' orders until late the night before they were to be dispatched. Lying in his bunk in the barracks, Tadek began to roll and groan, disturbing the entire platoon. He held his side and complained in wild-eyed pain. His captain, a Byelorussian, came to stand over his bunk and swear at him, calling him a coward, a traitor. He said he would have him shot. But the captain could scarcely believe that anyone would go to such extremes just to avoid driving a tank to Prague. After Tadek ignored his captain for an hour of unceasing moaning, the captain, still vowing to court martial him and have him shot when his fraud was exposed, finally relented and sent Tadek off to a medic, who in turn relayed him to a hospital.

At the hospital, orderlies carried Tadek on a stretcher into a room where a doctor, a tall man with a long, seamed, monkish face, probed his stomach. Tadek flinched and shouted in pain whenever the doctor touched his side. "Appendicitis," he said in Polish and then in Russian. "We'll have to take it out." With Russian efficiency, the orderlies then carried him down a long dark corridor where they set his stretcher on the floor and forgot about him for over an hour, during which time he kept up a dutiful moan, in case anyone should be listening. Finally the orderlies returned, placed him on a gurney, and wheeled him into a room where someone stuck a tube in his arm. He felt fuzzy all over, then very warm, then his brain was muffled in shadows.

He awoke in a hospital room with his surgeon above him. It was the same doctor with the monkish face, now lit by a light of humor in his eyes.

"You're lucky in your surgeon," he confided in a low voice to Tadek, again in Polish. "I've never seen a healthier appendix than yours in my life."

When quizzed by the army authorities, the doctor shrugged and said, "Sometimes appendices can be dangerously infected with surprisingly little swelling."

Tadek stayed in a hospital bed for a week, but when he was released, the troops were still in Czechoslovakia and he was ordered to join his battalion. The violence was over and they were now just window-dressing in a show of force. Tadek spent two weeks atop a tank in Prague, flashing the peace sign to the Czechs and shouting "*Mir!*," "*Laska!*" and "*Svoboda!*" to everyone. The Czechs who still had the spirit cheered back, understanding his support. He brought home postcards and souvenirs for each of his children.

* * *

Any further education was forbidden Tadek as an ex-zek, but, building on what he'd already learned, and working with a friend after his job at the textile mill was done, he learned the skills necessary to become licensed as an electrician, and finagled a job working for the government, like everyone else. This job gave him enough spare money to eventually buy a BMW motorcycle, his prize and pride, with a sidecar. Never liking to stay still for long, on weekends he'd stuff two kids in the sidecar and hang one behind him on the seat and rocket down side roads and over the fields to find the best mushrooming spots, until he knew the roads in the entire area better than anyone, as he'd used to know the alleys and narrow paths of Liaski on his bicycle. Eventually the government put in a gravel road that wound its way along the opposite bank of the Niemen. Previously, there had been only an overgrown road from the Commonwealth days, unraveling itself into confusing, deadend timber-cutting lanes.

Sometimes he'd detach the sidecar to rocket on his motorcycle up the rough, new road, between the forest and the river, up past Shabany on the other bank, up to the outcropping of rocks where the partisans had come down to the river to get messages from Jan, where he'd skated that winter night pursued by wolves. From here, if it was dry enough, he could pick a route on his bike through the marshlands, to the place where the partisans had camped. There he could still make out the scattered indentations in the earth where they'd made their huts. There were still shattered trees and overgrown craters from the bombardment of the Soviets. More than once he'd come upon a rusted-out rifle or mortar shell. Once, further afield, he discovered a skeleton, stretched out in the marshy land, shot through with weeds. He'd arranged with the town to have the body removed and with the priest to have the unknown partisan buried in the village plot.

Tadek eased off in his drinking as the years went by, making some necessary internal adjustments to the life of the village and marriage, but Roman began drinking more and more. He had been left with a constant cough from his years in a coal mine, and after the expenditure of what energy he had left building the house with Tadek, he spent most of his time fishing along the banks of the Niemen. When Tadek would find time to take out a little boat he'd bought, they would go upstream together near Grodno and then float back down, fishing each nook and eddy along the way, recapturing scraps of what closeness they could before Roman died of cancer in the '60s. Helena had immigrated to Poland with Kazimierz's two children. Jadwiga moved back to the cottage she'd shared for years with Janusz, reaching an accommodation with the bitter events of her life and dying after a peaceful decade on her own, always delighted when Tadek stopped by with his children. Krystyna, a gradually eroding beauty, lived in isolation and austerity into her nineties, holding herself apart from the other villagers and devoting herself to gardening and tending the orchards with the discipline of a nun.

Years passed and Krystyna died. Tadek's children grew and moved away into Grodno, and one to America, and they had children of their own. Tadek smiled to himself in August of 1980 when Solidarity arose, and again in 1991 when the iron curtain fell, feeling that work to which he had contributed was being completed. Though the weight of authoritarianism remained heavy in Belarus, his contempt for the government seemed to provide an elixir that kept him vital, as contempt for previous governments had done for his grandfather.

Change came even to Liaski. The government—which the Belyawskis and now the Gradinskis had never considered anything but a gang of banditos—had not only stolen Zygmunt's land, but had the bald-faced shamelessness to steal his idea and to put in a ferry across the Niemen to connect to the new road. So years later when Tadek retired from his electrician's job in Grodno, but was still too restless to do nothing, he took a part-time job manning the ferry across the Niemen. The bored or convivial among his village friends would come to talk with him between crossings, and play some cards, or share a story and a little homemade vodka, if it wasn't too early in the day.

He was always ready to pass the time while he waited for the buzzing of the electrical bell that signaled someone waiting on the other side. When they buzzed, he'd start up the smoky diesel motor and let it pull them across. The flat-bottomed twenty-foot ferry was hooked up to a taut, frayed steel cable that slung across the restless river like a bowstring always threatening to snap and send them spinning away in slow but relentless motion downstream.

He listened to BBC radio for an hour every night to stay informed of the politics around him, which had enfolded his entire life like an edict of destiny, but more and more he focused on life on a granular level—noticing the copper butterflies in the cemetery, the new nest of storks across from the ferry landing, the unusual size and feistiness of the pickerel in the Niemen this year, and the patterns of cloud shadows sweeping over the tops of the forest trees.

For a while Pawel and Halinka came with their family to visit once a year, and there would be a big dinner with much drinking and reminiscing. Tadek tried not to look overmuch at the growing blond boy, short and stocky with a squarish head like himself, who grew restless squirming at the table before he was excused to run outside to play. Pawel and Halinka both had maintained their studious sides and managed to acquire an education in Poland that would've been unlikely in Byelorussia, with Halinka becoming an obstetrician and Pawel ending up with a doctorate in agronomy, doing government-funded research on different strains of wheat, work that eventually achieved international attention. Tadek liked to boast particularly about Pawel's successes as he heard of them in letters from Halinka to Sabina, even as the Karposovichs visited Liaski less and less frequently after their parents' deaths.

In the summer Tadek and Sabina's daughter who had escaped to America was back for a visit with her eight-year-old daughter, Krystyna, who was going to tag along beside Tadek when he walked through the garden. She knew as little Polish or Russian as he knew English, but somehow they communicated.

They stepped out of the house. Low clouds had been sweeping over the village all day, dragging with them showers, but now the sun broke through.

Tadek gestured to the side of the house for Krystyna's benefit.

"See these bullet holes? These are from the Nazis," he said in Polish. She looked at him, puzzled. He pointed again to the bullet holes and repeated, "Nazis. Nazis. Germans." His hands formed guns: "Rat-a-tat-tat."

Her eyes lit up and she nodded. "Really?" she said in English. He grinned. She got it. They both laughed.

He headed down the path, holding her hand. First he stopped in the barn and lifted the lid to one feedbin.

"What's in there, grandpa?" his granddaughter asked,

craning over the edge to peer at the contraption of whirled copper tubing and tin containers. It grew more fantastical every year as Tadek added segments and reshaped others till it now presented the metaphysical question as to whether it was the same still that his grandfather had built, having occupied the same space but been tinkered on till only an original cork or screw remained, like a man whose every body cell has been replaced over a decade, or a man whose every memory and experience had been replaced and crowded out with new ones, which were replaced again in turn. Still, Tadek felt that its essential identity persisted, and he continued to think of it as Zygmunt's still, just as he thought of the bees as Zygmunt's bees and the apple trees, which he also replaced periodically, as Zygmunt's trees.

"This is my money machine," he said. Sometimes he sold a jar or two of vodka, but usually he gave it away to friends.

She peered inside and laughed, not understanding what he said or what purpose the strange agglomeration of random parts, hanging together in defiance of gravity, could possibly serve.

They walked back through the orchard and Tadek plucked one of the ivory-white apples off a low-hanging branch of a tree that he'd grown from a cutting from his great-grandfather's original tree. He withdrew a pocketknife and cut the apple in half and passed half to his granddaughter.

She shook her head, no. "I don't like apples," she said in English.

"The original tree here was planted by your great-great-great grandfather, you know that?" he said in Polish. "But it doesn't bear any apples now. This one. This one we planted as a seedling, and now it's mature."

Unimpressed by his foreign babble, she shook her head again. He lifted his hand in a "wait and see" gesture and grabbed a beekeeper's hat from the wall of a shed. They walked further on the well-worn path. They passed the thick hollow trunk from the original hive that stood like a primitive totem in a corner of the garden. He told her in Polish that his great-grandfather had found this hive in the woods, full of bees, and had brought it here in the winter, and that spring he had a hive. She looked at him politely. He couldn't quite believe that she didn't understand him. He kept expecting the intensity of meaning to burn through the opacity of individual words. He wanted to tell her so much. He wanted to tell her all about Hitler and Stalin, how they were nobody's mama and papa, but her mother said that she wasn't interested in history but liked playing video games and going to the mall, neither of which pasttimes Tadek completely understood.

He held up a hand to stop her and fit the beekeeper's hat on her head. Its much-patched gauze came down to her shoulders and it tilted on her head in a perilous fashion, but she smiled and straightened it with a hand, game for anything. He stepped up to a hive, directing his granddaughter to stay away. Ignoring the orbiting bees, long since immune to stings, Tadek with methodical moves lifted a frame of waxen comb and with his knife blade unsealed a few cells of honey, letting it drip on the slice of apple before gently returning the frame to the hive.

"Here. Take it. Eat."

She very tentatively lifted the honeyed apple slice to her lips. Her eyes widened. He laughed.

"See? See? Pretty good, huh?"

She smiled and took another bite, a convert.

Sabina called from the house. "Tadek! Someone's here to see you!"

From where he stood he could just make out a figure at the gate.

"Who is it?"

"Someone who wants to talk to you about bees."

He remembered then that it was a Russian colonel to whom he had given a ferry ride a month before. The colonel had retired to Liaski for the inexpensive living, and had taken up hives as a hobby. They'd struck up a conversation, and since the colonel could see that Tadek was the village expert on apiary matters, he'd taken to dropping by to quiz him for tips.

Tadek walked back to the house with his granddaughter, who ran inside. He let in the colonel and they both walked through the hives together, Tadek pacifying the bees with a casual wave of smoke, pulling and inspecting the frames, heavy with honey. The colonel asked about the distinctive flavors derived from different flowers. All the time, in the back of Tadek's mind, was the thought that when he was younger, he would've been conferring with Ewa or Kazimierz about the colonel's movements and where they might expose him to a quick machine gun burst from behind a tree. But Tadek liked the man, despite or perhaps because of the fact that he reminded Tadek of the major, the one who decades before had stood in the Gradinski front room discussing Piłsudski and who had sent him to the Gulag. Clouds overhead clotted together, and gradually a mist turned to rain, forcing them back to the barn where they finished their conversation, standing in the straw-reeking shadows and watching the drizzle. Tadek had a ferry shift anyway that afternoon and evening, as he did twice a week, just enough of a job to keep him occupied. He walked the colonel to the gate and changed his boots and put on a slicker for work.

The misty rain still suffused the air as Tadek made his way by himself across the village square, where Chopin had been shot, where the bookish Ruth Friedlander had offered him a day-old fig-cake, past Pawel's old house and down to the river. He greeted the daytime ferryman, a young man, always with a cigarette in his mouth. He had a round head that bobbed atop a skinny neck. His long, skinny arms were always in motion. Tadek could see that he was impatient; he wished to hurry home to his new wife.

"You're late," he said.

"Three minutes," Tadek shrugged.

"Someone just rang from the other side. I waited to go because I knew you'd be here any moment, and now he thinks we've forgotten him," he explained as the bell in the ferry shack rang again.

"He'll wait." But Tadek hopped on board and started up the diesel engine, releasing the gears that began to wind up the cable and haul the ferry through the water. Immediately the thick river fog surrounded him. It was on foggy days like this, when he was by himself, going across or coming back, that the ghosts came to visit him, and then they served as company, twisting in the skeins of fog above the lusterless silver water.

Waiting on the other side was a farmer with a single horse drawing a two-wheeled cart. Tadek smiled to himself as he brought the ferry to a standstill. He'd been seeing similar carts since he was a kid. Change came one cart at a time to this part of Europe, and this cart wouldn't be abandoned until there was nothing solid left to hold a nail. The ancient cart driver grunted: "Been waiting fifteen minutes." He had long white hair trapped under a leather cap, a long white mustache and beard, and skin as leathery as his cap.

"I just got here," Tadek replied. "The kid's going home." He'd seen this man before and knew his grunts and complaints never amounted to much. Sure enough, by mid-stream, the man was complaining about the weather, and then his horse, and then the price of vegetables.

Tadek left him off and watched his horse slowly climb the hill away from the river. A pair of storks flew low overhead through the mist, headed for their nest across the river. Tadek released the brake on the cable and let the current edge the ferry out toward the river's center, where the mists were heaviest, and he let the ferry sit there, held against the tug and hiss of the current. He sat on a simple wooden stool, closed his eyes, and let his mind wander. They were all there. Both of his uncles, Kazimierz and Janusz, Kazimierz relaxed and talkative, engaged in a low-key celebration, seeming to think that he had won the wars against Hitler and Stalin, his teeth white in his dark beard, turning over his shoulder to Tadek, gesturing for him to follow, and Janusz, on the other hand, fretful and snappish, not wanting to talk as he brooded over the chessboard, searching for that lethal pawn move. Also in the mist, their voices in the lapping of the water against the ferry's bow, the Reznikoffs, the father, the mother, the two children, still disappearing trustfully down a village lane toward their betrayal and death. There was the young partisan Hipolit, striding down a country lane next to the forest, lord of the morning. There was Vasilenko, a look of strenuous patience on his face as he repeated a line of poetry over and over for Tadek; there was Lamaara, taking off her dirty prisoner's blouse as she knelt on a pile of potato sacks. There was Lev Kostrapov, peering at him from his under his scarf like a badger from his hole, discerning that Tadek just might live. Both his parents were there, reconciled, sitting at the kitchen table, his father reading a book of calculus, his mother looking out the window at the garden, her eyes full of unspoken dreams. There was always Zygmunt, presiding over them all somehow, extending his advice concerning the bees and the salubrious attributes of honey to all who would listen.

The bell rang from across the river, calling him out of his reverie to the far side. Even as the dusk deepened, the clouds had broken and the mists had lifted. Now he could see a group of people waiting, huddled together where the road emerged from the woods. Standing for a moment before starting the motor, he

570

looked downstream toward the curve of the river that led to where the partisan camp had been, a dozen kilometers away. He looked along the side of the village, toward the fields that his grandfather had once owned or conspired to own, looked along the edge of the forest and the rise of the river bluff. A wind swept the forest and rippled across the river before ruffling up the bluff on the other side. He felt a shiver that seemed to begin at the roots of the trees and to run through him. As free in his heart as any man, he felt that everything he looked upon was his.

Notes

The following poems from *Five Centuries of Polish Poetry* (second edition), eds. Jerzy Peterkiewicz & Burns Singer (Secker & Warburg, 1960) have been recited in this work:

Pages 63 (and again on 541), "The Prisoner's Return," by Adam Mickiewicz
Page 265, "Brother," by Boleslaw Lesmian
Pages 266-267, "The Poet and the Peasant Bride," by Stanisław Wyspiański

Page 11, *Pan Tadeusz* by Adam Mickiewicz, translated by Marcel Weyland (Verand Press: New South Wales, 2004)

Page 31: "*znacharka*": In the Polish eastern borderlands (the *Kresy Wschodnie*), some Byelorussian words were used.

Page 381: "Message to Siberia," Alexander Pushkin, translated by Max Eastman (New Masses: New York, 1926)

Page 382: "I had bread from the wives of the village/ and the lads saw me right for makhorka." *Gulag Archipelago*, Aleksandr Solzhenitsyn (Basic Books: New York, 1997)

Pages 382-384: "The Scythians," *Selected Blok*, translated by Alex Miller (Progress Publishing: Moscow, 1981)

Author Photo: Danny Vasilyonok

Charles M. Boyer grew up in Illinois and Wisconsin and went to Beloit College, but has lived in New England for thirty years. He has an M.A. in fiction from the University of New Hampshire, and teaches English and Humanities at Montserrat College of Art. He has received a grant from the Wisconsin Arts Board and a Fellowship from the New Hampshire State Council on the Arts, and has published poems and stories with *The Atlanta Review*, *Abraxas*, Livingston Press, *Literal Latte*, and other venues. He lives near Boston with his family.

History's Child is loosely based on the life of Charles Boyer's father-in-law, who worked with anti-Stalin partisans as a teen and was captured by the Soviets and sent into the Gulag at the age of seventeen.